Abused Trust

Abused Trust

GEOFFREY R. TIGG

Rushing Tide
MEDIA

Abused Trust
Copyright ©2013 Geoffrey R Tigg

ISBN: 978-1-939288-17-2
Library of Congress Control Number: 2013938020

All rights reserved. Except for use in any review, the reproduction or utilization of this work in whole or in part in any form by an electronic, mechanical or other means, now known or hereafter invented, including xerography, photocopying, and recording, or in any information storage or retrieval system, is forbidden without the written permission of the author.

This is a work of fiction. Names, characters, places, and incidents are either the product of the author's imagination or are used fictionally, and any resemblance to actual persons, living or dead, business establishments, events, or locales is entirely coincidental.

Acknowledgement to Diane Stickney and Stephanie Kurenov.

A special thanks to my fine editor Karen Kibler whose dedicated work has been invaluable in the production of this book.

Rushing Tide
MEDIA

Published by Rushing Tide Media, Imprint of Wyatt-MacKenzie
Contact: grtigg@rushingtidemedia.com

Dedication

This story is dedicated to Raymond Miller
and
to my wife Diana and my daughter Danica for their loving
support and encouragement.

Preface

The exotic petite Asian woman straddled the overweight man with thinning graying brown hair, watching the pleasure on his face, as she gently rocked her pelvis encouraging his orgasm. Brian inhaled sharply, as he cupped the woman's small youthful breasts with his large sweating hands; his large-boned frame breathed heavily to the young woman's seemingly effortless stimulation. It was early Friday evening, and the young woman knew exactly how to please the large man lying beneath her, as she had had sex with him many times before. This was not their first time at the *Fraser Head Hotel* in room 210.

She was going to be busy later that night, so she took less time to bring the encounter to climax, touching herself while having intercourse, not wanting to leave the room unsatisfied.

"You're rushing, Carolynn! ... ah ... ohhh!" he exclaimed, grabbing her smooth soft buttocks to slow her movement on him, as she rapidly rubbed her crotch with three fingers.

"No! Make me come now! Oh ... ah ... ah!" she yelled, watching the sweat run from his forehead, and fighting his controlling hands by rapidly rotating her pelvis, encouraging the sensation within her.

"But ... ah ... Carolynn! ... ahhh," he exclaimed in a short breath, as his orgasm released from within him.

"Ah ...." she pulled from him and rolled over beside her exhausted partner, both of them gasping for breath as their bodies started to recover from their strenuous experience.

"You ah ... always know how to ah ... please a woman, and know just what I like!" she gasped, still breathing heavily, stroking the thinning brown hair on his chest.

Brian just smiled, needing a little longer to regain his breath, his heart still pounding feverishly.

Taking another moment to calm herself, she turned her inquisitive green eyes to look up into his face. "How are the projects for Larry going—still on track?" she asked as she was always curious about Brian's work and plans.

"Right on target, Carolynn, right on target," the labored voice replied as he ran his index finger around her firm breast toward its stiffened nipple.

"So sorry, lover," she whispered with a smile on her soft round face, "but tonight we must cut our time short. I've got another commitment and I can't be late!"

"Oh ... so soon ... we've just started ... yea, I understand," he sighed as he watched her slender petite body slip off the bed and disappear into the bathroom.

♓

Larry Langstone sat in a black, winged-back leather chair sipping brandy from a crystal glass as he studied chess pieces on a plaid, inlaid wooden board. His lavishly furnished home office was a refuge where he came to think and scheme about getting ahead in his business career.

"It's all about the strategy and the skills of the players. Preplanning the moves and anticipating the opponent is the key. Oh, I love this game!" Larry thought as he peered at the chess pieces on the checkered board.

His *ComTek* business strategy was being played with the same cunning, preplanned moves as a chess master playing a world tournament. Lost in thought, he picked up an opponent chess piece from where it rested beside the board. "Hmm ... I've the Fred Hawthorn and the Thomas Howe pieces taken out," he muttered, looking at the white knight, then returning the piece back onto the edge of the board out of play.

"Just a few more moves and I'll have the Will Richards piece eliminated, too," he mused, turning his attention to a white chess piece still on the board. "It's just a matter of time."

He thought about the contest as he enjoyed his brandy, satisfied with the moves he'd planned to make in the coming week at the office.

His game was on track, and he knew that his opponent wasn't ready for what was coming.

Chapter One

It was snowing, and it was only late November! Vancouver was considered a prime place to live in Canada as it rarely had snow and severe winter conditions. Winter weather patterns had been changing over the past few years and snow before Christmas was becoming more common than ever before; this storm was unusually early.

Will Richards was awakened by the ringing sound of his bedside telephone. It was very early Sunday morning, and the high-pitched ring could be heard throughout the house. Will worked long days and it was important to have the ringer turned up to ensure that he would not sleep through any incoming call.

"Shit," he grumbled in a dazed tone and picked up the receiver.

"Is that you, Mr. Richards?" the caller inquired in an East Indian accent.

"Ah yea, what time is it?" he inquired, still groggy from the interruption.

"Two thirty, Sir. Sorry for the early call. It's *ComTek* security! There's been a cave-in at the mill and the alarms went off! I have to call you when the alarms are triggered, Mr. Richards. I've turned the alarm off but I think ya need to come down here and see the mess!" the guard exclaimed, concerned about what he had discovered.

"What cave-in?" Will inquired in a higher-pitched voice, now fully awake and trying to process what he had been told.

"The snow's been coming down quite heavy and the cover of the mill has fallen through. It pulled the entire frame with it, Mr. Richards!" The guard continued, "Are ya goin' to come down?"

"Okay … ah, see you in about an hour. Call me on my cell if you need me again in the meantime. Ah … who else is there?" Will asked as he jumped out of bed.

"Just me so far, Mr. Richards! I just was doing my rounds when I saw that the roof had fallen in, and called ya right away, just as Mr. Sanchez says! Geez, what a mess. The roads are covered in snow out here so drive carefully. See ya soon," the guard warned and then hung up.

Will Richards was a tall, slim man, in his late forties with steely blue eyes. He had a drawn face and short brown hair that needed a cut. Will was a product of a large farming family, and as one of nine, he had learned early how to look after himself. He had sired four children of his own, most still living in the family home in Aldergrove. The youngest, now 17, was becoming a young woman, but was still catered to by his wife, Helen. Will was a good hardworking, trusting man with a kind heart, and was skilled with his hands—but his business skills were a different matter!

Will shuffled about his room that was furnished with a single bed, a small chest of drawers, and a throw rug on the old wooden floor. The bedroom had belonged to his eldest daughter who was now 22 and had left the house to live with her boyfriend downtown, and Will had been banished to this small basement room by his wife a number of months prior. His wife, Helen, slept in the master bedroom upstairs and she had grown apart from her husband, craving an easier and less stressful life. They often had heated arguments about his business and the lack of money. She had begun to press Will to close down the mill and get a job working for a company that would pay a decent wage and provide benefits. She worried excessively about money and the amounts that were owed to the bank, fearing that she would lose her house and end up with nothing.

He pulled on an old pair of blue jeans, a clean new long-sleeved plain shirt and heavy white socks. He walked into the bathroom that was across from the bedroom, brushed his teeth, and straightened his hair. His face needed a shave, but Will passed on the effort as he hurried to see what had happened at the mill.

Will's house was a back-split that he had renovated about five years earlier so that each of the four children could have their own space. The basement bedroom had access to the large south-facing backyard; on a clear day he would've been able to see Mount Baker in Washington State, but not today.

He pulled on his work boots and a heavy jacket, grabbed his cell phone and went out the back door. The yard was covered in a heavy blanket of wet, white snow. A sharp, cold wind was coming from the west as he pulled up his collar, turned his back, and carefully walked to the side of the house where he had parked his truck. There was no garage, just a carport; he surveyed the driveway conditions as he came around to the front of the house. The streetlights lit the area and Will determined that the snow on the downwardly sloping driveway would not be a problem for his light-duty green truck. He jumped in, ensured that his cell phone was turned on, placed it on the passenger seat and started the vehicle's engine. It was very cold and his breath began to fog the cabin while he waited for the windshield wipers to clear the glass and the engine to warm the inside of the two-seat truck.

"Damn," he thought, "the last thing I need now is a problem at the mill!"

Abused Trust

Aldergrove is a small community on the eastern outskirts of Vancouver; the community attracted many people as it offered more reasonable property values and taxation rates than most other areas of Vancouver. The cost of living was more reasonable, but the residents had to suffer the daily commute to and from work, like everyone else who lived outside the Vancouver core.

"Thank God that today's Sunday!" Will thought as he backed his truck out of his driveway. "It'll be a bitch for everyone if this snow doesn't clear for tomorrow's morning rush!"

Will's truck picked its way southward toward his mill that was located on *ComTek*'s property in Surrey, a forty-minute drive. He worried about what he might find, and what it might cost to fix! Will and his wife owned *Service Pole Recycling Limited*, a company they had started twelve years earlier. It had been his idea to recycle old hydro and telephone poles, recover the marketable wood while reducing landfill waste, and he loved doing it. Will had presented the idea to *ComTek* in the beginning, and a trial mill had been placed at the back of the lot where the new poles were stored, waiting to be supplied to *ComTek*'s many customers.

ComTek Supplies Corporation was a large logistics company that provided an entire supply chain suite of services that included procurement, warehousing, distribution, and in some cases disposal, for their clients. Throughout British Columbia, the company served large customers who had decided to outsource this activity, and the company's customer base had grown to include power, gas, and many telecommunications organizations.

Will's relationship with *ComTek* had been strong and trusting until a couple of years ago, when Fred Hawthorn retired. Will and Fred had put the project together, and Fred had been a strong supporter of reducing *ComTek*'s utility customers' environmental footprint and improving public safety.

Fred's successor, Brian Quest, didn't share those views and had made the relationship strained and frustrating after Fred's retirement. Will refused to think Helen was right, that the time had come to shut the operation down. He agreed that the business barely provided an adequate income for his family, but he loved the freedom to run his own show, and was convinced that things would get better. The interactions with the public and corporate customers were what he loved best, and even though he had a staff that was mostly transient and a pain in the ass, he loved going to work. Will's operation was well known throughout the province, and his talkative social nature encouraged everyone to stop and chat while they waited to have their recycled wood order filled. He knew lots of things about lots of people, and that fact worried those in power at *ComTek*.

The trip to the mill was slow, and it was almost four in the morning by the time that Will Richards arrived at the *ComTek* pole yard. The snow had stopped some time ago, but the sky still threatened. The security guard shack was located west of 148th Street, and Will waited for the traffic light at 66th Avenue before he turned into the entrance roadway. The guard who he had spoken to earlier was still there, and Will stopped to get an update on the situation.

"Hey, Mr. Richards, glad to see that you finally got here!" the Indian guard growled in the cold. He was wearing a standard issue yellow winter coat with a *Metro Security* logo printed on the back. His red turban was wrapped neatly around the top of his head but it didn't help protect him from the cold wind of the early morning. His long gray beard that ran down below his neck didn't provide much protection from the weather, either. His complexion was a light brownish shade, but much of it didn't show through the beard and the turned-up coat collar. The guard, born in Ralpur, had come to Canada three years ago to provide a better life for his family. He still hadn't become accustomed to the cold winter days in Canada, and this morning was unseasonably cold. His guard shack wasn't designed to protect anyone from the cold, only from the rainy weather that was more typical for Vancouver.

"I've called my office, and Mr. Sanchez will be here later this morning," the guard continued. "Hydro already has a crew down at your mill." The guard eked out a smile, and returned to his shack that was positioned at the entrance gate to the *ComTek* pole yard.

There was a small community substation fenced off in the northern corner and a large power transmission corridor ran along the backside of the lot.

The property was used to store emergency transmission tower components and also functioned as the prime pole storage yard for *ComTek*. Across the 148th Street roadway, and on the east side of the traffic light intersection, was the main entrance into *ComTek*'s main distribution warehouse and administration offices.

A metal-clad building was located close to the pole yard wire-fence gate entrance, and a sign reading *ComTek Pole Office* was placed over the front door. The office was where the pole employees and foreman handled the daily activities of receiving and shipping out new poles. A large, yellow log loader was parked in the lot beside the office. Terry Peters was *ComTek*'s pole yard foreman who had worked for *ComTek* for over twenty-five years. Terry wouldn't be in today, but Will knew that he would see him first thing Monday morning.

Will sighed, and turned his green truck into the pole yard entrance way. The wire security gate was open, and vehicle tracks could be seen pressed into the snow on top of the gravel roadway that led to the mill. He slowly drove past small, neatly stacked piles of new poles that were placed between small aisles. Will eyed his large pile of unprocessed retired poles that were covered in snow, waiting to be sorted and run through his mill. He was nervous as he followed the vehicle tracks in the still crisp white snow.

A *PowerOne* line-crew truck could be seen parked outside of Will's office trailer. A lineman was straddling the top of the service pole untangling some lines that had brought power to the mill site. The lineman's partner was standing underneath, at ground level, checking the electric meter.

"Hey, Will!" the lineman called out, when Will stepped from his truck. "I got a call to disconnect your service for safety reasons! The snow sure has created a mess, eh?" he yelled, as he rubbed his hands together. "Guys have been out all night with this storm. The MVAs and the heavy snow have taken power out all over the city. No one wanted you poking about this wreckage with the juice on, so you're a priority stop," he continued as he climbed down the pole. "Freezing your ass is a tough way to make an overtime buck, I'd say!" the lineman growled as he turned to face Will.

Will focused his attention on the lineman, who he knew well. "Hey, John, thanks for coming out! I really appreciate all the help I can get. It looks like it's going to be a long day for all of us, eh?" he asked without his normal smile and easy tone.

Will just wanted to get a closer look at the situation at the mill. "Stop by the next chance you get, and we'll talk about your day. Thanks again, John!"

"Sounds good, bud ... take care ... see ya later," John replied, waved, and joined his partner in the line truck. Will watched the crew pull out of the yard and he sighed, looking at the disastrous mess.

He took a deep breath, stared at the scene for a moment, and muttered to himself, shaking his head. Even at this early hour, Will could feel the weather pattern change, and knew the rain was not far away. The entire roof structure of his mill had collapsed under the weight of the heavy moisture-laden snow. This type of snowstorm was not common for the Lower Mainland, and his building structure hadn't been designed for such a wet load. The thin tubular structure that carried a tarp-like cover had been intended just as a shelter from the rain. The electrical control panel that formed one of the end walls of the tubular shelter was now fully exposed, and stood as a reminder of why the power technician had been at the mill. The only equipment not buried in the debris was the head rig, which was covered by a separate makeshift wooden roof that had been placed alongside the covered product-finishing area. It was Sunday, so Will's mill crew wouldn't be in today. "Just as well," he thought. "I need time to decide what to do with this mess!" Will muttered as he opened the office that was in an old trailer. "I need to warm up!"

The office was an old construction portable trailer that had been purchased by *ComTek* when the mill was first set up years before. It sat on large wooden blocks and a heavy duty padlock wrapped in a steel bracket was on the door to keep intruders out. The mill site had a history of break-ins by thieves looking for copper and tools to steal, so they could trade their loot for money to feed their drug habits. Will had also installed a security alarm a number of years before, hoping to deter future intruders. He knew that the disconnection of the power made the alarm system inoperable, and exposed the mill to pilfering thieves once again. "Can't deal with that now though," he thought as he prepared to make a coffee in the back room of the cold trailer.

The trailer didn't have a city water supply, so Will purchased bottled water for the crew. The trailer housed his office on one side of the unit, and the crew lunchroom was on the other, separated by a thin, wooden wall and door. His office was simple with an old chair that had been donated to him by his friend Thomas Howe, and his desk that was covered in paperwork that almost buried an old dirty, black telephone in the back corner. There was no computer Internet access, as the cost to install the line was too expensive, and the business couldn't generate adequate profits to cover such a cost. The used trailer was on the south side of the lot, with windows facing out toward the de-nailing pit and main head rig. With the power now turned off, the electric heat radiators had turned cold, and the office no longer served as a warm haven from the weather conditions outside.

"Shit. I forgot the power was out and I can't make coffee!" Will growled as he stopped looking for the coffee can in the frosty lunchroom. "Humph!"

Will Richards returned to his truck, and slid into the driver's seat, started the engine, and turned up the heater. It was still too early to call anyone, so he sat and contemplated what Helen would say when he got home. He could hear her now, "I told you so! I said you should've never renewed that agreement. We never make enough money to justify the

Abused Trust

bullshit and hard work. Damn bastards anyway! Now this! Get out and work for someone else who can have the headaches and the bank pressures!"

Even though he knew that lots of what she would say would be true, and that things should've been better than they were, they weren't. He still liked what he did, and believed the program was the right thing to do! He knew things could be fixed, working even better than before, and that *ComTek* would see that his project was still good for everyone. He trusted his instincts and his past experience and he was sure that things would work out! He had a lot of friends, and he knew they would help in any way that they could.

Will Richards knew of a 24-hour *Tim Hortons*® close by, and decided to get a hot drink and donut there. He pulled his truck out of its spot and headed down the snow-covered gravel pole yard roadway toward the guard shack.

"I'll be back in half an hour; I need a coffee. You want one?" Will asked, knowing the guard was likely freezing cold.

"Thanks, Mr. Richards. I'd appreciate it!" The guard smiled, looking thankful and chilled to the bone.

"If anyone comes by looking for me, just have them call my cell. I expect to be back soon and I'll continue to look around for a while when I get back. See ya in a bit!" Will rolled up the window of the old truck and drove slowly to the stop light that was a short distance up the service road from the guard shack.

It was seven o'clock that morning before Will Richards had returned to the mill site, refreshed and warmed up. He passed a fresh coffee to the guard, drove down the cold quiet gravel road and parked in front of his trailer office. He decided not to call Helen as it was early, and he didn't know what to tell her yet anyway. He needed to assess the detail of the destruction, and formulate a plan to keep her off his ass.

Will unlocked a storage container that had been placed three meters from the office. The large, old, steel box was three meters long, two meters wide, and almost three meters high. He jumped into a yellow log loader that had been parked in the yard beside the de-nailing pit on the prior Friday afternoon. The log loader belonged to *ComTek,* and they provided the fuel and maintenance, an agreement he'd made when the project had first been structured. The engine started with little effort, even though it was cold. "John Deere makes great stuff," he muttered, his breath visible in the small cab as he spoke.

The storage container had a large concrete curb that had been placed in front of the old steel door. Will had learned early that thieves liked looting his place, as it was very secluded and his equipment that was inside was always marketable. Will soon realized that the only way the container door could be prevented from being accessed, was to place a large heavy object, that couldn't easily be moved, in front of the steel doors, and the concrete curb was an ideal and cheap choice. He placed the log loader's long steel forks under the curb, and the heavy object was moved aside. Will put the log loader back into its prior parking place, pulled aside one of the doors of the container, and proceeded into the dark ice cold space inside.

The steel box was loaded with equipment. A half dozen chain saws were placed on a wooden bench, fuel containers were stacked neatly along one of the walls and an assortment of safety gear was hung on a pegboard and stacked on a wood shelf running the length of the space. A light switch had been installed, and the power line ran from the office trailer; but with the power disconnected, it was a good thing that Will knew where everything was placed. He removed a large industrial broom and a crow bar.

Will didn't notice the cold as he labored to clear the debris and wet snow from the mill's processing floor. The tarp roof had been torn into small pieces, and once the snow had been removed he easily dragged the torn tarp away into a corner. "Hmm ... the damage seems to be restricted to the shelter ... at least one break I've got anyway!" he muttered, happy that the equipment didn't look damaged, as he worked around the power lines and exhaust ducts that ran above the mill's concrete floor.

With the power service disconnected, and the security alarms not operational, Will knew that it wouldn't be long before looters would discover the opportunity. The largest risk was the copper power service cables that ran from the control panel to the mill equipment. This was prime gold for thieves. "The sooner the power can be restored, the better!" he thought. "I can't be exposed any longer than necessary, and I need to get *ComTek* to replace this building ASAP. I'm glad it's their problem and not mine!"

It was now early afternoon, and Will decided to take a break as he was cold and hungry. *McDonalds*® was only a few blocks away, and was a great place to grab a Big Mac® and a coffee.

Will laughed to himself, as he remembered when he first started with *ComTek* and installed the mill; the pole storage yard had just been relocated from the lot that now housed the small strip mall where *McDonalds*® now stood. There was such a controversy at the time, and many managers at the *ComTek*'s warehouse didn't agree with the proposal to sell off the property. From a logistics perspective, why move the pole operation across the street and disrupt the operational efficiency, let alone have unsupervised union employees away from direct eyeshot? Political opportunists' agendas within the organization took priority over operational efficiencies, and local management opinion, so the property was sold. The soil that had been scraped off the property by the purchaser had been relocated across the street to be sold. It still sat in large piles behind the mill, the top soil remaining largely unsold, and the location now served as a great place for would-be looters to hide, and monitor activity at the mill and the *ComTek* storage site.

Will stopped at the security shack and inquired through his truck's window as the guard met him at the gate, "Is Mr. Sanchez expected to appear today?" Will asked.

"I don't think so, Mr. Richards. The office says that things here can wait until tomorrow," the guard replied and with that news, Will decided that he no longer had a reason to stay at the site. He turned his truck around and decided to close shop for the day. He put away his tools, and replaced the concrete curb in front of the storage container, locked the office trailer and jumped back into his truck to go home. He sat in his vehicle for a moment, and thought, with his head in his hands, "What to say to Helen! Humph, my tough day isn't over by a long shot!"

It started to rain. The roads became slushy, and the streets began to clear of snow, as Will turned his truck toward the security guard shack and headed for home.

✵

Pablo Dominguez' large husky frame crouched by a small, open basement window, quietly watching, as three men were packing small plastic bags of heroin into cardboard cartons. The old run-down, pre-war, single-level house sat in the north part of Surrey, only blocks away from the footings of the Port Mann Bridge. Patches of snow still lingered on the ground, and the chill in the night air was an unwelcome reminder that winter had started early.

Pablo's narrow, black, beady eyes frequently darted around the property, and then focused back again on the activities taking place in the dimly lit basement. He strained to hear the conversation of the three men, as they quickly moved about the small space under the house.

"Juan, stop bitching! You can go out to have a smoke once this stuff gets packed," a short, stocky, heavy-set man grunted, as he continued to pack a cardboard carton. "How the hell was I to know that this house's located in a middle of a war zone!" Giermo Hernandez' round face showed the stress of the situation.

"Too bad ya gotta move from this place, eh boss? It's a lot closer to our transfer station than the new place's goin' to be!" a scrawny narrow-faced man grumbled, as he gathered the small plastic bags from an old metal shelf.

"Antonio, we're the new guys in this market, and I don't want to be caught in the middle between the *Black Widow* and the *Los Chinche*, that's suicide man! It's better for us to let them have their war, and we can go about our business in the background, somewhere else." Giermo Hernandez grimaced as he stretched his back. "It's a bitch though, now I've got to find another spot ta process this stuff!"

"What about the new place that we're taking this stuff to tonight? Isn't that going to be our new processing lab, boss?" Antonio asked, looking confused.

"No mano! That's only temporary, and just a place to finish putting together this shipment, that's all. I don't want to process 'H' there permanently. Stop asking questions, and get on with finishing this job! I want to be out of here as fast as I can," Giermo explained, as he began to tape a small cardboard box closed.

"Juan, you get those last two cartons finished, and Antonio, you start getting the stuff loaded into the van! Don't forget those computer housings, either! I'm goin' ta chat with Pablo," Giermo directed, as he started his way up the old wooden staircase from the basement.

Giermo Hernandez lit a cigarette as he exited the house, and worked his way around to the side where his friend was watching with interest. "Hey Pablo, thanks for coming, and covering our ass tonight!" he exclaimed, blowing cigarette smoke into the crisp air.

"Hey mano, it's what I do," the tall Colombian replied, standing up, towering over Giermo. "I get a call to assist, and I'm here, as always! Besides the family would be pissed if this business venture got screwed up. Ya want ta make a good impression, right?"

"Yea, sure. I just about shit when I found out that I picked a place right in the middle of a heated gang war! Man what crappy, shit luck!" Giermo exclaimed, annoyed with the whole thing as he took another drag from his smoke. "It's sure great to have contacts that are watching our backs!" he grunted, slowly blowing the smoke out of his nostrils.

"Well, just get his thing done, Giermo! I'm freezing my ass out here!" Pablo grumbled, as he rubbed his cold hands to warm them up.

Chapter Two

The offices of the *Central Logistics Group* opened at seven. The majority of the CLG management parked in the front of the building, which was accessed off 148th Street, just east of the traffic light. Those in management were given named parking stalls, and Brian Quest's was vacant, as he hadn't yet arrived. Everyone looked for the sleek, black 310ZX sports car before they entered the building, checking to see if the boss had arrived early. Brian had been offered a company vehicle, but the *ComTek* nondescript white sedan wasn't his style, so he chose to drive his own car.

The union staff parked in a lot behind the main warehouse facility, and they needed to pass the security guard station that was located on the side road, that ran along the south side of the building off 66th Avenue. Their parking area was on the north side of the complex, in a paved space that had once held stored materials waiting for disposal. The parking lot was a short distance from the rear entrance of the large warehouse and truck-loading bays.

The weekend snow had been washed away by Sunday night. Good thing, too, as Surrey drivers were no better than the average lower mainlander. Monday morning pilgrimages to work were bad enough without weather conditions that required adjustment in driving skills and attention, let alone the distractions brought about with cell phone calls and texting.

The CLG business operations were located in the middle of Surrey, the largest municipality in British Columbia. The area had grown steadily in the past three decades, and the once remote industrial area had now become prime real estate.

Brian Quest, the manager of the CLG operation, entered the administration office shortly after eight fifteen. "What a drive!" he exclaimed, frustrated at the lengthy commute. "Richmond has traffic backed up past the Steveston interchange! Sure glad the snow's gone ... what a weekend!" he grumbled as he turned toward his trusted receptionist, sitting at the front entrance. "Hey Georgina, how're you this Monday morning?"

"Okay, Boss," she replied curtly.

The receptionist, Georgina Davidson, was seated by the front entrance to the office, wearing a casual red sweater and yellow scarf. She lived in Langley, and the daily half an hour trip into Surrey had become a strain over the past few years. The woman, now fifty-seven, was a long-term employee and had worked for the *Central Logistics Group* for the last sixteen years. She had seen the comings and goings of many managers, and she didn't like Brian Quest very much—something about him just didn't gel with her. Her old boss, Fred Hawthorn, had been much more personable, and really had been interested in each employee who had worked at the CLG when he was there. Fred's sudden retirement had been a surprise for most— but not for Georgina. She knew the issues involved in his retirement, but didn't breach Fred's trust and had kept things to herself. She also knew a lot about Brian Quest. He'd been brought into the operation as one of Fred's political moves, as an attempt to control materials purchasing twelve years earlier. Fred knew that Thomas Howe was the better choice to run the operation, but Brian was the best political selection at the time. A political choice had been the only choice at *ComTek* at that time, and things hadn't changed in that regard since then.

Brian believed that he knew how to play the game; he had played Fred Hawthorn quite well and had been rewarded by

Larry Langstone for his patience. Brian had spent the last few years working on dismantling Fred's political achievements, as Brian tried to work himself out from Fred's stellar corporate shadow. Fred's legacy at the CLG had been remarkable; Brian wanted to make his own mark, and at the same time discredit Fred's achievements.

"I received a call from Larry Langstone this morning. I said that you hadn't arrived yet, but you would return his call when you got in," Georgina informed Brian stiffly as he walked past her toward his office.

"Hmm ... give me five minutes to get settled and then call him, please," Brian directed, and continued to walk through the open-concept office space, ignoring everyone else who was working in their small open-concept walled cubicles.

The administrative office had been designed before Brian had moved into the Surrey warehouse operation. Office cubicles had light green, fabric covers and were placed in clusters. The office was a large rectangle, with windows on the east and west sides, facing either the front street entrance or the storage yard and the Investment Recovery Department building in the back. Three managers had an enclosed executive type office: each one was in a corner of the concrete building that was attached to the large warehouse. Brian Quest's office was in the back northeast corner, and had a view through large windows that overlooked the entire outside paved storage yard. The office had a private, adjoining conference room, which could also be accessed from the front office.

Brian unlocked his private office door, removed his winter coat, and hung it on a coat tree in the corner. He placed his briefcase in one of the visitor chairs in front of his desk.

The office had once belonged to Fred Hawthorn, and it was as much a prize as was the job position! This was the only office that had four concrete walls and was secluded from the rest of the administrative work area. It was very private. In the centre of the room was a very large, wooden desk. Brian knew that executive office furniture like that wasn't made anymore and the size and grandeur seemed to intimidate visitors, which suited Brian just fine.

A framed, colored map of the Province of British Columbia was hung behind the credenza, and there were fifty-two red dots scattered on the surface. The dots represented locations where *ComTek* had material field-distribution mini-warehouses and offices that serviced the local communities. There was a keyboard and a computer monitor on the edge of the old, wooden desk with a *ComTek* logo moving about the screen. A large printer was positioned on the credenza behind the desk, along with a number of photos of Brian in golf attire, and a large, silver-colored trophy with a golfer in mid-swing that had his name engraved on a brass plate in small script print.

Brian was a large-boned man about two hundred and ten pounds and five-ten in height. He had thinning brown hair, turning grey on the sides, and had designer black-rimmed glasses supported by his broad nose. His face was round with heavy eyebrows, which seemed to camouflage his brown eyes from direct contact. He wore a light brown, tailored pinstripe suit, a plain blue dress shirt and a red-striped tie: an outfit that he thought demanded respect and attention.

※

Carolynn Gingell knocked on Larry Langstone's office door, and then entered. Larry loved his office on the tenth floor of the *Central City Tower*, where *ComTek* had its executive offices. He was responsible for all the logistics operations of the company, which was the core of *ComTek*'s business. He sat reviewing his appointment schedule for the day, and looked up at his secretary, as she delivered an envelope.

"What's that, Carolynn?" the tall, well-dressed man asked, as he looked up from his computer monitor.

"A courier just dropped it off for you, Larry. There's no return address, though. Strange, eh?"

"Thanks Carolynn, I'll see what's inside after I finish reviewing my schedule. Have any new meeting commitments been added since Friday?" he asked glancing down at the envelope.

"No, there's nothing new on your calendar, Larry, since Friday," Carolynn replied with a smile, and then closed her boss's door, knowing that he needed his private time to get organized for the day.

"Hmm ... I wonder what I've in here! That investigator sure does fast work!" Larry spoke softly to himself as he slit open the large brown envelope. "Ah ... perfect, I love pictures! It's the best insurance I can have to ensure that I get what I want!" His face wrinkled around his eyes when he smiled.

Larry was an astute businessman, and knew the value of politics and manipulation. These attributes had served him well, and if he continued to play the corporate game smartly, he was sure that he would one day replace Peter Fisher, the executive vice-president of *ComTek*. Larry had a plan, and it was in full motion!

♓

Brian Quest's office phone rang and he leaned over his large desk and picked up the receiver. Georgina was on the line. "Got your call for you, it's Larry on line two," she informed him and hung up.

Brian selected the line. "Good morning Larry, sorry I wasn't here for your call earlier. The traffic from Richmond was nuts this morning," he said in an apologetic voice as he moved to sit in the large chair behind the desk.

"Have you been told of the *Service Pole Recycling* building problem yet?" Larry's voice was intense for a Monday morning.

"No, I haven't talked to anyone yet, and Georgina said nothing when I arrived," he replied with interest. "What happened?"

"I got a call from Tom at *PowerOne's* dispatch this morning. It was another crazy weekend with the snow and *PowerOne* lost a lot of customers Saturday night and early Sunday morning. Tom apparently had crews all over the Lower Mainland from Chilliwack to West Vancouver. Anyway, he had to divert a crew to the pole yard early Sunday. The recycling building collapsed under the weight of the wet snow, and they needed to turn the power off to avoid anyone getting injured. I think we got the break that we've been looking for, Brian!"

"Hang on a sec," Brian got up to close the office door. A smile crossed his face as he returned to his seat. "Okay, Larry!"

"This situation will certainly put pressure on Will Richards!" Larry continued, "The report I got this morning says that the mill site is a mess, and the entire building frame came down. I also understand that Richards was at the site early Sunday, once our security guard called. Things will be tough for him with the power off!"

"Hmm," Brian thought for a moment. "You know Richards will want help, and will likely be in my office later today begging for assistance ... I guess I'll need to be sympathetic!" he replied with an open hand motion. "Let's see what develops. I'll keep you current, Larry!"

"Well, all of Richards' talking and nosing about is making me nervous. It's certainly time to deal with him now, Brian. While we're talking about *Service Pole*, where are we on the proposed changes to our pole return practices with *PowerOne?*" Larry changed the subject. "I expect to see the policy rewrite on my desk no later than tomorrow."

"It's almost done. I've John Humphries finishing it up, and I expect to get it for my review this morning," Brian replied as he leaned back in his chair. "I'll send you an e-mail and let you know when it's completed. I'll touch base later. Bye, Larry." Brian placed the phone back into its cradle and logged onto his computer to view his schedule.

Outlook® was a critical planning tool to keep Brian's days organized. He was able to see what all his managers were planning, and he was also able to schedule personal events, and block the time period details from everyone's view. Georgina was responsible for keeping his schedule current, and she had been instructed to let him know of any changes that she had made, or any conflicts that needed his resolution. This morning Brian had a managers meeting at ten o'clock, which was to be held in his private conference room. He opened his e-mail and searched for the agenda that Georgina had prepared. He printed a copy, and placed it into a folder with "meetings" printed on the label tab; returning to his Outlook® schedule he noted a meeting entitled "Chilliwack," which was a luncheon meeting that ran through the rest of the day.

Brian peered through the large window in his office and noted that it was still raining. "Just as well," he thought. "I don't need to drive in the damn snow this afternoon!" He knew that Chilliwack was up the valley, and the east usually got the brunt of the cold weather storms. Highway One could be treacherous when it snowed, and it often iced up and became quite dangerous, especially with the idiots on the roads who appeared to be oblivious of any change in road conditions!

The TransCanada route was the only trucking corridor to the interior and northern part of the Province. Truck spray and icy conditions didn't mix well, and in a small sports car like his, Brian knew that he had to be extra cautious, so he decided that it would be wise to leave early for his meeting in Chilliwack.

"I need to ensure that I have all the paperwork for the meeting," he thought as he began to unlock the credenza and open the drawer that had labeled folders that Georgina had laid out neatly. A folder labeled *BC Transformer Inc.* was pulled from the file set and placed on the desk. Brian briefly thumbed through the contents in the folder, and seemingly satisfied, he grabbed his briefcase from the chair in front of the desk and placed the folder inside it.

It was almost ten when Brian went into the small utility room that had been set up as a lunchroom for the office staff, and grabbed a coffee. There was a small platter of muffins on the counter top which Georgina had purchased for the meeting. His operating budget funded the coffee and the meeting food trays, and Brian grabbed his coffee cup that had "BOSS" printed in large letters on the side. Georgina had given the porcelain cup to him on his first day as manager of the unit, when he replaced Fred Hawthorn. Brian had liked the message and kept the cup.

The five managers filed into the conference room sharply at ten o'clock. Each section head carried a China cup filled with coffee that had "CLG Team" printed in blue, and each had a leather-bound, black binder that had a *ComTek* logo etched into the leather front cover. There had been a big push in *ComTek* five years before to eliminate Styrofoam coffee cups, and Brian had funded the replacements though his operating budget as an environmental initiative; but he really had done it to make political points with Larry Langstone. Back then, environmental initiatives had been a political bonanza for managers wanting to be noticed, and Brian had taken every opportunity to get onto the bandwagon. The political landscape had changed since then, and environmental activities took a back seat to other priorities that showed quicker and shorter-term personal gains.

The *Central Logistics Group* continued to operate with a small group of managers, just as it always had done under the direction of Fred Hawthorn. Brian didn't want to follow the current *ComTek* trend and enlarge the management team, as he wanted to keep his budget available for other opportunities that often arose. With the large number of management and skilled staff retirements of the past few years, *ComTek* was left with many inexperienced employees; to compensate for the loss of key people, *ComTek* was now operated by management committee, allowing accountabilities to blur. This approach to management decision-making created a lack of accountability but covered everyone's ass when mistakes were made.

The logistics management team also suffered from a lack of long-term experience in many areas and subject competencies, but Brian was able to cover the gaps with his strong directive nature and long-term internal *ComTek* contacts. Brian hated to deal with detail, and expected his managers to have the experience and capabilities to handle detail by themselves, but too often that expectation proved not to be realistic.

"John, you're up first!" Brian directed, as everyone got settled in the small conference room; Brian didn't like a lot of chitchat before his meetings. Georgina had placed the plate of muffins in the centre of the table earlier, and each manager took one before John started his report.

John Humphries had an average build, and was less experienced than many in the room. He wore wire-rimmed glasses that looked more like an accessory than a necessity. He wore a denim shirt and blue jeans, and his tie looked like it was a reject from *Value City* and looked out of place. He squirmed as he opened his portfolio and extracted his report.

"I've completed the new policy on pole removals and returns, and have a copy for each of you." He quickly glanced up at Brian as he reached for a stack of reports that he had brought with him. "The report is structured as you requested, Brian, and I've already vetted the plan with the distribution office reps," he continued. "All that's remaining is to have your review and Larry Langstone's signature authorizing the implementation."

Brian Quest was well aware that this new plan was really intended to push Will Richards out of business, by transferring *ComTek*'s costs to Will's operation. The disposal cost agreement had been developed when *Service Pole Recycling* had been established fifteen years before, and had never been updated to include changes in business practices or environmental stewardship costs. Many things had changed since the project was launched, and Brian now had other projects and political interests that required the elimination of Will Richards from the *ComTek* site.

"Great work, John!" Brian praised. "I'll do a final read and let you know tomorrow morning if the report can be couriered over to Larry's office. I'll be tied up most of the rest of the day, so I'll review your report the first chance that I get, and advise you accordingly."

"Okay, Brian ... so ah ... you all hear about *Service Pole* and the collapse of their building on Sunday morning?" John inquired as he slipped his report back into his binder.

"Yea, I had a call from Terry Peters this morning and I heard the news from him. All the guys are talking about it! Terry said that everyone at the pole yard has been down to take a look," Sandra Willows piped up. "All of the guys really like Will, and many have bought recycled wood for their fences from him ... Brian, are we going to able to help him out?" Sandra inquired, as she looked straight at him across the table.

"I'm going to have John go over there to look over the situation and have a talk with Will after the meeting," Brian responded without hesitation. "This situation will sure be tough on the guy!"

Brian glanced over at Sandra, and then returned to his agenda. "So ... Allen, what's happening on the transformer tender and *BC Transformer Inc.*?"

Allen Harwitz had not been with *ComTek* for very long. During a *ComTek* reorganization five years before, the decision-making on procurement contracts had been shifted from the CLG back to the corporate head office, to the dismay of Brian. This action reduced his control on supplier awards, and demanded that he expend more effort to have his preferred suppliers win the contracts. Brian had wanted new blood from the outside to allow him to be able to mold the employees to his way of doing business. Having a new manager in this area made things easier, as the new person didn't have the experience and background on prior practices; therefore, Allen took Brian's lead easily.

"Well, the tender analysis has been reviewed by corporate purchasing, and our recommendation seems to be okay with them. They said that the contracts will be prepared by legal and ready sometime next week. I think that you should call corporate, Brian, and see if you can release the information and directly advise *BC Transformer* of the pending contract," Allen replied confidently.

Allen was a younger man than most of the managers, in his early forties. Allen's staff was responsible for reviewing the inventory replenishment process for the main distribution centre and mini-warehouse operations, and Allen was kept busy dealing with supply problems and customer complaints.

Brian looked at his watch, knowing that it would take longer to get to his meeting in Chilliwack because of the weather conditions. "I need to adjourn this meeting early so proceed with your duties and assignments," Brian announced somewhat rudely and left the meeting; as he entered his office, the door closed behind him.

John Humphries was on his way back to his office and Georgina called out as he passed her desk. "Will Richards has called three times already!" she said with a concerned voice. "He seems quite upset and needs to talk to you about his processing shelter that collapsed on Sunday morning," she continued. "I know the guy drives you crazy, but he really means well."

John had been told to go down to the pole facility anyway, so John returned Will's call as soon as he reached his office. "Hey, Will, got your calls. I heard about the catastrophe on Sunday morning. I was planning to come right after my management meeting." John paused, then told Will, "I'll see ya in five," and with that short call he hung up. "The guy will talk your ear off if you give him an opportunity," he thought, "and since I have to go there anyway, I may as well save the conversation for when I get there."

John didn't like to walk over to the pole yard that was across the street. The light at 66th took a while to change and he also didn't like getting dirty. The pole operation always seemed dirty and messy! He stopped at Georgina's desk. "Can I have the keys to the beast, please?" he asked in a hurried tone.

Georgina glanced up at John, opened a draw at the side of her desk and fished out a set of car keys. "Here you go. Drive safely," she replied in an offhanded way.

The beast was a nickname given to the office vehicle. It was an old, white Chrysler purchased by Fleet many years ago, and was now waiting for recall. Fleet had let Brian have the vehicle, as managers often needed to travel to meetings at corporate headquarters, located in the new *Central City Tower* in the northern part of Surrey. The company preferred that employees not take their personal vehicles if they intended to return to the office before the end of the working day. The beast was perfect transport for John to go and see Will Richards.

John opened the creaky door and slid into the driver's seat. He pulled the seat forward, thinking that Allen must've used the car last. "Another scratch on this beater and no one would ever know," he thought, and started the engine.

John pulled out of the managers' parking lot, and headed across 148th Street. He waved at the security guard as he reached the gate, but he didn't stop. He glanced over at the pole yard office, but John didn't stop to chat with Terry Peters. "I'll catch up with Terry when I finish with Will," John thought as he passed the steel-clad building and travelled down the gravel road toward *Service Pole Recycling*.

John noticed that a pole delivery truck had just left a load of full-length, used poles along the side of the narrow roadway. "I'll have to remind Will to keep this roadway clear," he thought as he let the logging truck pass, now empty.

Will Richards was returning to his office after completing the pole count of the load that had just been dropped off and he heard the Chrysler coming behind him. It had a very distinct rumble, and Will was sure that John was likely driving.

John rolled down the driver side window as he approached Will who was walking through the mud. "Christ, what a mess, Will; those pole deliveries need to be kept out of this road ya know! The public comes down here, and we don't want any problems, do we?" John loved to take any opportunity to poke at Will.

"I know!" Will responded, exasperated. He knew that John was fully aware that he had little control of the drivers delivering the poles to his yard. "I was going to get one of the guys to clear it up!" Will choked out.

"Hey, Ray," Will yelled at a burly-built man standing in the de-nailing pit across from the trailer. "Jump on the loader and clear that mess that just arrived, okay?"

Ray Patterson was the mill's sawyer. He was a big man and had been a logger for most of his life. Ray joined Will when the mill was first set up. He was a skilled log sawyer and operated the head rig like he was expertly playing a piano. Today the mill was inoperable, but Will had decided to keep

Ray and Jack Hollands on site, having sent the rest of the crew home. Will knew that it was a tough time to send guys home with Christmas approaching, and his annual season shutdown was also rapidly approaching.

Jack Hollands was another strong and big-boned man. He also had spent many years in the forest, and operated mill and forestry equipment with skill and expertise. Will knew that he was lucky to have good men like Ray and Jack working for him, and Will made every effort to keep both men on the payroll. Jack was on the other side of the pole pile with a chainsaw and he was cutting out the junk, and getting it ready to load into disposal containers.

John Humphries pulled the dirty white car next to the front of Will's office trailer. "Holy shit, what a mess!" he exclaimed, as he peered at the shelter wreckage through the open car window. It was still raining and John refused to get out and get his shoes muddy and wet.

"You should've seen it Sunday morning before I cleared most of it up!" Will exclaimed, as he peered at John sitting in the car. "You guys need to help me get this facility replaced ASAP. I've got to get this mill running."

The wipers of the old Chrysler made a continuous noise as they scraped across the glass, partially drowning out John's reply. "Well, I'll have to see what can be done, Will. I don't know if I've got the budget to replace this, or even fix it!" John responded unsympathetically. "I'll have to talk to Brian. Why don't you begin to get quotes on fixing this, or a cost estimate for replacement, before I go to Brian looking for money?" John continued, "It's sure an unbelievable mess, Will." With that observation, John placed the car into gear and turned to leave the yard.

Will watched as John pulled out of the mill's yard and drive through the open wire gate. "What an asshole," he muttered. "Brian better come through, and he'd better not drag his ass about it either!"

⯎

Larry Langstone was returning from a budget meeting when he received a text on his BlackBerry®. "Hmm," he muttered as he looked at the message on the small screen. *Call tonight! We need an update on the meter agreement. Our client's getting anxious.*

Chapter Three

Will Richards was in his office calling suppliers who manufacture and repair hoardings, like the one that had been destroyed. He needed a cover that was twenty meters long, three meters wide and it had to be able to withstand a snow load that exceeded Sunday's unusual storm. He couldn't afford to go through the same experience a second time.

"Can you send someone to my site this morning?" Will inquired of the person at the other end of the line. "I understand that you've been getting calls from others who have had major damage too, but I would really appreciate some quick assessment as to what my options may be!" Will pleaded and held his breath waiting for a reply. "Oh, thanks a lot, I appreciate your help!" Will responded to the positive news he'd received. "Ah ... yes, 66th Avenue, and turn into *ComTek*'s pole yard at the 144th Street light. I'm at the back of the yard. See you shortly," he said with relief and hung up.

Will was reaching for the dial to make another call when Terry Peters pushed open the trailer door and entered. "Man what a mess, eh Will," he said in a harassing way as he slammed the door shut.

Terry Peters was the *ComTek* pole yard foreman, and controlled all the activities of the yard. He was left alone by the *ComTek* management across the street to do what he wished. His boss rarely came to the pole yard, and this afforded Terry a great deal of flexibility.

He was a scrawny little man in his late fifties with graying hair, a clean-shaven face and a broad nose that supported large wire-rimmed glasses. Terry had been with *ComTek* for over thirty years in one capacity or another; he was a strong union man who knew his way around the collective agreement, and understood just how far he could push Sandra Willows, his boss, and Brian Quest for that matter. Terry supervised one other employee at the pole yard, and as the workload was erratic, they frequently spent a great deal of time in the pole yard office or by the front gate talking.

Terry's eyes quickly scanned about Will's trailer and confirmed that no one was lurking inside, and without hesitation focused his attention on Will. "This doesn't mean our arrangement is off, ya know! I still expect my payment at the end of the week. Think of it as insurance—you still must pay no matter what, eh!" he growled.

"I won't be in production until this mess is cleared and Quest replaces the building!" Will replied, annoyed at the demand and Terry's insensitivity to his situation.

"Tough shit, Will, I got my own problems! I could arrange to have my log loader go into *Ernie's* for maintenance, and then I'd need yours. So buck up, it could be worse," and with that reminder, Terry turned around, opened the door, and vacated the office.

"When it rains it pours! I don't know how much longer I'll be able to tolerate that jerk," Will muttered as he became more annoyed, thinking about the predicament that he was in.

Will Richards knew that he was stuck with the situation. The payouts to Terry had been going on for over two years. The agreement with *ComTek* included the right for *Service Pole Recycling* to use the second log loader that had been purchased as a spare, to ensure *ComTek* could continue operations should the prime loader break down. That was the political story that Fred Hawthorn had used to justify the purchase of the second machine, which had really been intended for Will's sole use.

Losing the log loader was a major operational blow to Will's business when it occurred. The disruption was expensive, and paying to reduce that risk seemed justified somehow—but the situation gnawed at Will's ethics, and he hated the no-win situation.

Will's operation was non-union, as that was the only way he could operate and market the recycled product at a competitive price. People love recycled goods, but don't like to pay the same price as virgin product—in fact they expect to pay less.

Terry's strong connection with the union provided him an opportunity to make it difficult for a non-union operation on the *ComTek* site to carry on business. Will knew that this circumstance did present some risk to both the operation and his workers, so he buckled down and paid Terry his blackmail money.

Will had always kept this little secret between himself and Terry, but today had pushed the issue. "The day will come to resolve this problem!" Will vowed to himself, and he returned his focus to the problem of restoring his operation.

Service Pole Recycling continued to carry on business activities with the reduced workforce. A new load of used poles was being off-loaded; Jack was operating the log loader, picking a few poles at a time and placing them on the pole pile, to ensure they were stacked safely. The roadway by the large pile of used poles was narrow, and the loader operator needed to be skilled in handling full-length poles. Jack took the pole count and made the office notes for Will, which included the date, quantity, and delivery driver's name.

The pole count was extremely important to *ComTek* and *Service Pole Recycling*. The agreement included a delivery penalty that *ComTek* had to pay should a minimum number of poles not be provided to *Service Pole Recycling*. At the time, when the agreement had been conceived, the parties were concerned that insufficient poles would be provided to make the recycling operation financially viable; as a result, a penalty payment to reimburse *Service Pole Recycling* for lost revenue was implemented. If a shortfall was recorded at the end of each business year, the penalty payment had to be made by *ComTek*.

Historically, *ComTek* had paid some volume penalty every year, and often the penalty income was needed to show any type of business profit for *Service Pole*. Will took a meager salary for his effort, and the operation ran on a shoestring most of the time.

The rain had stopped, and the last remnants of the snowstorm had been washed away, leaving the typical wet yard and gravel roadway with lots of potholes. Will was constantly pressing Terry Peters to have new gravel brought in to the yard to maintain the roadway, but little had been done in the past few years. Will's crew could often be seen manually moving gravel about to fill the large holes, because the holes made operating a loader full of poles more difficult and dangerous.

Ray Patterson was out talking to the driver from *Bin Services*, who was preparing to load a full bin of wood waste, and transport it to a special waste landfill in Delta. He walked away from the *Bin Services* driver after he directed him where to leave the newly delivered empty bin, before picking up the full load that was ready for the landfill. Ray entered the office with mud up to the top of his boots. "Hey, Will, that driver just told me that he heard there's some kind of pole handling change coming from *ComTek*! Have you heard anything?" Ray inquired with a booming voice.

"Nope," Will replied, surprised. "John was just here, but said nothing to me about any pole handling changes. Those guys are always up to something. If it's anything to do with delivered poles, it's designed to screw us!"

"Just thought that I would pass it on," Ray commented and exited the office to return to work.

Will sighed, thought about what Ray had told him, and wondered what type of change *ComTek* could be planning. They had not said anything to him, so it was a big concern. He had sent John a report earlier in the year, making recommendations on how to cut costs and improve the efficiency of the processes. Thomas Howe had helped him with the preparation of the report, to make sure the financial projections and presentation were done correctly. Will had inquired numerous times as to the whereabouts of the report, but hadn't received any response. John Humphries didn't help either, even though John had been given a copy of the proposed cost-reduction projects.

"Perhaps they were going to implement one of the recommendations, but then why not talk to me about it first?" Will growled, frustrated.

The ringing phone on his desk pulled him from his thoughts and he swiveled in his chair to answer it. Will recognized the phone number on the call display.

"Hey, Will, it's Steve at *BC Parks*. How's it going over there?" the long-term customer asked.

"Not good," Will admitted. "The snowstorm on the weekend collapsed the mill roof and everything's shut down. Thank God it's warming up, or I'd be freezing my ass in the office here!"

"Wow, sorry to hear it. I need some stuff. Can you see if you have any of it in stock?"

Will scribbled down the order and promised to call back once the inventory had been checked. Will's recycled product had become a preferred construction standard for *BC Parks*, as it had for a number of other governmental agencies and local municipalities. Will had worked very hard in building his clientele, and his operation was well known in the lower mainland; but his margins were small, demanding that Will maintain high volumes to make ends meet.

He was getting chilled, and decided to grab a coffee from *Tim Hortons*® up the street. He put the *BC Parks* order on his chair, and planned to check the stock for Steve when he got back. Will was putting on his coat when the trailer door opened.

"Hi, Mr. Richards, I'm Ricardo Sanchez, the new security manager for *ComTek*. I finally got here to see how you are doing with the situation," Ricardo started. "I got a call from my office on Sunday, but everything seemed in hand and I didn't think I needed to come straight away. What a bugger eh?"

"It's good to meet you, Ricardo. Hey, I was about to get a warm coffee at *Tim Hortons*®. Why don't we go and have a talk there? It's too cold in here!" Will suggested.

"*Tim Hortons*®! Shit no, I'll buy you a late breakfast at *Denny's*® up on King George. Okay?" Ricardo suggested, "Let's take my truck," Ricardo grinned, "and use *ComTek*'s gas."

As the men left the office and headed toward Ricardo's company truck, Will saw Ray Patterson finishing up with the *Bin Services* driver and yelled, "Ray, going out for a bit. Watch the shop."

The two men jumped into the new white Ford Super Cab displaying *ComTek* markings on the doors, and headed out for breakfast.

Ricardo Sanchez was a strapping man who had been an RCMP officer in a previous life. The man had broad shoulders and his jet-black hair was cut short and was well manicured. He'd joined *ComTek* as their Security Manager a couple of months earlier. He had told everyone in the company that the demands of a cop's life had become a strain. It wasn't true, but it was a plausible story, and he knew that no one would check his references very closely. He had left the force two years before, as a result of a breach of conduct charge and a disciplinary hearing. His personal interests had occasionally come into conflict, and a graceful departure had been worked out, saving face for all concerned.

They sat at a quiet booth in the back of the restaurant. Will didn't know anything about Ricardo so he asked, "How do you like working for *ComTek*?"

"Sure beats the demands of the RCMP," Ricardo replied with a smile as he peered at Will who was wearing a well-used, dirty baseball cap. "I seem to be still getting to know how things are done in this company, and have a lot of people to meet. My office in the *Central City Tower* is great, and the facility is a nice place to work."

"Are you of Latin decent? You don't have much of an accent, but your last name is Sanchez," Will asked curiously. He paused and added with a smile, "I just wondered."

"Yes, well my parents are Colombian. My dad died when I was three and my mother moved from Bogotá to Canada after his death. We lived in a small apartment in the East End for years. I still speak Spanish with my mother, but other than that, I'm pure Canadian now," Ricardo answered, recalling his early childhood. "Canada's a great melting pot for those looking to find a new and better life. I joined the RCMP in my late teens, after finishing the mandatory High School requirement. What about you, Will?"

The waitress came by to take their orders. "Sorry to interrupt you guys, what can I get you two for breakfast?" she asked, holding a notepad.

"A Grand Slam® omelet with brown toast," replied Ricardo.

"I'll have the two eggs sunny side up with bacon and white toast. Coffee for both of us, thank you," ordered Will with a smile.

The waitress quickly brought the two coffees and returned to the kitchen to place the two orders as Will started to answer Ricardo's question. "My family was farmers in the old days. There were lots of kids to do the chores and the hard work. We lived in the Abbotsford area, and had quite a tract of land there. I left home early and went to work. I've operated lots of types of heavy equipment in my days." Will continued, "I came up with the idea to recycle the old hydro and telephone poles that were taken out of service, and presented the idea to Fred Hawthorn at *ComTek* in 1994. It's been a great idea, but it's become a lot harder to make a buck in these economic times. *ComTek* has become a bigger pain in the ass, too, especially once Fred Hawthorn retired!" Will replied, frustrated.

"I was concerned when I received my office report about your situation," Ricardo refocused the conversation. "What can I do for you while you get things sorted out?" he asked, looking closely at Will.

"Well, my biggest concern at this point is the exposure the mill has to local thieves. They often come snooping around my place looking for equipment, and the copper power cables that *ComTek* stores in the pole yard. Copper is a good cash item that can feed the druggie's habit for a while. With the power cut, the alarm isn't functional, and it won't take long for those guys to figure that out!"

"Hmm ... I'll have the guards be more diligent, but their guard station's quite a distance away from your operation, Will, which is well hidden behind the piles of old poles. It's very hard for the guards to see what's going on at your place with the power and lighting disconnected," Ricardo pointed out.

"Yea, well, I'd set up generators, but those bastards would steal them, too, and I can't afford them anyway. I appreciate your concern and help, though," Will replied, feeling hopeful. "Your support in increasing guard inspections at night would help until I can get the power turned back on."

"I'll see what I can arrange," Ricardo replied as the two breakfasts appeared.

Chapter Four

The spray of dirty water was difficult for the windshield wipers to keep clear, as the sleek black sports car headed northward up the TransCanada Highway. The vehicle was just passing the Mount Lehman interchange, and the highway conditions were still treacherous; Brian Quest, sitting low in the sports car front seat, could feel the patches of ice and slush on the roadway through the steering wheel. The conditions of the expressway deteriorated as the elevation climbed from the Fraser River crossing of the Port Mann Bridge. Highway One shadowed the Fraser River on its northbound route toward Hope, where the flatlands of the Fraser Valley ended and the landscape became mountainous.

Chilliwack was halfway between Abbotsford, where Brian Quest was currently navigating the expressway, and the town of Hope. Locations like Chilliwack were attractive sites for new businesses to set up shop. The cost of living for potential workers was considerably lower than adjacent Vancouver cities, and commuting for out of town employees would be in the reverse direction of the heavy traffic heading into the city. The TransCanada afforded an attractive transportation route to the United States through the Sumas border crossing, to the eastern parts of Canada, and to the Vancouver shipping ports serving Asia, China, and India. *BC Transformer Incorporated* selected the Chilliwack area for those key reasons. An attractive arrangement with *ComTek* had been worked out eighteen months earlier, making the investment viable and low risk for the overseas owners.

The transformer manufacturing plant was brand new, and funded with offshore capital looking to Canada for investment opportunities.

Brian took the exit onto Luckakuck Way, and travelled along the winding road to his destination. His appointment was for noon, and he was on time despite the driving conditions of the late morning. He parked his vehicle in a visitor's parking space outside the main entrance. Grabbing his briefcase and BlackBerry® from the seat, Brian ejected himself from the black, low-slung car. He placed his phone in his pocket and locked the car door with the remote.

The front entrance of the building was all glass, and the glass encased the two-story office and large foyer. Opening the heavy glass doors, Brian proceeded directly across the gray marble floor to the receptionist counter.

"Good morning, I've an appointment with Mr. Lee," Brian informed the young woman.

"Oh yes, Mr. Quest. Mr. Lee is expecting you," Sandra, the woman with her name on a badge, replied politely. "I will inform him that you are here. Please take a seat." She gestured toward a cluster of large, white leather chairs situated to her left.

Brian nodded, walked to the set of chairs and eyed the business magazines on the glass table. The room was bright, even for the dull day, and the décor was new and inviting. Two large paintings in black frames were placed on the wall down a short distance from the receptionist. He sat down, placed the briefcase next to him and pulled his cell phone from his pocket. He had just started to review his messages when the receptionist walked over to him. "Mr. Lee can see you now. Please just take the elevator to the second floor," she smiled, and pointed to the stainless steel door across the foyer.

Brian placed the BlackBerry® back into his pocket, grabbed his briefcase, and rose to his feet. He could hear the echo of his footsteps as he walked toward the elevator door.

He rode quickly to the second floor. The door opened to an exclusive entrance to the executive suites. It was a private entrance; the office staff employees entered the second floor offices through a different elevator, accessed through a hallway running behind the main foyer.

Facing the executive elevator door was a well-appointed waiting area, which opened onto the large glass windows in the front of the building that Brian had seen when he arrived earlier. West Coast native carvings were on display, placed on the wall behind the reception area.

"Good afternoon, Mr. Quest," the executive receptionist greeted in a soft voice. She was a stunning petite Asian woman with an inviting smile. Her hair was pulled back from her face, and she was dressed in a tight, red dress that clung to her shapely body. "Mr. Lee is waiting in his office. You know your way down the hall."

Brian reached the executive office and knocked politely on the door. The door had an elegant brass plate with "Tom Lee, President" inscribed and appropriately placed. Brian was aware that the Asian culture was very formal and respectful, and that proper protocol was expected at all times.

"Ah Brian, come in and sit down," the voice from the office invited him in, and continued as Brian entered the room, "It's always a pleasure to have you visit."

The office was tastefully decorated, with a large, black executive desk in front of a matching credenza. The executive furniture had carvings of Chinese symbols and figures, and was as much a piece of art as it was functional. Alongside the office large, glass windows was a small sitting area with two black leather sofas, separated by a black, glassed table with hand-carved legs that looked like serpents' tails.

A large computer monitor was on the edge of the large desk, turned away from the window glare. A printer sat on the credenza along with gold-framed, family photographs. A large Asian painting in a thick black ornate frame was hung above the credenza.

"I have taken the liberty of ordering lunch," the thinly built man said stiffly. "Ho Lin will set up a place for us in the conference room. Would you like to see our new line of transformers after lunch, or will you need to depart immediately after our discussion?" Tom inquired. "Unfortunately, I've a pressing situation that will need my attention after we eat, so I won't be able to accompany you if you choose to stay, however."

"That's a wonderful offer, and I'd like to see your new production line, but I'd prefer to postpone the tour and see it next time. With the road conditions today, I think I should leave directly after our meeting," Brian replied respectfully.

"Well then, let's have lunch and talk," Tom replied, and pressed the intercom button on the telephone, buzzing the front receptionist. "We are ready to start our meal now," he said, and pointed Brian toward the room next door.

Ho Lin came into the conference room with a large silver tray of Chinese food, Wonton soup and a pot of green tea. The conference table had two place settings with chop sticks, and small tea cups set across from each other at the end of the table.

The oval, red oak table had carvings skirting the edge and could seat sixteen executives. The chairs were square in design, were also of red oak, and were very heavy. They had silk-pad seats that tied around the chair legs, and had carvings at the top of each chair that matched the table. The room had a large, flat screen monitor affixed to the end wall, and the long side walls had framed photographs of the manufacturing plant and transformer products.

Tom Lee was a small, thin man of Chinese origin. He was born in Hong Kong and learned English as a course of the culture. The English language was a mandatory skill if anyone wanted to be in business with the North Americans. Tom was turning fifty-eight in a few months, and had thin, balding hair that was immaculately groomed. He wore a dark gray, pinstripe suit, black shoes, a black executive long-sleeved shirt, and a narrow, black and gray tie. He had a typical Asian complexion, and narrow, piecing, dark eyes that were surrounded by thin, wire-rimmed glasses.

Brian spoke first, once the men were seated and Ho Lin had left the room and closed the door. "I appreciate the hot lunch. You know it's one of my favorite meals," he said as he looked directly at Tom. "Based upon our recommendations, the expanded transformer tender has been approved by *ComTek*'s procurement group, and you'll be receiving confirmation within the next week. It's been a long road Tom, but we've prevailed!" Brian smiled as he informed his host.

"Ah ... very good, Brian! I knew that you would be able to make this come to pass as you promised us. I guess I need to keep my end of the bargain now," Tom replied with an expressionless face. "Our Hong Kong people will be pleased to get the news. Do you know when the details of the first revised order will be given to us?"

"My office is working on that now, Tom. I've had my staff plan for this contract for some time now, and the requirement lists and delivery schedule forecasts are expected to be on my desk by the end of the week," Brian replied with a large grin. "I've planned for this far in advance, you know!" he added, speaking in an overconfident voice.

The men finished their meals without much more conversation. After the tea had been finished, Tom rose to indicate the meeting had been concluded. "I'm glad that our meeting has been successful," Tom said as he faced Brian. "Please ask Ho Lin to give you the envelope that I left with her to give to you." Tom turned, opened his office door, and looked back at Brian, "Please schedule another meeting with Ho Lin. We should meet next month and see where we are with the orders and other business," he said stone-faced, and then closed the door.

Brian got up from the table, grabbed his briefcase, and proceeded to see Ho Lin. "You've an envelope for me."

"Oh yes, Mr. Lee informed me that you may be picking up this package today," she replied and handed Brian the white envelope.

"Thank you. Mr. Lee has requested that you schedule another meeting for us later next month. What's available in the early part of the last week?" Brian inquired stiffly.

"Let's see," Ho Lin replied as she searched Mr. Lee's schedule for available dates that suited Brian's request. "I have Tuesday the twentieth. The entire afternoon is free. How does that work for you, Mr. Quest?" she asked, looking up from the computer monitor.

Brian pulled out his BlackBerry® and checked his schedule. "Great. Let's schedule that time," he told the young woman and made a note on his calendar, marking it "Chilliwack." Brian opened his briefcase, shoved the white envelope inside, and headed for the elevator.

He returned to his car, and pressed his lips together tightly as he surveyed the white colored road mess covering his beautiful ride. He unlocked the door, entered the driver's seat and got himself comfortable, fishing out his cell phone from his pocket. He punched a speed-dial number and waited for an answer.

"Hi, I've been waiting for your call all day!" the female voice came from the phone.

"It's going to be too late today, so how about tomorrow after lunch?" Brian asked.

"Uh … yea that works for me, too. I'll block my calendar," the voice replied in a low tone.

"Great, we're on then." Brian smiled, hung up and started the sports car.

Chapter Five

Thomas Howe was sitting in front of his computer in his home study. He had retired from *ComTek* a few years earlier, and was now a business consultant working with owners and Boards of small businesses. He was fifty-eight, a relatively short person, and sported the typical mid-aged tummy bulge. He had a fair completion, common of someone with an Anglo-Saxon heritage, and thinning, blond hair and a small mustache.

His home office was well suited for his practice, and was in a room at the back of a three-story house in White Rock that overlooked Semiahmoo Bay. The office walls were covered in framed certificates, diplomas, and reminders of his parents, now passed.

A large, brown, leather easy chair was in an end corner. A cluttered bookshelf matching the blond-colored office furniture sat beside the arm chair. The main office desk was a small, oval tabletop that was designed for a small office space.

Thomas was doing his biweekly accounting for his consulting firm, and the desktop was full of receipts and invoices waiting to be processed. He sat in a comfortable, black, swivel, executive-style chair as he processed the paperwork. He tended to peer over his eyeglass frames that were perched on the edge of his large nose. He was nearsighted and often looked over the rims of his glasses to see the small print on the screen. He was contemplating the appropriate transaction for the receipt at the top of the pile when the phone rang. The call display announced that it was Will Richards on the line. Will frequently called to chat about some issue of the day, or something crazy that he had heard about *ComTek*.

"Hi, Will. What's up?" Thomas inquired as he picked up the phone, continuing to stare at the computer monitor.

"You won't believe it, but the snowstorm collapsed my mill building's roof! It's a mess and John Humphries seems to be stalling on agreeing to pay to fix it!" Will replied, exasperated. "*PowerOne* has yanked the power, too. I expect to get a cost quote to fix the place later today, though," Will blurted out his situation as his voice began to raise an octave, "Those bastards just don't get it!"

"The storm went through White Rock like a freight train, but I never expected it to do that sort of damage out your way! How long do you think it's going to take if we press John?" Thomas inquired, concerned.

"Oh, a week at least, I expect. I cut the staff down to Ray and Jack, and expect I can keep them busy for a while, but Helen will be up my ass if it's any longer," Will replied, sounding exhausted and speaking faster with every word. "There's a rumor going around here that those assholes are also planning some type of pole-handling process change or something. I thought that it might be because of our recommendations, but I doubt it. They've never called me on that report we did, ya know! Can we have lunch tomorrow?" Will rambled on.

"Ah ... okay. I'll come to the mill site, and you can show me what's left of the building, and then we can go to lunch from there. How about I show up at about eleven in the morning?"

"Well, make it eleven thirty, as the power is out and the office is cold. We'd be able to see everything in half an hour anyway!" Will replied.

"Okay, eleven thirty then. Don't worry, we'll sort this out," Thomas replied reassuringly, and he hung up the call.

The relationship between Will Richards and Thomas Howe went back to when the mill had just opened and Thomas had become responsible for the recycling project. Thomas was the Business Support Manager for *ComTek*'s logistics group, and had been asked by Fred Hawthorne to oversee the business venture between *ComTek* and *Service Pole Recycling*. Thomas was the only professional engineer on staff at CLG and Fred thought that Thomas had adequate time to fit the recycling project into his responsibilities, which included the information technology strategy and process changes for the growing operation.

Thomas always had enjoyed working with Will, and as the environmental project was a legacy of his earlier days with *ComTek*, he wanted to continue to help Will succeed with the project.

"Hey hon, who was that on the phone?" a woman's voice inquired from down the hall.

"Oh, just Will Richards with a problem at the mill. It seems that this weekend's snowstorm severely damaged his building, and he needs me to go out there and see it tomorrow," Thomas answered his wife.

"Always some disaster over there, it seems to me!" Jennifer commented with a sigh, as she joined Thomas in his office.

"Yeh, that's Will. It sounds bad this time though, and I might have to get involved. *ComTek* seems to be becoming more difficult than ever!" Thomas exclaimed, pondering the situation.

"Be careful. Remember you're retired, and *ComTek* hasn't treated you well in the past either!" she warned, sounding concerned as she walked out of the office and down the winding staircase toward the kitchen.

Jennifer Howe was a fabulous-looking woman, now in her early fifties. She was a petite brunette with her hair cut short. Her clear, youthful face radiated a kind and calm personality. Her blue eyes sparkled as she talked to her husband of twenty years. They had a daughter who now attended University, and with her away at school, the large house seemed very quiet. Thomas needed to have a project or two to keep him busy and focused. *Service Pole Recycling* was one of those distractions that kept his business juices flowing and his hand engaged with the *ComTek* antics.

Thomas had worked for *ComTek* for almost twenty-five years, and had enjoyed the challenges and rewarding projects for most of his time there. Empty promises and vindictive actions, blamed on policy or circumstance, had stripped him of promotions and influence in the last few years of his career, and had left him bitter and untrusting. He eventually was offered an opportunity to retire, a more dignified life than the stress-imposed political *ComTek* nightmare. He never forgot how he was played by the politically influential, and those who were involved. He wanted to ensure that the same fate didn't happen to Will Richards and he had his own agenda to get even with those in *ComTek* who had betrayed his trust.

♓

It was a very cold night, and the rain had finally stopped earlier that evening. The sky had partially cleared, but no moon had appeared in the skyline. An old, black minivan turned off 144th Street onto a poorly graveled lane, where some new low-rise buildings were being constructed. The vehicle passed the construction area and wandered to the back lot, then turned away from the construction and crept behind a large pile of topsoil overgrown with weeds. The driver knew that these piles of soil had been abandoned some years ago, and they afforded a great hiding place to park. The headlights were off as the vehicle turned around so that the front faced the route back.

Two men exited the vehicle and carefully closed their doors. The taller man wore a dark coat that covered only his upper body, exposing his worn blue jeans, and heavy industrial boots that laced up past his ankles. The shorter, second man wore a dirty cap, a heavy, black overall top, a pair of unwashed blue jeans that had a rip in the left knee, and rubber boots. The shorter man carried a bag of tools and a flashlight.

The flashlight was pointed directly toward the muddy ground as the men walked in single file away from the old van. The short man carrying the flashlight slowly picked his way along an old road that had been washed out over the years. A heavily wooded area was on the men's left side that blocked their view of a small, local, fenced substation, but it also provided adequate protection from anyone noticing their approach. They knew that a locked fence gate would be about ten meters from their starting point and was secluded from view. The muddy roadway skirted a transmission right-of-way, adding to their comfort that they would not be detected. They had been at that place before, and they were familiar with their route and target, which lay ahead in the dark, cold, early morning silence.

"We're here!" the short man said in a low voice as he opened the tool bag and grabbed the bolt cutters from the bag. The fence gate was locked with a chain that wrapped around two old metal posts, and it was affixed with a padlock that joined the end links together. The site was deserted, and the only person awake was a guard some one hundred and fifty meters away, at the entrance to the *ComTek* pole yard. It was two thirty in the morning and the men cut through the gate chain, pulled the gate open, and slipped into the muddy yard.

The flashlight beam remained pointed to the ground. The intruders walked along, and eventually reached a dimly-lit log bunker housing a large saw blade. They remained concealed by high piles of logs and a heavy lean-to constructed of old power poles. The men knew that not making a noise was the key to their success, and they had to be diligent not to attract the attention of the attending guard up the road! The street lights running along 64th Avenue and 144th Street were totally obscured by the buildings and trees surrounding the mill site, and the men's eyes strained to see in the darkness.

The two men approached the silent mill building. They had frequently checked the mill location many times before, posing as customers, and knew that it had been damaged in the snowstorm and that the power had been disconnected. This time the alarm could not announce their presence, and they now only worried about the unsuspecting security guard.

In the protection of the dark, and cover of the remote location, the men worked their way to the electrical control panel where it still remained erect after the collapse of the roof. The site had been cleared of the debris from the mill floor, and all the power cables feeding the equipment had been exposed, leaving them now easily accessible.

"Eh man, the stuff's open and it'll be like taking candy from a baby," the taller man spoke in a low Hispanic tone.

"Yea, let's get this done and get our asses out of here!" the shorter man replied, and they began cutting and stripping the site of the valuable exposed copper cables.

The cables were cut into pieces and the lengths didn't matter, just the copper was the prize. Cutting the cables enabled them to carry the heavy metal, and they quietly placed each piece in a pile alongside the log bunker. Their eyes had adjusted to the darkness; they were able to see enough with the light of the clearing sky and no longer needed the flashlight.

In less than an hour they began to carry the loot back to the parked minivan, still protected by the early morning darkness. They piled the wire into the back of the van making a number of trips, walking carefully back and forth through the mud until all the lengths of cables had been transported.

They jumped into the front seat of the van, turned toward each other and smiled.

"Off to payday!" the shorter man exclaimed and started the van's engine. The vehicle wound back along the muddy roadway as it had done earlier, with the headlights still off. The last thing they needed now was for a cop to see them coming out from behind the large pile of dirt!

As the vehicle approached the construction site it became easy to see the well-lit, paved roadway ahead. No vehicles could be seen travelling along the street and the van's headlights were turned on as it pulled into the roadway. The vehicle quickly travelled southward, away from the *ComTek* yard. "Thanks, guys!" the taller man said as he glanced through the van's side window and watched the passing buildings zip by.

Chapter Six

Will Richards had awakened early in the morning, and was sitting at his home desk trying to figure out how to save his e-mail notes into named folders. He wasn't very good with the computer, and he had been given the Toshiba® laptop by Thomas Howe only a few months earlier. His customers frequently wanted to get prices and quotes from him via e-mail, and he knew that it was time to figure out how to use the computer.

He and Helen had had an awful argument the night before about the mill. She had insisted that he close the entire mess down, especially in light of the disastrous roof collapse. She was verbally abusive and demanded that she be removed from the company's Board, and that any business losses be his responsibility only. He had agreed, just to stop the yelling and screaming, and he had retired to his small room downstairs, frustrated and upset.

Will had moved his office downstairs many months before, and he was sitting at an executive desk that Thomas Howe had sold him when Thomas' father passed away. "God damn computer e-mail," he grumbled under his breath. "I'll have to get Thomas to help me when I see him next at his home, and I'll bring this damn machine thing with me!"

Will had decided to stay home and work from the warmth of his basement office. The mill trailer was cold and there was little he could do there at this point. He had received the quotation for the replacement of the hoarding cover, and the thirty-six grand was way more than he'd expected. The existing tubular structure was scrap and an entire new building would be necessary, especially since the load capacity needed to be significantly increased to meet current standards.

Will had passed this news on to John at *ComTek* the day before, and had received a very cold response. John agreed to let Brian know, and have a decision on any funding that might be made available confirmed quickly. Will explained that he needed the mill back in operation! It was still too early to call John, so Will continued to fight with his computer in the meantime.

The basement office was a good get-away from Helen, and it was outfitted with an old sofa and a TV. He loved to watch Nascar® and football with his son, now nineteen and becoming a young adult. Will desperately wanted to leave Helen, but he was very close to all his kids and he wanted to wait until the youngest had come of age and could function on her own. He certainly was stuck, and the situation at the mill and *ComTek*'s attitude didn't help any.

It was now eight thirty in the morning, and he reached to phone John Humphries to get an update.

"John here," the cold voice growled at the other end.

"Morning John, it's Will Richards," Will apprehensively started the conversation. "I'm just calling to see if you had an opportunity to talk with Brian Quest concerning the quote I gave you yesterday for replacing the building," Will continued, holding his breath.

"Yea, well, I was going to call later this morning. We talked everything over and Brian has decided that it's not *ComTek*'s responsibility to pay for the damage or any replacement. You're on your own, Will." The voice sounded its usual indifferent tone. "I guess you'd better figure something out, as we'll still be shipping used poles to your site, as spelled out in our agreement!"

"What do you expect me to do, John? You guys supplied the initial building and it's on your property. You have to replace it!" Will responded in an angry tone, almost yelling.

"Not us, man! You've to figure this out yourself, Will!" and John abruptly hung up.

Will sat in his office, stunned. He knew that John was a prick, and that *ComTek* was being difficult, but he'd never expected this! He immediately picked up the phone and called Thomas Howe.

"Hey Thomas, it's almost nine, and I had to call!" Will knew that he wasn't supposed to call before nine in the morning, and his voice was a higher pitch than usual. "*ComTek* won't pay to replace the mill building! Brian's being an asshole and they told me it's my problem. I've been busting my ass for all these years for them, and this is the payback I get! I trusted them to support the project and do the right thing!"

"Hold on, Will! Slow down a notch. Bring me up to speed," Thomas asked, taking a breath.

"Ah, I got the quote to replace the building. It's thirty-six grand and I told John yesterday."

"Wow, thirty-six grand!" Thomas inhaled with surprise. "That's a bit pricy don't you think, Will?" Thomas exclaimed, concerned at the amount.

"I pushed the supplier to even get that price! The new structure must be brought up to code for the snow load, and a stronger and more stable wall is required to bolt down the infrastructure. I also need to have large wind vents placed at the back to ensure the wind can flow through and prevent the roof from being pulled off with any future updraft," Will explained, speaking quickly. "I don't have thirty-six Gs and

Helen will never agree to extend our line of credit. She's already told me to quit and find a real job!" Will exclaimed loudly and frustrated.

"Okay, okay, take a breath. Let me sit on the situation for a bit and think what approach to use here! Christ, thirty-six grand—that's a lot of money, Will! Are you sure you want to keep on doing this?" Thomas prodded for confirmation.

"Sure do, and I know I can make money with this project! Once *ComTek* backs off and starts to support what I'm doing, as they have in the past, all will be good. Besides, *MiTel* and *InterLink Cable* have always supported me, and maybe they can put some pressure on *ComTek*. Those telecommunication companies have a stake in this, too, ya know!"

"Yea, well, *MiTel* and *InterLink* have never shown the balls to stand up to *ComTek* before. They've always played the silent partner game, and they avoid pissing off *ComTek* at any turn—you know that, Will!"

"Look, I'm working at home today, as the trailer's without power and I can get more done here at the house. Let's postpone our lunch to another day later this week, okay?" Will asked, recalling his date with Thomas. "By the way, I called close to nine," he said in a calmer mood and a smile on his face.

"Yea, close enough. Let's touch base later!"

Jennifer passed by Thomas' office as he hung up the phone. "Will in crisis mode again?"

"Yea, it sure looks like it. The replacement building's thirty-six grand and *ComTek* told him they aren't going to help. They sure have turned into self-centered bastards; it's not the place I knew!" Thomas replied, as he sat in his office chair and pondered the situation. Jennifer left Thomas's office and headed downstairs as Thomas sat lost in thought. "Hmm …

what would be the best course of action?" Thomas mumbled to himself.

"I'm going down to make breakfast and grab a coffee. You want anything?" Jennifer asked as she reached the bottom of the stairs.

"No thanks, Dear, not right now. I need to think a bit," he replied, turning the situation around in his head.

♓

Terry Peters sat in his office and glanced at his helper, Andrew Sayer, as he loaded a log trailer with an order of new poles. The truck driver was standing next to Terry's desk, watching Terry prepare a set of shipping documents.

"The boss told me to give you this package when I arrived this morning," the East Indian driver said as he handed the *ComTek* foreman a small manila envelope with "Terry" scribbled on the face.

"Okay." Terry glanced again outside, took the envelope, and then completed the shipping documents for the pole load. "Sign here," he instructed, and pushed the shipping document to the corner of his desk.

The driver signed at the bottom of the sheet; Terry pulled a copy from the document set and handed the driver his copy. "Hey, I've a new shipment of BC Gold; ya know we only supply the best weed in town, eh Peters," the driver sneered as he took his copies of the shipping order. "Let your contacts know and call with your order."

"Humph! It's about time!" Terry growled. "I'll let ya know in a few days."

"Yea, ya do that Peters!" the driver replied, and retuned outside to wait for Andrew to secure the load.

Terry slit open the envelope and extracted a sheet of paper. It looked like a bank statement but it wasn't. It was a summary of his loan transactions with Ray Slider Hanson, the Surrey boss of the *Los Chinche* gang. Terry loved playing the stock market, and had often bought on margin. The economic downturn caused by the crisis in the US had forced Terry to cover his increasing losses. Terry had turned to Slider for some short-term cash, thinking that the stock market would quickly recover. It hadn't yet, and his debt had grown to an alarming level. The statement was a chilling reminder that another interest payment was due, and that Slider never took no for an answer.

"Shit!" Terry grumbled as he looked at the outstanding balance at the bottom of the page. He glanced up to ensure that everyone was busy outside, placed the reminder back into its envelope, and slipped it into his briefcase by the side of his desk.

He turned to his computer monitor and continued to read his e-mail, but he couldn't concentrate. He knew Slider's reputation, and knew time was running out. "I'd better press Will for his payment today! That'll be a start anyway," Terry thought as he peered out the office window to check on Andrew's progress. "With the activity around here in the last few days, there hasn't been an opportunity to pull Will aside and get my cash."

♓

Candice Parks was reading her e-mail in her Investment Recovery Department office. She was one of the CLG management team, and was a distraction each time she entered a room. She had a full seductive figure, and she often wore v-cut tops and push-up bras to enhance her cleavage and large breasts. She was blond with shoulder-length hair, parted on one side, which she curled and allowed to dangle on each side of her face. Her physical attributes were a large part of her resume, and her smile and accommodating personality usually overshadowed her lack of formal education and technical skills. She knew what she had, and she used it to her greatest advantage.

She had worked very hard to get the promotion to a management position at the CLG. Fred Hawthorn liked her work ethic, and knew that things had been very tough after her divorce that left her with a teenage daughter to support. She had been the only woman manager on Fred's team, and he just liked having her around. Things had been tough for Candice, and with Brian Quest now running the show, things were a lot more complicated.

The investment recovery operation was responsible for the disposal of all *ComTek*'s customers' unneeded, obsolete, or damaged assets. The operation sold these assets directly to the public, and anyone was allowed to come to the Surrey site and view the on-hand inventory that was for sale. Old computers and short pieces of copper wire were very popular, and the selection of items for sale changed frequently.

Candice had five employees, and the operation ran like a small retail store. Specialty IRD business software had been designed and constructed under the supervision of Thomas Howe a number of years before. Due to its unique function, the application had not been replaced when *ComTek* decided to purchase a new commercial business software package. There had been no capability to handle retail in the new package, so the specialty software had been retained.

Corporate didn't like the situation; there were major control gaps and financial risks in accounting of sales and asset receipts, as the system was now not integrated with the rest of the company's financials. Candice frequently had to ease these concerns with her smile and soft persuasive nature, as she wanted to keep the home-designed software that she knew very well.

Her employees were unloading another shipment of returned project materials from a mini-warehouse up-country. Each shipment had to be sorted through, and any items that were current stock and reusable were separated from the rest. The remaining items were recorded on a separate form, which would be processed into the IRD retail sales system so that they could be sold to the public.

♓

Will Richards was sorting business paperwork that was scattered all over his desk at home. He hated paperwork, and with Helen being such a bitch, he knew that he would be stuck with the office chores, as well as the operations of the mill and product sales. She wasn't going to do the business paperwork any longer or the payroll either, now that she didn't want to have anything to do with the company! She obviously hoped that the additional work pressure would force him to quit.

"Thank God Thomas has done my company books for the last five years!" Will thought, inundated in paper. He knew that so long as he kept all the types of paperwork together, Thomas seemed to get the year-end processed, even though Thomas kept threatening to stop doing the task. Will knew that Thomas would continue to do it anyway; that's what friends did! They had become good friends over the years and Thomas always came to the rescue when push came to shove.

Will's cell phone rang and he fished around the pile of papers and grabbed it.

"Mr. Richards, its *ComTek* security here. Sorry to disturb you, but we've another problem out here! Can you come right away?" an East Indian voice asked.

"Shit, now what!" Will asked himself. "What's the problem that can't wait?" he asked the guard.

"Well, it seems that the mill was broken into last night. I went down to check on things, as Mr. Sanchez said I needed to keep a closer watch on your place, and found that the power cables have been cut and stripped out. I think you need to come and see."

"Christ, I told Ricardo at breakfast yesterday that this was likely to happen. It sure didn't take those bastards long!" Will spit out the words, getting angry. "I'll pack up now and be there in less than an hour. Thanks for your call." He hung up and pitched the phone on the pile of papers. "This nightmare just keeps on going!" Will growled, and started to pull his stuff together to quickly tidy up before he left.

The phone rang again, and this time it was another number he recognized. "Hmm ... *MiTel*. I wonder what they want!" he muttered, then answered the phone again. "Hi Janice, its' been a while. How are you?"

"Crap, Will! Have you checked your e-mail this morning? The shit's sure going to hit the fan now!" she said in an excited, stressed voice. "My boss almost had a fit after I sent him a copy! What's going on over there? I didn't know your building was destroyed!"

"I was going to call you about that situation later today, once Thomas Howe had developed a plan. I haven't had a chance to check my e-mail yet today. I was just on my way out, as the mill was vandalized last night and the guard told me that the buggers took the all the copper power lines."

"Well, it looks like Thomas developed a plan all right! He sent an e-mail to me, John Humphries, *PowerOne* and *InterLink* this morning. It said that *ComTek* was acting unethically and irresponsibly, and that their position on not replacing the building was out of line!" Janice paused, then carried on, "He even said that he would fund the building replacement himself if they didn't have the balls to do it!" she quickly inhaled. "Some love note, eh?" she asked but didn't wait for an answer. "Wait until that note gets around *ComTek*! Thomas sure has brass rocks; I'll say that for him!"

Will smiled—Thomas sure came through! "You never know what Thomas will do when he gets pissed off!"

"Do you really think he'll follow through, and pay for the building?" Janice asked, not knowing what to tell her boss.

"Well, if it comes to that, everyone would be on the hook—big time! I don't know if *ComTek* wants him in their face going forward, though," Will replied, not sure himself if Thomas would carry through on the threat. "I've got to get to the mill! Let's talk later, Janice, after the e-mail circulates."

"There's going to be a shit-storm for sure now!" Janice remarked, thinking about the e-mail and the possible resulting reactions. "Okay, Will, call me later then."

It was almost noon by the time that Will grabbed his gear and left for Surrey. He thought about what Janice had said about the e-mail, and knew that John and Brian didn't like Thomas very much. Thomas knew a lot about lots of things at *ComTek*. They wouldn't like him returning in any way; they had been glad when he'd retired and was out of their space. The e-mail would be a shocking reminder that he could still get back into the picture.

Events rushed through Will's head as he drove to the mill site. "Damn, all I need is another cost to get the mill up and running!" he choked over the thought of the cost to replace the power cables. He recalled the expense the last time, and the price of copper had skyrocketed since then!

Will had a remarkable ability to remember things and numbers, and he knew lots of people. He picked up the cell phone and carefully dialed, while driving. "Hey Pete, I need some help. Thieving bastards apparently broke into the mill site last night and stripped out all my cables. I'm on my way to the mill now. Can you meet me there?" Will inquired of his local electrical contractor friend.

"Well, I've a job I'm finishing, but can be down in a couple of hours. Will that be okay?" the husky, rough voice responded.

"Yea, that's good. It'll take me some time to assess the situation anyway. See you when you get to the mill." With the confirmation he hung up, hoping he would find that the situation at the mill was not as bad as he expected.

Will didn't want to call Thomas just yet, as he first wanted to see if there would be a response from *ComTek* towards the e-mail. He was sure they were running around, and trying to decide what to do with the pointed note. He wished that he'd taken a moment to read the e-mail himself, but the situation at the mill had taken priority. He recalled that he needed to get back to *BC Parks* with a response on their wood order, too. He made a mental note to pull the order sheet and check before the end of the day.

♓

Larry Langstone sat in his executive office considering the recommendations described in the report that he was reading. He pressed the intercom on his phone. "Carolynn, please get me Peter Fisher on the phone."

Larry's phone rang moments later.

"I've Peter on line two," Carolynn said, thinking that it was very unusual for Larry to call Peter, so she decided to listen in on the conversation. Peter Fisher was an Executive VP and very influential. Larry only called when Peter's brand of politics was required.

"Good morning, Peter, it's Larry."

"Hi Larry, how's Sanchez working out?" he asked in a monotone voice.

"He's a great find. He'll serve us well I think, Peter."

"How's the pole recycling situation shaping up?"

"Ah ... a wrinkle or two. Did you know that Thomas Howe has got his face in things again?" Larry asked.

"I thought we took care of him a number of years ago. It took some strings to get him pulled from that Fleet manager's job, and moving forward that reorganization a month early sure screwed him!" he chuckled.

"Yea, well that really pissed off a lot of people besides Howe; anyway, he's still stirring up issues! People never change. He'll be gone for good once Will Richards is eliminated. Anyway, I called about an opportunity to sell off our Fleet Services division."

"Sell Fleet! That's interesting ...."

"There's a big opportunity for both of us, Peter. I've seen the numbers, and it wouldn't take much to put together a strong proposal. With your support and influence it'd be a slam dunk!"

"Hum ... okay Larry, I'll come to your house tonight and we'll discuss your thoughts and rationale in private. Oh ... you'd better watch your step with Howe. We caught him off guard once, but he'll be wiser this time!"

⯎

Will's green truck turned into the pole yard entrance, and he stopped at the security shack. "Thanks for the call," Will said to the guard as he rolled down the driver's side window.

"It's my job, Mr. Richards," the bearded man replied with an expressionless face.

The small truck turned into the pole yard roadway and travelled directly to the mill site. The property was vacant, as Will had called the boys the night before and told them not to come to work. Following the fight with Helen, he decided to have his men off for the rest of the week.

The cell phone rang, and Will reached for it as it lay on the cluttered passenger seat. Chainsaw pieces were scattered on the passenger side floor, and loose change rattled in the cigarette tray as he travelled over the gravel road and parked in front of the trailer. "Hello, Will here."

"Will, it's John. I received a note from Thomas Howe earlier today," he said curtly. "I've been discussing your situation again with Brian for the last hour! We've decided to pay to replace the building to a maximum of the thirty-six grand. The deal is that you must keep Thomas out of this! After all, he's retired and things would become too complicated with him involved. We'll work out something separate with *MiTel* and *InterLink*," he informed Will with a frustrated, grumbling demeanor. "I'll send you an e-mail confirming our agreement and you get the building put back up!" he growled and hung up abruptly.

Will sighed with relief. "Thomas sure pushed someone's button with his note! I'll bet that someone's really pissed," he thought and smiled. "Great!" Will exclaimed, and he began to dial the supplier to schedule the building replacement.

"Now, to deal with problem number two!" Will muttered after completing his first phone call. He exited his truck and began to survey the damage done by the overnight intruders.

The heist had been very thorough, and all the power cables had been cut at the padlocked control panel. The noise to break the panel lock would've been too risky for the thieves and they elected to cut the cables, rather than break the box and disconnect them from the main bus bar. The difference in the amount of copper was irrelevant, and an undetected visit obviously had been more important.

He was sure that Pete would arrive soon and he'd have some estimate of the cost and time frame for the electrical replacement before he went home. Will opened his office trailer, and retrieved the *BC Parks* order sheet. He grabbed the paper and went to check the stock to see if he could supply the order from what was already cut. He counted the boards and posts sitting in strapped piles placed in the yard.

"Okay, great. I've got enough to fill this one!" Will muttered with a smile.

He returned to his warm truck and dialed *BC Parks*. "Hi, it's Will. I've got all your stuff in stock. When do you want it, Steve?"

"I'll send a truck tomorrow—we need the materials right away. Thanks, Will, for getting back to me so quickly. We just love using your stuff, you know!"

Will decided it was time to call Thomas to check on the aftermath of the e-mail. "Thomas, it's Will—I hear that you sent a bombshell out this morning!"

"Yea, what'd you think? I got pissed off with all the bullshit at *ComTek* I guess, and let it rip."

"Well bud, it hit the spot, and they backed off and agreed to pay for the building! I guess you pushed the buggers into a corner. I haven't read the note yet, but got a call from Janice and John. Thanks a lot, but you didn't have to commit to funding the thing, ya know!"

"Well I needed something to show that I was serious about what's going on. I didn't really want to fund the building, but would've if it came to that! They sure responded quickly I see, so now what?"

"Well ... the mill site was hit by crack-heads last night. I asked Ricardo Sanchez, the new *ComTek* security manager, to take extra precautions, but you know how things work! I've a contractor coming here soon to let me know the financial hit I'm going to take."

"Two steps forward and one back! Sorry bud, but I can't help you with that problem."

"Look, I'll call later, but I wanted to pass on the news and my appreciation for your little love note. Oh ... the electrician guy's here. Gotta run!"

Chapter Seven

His hands followed the curve of her body, as he ran them along her smooth waist and to her hips. She was on her knees and her soft buttocks were raised above his head. "Oh ... ah ... ah!" she inhaled softly, as his movements made her groan and she wiggled a little to encourage him further.

She lifted her head from his crotch, as she stretched her body upward, extending her long thin arms to catch a fresh breath of air, then again lowered her torso. "Mmm!" she muttered.

She wanted him inside her, as she felt her heart pound and her nipples harden at his electrifying touch. "Ah ... ah ... oh!" she gasped, as she crawled down his frame on her knees eyeing his erection as it pointed toward her. She reached his pelvis, and quickly turned her body and straddled her buttocks across his perspiring frame, so he could see her face and her engorged breasts and stiffened nipples. "I know you like to play with my tits when we make love!" she whispered, and slowly lowered herself onto him, watching his face as she felt the rush of the sensation of him through her body.

They climaxed together, their hearts pounding between labored breaths. Neither of them spoke as they recovered and savored the experience.

"You just get better and better!" she finally gasped, still in an exhausted voice.

"You haven't lost your touch either, woman," he responded, still winded himself. "I got an e-mail from Thomas Howe this morning!" he changed the subject, still breathing heavily.

"Thomas Howe! I haven't heard that name for a while! What did he want?"

"Oh ... getting his interfering face where it doesn't belong, and pressing my decision to hang Will Richards out to dry—you know, my decision not to pay for his damn building replacement! It was a perfect opportunity to shut Will up and all his yakking!" the naked, big man replied angrily.

"What did Larry have to say about the e-mail?"

"I didn't tell him any details! He'd be pissed big time if he knew the specifics, so I dealt with the meddling asshole myself! Anyway, I had to keep Thomas out of our business, so I relented and agreed to fund Will Richard's new building. The other things we've in store for Mr. Richards will push him out anyway. You know what I mean, eh Candice?"

"Yea, Bri, I know. He'll certainly come snooping around my operation looking for stuff to fix his mill, soon I'll bet! Okay to let him have what he picks up?" she asked, putting her hand on his that was fondling her breast.

"Yea, it's okay. It's nothing to us, and I can't afford Thomas back with another damn threat or something else that will screw things up!"

Candice rose to get out of the bed, peeked out the window through the thin sheer coverings, and spotted the "Beast" in the parking lot.

"I need a shower! I can't go back to the office smelling like you!" she exclaimed as she sauntered her way into the small bathroom, turning on the light.

Brian could hear the glass door of the shower stall slide open. The water tap squeaked as it was turned, allowing the flow of water to begin. Candice stood naked, and looked at her shapely body in the mirror as she waited for the hot water to reach its destination. Her nipples were still hard and erect, and she realized that she still felt sexually aroused as she climbed over the tub lip, and slid the glass door closed to prevent the water from spaying onto the floor.

"Mmm," she muttered, as she placed her head under the stream of the warm shower water and felt it run down her back. She smiled as she heard the sound of the glass door side open behind her, as she faced the spray of water running from the nozzle. "Hey!" she uttered as she turned, and looked over her shoulder and saw Brian joining her with a big grin on his face, using her hips to stabilize himself as he climbed in behind her. He placed his mouth to her neck, and breathed on her as he pulled her wet behind toward him.

"Ah!" he exhaled as he entered her as she bent forward, with the water now pounding on her backside. "Ah!" she moaned again at her rush, as she quickly released another orgasm.

Both bodies remained in the shower stall, and they soaped each other, washing the sweat and body fluids from the surfaces of their skin. Their racing hearts had returned to normal as they completed their clean-up, and each stepped from the shower, still not saying a word. They dried each other, and returned to the small bedroom.

Pulling on his pants, Brian spotted Candice buttoning her blouse that was straining to stay closed between her enlarged breasts.

"My boobs always get larger after sex," she stated as she noticed him peering at her straining blouse. "My nipples stay hard for quite a while, too, and that's why I wear a dress jacket back to the office when we're done, to cover those things pointing through my bra," she said with a smile, as she put her index figure on one of her stiff nipples that pushed through the bra and white blouse.

Candice finished dressing first and prepared to leave; she grabbed her car keys and her purse. "Don't forget to lock up," she teased. "See you later."

She turned to look at Brian, to ensure that he was listening, opened the door, and left the room.

They both had a key to the room. It was their room, number 210 in the *Fraser Head Hotel*, only ten minutes from the office. The special client key allowed monthly prepaid customers to enter the locked security door at the back of the hotel as well as their room, so the privileged customers could come and go without passing through the front lobby if they chose to do so.

Monthly customers received this special key with FH stamped on the head of the key, and an etched ID number on the other side, so that the hotel could identify the specific lock that mated the key. The key looked like any other office key, and it was selected by the hotel so that its shape and color wasn't easily distinguishable from any other common keys that may be on a client's key ring.

Their room was paid monthly, and by cash, funded by Mr. Lee as a little perk and gesture of Brian's relationship with *BC Transformer*. It also served as a good place for Brian and Tom Lee to meet if Brian was unable to drive to Tom's Chilliwack operation.

Brian loved having sex, and Candice wasn't the only one who he regularly screwed in room 210. His wife was a cold bitch, and was more interested in her social life than spending time with her husband, in bed or not. She hadn't been able to have children and her desire to have sex had faded many years earlier, so Brian had been forced to find satisfaction elsewhere for a long time.

He peered out the window, to confirm that Candice had left. The old white company car was no longer in the parking lot, so he reached for his BlackBerry® on the dresser. "Georgina, my meeting's running later than I expected, but I'll be in shortly. Have there been any urgent calls?" Brian asked as he sat on the messy bed.

"Larry Langstone called about an hour ago, but he said that it wasn't urgent and you can call him later."

"Okay, thanks," Brian replied, and looked at the time before he placed the cell into his pocket.

Brian had missed lunch and was hungry. He needed to arrive back at the office a while after Candice did anyway, so he decided to grab a quick bite at a *Denny's*® next door.

♓

Candice Parks drove down the side road of the *ComTek* warehouse and stopped to acknowledge her return with the security guard, parked the car outside of her office, and pulled her BlackBerry® from her purse that had been placed on the passenger seat.

She dialed a phone number from memory, and the call was answered in a gruff voice. "Yea, who's callin'?"

"Giermo, it's me Candice, that you?" she always confirmed that she had the right person when she called this specific number.

"Hey, señorita, been waitin' for ya call," the reply came back in a strong Spanish accent. "The shipment's almost ready, and it should be out to ya manaña!"

"Okay, I'll watch for it in the morning. Bye." Candice hung up quickly, as she disliked talking to Giermo on the phone. She returned the BlackBerry® into her purse, grabbed her briefcase that she had left in the car earlier, and exited the white company vehicle. She returned the second set of car keys to her receptionist, and dropped the briefcase and purse in her office.

Candice walked through the small working area of her operation, past the conference room and through the back door, leading to the racks of stock that were labeled and priced. The receiving area was full of goods that needed inspection, identification, and labeling, and was at the far end of the building.

"What have we got today, Stewart?" she asked the young man who was pulling bolts from a box.

"Oh, just another shipment from *LM Distribution*, Ms. Parks. These guys sure are able to find lots of excess stuff around; I don't know how they do it!" he answered, as he pulled more items from the large cardboard box.

"Well, lucky for *ComTek*! We get current new stock at discount prices. Keep up the good work, and let me know when you've processed all this stuff," she replied and turned to head back to her office.

Stewart watched her shapely figure turn away from him, and took a breath as he watched her behind disappear from view. He mumbled something obscene and then returned to his task.

"Hmm … when Brian returns, I'll let him know that the shipment's almost processed," she muttered with a grin, as she thought about the satisfying sex that she had just enjoyed. In the meantime, she sat at her desk and entered her password to clear the screen saver on the monitor. She had been out of the office for a couple of hours and needed to check her e-mail, and see what was going on. Her face almost flushed as she recalled her last few hours screwing her boss, and then thought about the *LM Distribution* company that she and Brian had set up a number of years before.

The *LM Distribution* company was a front to process material returns of new distribution, power line stock that had been over-supplied to *PowerOne* line contractors in the Lower Mainland. *PowerOne* generated materials lists from their work management system for each new field job, and the contractors were billed for each stock item supplied by *ComTek* for the job that was listed on the materials job list. Small items that had low value were classified as "exempt" and had not been included in the billing, as the hassle to track the individual items often cost *PowerOne* more than the items were worth.

The contractors began to build large inventories of exempt-type materials, but they didn't inform *PowerOne* of these growing inventories and the buildup of the oversupplied materials. Historically, these inventories were not large, and the work management materials lists were frequently monitored. Whatever excess materials they gathered, the contractors used on new private-line installations and pocketed the profit. But now, the amounts of excess materials being collected by the contractors were a lot larger; this was one of the weaknesses of the new work-management system that had been installed at *PowerOne* a few years before. The situation pushed the contractors to find an alternative method to convert the stock into cash. The materials were unique to the power industry and there was little market elsewhere, so the contractors turned to Brian Quest at *ComTek* for help.

Brian was very aware of the exempt stocking process, and secretly worked with a number of large contractors to help them cash out their inventory. He knew that he'd to be able to process the materials without *ComTek* or *PowerOne* knowing that the contractors were the material source. Because the Investment Recovery operation controls were weakened with the new, unintegrated, *ComTek* control systems, he needed to run the side operation through IRD—and he needed Candice to be on board to ensure the process remained undetected by her staff and corporate finance.

Periodically, the contractors gathered their stock, recorded and listed the items under their name, and placed the materials into shipping boxes with *LM Distribution* imprinted on the boxes. The source information was used by *LM Distribution* to distribute the cash, once payment had been received from *ComTek*.

The *ComTek* CLG office staff, receiving the notification upstairs, was told that the *LM Distribution* supplier negotiated with manufactures to purchase excess stock, and that *ComTek* was able to obtain a discount on the received shipments. A document was produced, the materials placed into inventory, and a payment authorization was generated and sent to accounts payable at Central City; a payment to *LM Distribution* was cut at month's end.

Candice's thoughts were interrupted by Will Richards sticking his head into her office to say hello. "Hi Will, sorry to hear of your problems at the mill. If we have anything out back to help, let me know." She smiled.

"Thanks, I really appreciate that!" Will grinned back. "I've a list of power cables and connectors that I need to replace the lines that were taken by the druggies. I'm going to put the cables into conduits this time, and cover them to make it tougher for the thieves to get at them in the future!" he explained, but she didn't care.

"Just let my guys know out there what you're doing Will, and they can get a pallet if you need one. Stewart's sorting boxes out back. Talk to him."

Will smiled and left Candice to return to her work. He headed toward the back of the building, looking for Stewart.

Chapter Eight

The *Wheelhouse Pub* was busy. Thomas Howe could hear the buzz of conversation and the voices of customers ordering their drinks and food. It was just past noon, and Thomas was sitting at a round table by the window waiting for Will Richards to arrive. The two men usually met at the pub for lunch and a pint of Bud®. Thomas checked his cell phone for the time. Will often was late, and Thomas was accustomed to ordering his beer and waiting for Will to turn up.

Will appeared, wearing a dirty cap and a large smile. He approached the table, wandering through the maze of people having their lunch. "Sorry for being late. The guys arrived this morning to begin constructing the new building. A semi came to drop off the concrete blocks that'll form the back wall and the anchor for the back frame. I had Ray and Jack come back in to the mill to help, and ensure the setup was right. How ya been?" Will rambled as he found a seat.

Will sat down, glad that the table was by the window. He liked well lit places, as he usually had scraps of paper with notes that he brought along for discussion. He stood up to ensure the waitress saw him, and ordered a pint of Bud®. "I got lots to talk about today, Thomas. You won't believe some of the stuff!" he said and placed his cell on the table.

Will Richards always had lots to talk about! The ice cold beer showed up, and as the pint glass was close to overflowing, the waitress placed a coaster on the table. "You boys want to order lunch now?" she inquired, looking run off her feet. The pub was shorthanded today and the lunch rush was in full swing.

"Give us ten or fifteen. You're not in a hurry are you, Thomas?" Will glanced over at Thomas and then looked up at the waitress and smiled.

"I always plan a full afternoon when we get together for lunch, Will. The conversation's always entertaining, and we haven't gotten together for a while," Thomas replied, as he took a sip of his beer, eyeing his lunch mate as Will leaned over the table.

"I haven't told ya, but that prick Terry Peters has been blackmailing me for cash for a while! I got the son a bitch now, though!" Will blurted out the news, and watched the concern develop on the face of his friend.

"What do you mean that he's been blackmailing you! What for?" Thomas choked out the question in disbelief.

"Well, it's a bit complicated, but he threatened to make it difficult to have ongoing access to the loader. He said he'd press his union buddies to create trouble as I'm a non-union shop, unlike the rest of the company," Will replied before grabbing his cold mug of beer.

"Jesus Christ! Are you paying that asshole cash?" Thomas yelled out, forgetting that the pub was full of patrons only meters away.

"Yea, but I got him now! I was in the pole yard office a week ago looking for Terry so that I could arrange my next payment. He wasn't there, but I saw this fax which had fallen from the machine onto the floor. I picked it up, and it was a listing of numerous shipments of new poles with quantities and dates that I know never took place. You know me, I know what happens around there, and the comings and goings of loads. I checked with the guard, too, and he didn't recall seeing some of the loads of the size and dates listed on the sheet. I stuffed the fax into my pocket and left before anyone saw me."

Will talked quickly with his eyes wide open, staring at Thomas, and continued, excited with the story. "I know that Terry authorizes pole delivery invoices for payment and sends the paperwork across the street for processing, based upon his signature. Those idiots in administration don't know what happens at the pole yard! I'd bet he's got some scam running!"

"Well, if that jerk has the balls to blackmail you, then I can believe anything else is possible. I think it's time to have a talk with *ComTek* security. I don't know the new security guy, though." Thomas said, shaking his head, amazed at the circumstance.

"I met him the other day. Ricardo Sanchez," Will replied as he leaned over the table again and spoke in a whisper. "He said he was an RCMP cop before coming to *ComTek*." Will settled back in his chair. "We had breakfast after the building fiasco. He seems like a nice guy!"

The waitress returned to the side of the table. "Lunch now, boys?" she asked, holding her note pad ready to jot down their request.

"Okay. Ah ... bring us both another Bud® and I'll have the special steak sandwich," Will replied, eyeing the waitress.

"And you sir, what can I bring you?"

"A clubhouse with fries would be great, thanks," Thomas replied, and waited for the young woman to leave. "Well, security will be able to get the facts well enough on that action, my friend. Any RCMP worth his salt should be able to find the facts quickly enough, once placed on a documented trail." Thomas paused for a sip of the cold beer and then pounded his forefinger on the table. "The next time you see Sanchez at your yard, you need to request a private meeting. You sure don't want it to get out that you were the source of the information against Terry! People already think you know too much through your conversations with everyone coming to pick up wood."

Will smiled at the comment. "Yea, I sure do hear a lot of things. Customers like to pass the time waiting for their orders to be loaded. You're right though, I'd better be careful as there seems to be fewer people that I can trust these days."

The fresh cold pints of Budweiser® appeared just as the last of the first glasses were emptied.

Will pulled a scrap of notepaper from his pocket. He scanned the scratched-out list and selected the next topic. "Huh ... the pole count looks like it's going to be a problem this year. The buggers are increasing the shipments and I think they want to ensure I don't get the subsidy this time. Truck deliveries have been coming like gang busters in the last few weeks. If that rate keeps up, they'll reach the minimum target volume and I'll not get any additional payment at the end of next month!"

Will continued the story, looking down at his beer with dismay on his face. "With the building and suspended production, I'm going to be in a lot of shit without that cash injection, Thomas! It's usually how we work ourselves out of the hole each year and have a little extra cash for Christmas. You know how it's been, Thomas."

"Who's cranking up the shipments, *PowerOne* or *MiTek*?"

"It's *PowerOne* for sure! I'm also beginning to see smaller pieces being dropped off, large enough to be counted, but not full length. They're a pain in the ass, as I have to handle and sort through them all to find usable stuff." Will looked up at Thomas. "There must be something going on between *PowerOne* and *ComTek*."

"Better watch that situation. Hmm ... you get your increase for the clean-up contract yet?" Thomas remembered the notices that he had prepared for Will, and that were to have been sent out a couple months earlier.

"Nope. I keep on getting the runaround from *ComTek* payables, saying they haven't received the notices. I've been distracted and haven't followed up yet."

Thomas grabbed his friend's arm across the table. "You worked hard to get *Service Pole* that separate contract with *ComTek* providing that clean-up service, Will!" Thomas pulled back his hand. "I know you're going to be focused on getting your building replaced and ready to start up again, but you need to get the rate increased for the clean-up deal. That's critical income right now, man."

Their lunches arrived along with a small rack of condiments and napkins. "Anything else, gentlemen?" the waitress asked, eyeing the two quickly disappearing beers.

"The conversation's getting interesting. We need a couple more pints, please," Will replied, giving the waitress a big grin. Will watched the waitress leave, walking toward the bar, and then leaned over the table again. "Hey, you ever hear of *LM Distribution*? I was over at Candice's operation yesterday, scrounging power lines and fittings to replace the stuff that got ripped off, and saw new stock being unpacked in the Investment Recovery's receiving area when I went back to arrange to have one of the guys get me a pallet. Strange—new stuff usually goes directly to the warehouse receiving dock, doesn't it, Thomas?"

"Hmm ... don't know for sure, Will. It seems unusual, as that wasn't the practice when I was there. Things have changed though, due to the new business system. Ah ... maybe something to do with that, Will." Thomas paused for a moment ready to change the subject. "How're things going with Helen? Still being a bitch?" Thomas asked, concerned with the living environment, knowing that Will often slept in the room down in the basement.

"She's becoming unbearable! We'd another heated yelling match the other night and she forced me to sign her resignation paper as director of *Service Pole Recycling*, and also had me agree to pay any losses myself if the business fails. She's protecting her ass and wants the house ya know."

"Man, you need to get some professional legal advice before she screws you out of everything, Will!" Thomas commented as the pair of fresh beers arrived.

"It's okay. I can put up with her shit for a while longer! I know it's just about the money; she has always been like that, but she's certainly worse now that things are tighter. The pressure we always get at year-end only makes things worse! You know, Thomas, we have this conversation every year!"

"Okay, but pulling that paperwork stuff is new! I'd bet she's still able to write checks on the bank, though, and I'd bet you haven't had her taken off the account, either. If she's not an employee or director either, she has no right being able to get at the accounts or write checks. Watch out!" Thomas took a deep breath to calm himself. "Let's finish eating before it gets cold."

Chapter Nine

A police officer lay hidden by the bank of the road, trying to remain unseen in the late afternoon light. It was almost dusk, and the hillside was cold and wet, the moisture was penetrating his pressed uniform and he was becoming chilled.

The roadway had expensive homes on one side of the hillside, and the place where the officer was hiding skirted a small lake area. There was a wire fence to keep pedestrians and bicycles from falling down the embankment on the lake side. Large pine trees guarded the edge of the quiet street that wound around the contour of the lake that was barely visible from the officer's position on the slope.

The officer's partner sat warm and dry in their unmarked cruiser at the end of the road, five houses to his right. The hidden officer was unable to see their vehicle from his vantage point, but knew his partner was there, as they frequently corresponded on the private RCMP bandwidth.

"Frank, I still don't see any movement at the target. When is KO expected?" the sprawled-out officer asked, as he was getting anxious to leave his uncomfortable position. He was watching for any activity at 905 Elvenden Row, a private house that was located quite a way up the mountainside; the house had a spectacular view of Stanley Park, the ocean, and the Lions Gate Bridge. West Vancouver was a wealthy area, and it was unusual to suspect a grow-op there, but a report came in from *PowerOne* that the power consumption for that address was off the charts, usually indicating an illegal marijuana operation.

This situation was different, as the entire neighborhood had had their old electric meters changed out to the new digital ones. It was an experimental project designed to check the new meter's accuracy before *PowerOne* implemented the new technology province-wide. The meter at 905 Elvenden Row could be faulty, but then again, it might be reporting accurately.

The house was protected by large trees, and it was difficult for the officer to get a good view of what was going on. He surveyed the driveway entrance that followed a curved rock wall leading to a double-car garage. The street didn't have many light standards, so the raid needed to be soon, while there was still light enough to see any suspects that might try to escape the trap. The large home was a rancher style, and was faced in a curved, Spanish-bricked motif. The white stucco sides needed a new paint job, and the home was well secluded from the view of any traffic, or the neighbors for that matter.

The evening was very quiet, and the officer hadn't reported any vehicles travelling down the street for some time now. The stakeout had been approved and set up an hour earlier, and the partner officer sitting in the cruiser had done this type of bust many times before. He knew they needed to be patient and wait for the assigned leading officer to arrive and direct the entry operation with the appropriate legal papers. He sat wondering if the entire thing would be a waste of his time, and secretly hoped not.

The stillness was disrupted by a fleet of four additional RCMP cruisers, two coming from the west to the left of the officer, who raised himself from the bush as he saw the marked cars, and the other two from his right. His partner remained at his vehicle at the street intersection, waiting for further instructions. The units converged silently, not wanting to warn any occupants of their arrival. It was critical that the officers take positions around the property before taking steps to access the house. Another vehicle, a white Ford Super Cab displaying *ComTek* markers, followed closely behind and parked at the corner, accompanying the unmarked unit posted there.

The lead officer stepped from the passenger side of the white cruiser, clutching the warrant needed to allow their entry of the premises. Officer Kelly O'Brian had been the lead officer at numerous grow-op investigations, and knew the drill and the proper protocols very well. All the people who knew her called her KO for short. She was a tall attractive brunette, and her arm-length hair had been pulled back from her face into a pony tail.

Closing the door of her squad car, she was joined at her car by the group of officers who came to receive instructions on the raid. The young officer who was climbing out of his hillside hiding place was a rookie, and this was his first experience in dealing with a potential marijuana bust. He was excited to be working with Kelly O'Brian, as she had a reputation of ensuring that all her team was as safe as possible, and the letter of the law was respected. Officer O'Brian looked about, seeking the first responding team members, and spotted the young officer with wet trousers and mud-soaked arms and elbows approaching her.

"Good afternoon, Sir, I'm Officer Sylvester Penner. My partner and I have been here since dispatch sent us out to observe that house, and watch for any occupants trying to leave the property," he informed the woman in a deep, stiff voice as he pointed to the suspect property. "My partner remains at our squad car at the corner, waiting for orders!"

"Okay, Officer Penner, thanks for the update. Tell your partner that I'd like the both of you to work your way quietly around to the back of the property. I saw a hydro line running through there, so follow that, and it should provide good access to the rear. Inform me when you're in position and you have a good view of the back of the house. Remember, this may only be a false report, Officer!"

"Yes, Sir!" the officer replied stiffly, focused on carrying out his assignment as he passed Ricardo Sanchez without a glance.

"Officer O'Brian, I was told you were going to lead this investigation," Ricardo smiled as he greeted the woman officer surrounded by the group of men.

Kelly O'Brian knew Ricardo very well from his days on the Vancouver police force. "Hey, Ricardo, heard you couldn't keep up, and joined *ComTek*. What a soft gig, eh!" she said, teasing him. "The uniform get too tight or somethin'?"

"Hell no, KO, just getting nervous with all you females trying to fill guys' boots! Besides, I thought I'd taught you all I knew, and I didn't want another woman understudy. A guy's got only so much patience, ya know!" Ricardo replied with a grin.

"Men, this is Mr. Ricardo Sanchez, the manager of *ComTek*'s security." She introduced him to the team that had gathered in front of her cruiser. The team members all had their protective gear on, and had extracted their hardware from the trunks of their vehicles, ready to carry out their assignments.

"*PowerOne* called the precinct this afternoon and told the Captain that this was a likely marijuana grow-op, as the power consumption far exceeds the normal usage for this type of area. The new *PowerOne* digital meters have been placed here by *ComTek* as a test, so this may only be a bad report. We must check it out anyway, so Officer Penner and his partner have been here for the past hour or so keeping an eye on the place. They've reported that nothing unusual has been going on since their arrival. I've dispatched them to the rear." Kelly looked about. "It's getting dark, so we'd better get on with it!" She paused, and then continued with dispatching her team.

"Williams, you back me up and you, Parker, work your way up the driveway and set a position outside the edge of the garage, making sure that you can see the front door. Peterson, take your partner up over this wall bordering the property line, and stay concealed by these large pine trees. Move toward the front and stay out about five meters, so you can see the front and side of the house." Kelly barked the commands clearly. "You last two, I want you to split up and take a position, one at each end of the roadway, about fifteen meters or so from the driveway, and ensure that any oncoming citizens are prevented from coming though this area until I advise. Remember it's getting dark, and approaching vehicles need to see you." The men nodded their heads in understanding compliance and began to move to the instructed positions.

Buzz, buzz. The walkie-talkie buzzed on Officer O'Brian's handheld. "O'Brian here."

"It's Penner. We're in position now, Sir. It's tough to see very well through the trees and poor light."

"Stay put, we're about to move on the house. Stay alert!"

Antonio Castillo was standing outside in the back of the house, by the edge of the tree line, finishing his smoke. In the dim light of the early evening, he thought that he had spotted some movement in the far corner of the treed lot. He peered through the darkness, taking a closer look at the spot where he'd thought he had seen someone. He sucked on his cigarette and peered out, squinting his eyes as he looked, thinking that he definitely saw some movement this time. His body stiffened, as he suspected the pending event, and without any hesitation decided to slip along the tree line toward the far edge of the back of the lot, away from where he had been looking.

"Holy shit the cops! If I move away from the house and close to the property edge I might be able to stay undetected," he muttered, taking the cigarette from his lips. "I can stay low until I see a chance to get out of this place," he thought, extinguishing the cigarette on the closest tree trunk.

"Sanchez, you stay here! Remember you're a civilian now, and I don't want an incident. You got it?" Kelly turned and stared directly at Ricardo in the dimming light. She pulled her service revolver from its place on her belt: a silver-colored 9 mm SW5946 with an RCMP logo stamped on the muzzle. "You can't screw around with drug guys!" she whispered to Ricardo, who knew all too well that she was right, and motioned Williams to follow behind, as she crouched and made her way up the winding driveway toward the front door.

The house was dark and no lights were on. It was dusk, and Kelly knew that most people turned on lights before the darkness fell, if they were home. Both officers reached the front stoop and took positions on either side of the large front door. The neighborhood was silent, and the moon could be seen from the porch rising over the lake.

Kelly briskly knocked on the door. "Mr. and Mrs. Dominguez, this is the RCMP! Open the door. I have a warrant to check your electric meter!"

There wasn't an answer, or any sign of movement in the house. She announced her request a second time and included, "We'll use force if you don't cooperate!" as she pounded on the wooden door.

Kelly stood on the stoop for a moment deciding what the odds were that the meter was bad.

With the decision made, a loud crack of the splitting door frame could be heard, as the door was kicked in. "Police! Come out with your hands in the air. Now!" Kelly demanded, with her weapon at the ready. Hugging the wall, she groped to find a light switch. She flipped the light on, and saw Officer Williams crouching at the door entrance, pistol drawn and pointing straight ahead, eyes wide open and darting around searching the room. The remaining officers outside held their ground, listening for any sound of movement in the dark. There was nothing!

The officers carefully continued their sweep of the interior, turning on lights and yelling "RCMP" as they continued to search for their prey.

Antonio heard the breaking of the door and the commotion of the cops entering the house. He'd found a good hiding space, but it was wet, and his tee shirt was becoming soaked with muddy, cold water. He was dressed for working in the humid basement, and the unexpected raid left him poorly dressed for his cold, evening dive into his protective shelter. He lay motionless, covered by the darkness and large branches of the pines. He apparently hadn't been spotted as two officers appeared from the far side. He was lucky, as his presence also hadn't been noted by either of the two cops in the front yard, who were focused on the front of the house and the police officer leading the raid as she entered the front door.

"RCMP," Kelly yelled as she stood momentarily in the foyer. She heard a noise from the basement below her, and she signaled Williams with her hand, indicating that she thought they had company downstairs. "RCMP! We know you're down there. Come out now, hands where we can see them!" Kelly yelled. "You've got five seconds, or I'm coming to get you!"

She heard a door creak open and a person yelled, "Okay, okay were coming out! Don't shoot!"

"How many of you are in there?" Kelly called out.

"Just two, we're coming out!"

The two officers stood, weapons drawn and pointed at the stairwell leading to the basement, ready in the event that the men came out armed. Two men slowly worked their way up the staircase with their hands in clear sight. As they reached the top of the stairs, the officers pushed each man against the wall, pressing their upper bodies and faces into the wallboard as they were searched. Handcuffs were quickly wrapped around their hands, now pinned at their backs.

"Hey, Peterson. See anyone out there? We got a couple in here!" Kelly squawked on her mike.

"No Sir, quiet out here!" the response crackled back.

"You and your partner come in here pronto. We need you to babysit these two guys while we finish checking out the house," she replied.

The two husky uniforms quickly abandoned their position and joined the party inside. The shackled men were pushed away from the staircase and into a corner at the far side of the room. Officer Parker remained glued to his position near the garage, itching to move, but continued to stay alert and scan the area. It was now dark, and the officers blended into the night.

Only one vehicle had travelled down the quiet road and had been stopped by the RCMP officer assigned to manage the access to the blocked section of street. A lone occupant of a black Cadillac hadn't been happy about being prevented from entering his home two doors down the street, and had been temporarily silenced with an official stare by the husky officer.

Ricardo Sanchez was anxious about the activity in the house. His cop instinct knew that a grow-op was going to be found in the house. He hated being on the sideline, especially since the operation included Kelly O'Brian! They had had a special connection a few years before, but she had cut it off before it became too serious. Definitely not his choice, but he knew not to mess with a woman cop, especially with Kelly O'Brian.

The rookie cop and his partner were getting cold in the darkness of the backyard. Officer Penner wanted action to test himself, but it seemed that this bust wasn't going to deliver the opportunity. He and his partner worked their way closer to the rear of the house, and they were now able to see the blackened windows of the basement.

Officer O'Brian carefully stepped down the staircase toward the basement entrance, vacated by the two captives. Her partner followed with his sidearm still drawn and directed toward the opening.

"RCMP! Anyone else down here?" she yelled.

There was no response, and the two officers slowly continued and entered the room that was brightly lit and humid. Eyeing the space, it was clear that the room was empty and the officers lowered their firearms and placed them back into their holders.

"Clear down here ... Parker, Penner, bring your partner and join the party!" Kelly commanded on her mike.

"Hey, Peterson," Kelly shouted upstairs. "Place that shit you've got in the car, and let the other guys on road duty let the citizens pass. Put on the flashing lights of all the cars, so everyone can see we're here! By the way, have Sanchez get his ass in gear and join us down here. He's gotta see this!"

The team swarmed the inside of the house that had been furnished with fine Spanish antiques and paintings of obvious Mexican origin. A piece of the smashed-in door frame lay on the front terracotta tiled foyer. Muddy boot impressions marked the uninvited intrusion, which led to the basement access through the large kitchen. A small hand-painted porcelain wall hanging placed over the staircase invited guests with the saying, "Mi casa es su casa."

Ricardo Sanchez worked his way through the group of officers, reached the basement, and spotted Kelly O'Brian staring at a huge, sophisticated expanse of marijuana plants that were growing in a hydroponically controlled environment. A power control panel was on the far side of the wall, which had a large cable that ran out the wall.

"Jesus Christ! We hit pay dirt this time, amigos!" Ricardo exclaimed. "Wow, look at this setup. Who would've guessed that this was below this elegant house buried in this exclusive neighborhood?"

"Don't go crazy in front of me, Sanchez!" Kelly tried to contain her enthusiasm.

The basement was closed in with blacked-out windows, and intense grow lights were installed and hung on wire supports from the ceiling, evenly spaced a foot apart. The humidity was controlled by a fan with an automated sensor, to ensure the correct moisture for optimal growing conditions, and which exhausted the air and excess moisture into the manicured backyard. The electrical switches were encased in stainless steel lockboxes, designed to keep the uneducated workers from electrocuting themselves. The engineered hydroponics demonstrated that this environment was created by someone with professional expertise.

"This place has been built to last for an extended period of time I'd say, and the growers obviously didn't expect us to find this one!" Ricardo remarked as he continued to inspect the facility. "Well, we certainly don't have a faulty meter reading here! What's the story on the homeowners, KO?"

"Don't know!" Kelly replied as she turned to face Ricardo. "We need to have the narcotics team in here in the morning. It's getting late and we've a couple of visitors in our cages outside."

Ricardo continued to look about and spotted three winter coats dumped in the corner. "Hey, KO. What's with the three coats? I thought you guys collared only two guys!" he exclaimed as he pointed out the jackets piled in the corner by the outside rear door.

"Hey Peterson, roust those two dirt-bags and get the story on the third guy!" she yelled upstairs. "Shit, I can't believe one got away!" she mumbled, annoyed with herself as much as with the situation.

Officer Peterson pulled one of the captives from the back seat of the squad car by the scruff of the neck, and slammed the captive's face into the roof.

"Hey shit head, who's the third hombre? We got his coat downstairs and need an ID pronto!" Peterson growled, pressing the man's head forcibly into the flashing light frame.

"Antonio, ah … don't know his last name. Honest!" he blurted out as his head began to bleed. "He went out for a smoke just before you guys arrived! He must've seen ya, and split, man!"

Kelly O'Brian continued to meticulously survey the well lit room. She spotted some powder on the table and a couple of old computers stacked in the corner. Two sizes of unassembled cardboard boxes were visible on a shelf, and they seemed out of place for a typical marijuana grow-op. "Hmm, I wonder what this is all about!" she muttered, walking more closely for a better look. "Ricardo, come here and take a gander. Something else is going on here!" She pointed to the powder on the table and the strange collection of tower-styled computers, and unmade boxes. "Sure is strange! Don't usually see this kind of stuff with weed plants. I'll have the lab advised to check it out and see what we got. I'll leave a team here until the lab guys can get here. Hum … maybe we can get one of those jokers out front to fill us in!"

"Hey, Williams, get the lab guys out here and you and your partner button up until they show. You'd better let HQ know that the door's broke, too." Kelly barked into her mike again as she worked her way upstairs.

"Let's see what we can get from these maggots when we get them to the station. All you guys, mount up—except the Williams pair." Kelly looked about to ensure that the rest of her team was preparing to leave, and then she turned her attention to the rookie and queried, "You see anything out back, Penner? It seems a guy got past ya!"

"We never saw or heard a thing, Sir!" The young officer replied, looking down at the floor.

"Hey, Penner. It's okay, good job! Go home and get changed. You look like shit!" she said with a smile and turned, preparing to enter her vehicle, and noticed Ricardo. "Hey Sanchez, see ya around eh?" She glanced at him and paused briefly to see Ricardo smile, and then turned toward her ride.

Ricardo watched Kelly's squad car speed off, pulled his BlackBerry® cell from his pocket and pressed his speed dial. "Hey, Mr. Langstone, I know that it's a little late but you asked me to call as soon as I had a report on that high-reading meter out here in West Vancouver. The problem wasn't the new digital meter, Sir, it was a grow-op—actually, it was quite a large one."

"That's good news, Ricardo. Thanks for the call," Larry replied abruptly. "Good night."

"Good night, Sir!" Ricardo hung up the call and prepared to go home.

The flashing lights of the police cars could be seen throughout the area. The colorful reflections danced off the smooth surface of the lake and drowned out the beam of light cast by the rising moon.

Giermo Hernandez was returning to the house after dropping off his latest shipment, and had just turned up Kenwood Road that skirted the lake on the south side. His disguised dark blue van had "New Wave Couriers" identified on the side panels. It had been easy to have a sign graphic company design, produce, and install professional-looking vehicle signs in a few days. Giermo knew that a courier van would not appear out of place, and loading and unloading activities wouldn't attract any attention out of the ordinary.

He was on his way to pick up his boys, who he had left to finish cleaning up and securing the property for the night. A frown crossed his face as he turned up St. Andrews Road, and he realized that the cops were camped outside of his destination. A police cruiser with lights flashing was stationed at the corner of Elvenden and St. Andrews, and an officer was stationed at the intersection. St. Andrews Road carried through northbound, and Giermo decided to pass the activity without stopping. He looked into his rearview mirror to ensure that he passed the cop without attracting any attention.

"Shit, how'd the cops find us here?" he muttered, not having ever considered that the power consumption would be monitored and trigger the power company's suspicions.

The van reached a "Y" in the road; he turned the wheel to the left and stopped at the next intersection. He decided to return home to his small flat in East Vancouver; he turned a sharp left and travelled back down the mountainside that connected to the expressway ramp, which would take him east toward his destination. He knew the route would be congested with the outbound traffic of the evening commute, but that would give him time to think about his next move.

The Williams team had returned their MP5s and flak jackets back into the trunk of their squad car, and had pulled out a duffle bag containing rolls of yellow "Don't Cross RCMP" labeled tape. They began to cordon off the perimeter of the entire property, as the rest of the team removed their protective gear and prepared to drive back to the West Vancouver precinct. It was getting late, and the dark streets were sparsely lit, allowing the brightness of the sprawling city below to radiate into the thousands of windows peering out, dotting the West Vancouver mountainside.

The prisoners sat back in silence in their separate back seats, as the officers navigated their squad cars along the route back to the station. The sound of the chatter on the RCMP radio constantly announced some event using numbered codes that described the activity. The voices of the officers were muffled, as the plexiglass separating the front seat from the rear insulated the conversation from the caged passengers in the back. Small computer monitors, mounted between the front seats, radiated a glow, and the two officers appeared as dark blue shadows in the front seat.

The large, two-story police station was on Marine Drive; the back of the building overlooked an old sailing club situated on the beachfront. The parade of white cars passed the front of the building, and proceeded to a fenced garage area behind the brick structure. The entrance gate motor was activated, and the steel, framed barrier rose to accept the returning officers.

The vehicles parked in their designated slots, marked with the number of the car that was boldly stenciled in large numbers on the roof.

Kelly O'Brian exited her vehicle first, and pointed to the officers now removing themselves from their front seats, "Lock those men in separate isolated holes, and get the paperwork finished before you clock out of your shift," she commanded, eyeing Peterson as he closed his door.

"Yes, Sir, we'll take nice care of these guys for ya!" the enthusiastic cop stiffly responded with a smile.

"I want a debriefing at 0800 tomorrow! Read them their rights and get the names of their lawyer, if they have one. We don't want to taint this bust with a screwed-up protocol," she uttered, giving them her last directive for the night.

Cop days were often long, and Kelly O'Brian knew the sacrifice that went along with the territory. She thought about Ricardo Sanchez, and was glad to have seen him; she had enjoyed poking at his change in profession.

"Good for him!" she muttered, as she thought about the impacts that leaving the RCMP force would make. "Not for me, though! I love the chase and challenge!"

Kelly had wanted to be a detective and shed the uniform. She had completed the program and all the exams, and was waiting for her results. She loved the streets, but there was a kind of attraction in figuring out mysteries and making collars through her smarts, rather than physical strength and a revolver. Her results couldn't come soon enough, but she had this job, and she wanted to do it properly in the meantime.

♓

Giermo Hernandez was exhausted as he arrived at his apartment. The Vancouver city traffic can drive anyone crazy, and there seemed to be an idiot every kilometer. He lived in a modest five-suite, single-story building, just a block from Commercial Drive in the core of the East end. The Port of Vancouver was just minutes north, but he couldn't see the waterfront from his small kitchen window. The area housed many immigrants from many countries that came to Canada for a better life. He was Colombian, but had chosen not to become involved in that immigrant community, as his business activities demanded that he remain invisible as much as possible.

He entered his two-bedroom apartment. The sparsely furnished front room had an old couch and a large flat screen Sony® TV, with multimedia components sitting on a shelf of the large cabinet. An IKEA™ table and four chairs were placed toward the end of the room, beside an un-kept kitchen that still had dirty dishes lying in the sink, begging for his attention.

One bedroom that had a single bed was used to allow one of his guys to crash should the situation dictate, but he was reluctant to have anyone visit. The second bedroom was larger and a queen-sized bed filled the room, with a small night stand beside it that was cluttered with cigarette butts and empty beer cans. The surroundings certainly weren't romantic, and women seldom were invited. Giermo was a loner and masturbation was an easy substitution, made easier with a library of porno flicks stored in the bedside drawer.

"That woman at *ComTek* sure gave me a hard-on today," he thought as he recalled his trip to drop off the shipment that morning. "Man, what a tight ass and set of tits! She can do me any time!" The wishful thought started to get him aroused.

Giermo was hungry, as it was late and the stress of the daily events seemed to have worn him out. He noticed the answering machine was flashing, so pressed the play button, and the first message screamed out. "It's Juan. The cops got us at the West Van station. Get us out quick!"

"Damn, I guessed as much! Man, this day just won't give me a break!" he sighed as he placed the palm of his hand on his forehead. "Shit, shit, shit!" continued to run through his brain, as he recalled the incoming shipment of heroin and the fact that he now had nowhere to take it!

Giermo ordered a pizza from the local pizzeria and turned on the flat screen to wait for the delivery. He didn't hear the sound of the TV show, as he began to think about the three amigos surely grabbed by the cops. His heart rate began to increase as he remembered the sight of the RCMP, and the grow-op that he had just lost. "What a mess. Humph! I'd better figure something out quick," he mumbled as he waited for his meal to arrive.

♓

"So Larry, tell me about this idea to sell Fleet," Peter Fisher asked as he sat in a large, leather easy chair, drinking a scotch in Larry's home study.

"I was looking at the financials for that division last month, and there'd be lots of opportunity to make money if that operation didn't use union workers with the type of benefit packages that *ComTek*'s paying!" Larry Langstone replied, sitting in an easy chair adjacent to Peter. "A third party could purchase the entire division and turn around and contract out the service back to *ComTek*. Long-term deadweight employees could be encouraged to leave, paid out by *ComTek* of course, and the operation streamlined."

"Hmm ... and we'd set up this third party, I assume, eh Larry!" Peter took another drink and pondered the suggestion. The heavyset man, with black-rimmed glasses, leaned over the side table that separated the two men. "We could embed that service with some of *ComTek*'s major suppliers, too, like *BC Transformer*, who'll be shipping directly to *PowerOne*."

Larry smiled, and his long narrow face studied Peter Fisher closely. "That's right. I've done some preliminary work on this idea and if you're interested, I could tighten up the forecast for further discussion. I've sourced the capital that we'd need, too."

"Sounds like something to pursue, Larry. So ... where are we on our meter project?"

"Well, *PowerOne*'s test meters are doing okay in the field. We had a scare when one of the meters reported a large usage spike. Anyway, I sent Sanchez out to check when the cops went to investigate a potential grow-op, and it was a grow-op—can you imagine—in West Vancouver!" Larry exclaimed. "Anyway, I've got a meeting with a potential buyer of *Power One's* used meters in a couple of weeks organized through a third party. They want to see a plan and schedule for when *PowerOne* takes them out of service and sends them to disposal at the CLG," Larry replied with a smile.

"Have you got all the information that you need from *PowerOne*?" Peter asked, taking another sip from his scotch.

"Yes, for this stage anyway. They've indicated that they want to accelerate the change out, even though the public is pushing back on the program! I haven't worked a plan for our Investment Recovery piece yet though, and I hope I don't have to get Brian Quest involved." Larry took a breath and picked up a chess piece from the board sitting on the table between the two men. "We've at least six months to work that end of the deal, so that's lots of time to work out the disposal details."

"Hmm ... and what about Richards? We need that property vacated by spring," Peter asked, finishing his scotch and placing the crystal glass on the edge of the wooden chessboard.

"That's not going to be a problem, Peter! I've got Quest pushing that guy. Don't worry, Richards' contract's ending and he'll be history." Larry smiled as he replaced the chess piece that was in his hand back onto the checkered board. "What we do with that pole disposal program after Richards is gone is still a problem though, but I'll work something out!"

"Okay then, Larry," Peter replied as he got up to leave. "It sounds like you've got things in control. Let me know when you've the details on the Fleet thing. I like what you've done."

"Sure will, Peter. I think we're going to have a very lucrative year coming up. Thanks for coming." Larry got up and walked his guest to the front door. "I'll call you, Peter. Good night."

Chapter Ten

The bedside alarm signaled that it was 0600 and that it was time to get moving. Kelly O'Brian's shapely figure pulled itself from the bed; she slipped off her nightgown and wandered into the bathroom. Her brunette hair flowed over her muscular arms, and covered the top half of her firm youthful breasts. She always took a run in the morning to get her juices pumping, and it was her daily program to maintain her stamina. She quickly brushed her teeth, wrapped her arm-length hair in an elastic band, and pulled on black lace panties and an old, worn pair of gray-colored sweats. Strapping on a white sports bra and yanking on a top that had had *Top Gun*® stenciled on the front, she laced her Adidas™ sneakers, snatched her keys from the front counter, and exited the apartment, locking the door behind her.

She chose the Kitsalano area as the place to live, as it was vibrant, had a hot singles scene, and a casual atmosphere. The view of English Bay seemed to raise her spirits, and her run around Hadden and Vanier Parks reset her mood for the day. She thought that Vancouver was the best city in the world to live, and she appreciated the opportunity to protect it. The drive to the West Vancouver RCMP station required an early start, and the route through Stanley Park and over the Lions Gate Bridge took over twenty minutes on a good day.

Everyone in the neighborhood knew that she was a cop, advertised by the uniform that she wore coming and going from work each day. This fact seemed to set people living in the area at ease, somehow. She ran along the jogging path that took her around the parks, under Burrard Street and back to her cozy place on Maple Street.

Kelly performed her running circuit in less than twenty minutes. She tried to catch her breath as she fished out her keys, and returned to the task of getting ready for work.

The single-bedroom apartment was a common size for the district, and she outfitted her space with comfortable furnishings, and had even painted the suite a light yellow when she moved in, about three years before.

The RCMP uniform hung well on her body and the tailored style suited her figure. Her hair was returned to the tight ponytail pinned together at the back, a configuration that worked best for her as it was neat and out of the way. She went to the bedroom side table and withdrew her weapon from its safe-keeping location, hidden from any visitors who might stop by unexpectedly. Visitors were an infrequent event, as Kelly focused on her RCMP career and she left little time for socializing. She hoped that becoming a detective would fix some of that, but she was driven by other more deeply rooted reasons.

It was seven forty-five when Kelly pulled her old, white Nissan hardtop into the West Vancouver employee parking space. She was refreshed and ready for a new day that was to start with the debriefing session she had called the night before.

"Hey KO, the lab boys have already left for the West Van grow-op you busted yesterday," she was informed by Officer Williams who had arrived at 0730 that morning.

"I'm sure the findings will be very interesting. Hopefully some blanks will be filled in later. What's the story on the two guys in the cages out back?" Kelly asked, getting herself focused on the job.

"Not a sign of any lawyer for them yet, and no one's yanked their chains yet either!" Officer Williams replied flatly. "I hear that Detective Hal Mourin has been assigned to work with you on the interview."

"Yea, the quiet one, hmm! Did either of the two guys give you a lawyer's name, or are we going through the pain of a public defender handling their asses?" Kelly asked, interested in who might appear, as the lawyer usually was a clue to suspects' connections, and it gave her an idea of the direction to pursue during the questioning period. No clue was forthcoming yet, and she had to wait for the men's counsel to arrive before the games could begin.

Kelly's team gathered into a large room, usually used for debriefing sessions, set up with tables and chairs. It was exactly 0800 and yesterday's team was assembled as directed.

"We need to keep the documentation and the facts clean on this one, boys," O'Brian started the proceeding that was required after each bust. "We've a good collar here and there's no time for screw-ups!" She paused to ensure the message was clear. "I'll recommend in my report that the assigned detective team takes a close look outside in the backyard for evidence that might help us ID this Antonio character. I understand that's going to be Detectives Mourin and Anderson. I'll also suggest that they pay close attention to the powder on the tabletop in the basement. I'm sure it's some narcotic and we need to find out what these marijuana growers are doing with it!" Kelly paused and looked about the room. "So, everyone take a moment and recall the events of last night, then speak up if anything in your reports has been missed!"

"The two suspects that we hauled in were processed last night, and the usual fingerprints and photos were taken and filed. We got a hit on both of these guys and one is Ernesto

Rodriguez and his partner's Juan Vergara. Both of them have rap sheets for petty stuff, nothing major," Williams spoke out first. "We don't know too much about those two, but they've been arrested with others who are members of a new Colombian organization pushing heroin. That's all we got!"

"Hmm ... anything else?" Kelly asked, then paused, allowing the officers to consider the events and respond. The room remained silent. Nothing else was added.

"Okay then. I'll review your reports that I expect are on my desk by now. You're dismissed, and can return to your normal tours. Thank you, Officers," Kelly said with a smile. "Great work, guys! The file will be transferred to DEA and the detective team upstairs when I'm done."

It was almost 0900 before a lawyer came to the precinct office and asked for Officer O'Brian. The receptionist buzzed Kelly's phone, which Kelly answered while sitting at her small shared desk, reviewing the reports that had been left there for her the night before.

"Officer O'Brian, a Mr. Karl Kuntz is here to see you about the men you picked up last night," the receptionist said; she paused to listen to the response, and then hung up the phone.

"You can find Officer O'Brian down the hall on this main floor, Mr. Kuntz," the receptionist directed the visitor toward O'Brian's desk.

The man wore a light brown, inexpensive suit and had a stocky build. He was overweight and looked like he was over two hundred pounds and about five-four in height. His black hair was slicked to the side and it appeared as though it hadn't been cut for some time. His brown slip-on loafers were scuffed and about a size nine.

"Officer, I had a call from my client and understand that you're holding two men that you picked up last night. Is that correct?" the man asked, standing by Kelly O'Brian's desk.

She looked up from her paperwork, but didn't respond as she studied the man.

"I'm Mr. Kuntz, their lawyer. May I see them now, please?" he asked in a tone that was more of a command than request.

"Well, we want to keep them separated to ensure they have no chance to collaborate on their stories, Mr. Kuntz. We can meet with each one individually, though, in your presence, of course," Kelly said, picking up the telephone and punching in a few digits. "Yes, Detective Mourin, it's Officer O'Brian. I understand that you have been assigned to the Elvenden Row case. The two suspects' lawyer is here and he wants to see his clients." She listened to the reply and hung up the phone and got out of her chair.

"Okay, that's acceptable," Kuntz replied, and followed the woman officer as she marched off to the holding area and interview rooms down the hall.

An officer was stationed at the entrance to the holding area, who was instructing Kelly and Mr. Kuntz to sign the register just as Detective Mourin appeared. The officer buzzed the door lock, and Kelly opened the heavy steel door leading into a row of interrogation rooms. Two rooms were occupied, as the receptionist had arranged to have the two captives placed in separate locked rooms.

The first room was unlocked by the attendant and the trio entered the room. Karl Kuntz took a seat in front of his client while Kelly and Hal Mourin chose to remain standing.

"I'm your lawyer and it's been arranged for me to represent you today. Don't answer anything unless I nod my head. Okay?" the lawyer instructed, looking directly at Ernesto Rodriguez.

Kelly wanted to see how things were going to work with this lawyer who she hadn't met before. "So Ernesto, getting involved with the big boys now, are ya?" she asked flatly as she glanced over at Hal Mourin.

The small man raised his eyes up and looked at Karl, who shook his head in a negative gesture, discouraging the man from answering as Kelly stood and observed.

"Hmm … you only get one shot at working with me, Ernesto. You'd better take it! You never know, your buddy Juan next door might cooperate, and then you're screwed!" she paused for him to absorb her words. "Who's the boss you're working for? You guys sure don't have the skills to run that type of show yourselves!" Kelly pressed, hoping that she would get a name.

Once again the man didn't answer, following what the lawyer's gesture recommended.

The same routine took place in the adjoining room, with the same result. The two shackled men were extracted from the interview rooms and returned to their cells in the back.

"Ah, Mr. Kuntz, this is Detective Mourin and he will be handling this case going forward," Kelly said as the trio watched the two prisoners leave the room. "These men will have their time in a court proceeding later this morning, and will have to face charges relating to the marijuana grow-op they were involved in," Kelly informed the lawyer.

"You will have to deal with Detective Mourin the next time you come here. You can check at the desk for the details on your way out," she said, annoyed that she was unable to extract any further information during the short visit.

"Detective Mourin, I'll be in touch," the lawyer replied coldly.

Kelly escorted the lawyer back to the front desk, ensuring that his departure was immediate. Upon their approach, the receptionist looked up. "Hey KO, the Captain's been looking for you. He told me to ask you to go upstairs and visit with him as soon as you finished downstairs."

"Thanks," Kelly replied, "I'm on my way," and turned to go upstairs, curious about what was on the Captain's mind.

♓

Buzz, buzz. The door buzzer noise pierced his brain as Giermo's sleep was disrupted. The pizza and the excess beer the night before had resulted in him passing out, and he found himself sprawled on the couch with the TV still on. *Buzz, buzz.* The buzzer noise was never-ending, and it didn't sit well with his splitting headache and hangover. He still was wearing the smelly clothing from the day before that was now stained with beer and pizza sauce. *Buzz, buzz,* the sound persisted as he slowly became conscious, and when he finally reached the intercom he yelled in a groggy voice, "Yea, what da ya want?"

"It's Antonio! Let me in!" The voice sounded desperate through the tiny speaker on the wall.

"Christ, I thought you got caught by the cops!" Giermo exclaimed, surprised, and then buzzed the door to let the man into the building.

What a sight Antonio was when Giermo opened the door! The scrawny man was a soaking mess covered in mud, standing in the apartment doorway, almost frozen from exposure. His face showed signs that it had been covered in mud and that he had tried to wipe it clean with his hand. He had a long face that narrowed as it formed his chin, which sported a small blackish goatee.

"Hey man, it's a bitch to get here with only a few bucks in the pocket! Try getting a bus to stop, looking like this! Shit, I hate busses. I need a place to get this shit off and have a hot shower," the man croaked as Giermo let him inside. Antonio continued explaining, "I was having a smoke outside and I heard the cops! Juan and Ernesto were in the basement and I didn't have time to warn them. I split and hid in a mud hole, waiting for the cops to leave the area. All I had was a pack of cigarettes and five bucks in my jeans. I'll fill ya in with the rest after I get cleaned up."

While Giermo's Colombian compadre took a shower, Giermo racked his brain as to his options on handling the incoming shipment of "H" scheduled for the next night. He hadn't ever been pressured to improvise before, and his hangover wasn't helping! As options ran through his pounding head, a solution began to form.

"Brilliant, I got a way to make this work and keep the brothers at home from doubting me! I'll set it up later this morning," Giermo muttered, listening to the shower being turned on and the man in the bathroom bitch as he got undressed. "Hey, Antonio, ya want to go down the street for a late breakfast after your shower?" Giermo yelled over the sound of the running water.

"Don't care. So long as it's hot, mano."

Giermo picked up the empty beer cans strewn all over the floor, and found the empty pizza box hiding under the couch. Gathering the items, he dumped them in the trash bucket hidden under the sink. He rinsed the unclean dishes, and did a quick dry with an old dishcloth that looked like it had never been washed itself. He haphazardly shoved the cutlery and plates back into their designated places, and stripped off his filthy top and dumped it into the bedroom closet.

Returning to the couch, Giermo picked up the phone and dialed.

"Hello, *ComTek*," a woman answered the phone.

"It's Giermo, we have to meet. How about lunch time? It's easier for you then, right?"

The woman hesitated then replied in a low voice, "Things are busy here today, and I've a meeting at three this afternoon."

"Look, QE Park's halfway, and I gotta be in Vancouver later this afternoon. That work for ya?" Giermo pushed, hoping not to have to drive all the way out to Surrey.

The woman sighed then replied, still in the low tone, "Yea, okay, see ya at the dome then," and hung up.

Pleased that things were set up and a plan was in motion, Giermo turned on the TV and sat waiting for his turn in the bathroom.

⚹

The second floor of the West Vancouver RCMP detachment building was configured very differently from the main floor downstairs, which was designed for the contingent of uniformed officers.

The detective's floor looked like an open-concept workplace. Desks were placed in pairs and shared a small cubicle type barrier that rose about a foot above the desk surfaces. The south wall was encased by a full bank of large windows that overlooked the Burrard Inlet and Ambleside Park to the east. Small, thin, metal blinds were installed to keep the bright glare of the late afternoon sunshine from overheating the room.

The large, precinct Captain's office was at the end, and placed in the corner, sharing the south wall and the back of the room on the west side of the building. Along the north side, was a row of small rooms; windows facing Marine Drive could be seen strung along the concrete wall at the back of each one; the rooms each housed a table and a pair of chairs, and had a door and a window facing into the centre of the main workspace. The hard floor of the entire area had been designed for heavy traffic and a light gray, speckled tile was placed throughout.

Officer Kelly O'Brian walked directly to the back of the not-so-busy office, and knocked respectfully on the Captain's door. "Hey Captain, Sir, I was told that you're looking for me," she said, standing stiffly in the open door frame.

"That's right, Officer O'Brian. Close the door and take a seat," he instructed in a noticeable British accent.

The fit and trim, five-foot-six gentleman had reddish brown hair that was parted on the left side. He had narrow eyebrows, an oval-shaped head, fair skin and a well groomed, reddish mustache. He wore a blue suit with a subtle plaid pattern, a white long-sleeved, pinstripe shirt and a blue-striped tie.

Kelly sat as instructed and looked about the office, as she'd never been invited there before. A large, old, wooden desk was placed in the centre of the room, and a large, wooden credenza that was heavily scratched displayed family photographs and awards. A brass nameplate with "Captain Samuel Hollingsworth" inscribed was displayed in the front centre of the desk and large neat piles of file folders were stacked on each side of the wooden surface. A comfortable, brown executive desk chair supported the man, as he looked at

Kelly, who was sitting patiently, waiting for him to begin the conversation.

"Well, Officer O'Brian, I've been reviewing the preliminary report on your collar the other night. Looks complete and well prepared," he stated as his piercing dark blue eyes focused directly at her. "Good work!"

"Thank you, Sir," was all she could utter, as she nervously wondered why she had been summoned to his office.

"I'm well aware that you want to become a detective, and that you are waiting to see if you've made the grade. Is that correct, Officer O'Brian?"

"Yes, Sir. That's right, Sir," she replied stiffly.

The room went silent as Captain Hollingsworth reached for another file folder that was sitting on the top of the pile to his right; his face did not change expression. He opened the folder, paused, and glanced up at the young woman.

"Congratulations, Detective O'Brian," the Captain said as he stood up from his chair, smiled, and put his hand out to shake hers.

Kelly sat motionless in her seat for a moment. Her heart was pounding out of her chest with the unexpected announcement. She rose up to grab the congratulatory hand. "Wow! Thanks, Captain!" she replied, stunned at the news.

"I'm very proud of you, Kelly, and your achievement. I've been waiting for these results for a week or so, and have arranged for you and your new partner to be stationed here working with this office," the Captain said as he sat back down. He reached behind his chair, slid open the left credenza door and pulled a box from the space. He placed it on the front edge of his desk. "Open it!"

Kelly turned her focus toward the box. She took a deep breath, reached and grabbed the plain sandy-colored container that had an RCMP insignia stamped on the lid. Pulling the lid off and placing it on the desk, she reached inside and found a new holster and belt for her Smith and Wesson. Taking the prize from the box, she watched him pull out the front desk drawer and grab a shiny gold badge with his right hand. Sliding the drawer closed, he looked up, and facing her, placed the gold colored shield on the desk.

"A new detective shield for a new detective! Please hand over your officer's badge and then your appointment will be official!" he requested with a stern look.

"Yes, Sir!" Kelly responded, trying not to yell out as she removed her old officer's badge from her uniform. She placed it on the desk and took the new detective shield that had O'Brian and her ID number engraved boldly on the face.

"Go home and put that uniform into a storage bag and change into some street clothes, Detective O'Brian. Your new partner will be here after lunch. You need to report to this office at 1300. Good luck in your new profession. You're dismissed," Hollingsworth commanded, with a slight smile on his face.

Kelly O'Brian left the Captain's office clutching her detective's shield and new holster belt. It was almost 1100 and she had little time to change and be back to meet her new partner in just two hours!

Grinning from ear to ear, she knew her dream had just begun.

Chapter Eleven

It had begun to rain again when the dark blue courier truck pulled into the visitor's parking lot at the top of Queen Elizabeth Park. Giermo Hernandez parked with the front of the vehicle overlooking the vast city that could be seen for miles from that vantage point. The popular tourist destination had a few visitors who had come to see the *Bloedel Conservatory* attraction, and it was a good place to meet Ms. Parks, as it was unlikely anyone would recognize them here. He fidgeted as he waited for her to arrive, and the music on the van's radio didn't distract his thoughts from the issues that he had to resolve with the woman.

An old, white passenger car pulled into place a few parking spaces away from the courier van, and the attractive blond driver stepped out and closed her vehicle door, not bothering to lock it. She approached the driver's side of the van, and Giermo rolled down the window and told her, "Get in, on the other side."

Somewhat reluctantly, she sauntered around to the other side, entered the van's front passenger door, sat, and shut the door. "So, what's the panic and big mystery?" she inquired; she was concentrating on trying not to get her outfit dirty while Giermo was busy looking at her seductive painted lips. "I haven't processed the shipment you dropped off yesterday yet—you know that it takes a few days. I avoid taking any chances that any of my staff may get curious if I show too much attention to a specific shipment," she said, wiping the rain water off the sleeves of her jacket.

"I have …" then he corrected himself, "we have a bigger problem than that!" Giermo snapped as he saw her glare at him with her alluring eyes. "The place where I prepare those shipments was raided by the cops yesterday. They were all over the place when I returned from making the latest delivery to you!" he growled.

"So, what's that got to do with me? There wasn't anything to link us, was there?" she asked as her heart started to race and she looked closely at the man with his long, unmanaged, shoulder-length hair.

"No, relax, but I've a new shipment of uncut product coming in tomorrow night, and I now don't have a place to put it while I set up again! I want you to find a spot for that stuff for a few days, until I have time to make other arrangements," Giermo replied, lighting a cigarette.

"Me? Why me? I don't need that kind of shit problem!"

"Well, you got it! I don't have any other choice at this point, and I can't delay the shipment, either! You sure don't want cops at your place, do ya?" he blew smoke in her direction when he finished speaking.

"How'd they find your place anyway? Do you have any details on the bust?"

"No. One of my guys escaped detection while outside taking a smoke but he doesn't know much. I've sent a lawyer to get the other two sprung, but they're still at the cop's station. I need an answer now, so I can plan my next move!" Giermo pressed, getting anxious and starting to fidget again, as he took a long drag from the cigarette and opened his side window a little.

"Okay. I'll set something up and get a place to store the stuff—two days max. I'll call. I assume you're going to bring the shipment in this thing, right?" she asked as she waved her hand to move the smoke from her face.

"Yea, I think it'll all fit. Don't screw up and leave me hangin'," Giermo warned, worried that this arrangement would all fall through and he would be stuck with the shipment left in the van.

"You gotta be kidding me!" Candice exclaimed, climbing out of the van and slamming the door. "Christ, I'd better call Terry and figure a way to store this asshole's stuff without creating attention, and for that matter, without Will Richards seeing anything, either! His nose always seems to show up at the most inopportune time!" she mumbled, working on the problem as she climbed back into her *ComTek* old, white car.

Both vehicles departed the parking lot and headed down the QE Park hillside road toward their respective destinations.

"Terry got me involved with this jerk in the first place. He'd better help me now!" Candice grumbled as she headed back to her office in Surrey. "Humph!" Candice picked up her BlackBerry® and dialed the pole yard number.

"Pole yard, Terry here."

"It's Candice. We need to meet later. What works for you?"

"Well, Brian has been in your face—so to speak, so it would be better if our meeting appear as normal company business."

"Uh," she paused, "you're right. I've a meeting expected to be finished upstairs by four. Come to my office after then." She hung up the phone and continued her trek back to Surrey, feeling stressed about the unexpected risky situation.

⚹

The contracting crew was finishing the last touches of pulling the heavy, blue canvas cover over the new building framework at the mill. The electrical contractor had been working around the construction the best that he could, so the operation could be energized as quickly as possible. New power lines had been installed feeding each piece of equipment with cables that Will was able to scrounge from Candice. The cables were placed inside heavy metal tubing, and the ends were protected by large fittings affixed to each end. Will expected to have the lighting hung by the end of the day, too, and was pressing to be able to have the power reconnected before nightfall.

"Hey, Tom, it's Will Richards down at the recycling mill. Can you arrange to have a crew reconnect my service today? I've my electrical contractor indicating that he'll be finished within the hour and I need to have my security reactivated ASAP," Will asked the local *PowerOne* line-crew dispatcher.

"Hey Will, I'm glad to hear that you've got that place sorted out. Good for you! Sure I can have a crew drop by before the end of the shift. I'll make the arrangement," Tom confirmed, glad to help out a man who was always accommodating.

"Hey, Ray," Will waved at the man operating the log loader tidying up the yard. "We should be back in business in the morning. Start loading the bunker and clean up the de-nailing pit! We've got to rock and roll with all this stuff that's arrived," he said loudly, pointing to the mounting pile of returned poles.

Will surveyed the site, planning on how he was going to attack the loads of material that had arrived during the shutdown. He noted the increasing amount of smaller pole pieces being delivered by the *PowerOne* crews, and was concerned with the extra work that he'd have to go through to handle and sort the stuff into usable product. "I hope this is a short-term thing," he told himself, looking at the sea of dumped stuff laying all over his yard. "What a mess! I don't know about this!"

He looked over at his trailer. "At least I'll have some heat tomorrow," he mused, and thought about the mound of paperwork sitting on his desk at home.

The pole recycling operation was more complex than it appeared. The poles were delivered by contractors, or directly by *PowerOne* and *MiTel* line crews, and deposited in a designated dump zone that was placed outside the *Service Pole Recycling* fence line, located at the back end of the *ComTek* new pole storage yard. The piles of delivered materials needed to be sorted, have the scrap waste removed, and the full length poles gathered in safe, neat piles. Only cedar poles were selected for processing, because other types, such as pine and fir, were unsuitable for marketing as a finished product. It was mandatory that the area be kept tidy and safe, as the general public travelled past the area before entering the mill yard and office.

Usable poles were selected from the sorted piles, and the log loader moved them to a designated place called the de-nailing pit. Here, the poles were scanned with metal detectors, so as to locate nails and other metal objects that must be removed before the pole could enter the head rig saw to be processed. Any metal that was found had to be marked and removed by hand, with large clawed hammers. The now-safe log was cut with a chain saw into usable log lengths, which were later loaded onto the feed bunk, ready for the skilled sawyer to select and place into the handling rig.

The contaminated pole sides were sliced off first, and the ejected slabs carried by hand and placed into a scrap bin, that was located at the edge and side of the large fifty-inch-diameter circular blade. The clean uncontaminated core of the pole was then passed through a four-blade pony edger and finally cut into a desired length with a chop saw. The finished product was stacked by product type, and banded. The scrap and contaminated wood was boxed, so it could be shipped to a special environmentally monitored landfill.

♓

It already was past two o'clock, and Candice hadn't developed a clear plan on what to do to solve her problem with Giermo Hernandez. She'd been stuck in her office since returning from the meeting at QE Park, and wanted to check on Giermo's shipment that had been received the prior afternoon.

"Sure can't have anything else get screwed up!" she mumbled to herself as she left her office and started to walk toward the back of the office. "Good afternoon, Stewart. Still sorting out the shipment from LM?" Candice asked the young man as he pulled out metal materials from a box.

"Just about finished, Ms. Parks. There was a lot of stuff this time," Stewart replied as he continued to mark the list with items he was removing. "We received another shipment of old computers yesterday, too, but I haven't called the repair guys to pick them up yet. I'll be getting to that before the end of the day. Okay?"

"That's just fine Stewart, but let me know when they're picked up. I'm trying to keep those geeks busy and out of my hair."

"You bet, Ms. Parks," Stewart responded with a large smile, enjoying any poke at IT repair guys.

Candice knew that Giermo didn't receive his payment until the computer shipment had been received by his buyers, and that meant that she didn't get her cut until after that, so keeping everything moving as quickly as possible was in her best interest. She continued to think about what suggestions Terry Peters might have concerning Giermo's drug shipment, and hoped that he'd be able to come up with something practical and low risk. She walked back through the office, and returned to sifting through her e-mail, ensuring there wasn't any last request from Brian Quest before her three o'clock managers meeting.

Brian didn't usually have meetings late in the day, and the standard practice was to have his manager updates in the morning. It was curious to have a meeting scheduled at three. It would likely be quite short, with some announcement or something. That'd be a good thing, as she was becoming distracted and worried that having Terry in her office would arouse some unwanted attention to their discussion.

The three o'clock with Brian was as expected.

"I just wanted to get you all together to update you on the new business strategy that has been selected by the *ComTek* executives," Brian started, once all the managers had assembled in the conference room. The door was closed and the discussion was limited to those in attendance, which was Brian's usual mode of operation. Everyone sat silently and focused on Brian, who was sitting at the head of the table. There were no goodies today, indicating the meeting was going to be brief.

"*ComTek* has decided that they want to have key products supplied directly from the manufacturer to our customers, where possible. The centralized distribution warehousing practices will be discontinued for those items and we need to alter our business practices to accommodate this directive," he informed the group, watching for their reactions.

"You've got to be kidding!" Sandra Willows exclaimed in amazement. "Numerous studies have been carried out, even as far back as fifteen years ago, which continue to show that a centralized distribution logistical process is the best way to serve our customers and maintain optimized inventory investments in this province. What kind of dork came up with this!" Sandra carried on, very agitated.

"Well, that's the plan. You guys go think about what needs to be done to implement this directive and be ready to discuss this at our next managers meeting. I'll have Georgina schedule one. Party's over!" Brian paused then added, "By the way, we'll be beginning this process with transformers first, as we've approved and signed a ten-year contract with *BC Transformer Inc.* in Chilliwack." Brian abruptly terminated the discussion, turned and entered his office, closing his door behind him.

"Jesus Christ! This is insane! Someone has their head up their ass!" Sandra commented as the managers filed out of the room to figure out what they needed to do. "Wait until the union guys hear about this. They won't like it a bit!"

✶

Terry Peters was down to Candice's office shortly after receiving her phone call that the meeting was over and that they could meet.

"Shut the door and sit down!" she directed in a stern voice. The tone of the last meeting had placed her in a tenser mood than she had been before, and her stress level was highly elevated.

"Your three o'clock get ya all riled up?" Terry prodded to discover what had taken place upstairs.

"Oh, nothing that concerns you at this point, but I expect you and the guys won't like it when the story gets out!" Candice began to spill the news and stopped. "Anyway, we're here to fix something else right now. Let's focus on that! I had a short meeting with Giermo Hernandez and he needs a place to stash a drug shipment for a few days. You'll have to store it somewhere in the pole yard office."

"Are you kidding me?" Terry blurted out. "I'm not running a warehouse ya know."

"Well, that's the problem, and I said that I would provide a solution. I can't do it here. I've already got his computers on the receiving dock and I can't have my staff involved in handling an unknown shipment."

"Ah, okay ...." Terry sat and just breathed for a moment. "I believe that we must receive the shipment during regular office hours so nothing looks unusual if it must go to the pole yard. Giermo has a courier van, and that also shouldn't raise any eyebrows with his delivery. His merchandise will need to be moved quickly, and it should be done when Andrew's busy, so he's not hanging about during the transfer." Terry continued to outline his ad-hoc plan, "I'll have to create enough space in the back inside storage area of the pole office, so I'll arrange some type of clean-up project for Andrew today. What do ya think?"

"Sounds okay, so far. What about getting the stuff out, huh Terry?"

"Buggered if I know! Let's just get the shipment received without incident, and then we can work out something when we've more information about Giermo's timetables," Terry replied as he bit his lip, indicating that he had some stress about the plan. He didn't like having his activities placed at risk and this situation had all types of opportunity for getting screwed up.

"Okay. We need to have a story why you're in my office, too, just in case," Candice remarked, looking through her window up at the administration office above her. Candice knew it was unusual for Terry Peters to be in her office. She thought for a moment then suggested, "Let's say you came to see me to check on Will Richard's replacement materials you noticed on his site, and that you wanted to be sure that all the *ComTek* stuff had been given to him with authority!"

"Great idea! Yea that works. Candice, you arrange to have Giermo's shipment delivered to me at about three thirty tomorrow afternoon, and I'll look after everything else," Terry replied, and then promptly left the office.

Dealing with Giermo had gotten out of hand. Candice had been in financial trouble and an opportunity to make some easy money had seemed like a good idea when she started dealing with him. Her project with Giermo didn't include Brian, and she didn't want Brian to suspect that she was running her own scam and was using *ComTek* to handle her own personal business without his involvement. He would think that running something other than *LM Distribution* was stupid and far too risky. Brian's silent partners would be really pissed, too, if they got wind of it! Trying to stay calm, she reassured herself that she was a smart woman, and could look after herself, and really didn't have a choice on this new situation anyway.

Brian had been sitting in his office contemplating the issues that would need to be discussed concerning the new supply directive, and noticed Terry Peters leaving the IRD building situated below his window.

"Hmm ... I wonder what that was all about! I'll have to ask Candice when I see her next."

Chapter Twelve

Kelly O'Brian had returned home in a state of euphoria. She told herself that with her new job she needed a new look, as she decided what to wear. Her officer uniform had already been placed in a suit bag, and she would take it to the dry cleaners later, but right now she had to decide on other important things, like shoes and accessories!

She stood in her underwear in front of her bedroom mirror, knowing that she had to be ready in about an hour. That was a challenge for Kelly O'Brian, as she hadn't thought much about this day, and a change in clothing was the last thing that she'd thought about when envisioning the day that she would become a detective.

"Damn! This surely can't be that difficult!" she thought, fussing while holding the third different outfit over her body and modeling it in front of the bedroom mirror. "Think woman, think. I want to be stylish, not too sexy, be cop-like and professional and comfortable. Hmm ...." Kelly muttered at her reflection in the mirror, and then returned to her closet to look for another something that must be lurking in there! "It's going to be a big day and a new partner, too!" she told herself, pushing outfits around in the closet, hardly able to contain her excitement.

Finally a pair of stylish black pants, a trim black sport coat, and a tasteful white button-up cotton blouse were all placed on the bed. She changed her bra to suit her outfit, slipped into her bathroom, and decided to pull her hair into a tight bun. She grabbed a handful of hair pins and quickly pulled her long hair from her face and smiled. After a quick glance at herself in the mirror, she returned to her bedroom, slipped on her pants and blouse, leaving the top two buttons undone, exposing just a little cleavage. "Ah … a little color!" she muttered, searching in the cabinet above the sink; she clutched a lipstick and twisted the top, revealing a subtle light shade of pink. She found a pair of black onyx earring studs and poked them into place.

"Hmm …." she was stuck again, and searched in her closet for a pair of shoes that would work. "These old black flats are all I've got for today that isn't street–cop, heavy shoes, or heels!" she sighed as she slipped into the shoes and noted that her time had run out. "I'll have to buy new shoes later!"

"Oh, yea. I got to get this new belt on for my piece!" she thought, remembering that the outfit was not a standard issue uniform with all the gear. Kelly took a closer look at the belt she had been given by the Captain, and noticed that it was reversible, black on one side and brown on the other.

"Hey, how smart and convenient!" she noted, as she twisted the belt to the black side and slid the gun holster through. "Great," she said out loud; she clipped her new shield to the belt, placed her revolver inside its new home, and pulled the locking strap over the grip. She pulled on the small black dress sport coat, grabbed her keys, and left for the office.

Kelly O'Brian arrived at the detachment office and exited the second floor elevator. The room was filled with bodies now, working as pairs. The room was a hum of activity and noisy with the conversations and ringing telephones.

The room seemed to quiet down as Kelly walked toward Captain Hollingsworth's office. She felt the stare of eyes following her, as she tried to reach the office before anyone could make a comment. She knew all of these people through previous assignments, but knew they hadn't seen her out of uniform before.

"Holy shit, it's KO! Wow, look at that, eh!" John Burrows remarked before she reached her destination. Kelly just smiled to herself and carried on, without a word.

"Detective O'Brian reporting as directed, Captain, Sir," Kelly said as she politely knocked on Captain Hollingsworth's open door.

"Right on time, Detective. Close the door and please sit down."

"Yes, Sir!" Kelly replied as she sat next to a man who had already been seated next to the window. Through the corner of his eye, Hollingsworth saw her sit, and waited a moment before he turned from the other guest to face the young woman.

"Detective Kelly O'Brian, meet your new partner, Detective Simon Chung," Hollingsworth said in a monotone voice.

"Hi, I'm Kelly, just call me KO," she said and presented her hand to the man next to her.

"Yes, I'm Simon. Glad to meet you, KO," he replied with a smile, and took her outstretched hand and shook it.

"Detective O'Brian was made detective this morning, Simon, and I've arranged for the two of you to be partners, effective immediately. I've heard great things about you, Simon, and think you can be a great partner for Detective O'Brian here," the Captain said, studying the two and then continued, addressing Kelly. "Simon has just arrived at the office and needs to be introduced around. He's accepted his new assignment here in West Vancouver and you two will be taking that set of desks over there by the window. Get acquainted, settled, and return here in an hour. I've a case for you!" he said, pointing to the back of the main area.

The new partners departed the Captain's office, and Kelly started the rounds, introducing Simon to those detectives who were in the room.

"Hey, KO, moving up in the world, I see!" was the first thing out of John Burrows' mouth, hearing that Kelly had just been added to the detective squad. "Congrats on making detective and joining our West Van team!" he added.

"Thanks, no one's more surprised than I am!" she replied with a grin. "This is my new partner, Detective Simon Chung. Simon, this is Detective John Burrows, the smart ass of the group," she said with a grin. Turning around, she added, "and this is Burrows' partner Detective Frank Jansen, the only one crazy enough to tag along with JB!"

"Hey, Chung, you're goin' to have your hands full. Have fun and glad to have you aboard," Frank said as he eyed the new man.

The new partners travelled across the room and stopped at the pair of desks outside the Captain's office.

"Detective Simon Chung, meet Detectives Patrick Anderson and Hal Mourin. These are the serious guys in the room," she said with a twinkle in her eye.

"Glad to meet you, Simon." Hal stuck out his hand and shook Simon's. "This is a great precinct to work in—Hollingsworth's one of the best cops in the Lower Mainland."

With the introductions concluded, Kelly and Simon migrated to their new assigned work space.

"So, first things first Simon, do you like to drive or should I?" Kelly smiled, looking directly at her new partner.

"You drive, the streets are dangerous enough without me behind the wheel!" he replied, returning the grin.

They each selected a desk, placed their jackets on the back of the closest chair, and sat down, looking about the surroundings. Kelly pulled out her cell phone from the pocket of her jacket and looked at the phone number on the desk, placing it into the cell's memory.

"Simon, what's your cell? I should put you in my favs," Kelly asked, peering at the small screen of the iPhone®.

"Ah ... 604 ... 555 ... 2947," Simon replied, carefully watching his new partner. He was about five foot six, shorter than she was, and obviously of Chinese decent. He had the Asian skin coloring and a roundish-shaped head with black hair typical of his heritage. He had thin, narrowing eyes and eyebrows that were almost indistinguishable behind his thick black eyeglasses. He wore a dark blazer and black pants and shoes.

"Look ... we've an hour to get acquainted and I need to go shopping! The day's been nuts and I don't have the right shoes for chasing bad guys," Kelly remarked, pointing to the old, black flats. "Let's go to the mall up the street and fix that problem while we talk. Besides, you can see if your choice of driver was the correct one!" Kelly grinned as she looked up and grabbed her jacket. "Coming?"

Simon checked his watch and mentally registered the time. They had forty-five minutes left. He yanked his sports coat from the chair back and followed along, watching his new partner lead the way.

"We don't have our assigned ride yet, so my car will have to do!" Kelly continued to talk while she headed for the employee parking lot. Finding her old white sedan, she unlocked it and opened the front door. "This is it—jump in."

The *West Vancouver Mall* was only two traffic lights up the street past the Ambleside Park. Kelly found an empty parking stall and pulled in.

"Well, I'm still safe and in one piece!" Simon laughed as he vacated the car. "I guess you've passed your first job as my new partner."

"I'm even better with the lights flashing and siren blaring!" Kelly retorted. "Let's find some shoes!"

The two new partners approached the mall entranceway, and stopped at the end of the short corridor. Kelly located the mall map and directory, noted the shoe shops and marched in the direction of the first one. Simon tagged along behind, silently watching her confident stride as they moved quickly toward their destination. In less than fifteen minutes Kelly was wearing laced, black shoes on her feet and exited the shop with her old flats in a bag.

"That's better. Let's grab a coffee and talk before we head back," she suggested as she turned, searching for a *Starbucks* or something.

With coffees in hand they sat in the courtyard.

"Simon, what brings you to West Van?"

"Oh ... my partner caught a bullet a few months ago. He's okay but it was close. He only has a few years to go to retirement and he requested a desk job for the duration. I've been in a waiting pattern since then. I got this call, and have heard that Captain Hollingsworth's one of the best, so I took the transfer," Simon replied, taking a sip of the hot coffee. "The Captain said that he'd been shorthanded for some time and that he was saving the spot for an up-and-coming new detective grown from in-house. I guess that was you, KO," he continued after another mouthful. "I've been on the force for just over twenty years and Hollingsworth said that he wanted a seasoned detective to help break you in." Simon smiled with a twinkle in his dark brown eyes.

"One thing's for sure—I've been working my tail off becoming a detective! It looks like I've lucked out with my partner, too. It's been one hell of a day and I think that we'll get along just fine!" Kelly exclaimed and then quickly finished her coffee. "Let's get back and see what the Captain has for us!"

The two detectives arrived back at the precinct to find a set of keys and a blue folder on their desk with "Simon Chung" labeled on the tab. Simon opened the flap and thumbed through the papers and then looked up at Kelly. "Just administration stuff that I have to complete for this office—the bureaucracy lives everywhere!"

"Looks like we've our ride assignment, too." Kelly remarked, eyeing the car keys on the desk.

"Okay, you two!" a voice came from a short distance away. "You've had enough time to make nice! Here's your first jacket. You two finish the work on the Elvenden Row case. Detective O'Brian, I've reassigned it from Detectives Mourin and Anderson so fill in your partner. We need to find the head honcho of that grow-op. The lab's confirmed that the powder you found at the scene was heroin, and we need to find the new setup!" the Captain instructed, and handed them the file which contained the reports that Kelly had asked her team to complete the night before. "Keep me current," was the last command they heard as Kelly grabbed the car keys.

"Let's go, I'll fill ya in on the way," she said as she headed for the elevator.

Their assigned detective vehicle was an unmarked gray Ford Taurus SHO sitting in slot 2112. It was one of the newest vehicles in the fleet; the turbocharged 365 HP V6 engine was ready for action when the demand came.

"Sweet! I'm sure glad I got to be the designated driver of this team and I can't wait to see what this baby's got!" Kelly remarked as she unlocked the vehicle and the pair climbed in. Simon just smiled and studied his partner as Kelly pulled the vehicle from its space and headed for the security gate. She was excited and nervous at the same time as she cleared the gate and turned the vehicle into the street behind the precinct.

She twisted her head to face Simon as she navigated the vehicle toward the Elvenden crime scene. "Hmm … he's going to be the quiet one," she thought, turning back to check the road.

"Ah, I was asked to lead a team to a suspected grow-op yesterday up the mountain by *British Properties*. The electric meter was reading off the chart but that area had been installed with *PowerOne* test smart meters, so we weren't sure if the call was false or not," Kelly started her outline as Simon sat silently. "As you'll see, there was a very sophisticated marijuana operation in the basement and we caught two of three suspects during our raid."

"Hmm … high end part of town, I'd say for that type of activity," Simon replied as he opened the folder that had Kelly's reports inside. "Apparently the lab teams finished their work already as they've confirmed that the white powder you found was heroin! I see from your incident report that you also discovered a number of old computers in the corner of the lab. I think we need to give those a closer look-see," Simon said as he scanned the reports inside the jacket that Hollingsworth had handed over.

"So, Simon, where do you hang out?" Kelly inquired, taking the opportunity to find out a little more about her untalkative partner.

"I've a place in Chinatown and have lived there all my life. I'm a second generation Canadian. My grandparents immigrated to Vancouver, as it was the second-largest Chinese community in North America. They didn't want to be US citizens, so they came here. I love this city and want to protect our way of life, which is why I joined the RCMP as early as I could," Simon replied as Kelly travelled up the mountainside toward their destination.

The pair of detectives arrived at the house on Elvenden Row Street. Yellow tape surrounded the property and the door frame was being repaired so that the door could be properly locked. A blue and white RCMP cruiser was sitting in the driveway and Kelly swung the gray Taurus behind the police vehicle.

"Open the trunk, and let's see if the standard issue box of toys has been provided with this unit," Simon requested, knowing the items that should be in every detective's assigned vehicle.

Kelly opened the deck lid and found an MP5 with ammunition locked in an RCMP-designed security clamp, a set of raingear safety pullover slicks, flak jackets, an emergency band portable radio, and a tool box. Simon grabbed the red tool box by the handle, shut the lid, and said, "Yep, looks complete, let's go."

The pair flashed their detective badges to the repairman kneeling at the edge of the doorjamb and entered the premises. The house looked different in the light of day, and as they walked toward the kitchen, Kelly was greeted by a familiar face.

"Hey, Officer Penner, got the babysitting job, eh?" Kelly poked.

"That's okay … say, you were in an officer's uniform the last time I saw ya! I see you made detective since then!" the young officer replied with a smile.

"Yea, started this morning and got this case, too!" Kelly replied and smiled back. "Meet my new partner, Detective Simon Chung."

"Good to meet you, Sir," Officer Penner said stiffly. "Well, all's secured for you, and downstairs has been processed by the lab guys. I'll be up here if you need me, Detectives," the young man said and flashed Kelly another big smile.

Kelly led the way through the kitchen and headed downstairs.

"What a beautiful executive home! How did this high-end place become a grow-op and a drug-processing site?" Simon asked, shaking his head, but also knew the gangs were moving into secluded and new locales.

"Well, it's been here for some time!" Kelly exclaimed as the pair worked their way down the stairs. "Wait until you see the setup down in the basement!"

The pair entered the large room in the basement. *PowerOne* had already been inside to disconnect and tag the bypass. Kelly knew that the investigating team would've photographed the site and inventoried the plants for their report. The rest was left for the assigned detective team.

"Show me the computers that you mentioned in your incident report," Simon requested as they stood looking at the sophisticated plant environment. Simon pulled a small notebook from the inside pocket of his jacket. "You need to go to stationary and get yourself one of these small notebooks,

KO," Simon suggested as he began to put comments on a page of the small, black notebook.

Kelly walked over to where she had found the stack of computers. Simon lifted one of the cream-colored metal towers onto the table, and opened the tool box that he had brought from the car. He searched for a small screwdriver and after removing the tiny screws on the side of the metal computer case, slid the cover back and out.

"Hmm, I don't see anything hiding inside. There are six of these computer cases sitting on the floor for some reason. That's very unusual, I'd say, for a grow-op site," Simon remarked as he continued to eye the contents and look for anything out of place. He took a photo of the open case with his cell phone. He turned to continue looking around after making a few notes as Kelly watched her new partner closely. "Hey KO, these unfolded cardboard boxes are in two sizes!" Simon said as he made a note in his book.

"Yea, I know. My team noted those in the report."

Simon grabbed one of the larger cardboard boxes, placed it on the table and assembled it. "Look, this box is the size of the computer case and I'd bet the boxes are used to ship a number of computers inside." Simon paused for a moment. "Hmm!" he muttered, thinking out loud and reaching for a smaller cardboard box placed on a shelf. He assembled the box and looked at the shape and size. His face lit up with a smile.

"I know!" he commented, still talking to himself as he took the smaller box, rotated it, and slid it between the inside of the computer case and the motherboard. "I thought that it was strange for this computer to have only one printed circuit card. They usually have at least two or three. One is the main computer motherboard, one is the communications internet card, and a third is the graphics monitor card. This unit's only got the motherboard, leaving a large enough space to insert two of these small boxes, probably for the cut heroin," Simon said as he took another photograph with his cell, this time of a partially inserted box sitting in the computer housing.

"So ... where do the units go from here?" It was Kelly's turn to ponder the question. "I doubt the two suspects we caught will know!"

"Yea, KO. I suspect those guys were here to look after the grass, not the heavy stuff," Simon said as he surveyed the setup. "Let's do more snooping and see what comes up. You know it's not very common for drug sites to have grass and heroin together in the same operation!"

"Probably the operation has expanded from grass to 'H' and a permanent place to process the heroin hadn't been established yet," Kelly remarked, still poking around; she spotted a small bag that had fallen behind the shelving. "Well, what do we have here?" she asked as she grabbed the small duffle bag and placed it on the table.

It was already open and Simon began to pull the contents out, and place them on the large table alongside the computer casing. "Wide 3M™ box tape and a dispenser, black felt marking pens, and a roll of labels," Simon called out the items as he pulled them from the bag. He pulled the end of the label roll and found "Bug Busters Computer Services" imprinted on two-by-four-inch sticky labels.

"Bingo!" Simon exclaimed, excited with the find and took another photo of the items laid out on the table, then noted them in his black book.

"Hmm ... that seems to be about it in here! Let's take a look outside," Kelly said opening the door to the backyard.

The pair walked up a flight of concrete stairs that led to an unkept lawn. Simon spotted a yellow RCMP marker tape that had been left the prior night by the lab crew. Cigarette butts were scattered on the ground. "Hmm," Simon muttered as he picked up a couple of butts from the ground. "These might lead somewhere," he said as he placed them in a small clear plastic bag that he had taken from the tool kit before he went outside.

"Sure is muddy out here. The rain has ruined any hope of getting any boot prints though," Kelly said as she crouched down to take a close look at the markings in the mud.

"Let's wrap up, KO. We both have had a long day and we've something to work on tomorrow."

The two partners returned to the basement and relocked the back door. Simon placed his additional cigarette evidence into the tool box, gathered the duffle bag items from the table, and returned them back inside the bag. "KO, you take this bag of evidence and I'll bring our tool box," he said as he zipped the bag closed. "Let's go!"

♓

Giermo Hernandez's cell phone rang. Candice Parks was on the line. "All things are set for tomorrow afternoon at three. Come to the pole yard gate on the other side of the road from my office. Tell the guard that you've a delivery for the pole yard office, attention Terry Peters," she said quickly and hung up without waiting for Giermo to reply.

Giermo's drug shipment pickup site was a short drive along the waterfront docks, and he needed to be at the designated place at twelve thirty during the shoreman's lunch hour. He calculated, and figured the three o'clock delivery time was tight but workable.

Antonio Castillo was still in Giermo's apartment and had been told to help with the next day's work, so Giermo decided to let him stay for the night. Giermo didn't know if the cops had identified Antonio, and it was safer for all if Antonio remained as his house guest.

Giermo needed to find a new place to process the incoming shipment of drugs. He continued to make phone calls, looking for a small warehouse that he could sublease. The only place that he'd found so far was out in Port Coquitlam, but POCO was further out of the city than he had wanted. He preferred a subleasing situation as the documented prime tenant couldn't easily be linked to him. He had three grand a month to spend on the rent, which was the outlay he'd made for the Elvenden place. He had to find a suitable place quickly, as time was running out, and he didn't want to keep the shipment at *ComTek* very long.

He was spread out on the sofa watching football and drinking his fourth beer of the day. The shrill sound of the house phone ringer interrupted his mental evaluation of the POCO warehouse opportunity. "Giermo here," he responded to the third ring.

"Good afternoon, it's Karl Kuntz," the caller said without expression. "The cops have decided not to press charges and I expect that Juan and Ernesto will be released about five this afternoon. It seems that the cops are still fishing about and haven't charged them. Are you going to be able to arrange for their pickup Giermo, or would it be better for me to drop them off somewhere?" the lawyer offered.

"Uh … good job, Karl. I think that it would be best for me to stay out of the picture, so can you take them home, please?" Giermo replied as he sat up in the sofa.

"Will do! Be careful, there're lots of eyes out there, Giermo!" Karl warned and then hung up.

"Hmm … now with those guys out of jail and the cops watching, I'm going to get exposed if I'm not very careful,"

Giermo mumbled, assessing the situation and becoming more worried than he had been when they were at the cop shop. "Maybe I need to call Pablo!"

Giermo Hernandez had been born on a finca, a small farm outside the outskirts of Mosquera, a small village on the road between Bogotá and Medellin, Colombia. The Hernandez family was well known in the area and Giermo was one of five children, all boys, who worked the small family farm.

He was adequately educated for the family business, and it was mandatory that each of the brothers mastered English, the language of International business. A year ago the family decided to establish a foothold in the Canadian market, and Giermo had been selected to organize the venture, his first major family business assignment. He was provided with a list of contacts the family had cultivated in Vancouver, and he was sent on his way.

Giermo was well aware that the news of the bust at the Elvenden Row site wouldn't be well received by his family. He knew that it was only a matter of time before the word of his first major failure would reach Mosquera. His family had trusted him and he had let them down.

Chapter Thirteen

It had been a cold and stormy night, the wind had howled and the driving rain had pounded rooftops and filled road culverts to overflowing. It was Friday, and the morning commute had already taken its toll on unprepared drivers by six that morning.

Will Richards was out of bed and brushing his teeth. It was the day of a new beginning and he was going to be ready! He'd been up late the night before, thrashing through the paperwork demanded from owners of every type of business. Government agencies didn't wait for anything, nor did they care about excuses. It was the last days of the month, and Will needed to gather all the documentation for payroll reporting and tax submissions. He knew that he was slow and didn't like doing these tasks, so he started before the deadline, hoping something would not arise that would divert his attention and place his company into arrears, again.

Will had decided to call in his entire crew, even though it was Friday and a payday. He knew that keeping payroll costs down at this time of year was critical to keeping his line of credit manageable but he also knew that he had to get the mill up and running. Stock produced late in the fall often sat as inventory until spring, but Will was getting pressure from *ComTek* concerning the size of the piles of unprocessed poles, and the look of the un-kept yard. He had to get things restarted and deal with the financial fallout later!

"Well, it's a rough trip into Vancouver this morning, listeners," Will heard the six thirty *CKVR* traffic report on the truck radio. "Watch out for the flooding and hydroplaning, folks."

"Damn, what a day to start the mill. It's going to be a mud hole, especially since *ComTek* has done nothing to maintain the gravel yard all year!" he thought as he steered his vehicle toward Surrey.

"One good thing today though; the Canucks® play at home and I'll need the hockey game to relax me after the day I expect I'll have!" Will thought, as his mind continued to mull over the tasks ahead. He hadn't noticed that the pounding rain had subsided.

The *ComTek* security guard was wearing a bright yellow slicker, and waved from the protective shack as Will turned into the pole yard entrance. Will pointed the truck directly toward his trailer and observed the worksite as he travelled past the pole-unloading area.

"I'd better form a plan this morning so the guys are focused on the priority work," he thought, knowing that none of his crew had arrived yet, and he needed to get his head straight before everyone showed up. Will unlocked the crew trailer and turned up the electric heat.

"At least I won't freeze my butt today!" he muttered as he thought about the many times he had been forced to sit in the frigid office lately. He turned on the lights, and sat at his desk to make notes of tasks for his crew.

※

Terry Peters arrived at the *ComTek* pole yard office, parked his vehicle and entered the building. "I need to formulate a plan for Giermo's shipment!" he muttered, thinking about what he had to do to have everything ready and organized by three. He checked the pole shipment roster and there wasn't anything planned for the afternoon, and there were only two shipments scheduled for the morning.

"Hmm … it's going to be a bit quiet around here today," Terry contemplated the work timetable and went to the back to make coffee. "The first thing I need to do is to clean out some space for the shipment," he told himself, putting the coffee filter into position. "Hmm … let see! I wonder how much space I'll need for a van full of boxes," Terry muttered, as he poured water into the cavity of the machine and turned it on. He went to the back of the building to look at what he needed to do. He didn't know the size of the boxes that were going to be delivered, nor the weight. "That could be a big problem if we can't move the stuff really fast!" Terry scratched his forehead as he stood in the small, unused storage room.

The back storage area was almost empty and seldom had been used in the past few years, so Terry figured that it was an ideal place to hide the late-day shipment. "That's good—this will be easier than I thought," he smiled, happy not to have to do any manual work to move things out of the room.

Terry returned to the coffee which was now ready. "I'll come up with some excuse to send the log loader over to *Ernie's Equipment Repairs* for a maintenance check just before three this afternoon. That'll have Andrew away from the yard and it'll piss off Will at the same time. A two-fer!" Terry grinned as he formulated his plan, pleased with how it played out in his mind. He poured a cup of coffee and went to his desk with a large smirk.

♓

Giermo Hernandez concluded that he had to call Pablo. This was a last resort solution, but there seemed no other option, as Giermo didn't handle stress or changes in plans very well. There was a lot to do with the new shipment and all, not to mention that he still had to decide on a new heroin processing site. He'd no time to fuss with Juan or Ernesto, and it was a job that Pablo handled well. Giermo dialed the number displayed on his cell's contacts list. "Pablo, it's me, Giermo. I need your services tonight," he spoke softly so as not to wake Antonio in the other room.

"Okay mano. It's your dime, Giermo! What's the job?" the deep voice inquired indifferently.

"Look, not on the phone. I got company. Meet me at the coffee shop on East Pender and Commercial in about an hour," Giermo said quietly, and then hung up.

"Hey man, what's up?" a sleepy voice drifted from the guest bedroom.

"Nothing important, Antonio, just making calls to find another place for us to work from. I'll be finished in a minute!"

Giermo heard his guest go into the bathroom, so he decided to return the call from the realtor looking for an answer on the facility in POCO. "I'd better go and see that place tomorrow," he sighed as he looked for the phone number to make the appointment. "I sure don't have time today!" He made the call and agreed to meet the realtor at ten the next morning. "Hey, Antonio, I've to go out soon, so you'll have to entertain yourself for a while!" Giermo raised his voice so he could be heard over the sound of the running water in the bathroom.

Pablo Dominguez was sitting by the front window inside the coffee shop when Giermo arrived on foot. Pablo was a large, husky man, towering over two meters in height. His face was noticeably Spanish, and a few scars on his face and neck were reminders of his profession. He had narrow, black, beady eyes, curly shoulder-length hair and an unshaven, round face. His coat was pulled up covering the back of his neck, and a coffee and fruit square sat on a plate on the table in front of him.

Giermo went to the cashier counter and paid for his coffee. There wasn't a line at that time of morning and Giermo was able to go to the coffee urn and pour a black plain coffee without interruption. He pulled up a chair close to the big man and sat down, placing his coffee by the front window to cool.

"Thanks for coming on short notice," Giermo said in a low voice and glanced at the steam rising from his hot coffee.

"In my line of work everything's short notice." The husky man stared out into the street and watched the pedestrians dodge the puddles in the sidewalk.

"The cops busted Ernesto Rodriguez and Juan Vergara a few days ago. They were released last night and I had Karl take them home. I can't be connected to them ya know, and I don't know what they told the cops. Karl said that they told the cops nothin', but I think that they're both liability risks now!" Giermo said in a low nervous voice, looking out the window and not at Pablo. "I don't think I've any option now, and need to ensure they don't leave a trail to me!"

"Ya got a plan, or is it all my show?" Pablo's black, beady eyes turned from the window and peered at Giermo.

"Ah ... there's a hockey game tonight and transit will be crowded. I expect the cops are watching both of them, so I was going to have the guys lose the cops in the large crowds and meet me some place. They'll think that the meet will be with me to talk about next steps, or something. Instead, you'll be waiting!" Giermo described his simple plan and waited for a reaction.

"Yea okay; where will ya set up the meeting, Giermo?"

"Ah ... I figured under the Burrard Street Bridge, where the *Aquatic Center* is. It'll be deserted there, with the game and all." He continued, "The guys can get there by transit and a short walk, and I thought that by say seven fifteen tonight, the city will be glued to the TV and not out and about."

Pablo grabbed his coffee and a piece of his square. He turned to watch the people passing the shop, and it was clear that he was considering the plan and the selected venue. Giermo picked up his coffee as it had cooled enough to drink. He needed to have something to do while he waited through the silence.

"Hmm ... both guys, same spot, eh?" Pablo asked, still looking out the window.

"I could figure something to split them if you need," Giermo responded anxiously.

"No, it's not a problem. You set it up and I'll handle it from there!" The cold reply was a relief for Giermo. "Standard price, one for two as the place and setup's the same. That work for ya, Giermo?"

Giermo was prepared for the payment and had assumed the price. He pulled out an envelope and slid it under the table, ensuring no one was watching. "Right!"

Pablo grabbed the envelope, pushed the last piece of the square into his mouth, and gulped the remaining coffee. Without any further discussion he quickly joined the pedestrians in the street. He was out of site in a flash.

Giermo remained at the table and finished his coffee, needing time to regain his composure. He hated these types of things, and the thought of the assignment that he'd given Pablo sent a cold shiver up his spine. "It's for the best," he continued to convince himself. He sat working out a script for the phone call that he had to make on his cell. Antonio was at the apartment and he needed to remain unaware of the pending event. The timing was going to be critical!

Abused Trust

♓

Candice Parks was preoccupied when she walked into her office. She'd enough secrets without this mess with Giermo's shipment, and she was worried about having Terry Peters involved more than he was. She told herself over and over again that it had been Terry who had gotten her involved with Giermo in the first place, and she blamed him for her predicament. "I hate that Terry's involved again in my affairs!" she sighed. "Damn, he's making things too risky for me!"

She recalled how Terry had been well connected with everything that was happening at the CLG, and through some gossip or something, he'd found out that she had overwhelming financial pressures. Terry knew Giermo through other dealings that Candice didn't know anything about, and Terry also knew that Giermo had been looking for an undetectable distribution solution for moving his merchandise.

In the beginning, Candice had been unaware of the true nature of the contents of Giermo's shipments, and had been told that they were stolen computers that he needed to fence without hassles. She'd agreed to handle the shipments for a fee paid upon receipt of the goods by the *Bug Busters Computer Services* company. It seemed easy money at the time.

"It's too late to pull out now, and I still need those personal cash injections anyway!" Candice muttered, trying to convince herself to tough out the situation, "it's just another business arrangement like the one with Brian, only without the sex! Humph, I must keep things in perspective." She sat for a moment and sighed. Of course she knew better, about Brian Quest. Things between them had gone beyond casual business sex a long time ago, at least for her it had. She had wanted to tell him but he was still married, he was still her boss, and things were complicated enough already. "I've got to deal with

Terry and Giermo right now," she muttered and got out of her chair.

Candice walked to the back of the building to check on the computer shipment, and saw the boxes with *Bug Busters Computer Services* labels sitting in the shipment area.

"Hi, Ms. Parks. I've finally got this shipment ready to go, and I've contacted the courier to pick them up," Steward told his boss as she entered the packing area.

"Good work. Have you finished with the counts and processing of the *LM Distributor*'s shipment as well?"

"Yup, all done. I'm about to go up the hill and work on some wire cable we've just received from Prince George," he said, happy that the tedious counting task was finished for now.

Candice smiled and nodded her head, indicating that she had heard his status report. She then turned back to her office to think more about Terry Peters and how she might deal with her growing concerns about him.

♓

Allen Harwitz was sitting in Brian Quest's office; his leg was nervously bobbing up and down as he was outlining the problems that he was having in working out a solution to supplying the transformers directly to customers from the manufacturer, and bypassing the central warehouse system.

"Our Integrated Package isn't designed to handle this scenario!" Allen said, frustrated as he explained the findings that he had identified. "Everything has been configured to receive supplier shipments here, and then we distribute. The system looks at the stock requirements of our remote mini-warehouses and looks at our on-hand balances before it generates picking documents to refill those sites," he described the process that Brian should've known anyway.

"Well, talk to the IT guys and get a work-around! Systems should perform the tasks we want, not the other way around!" Brian growled, raising his voice to the point that most of the office was able to overhear the conversation through the open door.

"It's one of the down sides of off-the-shelf system software, Boss—you know that!"

"I don't give shit about that. Just fix it, and don't come back until you have a solution of some kind." Brian pointed to the door. "Shut the door on your way out!"

Brian glared at the man as he watched him get up from his seat and quickly leave the office. "I'm not going to let this shitty software get in the way of my deal," Brian thought, now pissed off at the situation as he stared at his closed door.

Brian knew that the Integrated Package solution was unpopular with his staff, including the field personnel, but it hadn't been his choice in the first place and he had to live with it as well. "Who would've guessed that the software would make everyone's lives so difficult, just to do their jobs? You know, Thomas Howe was right all along and we shouldn't have put this monster in!" he grumbled, hoping that Allen would figure something out soon.

♓

Will Richards stood by the fifty-inch saw blade, talking to Ray Patterson. "What do ya think, eh? Is everything working after the lengthy shut down?" Will asked, looking at the first product that had gone through the head rig.

"Yea, looks good to me!" Ray yelled over the noise of the equipment. "I'll put that piece through the rest of the machines and check that they're running properly!"

Will nodded and turned his attention to the activities his men were doing in the yard.

A thin anemic-looking man was working the de-nailing pit. Will had hired him a few months before the shutdown, and the work was tough and hard on the body. The man had a lit cigarette dangling out of his mouth, and he was straining to turn a large pole over to check for metal objects on the other side. He grabbed the metal detector in one hand, and a marking pen in the other, circling any object that needed to be extracted as he passed the head of the detector along the length of the cut pole.

Jack Hollands was bouncing in the operator's seat of the large yellow log loader as it travelled over the uneven gravel roadway, returning for a new load of poles to sort. The ground was soft from all the rain, and large pools of water made it difficult to navigate the large machine around the potholes.

"Hmm ... good! Everyone's busy and I got a start on getting this place back in order," Will thought, feeling better now that the operation was functioning again. I should call Thomas and have him come out and see the new place, and we can go for lunch later," he muttered, glancing to his right to admire his new facility with its new, shiny, blue cover. He smiled, opened the office door, and sat in his old office chair to prepare to make the call to his friend.

⚜

Thomas Howe knew the trip to Will's mill with his eyes closed. He always enjoyed going and visiting with the crew, and seeing the poles being turned back into useful raw product. Often there were customers waiting for their orders and standing around having a chat with Will; but not today, as it was late in the season and there was little demand for Will's product.

Most of the public was looking for a deal on cedar fencing panels and posts. The price was usually more important than the recycled aspect of the product, and Will ensured his prices were the lowest anywhere. The furor for fencing materials would not begin until the early spring, and Thomas knew that the majority of Will's current production would become inventory until then.

The light blue convertible Ford Mustang took the parking space alongside Will's green pickup truck. Thomas climbed out of the driver's seat and waved at Ray who was pulling levers of the head rig saw. The long-term employees knew Thomas, and his relationship with *ComTek* and Will Richards.

"The bright blue cover's a beautiful site, eh Will!" Thomas commented as he entered the trailer, not realizing that Will was on the phone.

"I've most of that order already in stock, and I can have the rest of your order ready to go tomorrow afternoon. Is that okay?" Will asked, as he made notes on an order form, listening to the squawk coming out of the telephone speaker on the desk.

"That's great, Will! I'm glad that you're back in business. You're our preferred supplier ya know!" the voice continued to vibrate from the speaker.

"Great—thanks for your support. You can pay in cash or check when you pick up the order. Hang on," Will said as he took a calculator, punched in the numbers, and scribbled the total at the bottom of the order sheet. "The total will be three hundred forty-two, fifty-six plus tax."

"Great. I'll expect your call letting me know when I can pick up my stuff." The caller hung up and Will turned to see his friend standing next to his desk, by the door. "Amazing—I'm still getting calls for fencing. It's late in the year but due to the big winds, old fences and posts have been pushed over and I've been getting lots of calls!"

"Back in the saddle again, eh!" Thomas poked with a smile.

"It took too long, my friend. I don't know what would've happened if you hadn't written your little love note! Hey, come and take a close look at the new setup," Will said with a broad smile across his round face, as he stood to go outside.

The unique sound of the large blade running through the pole could be heard throughout the surrounding area, and it was music to Will's ears. Thomas was taken on a tour of the new building and Will pointed out all the improvements that had been made, comparing it to the old design. The movement of the large John Deere log loader was noticeable a short distance from Will's fence line.

Completing the survey, Thomas turned and spoke loudly so he could be heard over the noise of the equipment, "Let's go to *Kennedy's* for lunch. Grab your coat and I'll meet you there."

Will nodded his approval and started toward the office, but stopped to advise Jack Hollands where he was going.

Thomas had arrived at the pub and had ordered two cold pints of Bud® before Will arrived, and the beers were sitting on the table with their cold sweat running down the outside of the chilled mugs.

"Sorry, the phone rang as I was picking up my coat. Another order. They want to use recycled cedar on a large wall of some community centre, and it'll be part of their environmental initiative. I've to give them a price and delivery date when I get back!" Will spoke quickly and the enthusiasm oozed out. "You know, this is a great project, and I appreciate your help, Thomas."

"I know—no problem. You know that I do what I can to help. You must make a living at this, too, my friend. It's not a charity project! Have you been able to find out what's going on concerning the recommended improvements to the operation that you submitted to *ComTek*?"

"No, I keep getting the run around, and every time I ask they say the report's sitting on someone else's desk waiting for review. It's ridiculous—the improvements don't cost much but the benefits are thousands a year. I don't get it!" Will responded, annoyed. "It almost seems intentional!"

The men ordered their lunch and another pair of pints of beer. The pub was not very busy and the bartender and waitress were leaning against the bar yakking. Thomas didn't want to dampen the mood, so decided not to pursue other sensitive issues that he knew Will hadn't addressed, and left them for another day to discuss.

"So, excited about getting everything going, eh?" Thomas asked grabbing his mug of beer.

"Yea, but Helen thinks I'm an idiot. I do love this project, though!"

"Hey, all our wives think we're idiots half the time!" Thomas remarked, trying to lighten the conversation. "Some of them just tell us more frequently than others." He grinned and grabbed his beer.

The conversation drifted to other topics and the Canucks® hockey game. Will was an avid sports fan and loved to talk about sports, or anything else for that matter, and the conversation carried long through the lunch hour.

"Hey, it's time to go!" Thomas couldn't believe the time when he checked the display on his cell.

"The conversation's always good when we get together over a pint!" Will smiled, pulling some cash from his pocket. "My turn, remember!"

The green pickup truck was reaching the light at 66th when Will saw the John Deere log loader preparing to cross the road. The large yellow machine turned toward the repair shop down the road. Will knew that his machine would've already been reassigned to *ComTek*. It was before three in the afternoon, and sending the machine over the street before the end of the daily shift implied that the equipment needed immediate attention.

"Shit, another problem! Hopefully my machine will be returned on Monday!" Will grumbled, thinking that he'd have to send the men home early.

♓

A blue courier van that had "New Wave Couriers" written on the side panel, stopped at the security guard post and the driver rolled down the window. "I've a delivery for a Mr. Terry Peters. I was told that I could find him here," the driver informed the guard while obscuring his face by looking down at the paper on his lap.

"Yes, sir. He can be found in that building over there." The guard pointed to the pole yard office and waved the driver through the checkpoint.

Terry was watching for the van from his office window. The courier van was right on time and Terry came out of his office to meet the oncoming vehicle. He directed the vehicle toward the side of the building, and it backed into the covered area that was hidden from the guard's view. The Colombian driver vacated the driver's seat, quickly reached the back of the van, and opened the two large doors.

"Right on schedule, Giermo! Let's get this stuff unloaded!" Terry exclaimed, concerned that some unexpected visitor might appear, like Will Richards whining about the loader.

The van was completely loaded with unmarked moving boxes. The small cube brown cardboard boxes were heavier than Terry had expected, as he lifted the first box and led the driver through an access door leading to the selected storage place.

"I hope that no one comes in here after all this stuff's unloaded. I can't hide a shipment of this size in this small space for too long," Terry said in a low and nervous voice as he put the first box onto the floor.

"I expect to be able to pick them up sometime Monday, Tuesday the latest. I've a new place but I still need to finalize the arrangements, hopefully this weekend," Giermo tried to reassure Terry, as he turned to get another carton from the van.

It took the two men fifteen minutes to unload the van, moving the cargo as fast as they could, both feeling stressed that they may be seen by the guard who was only a short distance away.

Terry gave the thumbs-up as the last box was withdrawn from the van, puffing to catch his breath from the strain of the exercise. Giermo closed the doors, jumped into the driver's seat and the dark blue courier van quickly pulled away. Terry grabbed the last box and stacked it with the others, locked the room, and returned to his normal activities, still worried about the what-ifs of his actions.

Chapter Fourteen

It was six o'clock in the evening, and Juan and Ernesto were getting ready for their meeting with Giermo according to the instructions given to them on their apartment landline telephone earlier in the day. Neither of the men had a cell phone, as Giermo wanted to keep the costs of his operation contained; besides they didn't have a need for one, since they were with Giermo most of the time anyway.

Juan looked out the front window of his apartment and didn't see anything unusual, but Giermo had cautioned him that the cops were likely watching his and Ernesto's every move, and that they had to shake any tail before they reached the designated meeting!

It was raining again, and the two men were spotted with their baseball caps pulled over their faces, allowing the water to drip down the backs of their hats, wetting their upturned collars.

"Hey KO, turn that thing off! Our guys are on the move!" announced Simon, poking her in the arm. Both detectives were listening to the hockey pregame commentary on the radio. It was going to be a big hockey game for the home team Canucks® and everyone in the city was tuned in.

The two detectives were staked out at the address they had pulled from Juan's rap sheet. Simon had instigated the men's release with the hope that one of them would lead him to the Elvenden Row operation's boss. Endless waiting was the norm in cases like this, but sitting in their new set of wheels made it seem better somehow.

The two suspects started to walk in the direction of the unmarked vehicle, and the two detectives slouched down to reduce their visibility. It was raining and the water running over the windshield further obscured their presence. The targets were walking on the other side of the poorly lit street in the direction of Hastings Street, a busy main artery leading into the city. The traffic was becoming congested with hockey fans rushing to get to the stadium before the seven o'clock puck drop.

"It's going to be tough keeping tabs on those guys tonight!" Kelly commented as she turned on the car's engine and swung the vehicle in the direction of the two men. Kelly knew that it required great skill to keep just the correct distance while shadowing a suspect and remaining undetected, yet maintaining visual contact, especially in a moving vehicle.

The two men reached a bus stop. The detectives pulled their gray SHO into the side curb, now about eight cars back, and waited for the bus. The bus stopped, loaded with hockey fans dressed in team colors, and picked up its passengers; no one exited at the stop. There was only standing room in the bus, and the two men held a hand strap as they travelled to the next planned stop.

The bus weaved through the heavy traffic. The unmarked gray vehicle had difficulty in keeping pace, but the saving grace was that the bus had to make stops, which allowed adequate time for the pursuers to make up the distance. The bus travelled another five stops before the two Colombians jumped off and waited under the cover of the glassed-in transit shelter. The two men looked at the bus numbers of each bus that stopped, and when they determined that the correct ride had arrived, they jumped on. The bus travelled an additional block then moved into the left lane, indicating a turn was imminent. The gray Taurus followed. The bus headed southward toward the SkyTrain station a few blocks ahead.

"Hmm … I think they're going to the Broadway Station. We'll lose them if we stay in this car!" Simon remarked anxiously, looking at the congested road ahead.

The city was a zoo with people trying to get to the transit stadium or a bar to watch the action.

"I know that there's a designated police parking zone close to the Broadway Station, KO," Simon said, concerned at the size of the growing crowd. "We've got to park and get to the transit entrance before our suspects' bus can navigate the route and complete picking up fares."

By the time the two detectives arrived at the SkyTrain station, there was a sea of bodies on the platform, many wearing Canucks® blue jerseys or blue and green painted faces; none worried about the wet night. The crowd crushed together and the detectives were unable to find their prey.

The monorail train arrived in the station, already crammed with blue-clad bodies. The doors opened and sucked most of the masses inside. The two cops remained on the platform with other commuters who were unable to get inside the packed train. "Damn!" wasn't audible over the rushing noise of the departing rail cars.

"I don't see them, do you Simon?" Kelly asked, frustrated and looking about in the crowd which was now growing again.

"Nope, I think they got onto that last train! Well, we're screwed for the night. Might as well go home and watch the game, like everyone else!" Simon exclaimed, annoyed with the turn of events.

The two detectives headed back to their car, not saying anything else.

♓

"Well Juan, if we'd any cops on our ass, we must've lost them in this crowd!" Ernesto whispered in the ear of his friend, keeping his comment from the earshot range of the next person pressing against him.

Juan smiled in agreement, and stood, holding on tightly, ensuring that he didn't lose his balance in the pushing and rocking motion of the train car as it zipped westward.

It was almost six thirty when Giermo was able to park his courier van outside of his apartment. Traffic was in gridlock on every route entering the city. It was Friday night, and with the game and the weekend, Vancouver's highways and side streets quickly choked as people tried to find a way to get to their destination. The wet roads from the rain didn't help either, and the radio was reporting accidents throughout the Lower Mainland.

Giermo was ready to grab a brew and sit and watch the game with Antonio.

"The drive seems to suck the life out of you on nights like this!" Giermo grumbled to himself, as he opened the door to his warm apartment.

"Hey, Giermo, you've had a few calls while you were out. I didn't answer them—I just let the machine get 'em!" Antonio told Giermo as he sat in front of the flat screen with an open Canadian® beer in his hand. "The game's on *SportsNet*® and this high definition screen's better than a seat at the stadium!"

Giermo dumped his jacket in his room and went to the fridge to grab a cold beer and returned to the phone to listen to his messages. The sound was turned up on the TV, and Giermo needed to concentrate to hear the machine over the broadcast.

"Oiga, Giermo. Necesito a hablar con usted. Es importante!" The message was brief, and Giermo recognized the voice from Colombia and stiffened up. He mumbled something in Spanish and punched out the numbers on the phone.

"Hey man, are ya going to watch the game?" Antonio yelled out, curious as to what was taking Giermo so long. "The first period's about to start soon, man!"

"Yea, yea, hold onto your shorts, I'll be there in a sec! I gotta make this call first. Something's up at home!" Giermo yelled back as he waited for the phone to be answered.

"Oiga, es Giermo, qué pasa?" Giermo asked the person on the other end of the line.

The caller told Giermo that the word had reached Colombia about the bust in West Vancouver and the arrest of Juan and Ernesto. He was also told that they were disappointed that he hadn't called to tell them himself. Giermo continued to listen to the caller and then gasped as his eyes widened.

The news took time to resonate with him, and he stood frozen while he processed what he'd been told as he hung up the phone. "Chinga!" he growled.

It was six forty and only twenty minutes to the face-off. Giermo heard the TV sportscaster in the distracted subconscious of his mind. His head was racing, thinking about what to do!

The SkyTrain reached the Stadium stop and spewed out its riders when the doors opened; bodies spilled into the station terminal platform. The train car emptied, and Juan and Ernesto were left with only a few other riders still sitting inside the car. They sat and waited for the train to pull out and take them to their destination at Burrard Station, two stops farther up the rail line.

Abused Trust

"I got to stop him!" Giermo yelled, darting into his bedroom to collect his coat. "See ya later," he yelled again, not stopping to lock the door or explain to Antonio. Giermo ran out of his apartment without a plan in his head. "How could I not know that Ernesto was my second cousin!" he asked himself over and over. "I have to stop Pablo at all costs, I got to!"

Neither of the boys had a cell phone, that had been Giermo's decision. He called Pablo's cell but got no answer. "He must've turned it off so the noise wouldn't attract attention! Damn, damn!"

Giermo knew that he'd little time to reach the *Aquatic Center*, exactly twenty-nine minutes. The transit system wouldn't be fast enough by the time he'd parked and transferred at Burrard Station. He had to drive through the chaos without getting into an accident.

"What a mess!" Giermo blurted out, blaming himself for not trusting the two men and for bringing in Pablo to mop up what he had thought was a mess.

The SkyTrain reached the Burrard Station, and the car was almost empty now. Ernesto and Juan jumped out, walked up the stairs, and headed across the street to the bus stop. Only a couple of people were waiting in the shelter from the rain as the entire city was engaged in the hockey match. The streets were becoming deserted as people were rushing to find a late venue that had space with a TV.

The boys waited for the bus that went south on Burrard Street, as they needed to get to the *Aquatic Center* at the edge of the bridge that crossed over False Creek.

Giermo gunned the accelerator of the courier van and darted out into the traffic. The roadways began to clear as the hockey game was about to begin, and spectators were in their spots ready for the anthem to be played, beers in hand. He pointed the vehicle southward toward Venables Street, which would take him along the most direct route toward the meeting place. Venables became Prior Street and flowed directly into Pacific Boulevard passing by the Rodger's Stadium® full of Canuck® hockey fans.

The roads were wet and it seemed that every traffic light turned red, delaying his progress toward stopping his paid assassin.

The Burrard Street southbound bus opened the doors for the two new passengers. The bus was empty. "You boys not watching tonight's contest?" the bus driver asked as the two men boarded and showed their bus transfers.

"Ah ..." Juan replied, "just running late to get to our friend's place on Beach Avenue."

"It's quiet now and the traffic's lighter, so you boys shouldn't be too late." The bus driver spoke over the noise of the portable radio playing the hockey game, which had already started. The loud crowd cheers could be heard through the small speaker, as the bus picked its way southbound down the main corridor.

It was seven minutes past seven o'clock according to the clock in the dash of the van. Giermo was just entering the ramp to Pacific Boulevard and he could see the large stadium filling his front windshield. He was glad that the game had started, as the majority of the vehicle traffic was now off the road. He passed the stadium and flew past the Cambie Bridge underpass. It was seven ten.

The two Colombian men got off the bus at the Beach Avenue stop, and watched the empty bus pull out, headed toward the bridge. The rain continued, and the men started their trek toward the meeting spot. The night was wet, uninviting, and even the avid joggers were at home. The pair of men saw the *Aquatic Center* ahead, sitting on the shore of False Creek. The area was dark, and the only sound was from screaming hockey fans watching the game in their Beach Avenue apartments.

Giermo was panicking. Time was up and he was just turning off Pacific onto Hornby, a block away from his destination. "I hope those two guys are a little late. Maybe with the game and all, they got delayed," the wishful thought crossed his mind, as he searched for a place to park the van.

He found a parking space a block away, dashed out of the van, slammed the door, and began running toward the pool facility. He didn't hear the screams of the fans that erupted resulting from a home goal. He heard nothing at all. The rain was now coming down heavily, and the air turned cold with a westerly brisk wind that cut across his face. His heart pounded, and his breath had become labored with the dash to save his cousin.

He stopped to catch his breath. He saw no one in the dark and his eyes were wide open searching for movement. It was pouring and quiet; he reminded himself that he had to be careful. Pablo didn't know that he was coming and might mistake him for one of his targets. "Shit, I didn't think of that!" he stressed at the thought.

"Hey guys," he decided to yell out to let Pablo know that he was there, and to see if he got a welcome response from either Ernesto or Juan. He stood still and waited in the heavy rain. Nothing, not a sound. He walked carefully now, more scared of Pablo than what he might find.

Giermo almost tripped on the two limp bodies that were lying on the ground motionless, as he came around the corner of the building. Pablo was nowhere in sight and Giermo realized that he was too late. He looked about. He was alone and tears began to stream down his face. He heard cheers emitting from nearby windows, but he'd nothing to cheer about. It was entirely his fault.

Chapter Fifteen

Kelly O'Brian was awakened from her deep sleep by a stream of sunlight pouring through her bedroom window. It was Saturday, and she didn't have her alarm set at the normal six o'clock mark signaling the beginning of a new work day.

It was almost eight, and she found herself still in the clothes she had worn the night before. She immediately recalled that she had been up late doing research, had gotten tired, and then had crawled into bed without changing.

Kelly had arrived home in time for the end of the second period of the hockey game. She'd been disappointed that the surveillance of the two Colombians had failed, and that the two men had been able to slip away so easily. It had been her first stakeout as a detective and it hadn't ended well.

The Apple® laptop computer was sitting on her kitchen table, still running, now displaying photographs as the screensaver picked images at random. She was hungry, as she'd not eaten much the night before, and decided that she would stop and pick up an Egg McMuffin™ during her morning jogging tour. She suited up in her running gear, closed the laptop lid, and placed her spiral black research notebook back into her bedroom nightstand drawer.

Grabbing her house keys and stuffing some cash into her jogging suit pocket, she reached for the front door handle just as the phone rang. She ran back to the phone and answered, "KO."

"Morning Kelly, it's Simon."

"Hey Simon, it's Saturday, what's up?"

"The Vancouver precinct found our two guys last night. They're in the morgue. Can you pick me up in an hour?"

"The morgue! Ah ... an hour's good, what's your address?" She listened, and responded "Yea, I can find that." She hung up, feeling responsible for the death of the two men. She was frustrated that the two men had been able to slip out of her grasp and that she hadn't somehow tried harder to find them in the crowd. Her job was to serve and protect, even those two, and she had failed them. "I mustn't give up so easily. I won't the next time!" she sighed, determined to be a better cop.

Kelly skipped her jog, and thirty minutes later she made her final check in the mirror. She stood five-feet-eight in bare feet and carried fitted outfits like a model. She'd pulled on a purple turtle neck sweater, black leggings, had placed small diamond stud earnings in her earlobes and let her hair flow freely around her shoulders. It was a beautiful morning but cold, so she searched in the closet for her lined jacket.

"Simon's address will be on the left, according to the numbering on the shops," Kelly mumbled, thinking about where she was going, noticing that the street was jammed with cabarets, restaurants, and cultural buildings. "What a vibrant place to live!" Kelly thought. Simon Chung was already at the crosswalk across from his Chinatown apartment as Kelly appeared in the gray Taurus.

"Beautiful drive this morning and this weather sure shows Vancouver at its finest," Kelly announced as Simon jumped into the car. "I feel so bad about those two last night—so what's the story?"

"It's not our fault!" Simon replied as he glanced over at his partner. "A pair of joggers found our guys at the *Aquatic Center* on Beach Avenue. The joggers were quite shaken up and were allowed to go home after making their statements. The coroner has indicated that the bodies had been dead since about seven or seven thirty last night, and he has already taken the two corpses for further examination."

"We lost them about six thirty. They must've been on their way to a planned meeting. Hmm ... it must've been a setup by the killer! They must've known something that made someone nervous, eh?" Kelly surmised, as she watched the road. "Have we got anything new from the lab concerning the Elvenden Row findings?"

"We should have the report Monday—the lab guys don't work our hours!" Simon replied as he continued to look over at his new partner. "Let's visit the Medical Examiner and see if any blanks can be filled in."

The drive to *St. Paul's Hospital* in Vancouver took the detectives fifteen minutes. The sunny weather and weekend break from work brought out everyone wanting to enjoy an outside activity or to catch up on daily living routines, often using their cars.

Kelly hadn't experienced visits with the coroner, as her uniform duties had always been transferred to the detective squad in cases that involved corpses.

"I guess this'll be one of your first experiences with dead people in a coroner's examination room. Will you be okay with it?" Simon asked, as he was sensitive to new detectives working through this experience and wanted to know her state of mind before the visit started.

"Yup, I'll be all right. Let's see what we got!" Kelly replied confidently, even though she wasn't really sure herself how she'd react.

The pair of detectives took the elevator down to the morgue that was located in the basement of the old brick hospital. It was an unnerving place for most people, and many detectives disliked the experience. They reached the glass-faced swinging doors and knocked to attract the attention of the medical examiner, who was leaning over a body that was lying on a table. They were waved in with a hand gesture.

"Good morning, we're Detectives Chung and O'Brian. We're here to see what you've been able to determine about the two Colombian men brought in earlier this morning," Kelly said quietly.

"It's okay, Detective, you won't wake them!" the coroner replied with a smile as he noticed the apprehensive look on Kelly's face. "Ah, yes, the two bodies from the *Aquatic Centre*. They're over here."

He walked toward two gurneys with white sheets covering the corpses. "Both men had been stabbed. One had his throat cut, likely the first victim. Looks professional, as the blade targeted the most vulnerable places. Deaths were almost instantaneous," the coroner said as he revealed the men's wounds for the detectives' inspection.

"Were you able to find any clue as to the killer?" Kelly choked out, managing to keep her composure by focusing on the mystery rather than the stiff bodies.

The coroner re-covered the bodies with a white sheet. "I couldn't find anything on either of these two. It was raining hard last night and no evidence could be found about their killer, no clothing transfer or hairs. It was a very neat job."

"Thanks, Doc. When will all your photos and the report be ready for us?" Simon asked as he turned away from the gurneys and glanced over to see how Kelly was handling the experience.

"You should have all my findings Monday," the coroner replied as he returned to the body that he had been examining when the detectives arrived.

"Well, I think that we should drive out to the scene and see what we can find out there. Hopefully the crime location hasn't been too contaminated by now!" Kelly suggested as the pair exited the examination room. "The *Aquatic Centre's* a busy place on sunny weekend days; I know, as I can see that area when I jog each morning!"

"KO, you handled your first corpse examination better than some I've worked with! Are you feeling all right?" Simon asked as the pair exited the basement. "I know that you feel we could've prevented this, but their deaths aren't our responsibility. It's the lives they chose KO, and it's the murderer's responsibility, not ours!"

"I'm all right! Let's see what we can find about the perp," Kelly replied, but was glad to be leaving the basement and wasn't in a hurry to return too soon.

Kelly drove to the scene, found a parking space on Beach Avenue, and the detectives noticed that the perimeter of the crime scene had been established and marked off with yellow tape.

"Good morning, Officer, we're from the West Vancouver detachment," Kelly said, showing her new gold shield to the woman officer. "The two victims that were murdered here last night are part of an investigation that we're handling. May we take a look about?"

"Ah … sure, Detective. I have to wait for our people to release the site, so please don't disturb anything."

The pair separated and began a careful inspection of the area and grounds surrounding the building. Numbered tags remained from the first responding team, marking spots that would later be referenced in photographs and reports.

"Hey, Simon, come here and look at this!" Kelly exclaimed, calling for her partner to join her at the front of the building. "There appears to be two different sets of smudged shoe prints that head away from the crime scene. One set behind the building and one out here in the front, heading toward the street. They were definitely made last night, as the prints from this morning aren't so deep and wet! Curious—I thought the coroner indicated that the attack was by a single killer, not two."

"Yea, the stab wounds and locations on our vics would indicate a single attacker. If it was a citizen happening by here after the killings, we would've received a 911 call last night, not this morning from passing joggers. One of those smudged prints might belong to one of the vics though," Simon replied as he pulled his cell phone and took a photo of the find.

"Hmm … I think that we're done here. Should we go?" Kelly asked, looking out over the water and seeing joggers running along the path that she knew so well. "We can get what we need from the Vancouver detective team, now that we've had a look at the scene ourselves."

"That sounds good to me. We'll have all the reports on Monday anyway, so I guess that we really can't do much else until then," Simon replied as they turned to leave the marked area.

It was approaching lunch time by the time Kelly returned home, having dropped Simon off in Chinatown. She still hadn't eaten, and decided to quickly clean up and walk to the diner down the street. She wasn't in any mood to make something at home, and wanted to be outside in the fine clear weather.

Kelly sat at a table at a street-side café, and her attention turned from her RCMP case to her own private research activities, that she had been working on the night before. She loved the outdoors and took advantage of the opportunity to eat outside, even in the chilly outside street patio. She thought that the fresh air would clear her head.

"I've your order, madam," the waitress disrupted Kelly's thoughts. "Here's your cranberry and soda, and your clubhouse and fries. Can I get you anything else?" the young woman asked, sporting a large smile and rubbing her hands together to keep them warm.

"No thanks, that's great," Kelly replied as she pulled her coat up and over her shoulders. The weather was cooler by the beachfront and the breeze reminded her that it was late November.

Kelly had a date that night. She didn't go on many dates; her job and detective class studies had taken priority and there often wasn't time for dating, let alone a relationship. She was excited and apprehensive at the same time. She knew that it was time to get involved with someone, and she hoped that her detective career would provide a better social opportunity than her street cop schedule had allowed!

The date was with Ricardo Sanchez, and she had considered his invitation with mixed emotions before she had agreed. They'd started a relationship a number of years earlier which she ended after only a few dates. At that time, she had wanted to put all her effort into becoming a detective; with the demands of a street RCMP officer, her career commitments had consumed everything she had to give, and there had been nothing left for a social life.

She did feel something when she saw Ricardo at the Elvenden Row scene, and she needed to find out what that was. It was just dinner, she reminded herself, getting edgy thinking about the scenario with Ricardo. She remembered that he liked classy restaurants, and she knew that she should dress up for the evening.

Kelly started to get ready at five, even though Ricardo wasn't planning to pick her up until seven. The closet didn't offer many evening outfits and her selection was limited.

She entered her shower stall and appreciated that it was one of her favorite places to unwind. The hot water seemed to relax the tension from her body and mind. After toweling off and blow drying her long dark hair, she slipped on sexy black sheer lace underwear. She pulled out her makeup accessories and selected a dark shade of red gloss lipstick.

Manicuring her eyebrows and nails, she selected the appropriate nail color matching the lipstick. She took her time applying the glossy paint, and thought about her date as the polish dried. She then wound her hair up in a bun, which showcased her long sexy neck and showed off her high cheek bones. She slipped on a black elegant evening dress, which had a scalloped neckline and long lace sleeves. Her black heels and black clutch bag, along with a black shoulder jacket, finished the outfit. She stood in front of her mirror making her final check as her heart pounded in anticipation.

"All right, not bad!" she exclaimed as she smiled, turning around and checking her reflection once again.

The doorbell rang on the stroke of seven. The tall, six-foot-one, lean man stood at the front door with a large smile and a bunch of red roses clutched in his fist. "Wow, you're the hottest-looking cop in the city in that stunning dress!" was the first thing that Ricardo could utter, staring at his date standing in the doorway.

"Well, thank you sir! Come in while I put those flowers in water. They're beautiful!"

Ricardo stood in the entranceway of her apartment, and waited for her while she quickly arranged the roses in a vase. He wore a dark gray, slim-cut suit and a black dressy shirt unbuttoned and slightly open at the top, and peered about the sitting room while waiting patiently for his date to return.

He finally heard the tapping of high-heeled shoes returning from the kitchen, and he turned his attention back to his date. "Shall we go then?" he asked and took her arm.

The white 4x4 truck was parked out on the curb, and he assisted Kelly into the front seat. "Sorry, not a limo, but I didn't have to buy this one!" he chuckled as he pulled himself up into the front bucket seat. "Have you ever been to the *SandBar* on Granville Island?" Ricardo asked, to find out if the restaurant was going to be a surprise first visit.

"Nope, it'll be my first time there," she responded, her heart pounding in her throat, as she was still somewhat nervous about the entire dating decision.

The drive was less than ten minutes, and Granville Island was always alive and active on Saturday nights. The small downtown island was an interesting mix of industrial companies, artistic studios, playhouses and restaurants. The public market was one of the best of its kind in Vancouver and many people came to the island on small walk-on ferries, so they didn't have to drive and find a place to park. The *SandBar* was a hot spot, located directly underneath of the Granville Street Bridge and offered a breathtaking view of an inner marina and harbor of False Creek.

The couple was taken to their reserved table by a window, overlooking the calm water that reflected the lights of the condos and restaurants hugging the shoreline. The occasional boat could be seen with its navigation lights on, weaving a trail toward a berth in the distance.

"Do you wish to select a wine this evening?" the wine steward inquired, handing Ricardo a list.

"Kelly, would you like red or white tonight?" Ricardo asked as he looked directly into her eyes.

"White, please," she responded, blushing slightly in the dim light.

"Okay ...." and after skimming the list, he ordered a pinot grigio from the steward.

"What a beautiful place!" Kelly started the conversation. "So Ricardo, what's the story with *ComTek*? I thought that you were RCMP to the core, at least you were from what I remember!"

Ricardo sat for a few moments not answering her question, seeking the right words to say. "Look, I believe that our relationship, if we're going to have one, must be honest, upfront, and trusting," he started, deciding on how to answer the apparently easy question.

"Okay Ricardo, that works for me, too," Kelly replied, curious as to his answer as she looked directly at his tanned face.

The wine steward returned with the chilled bottle of wine, removed the cork and placed it on the table in front of Ricardo and poured the wine.

"I'm still RCMP! The *ComTek* position's an undercover operation that I've been assigned. Very few know about this taskforce, and there's been a lot of effort to set this whole thing up," Ricardo confided in a low whispering voice. "We think that there're illegal activities taking place at *ComTek's* CLG, and I'm working on that case."

Ricardo wanted to ensure that he was able to gain her trust over the evening. "I can't tell you anymore now. I've already told you too much, and you must keep it strictly between us. Promise, KO?"

"I understand. I'll honor your trust," Kelly replied with a smile as she searched his dark brown, almost black eyes.

They both picked up the menus and realized how difficult it was going to be to select from the list. The assigned waiter took their orders and trotted off to the kitchen to advise the group of chefs behind the stainless steel open counter.

"So … tell me a little more about you, KO. We never got to know each other that well the last time we were together," Ricardo prodded, taking a sip of his wine. "Wow, she looks stunning in that outfit!" he thought as he stared directly at her seductive dress that seemed to enhance her figure.

Kelly could feel his inquiring look, and thought she'd better say something quickly before she blushed. "Well, my family lived in Kerrisdale and I went to *Croften House*, a girl's private school. When I was fifteen, my parents divorced. Dad's business was bankrupted and he had to sell everything to pay the debts," she said; having never before told anyone her story, she wasn't sure how much more about it she was prepared to say.

"Sorry … what made you want to be a cop? It's not a common choice for a young woman coming from that kind of neighborhood," Ricardo asked as he leaned over the table.

Just as Ricardo had earlier hesitated to answer a seemingly simple question, Kelly now had to decide if she wanted to honestly answer the question. She took another sip of her wine, leaving her glass now almost empty. "I once heard my parents talking when I was young. They thought that I was in bed, asleep upstairs, and I heard my mother say that I wasn't her child." Kelly paused again, a little upset. "I wanted to be able to solve the mystery as to who I really am, and thought that by joining the RCMP I could learn the skills to do that," Kelly replied with tears welling in her eyes. "Excuse me Ricardo, I have to freshen up," she said, got up, and rushed toward the bathroom.

Ricardo sat stunned by the intensity of the conversation. He attracted the waiter and ordered a second bottle of wine.

The evening ended with a good night kiss and Kelly smiled as she closed her door, feeling that her date with Ricardo hadn't been as stressful as she had first imagined it would be. In fact she was energized by the possibility of having a renewed relationship with the man and looked forward to another opportunity to get to know him better.

Chapter Sixteen

It was Monday morning and many people hate Monday mornings! The rush to get to the office for that paycheck that never went far enough and the dream of purchasing a winning lottery ticket to say "screw you," to the boss, and have an easier life, all started again.

Some people relish in the adventure, the challenge, of serving and contributing; some plot on how to get ahead and screw their workmate or a friend for a better life. It's the Monday rush and the games began once again for another week!

It was a particularly ugly morning start, with rain pelting down in an almost-frozen state, frost forming on the soft shoulder of the roadway, and the calendar turning to December without a warning.

Will Richards had expected to begin his day behind the eight ball. He knew that the log loader that went for servicing Friday afternoon would likely not have been returned for the Monday morning tasks.

Another delivery truck of full length poles from *MiTel* was being dropped off too close to the centre of the gravel roadway at the end of the pole yard. The drivers knew the rules governing where to drop their loads, but usually didn't care. It wasn't their problem, and any safety risks for passing vehicles would be someone else's concern.

"Damn, I knew I'd need that loader this morning!" Will uttered, annoyed with the miserable weather and the frustrating situation. This weather condition made it difficult for his people to work outdoors, and the sloppy ground conditions could easily become unsafe for workers with power tools in their hands. Most of the crew had already arrived, but they were not to be seen when Will reached the gate of his mill. "Likely warming in the trailer!" Will muttered as he entered the warm trailer, glad to be dry and out of the rain. He hung up his coat and wandered into the crew section of the trailer, seeking a coffee.

"I don't know if we're going to be able to work all day in this or not guys! *ComTek* has our loader today, so we need to improvise and see what's best to do considering the circumstances. As you know, I usually lay most of you off this time of year as we don't sell much and money's tight. We're going to play things by ear this week, and see what comes up," Will growled as he outlined the situation to the staff who all knew the situation as well as he did. "Ray, you get things organized this morning—I've some paperwork that I need to focus on first thing."

Will returned to his office, grabbed a stack of tally sheets, and began to copy the pole receipt numbers into his permanent record log. December brought on his fiscal year end, and he wanted to determine if there was going to be a pole financial subsidy this year or not.

※

Terry Peters was still tense from the knowledge of the hidden drug shipment sitting in the back of the *ComTek* pole building. He unlocked the pole yard office, and rushed inside to avoid becoming soaked by the downpour of rain.

"The weather's going to be a pig today, but it's a wonderful day to harass Will Richards! The loader story was sure a stroke of brilliance on Friday," Terry thought as he started to make the morning coffee. "I think I'd better go and press for my payment today, and that'll only annoy Richards even more!" he muttered as he left the coffee machine and checked for incoming pole orders.

He grabbed a fax that had numerous pole shipment orders, indicating that the day would be busy.

"My marijuana contact will be here early this afternoon picking up a pole shipment, too, so I'd better think about what I'm going to do about my weed order!" he thought, remembering that he'd his own operation to manage besides dealing with Candice's problem. "Humph! I'd better get that cash for Slider, too, or I've got a bigger problem than Giermo's God-damn shipment in the back!"

A large load of new *ComTek* poles pulled into the yard and distracted Terry's thoughts. He knew that he'd better warm up the loader for work, so he went to the large machine and climbed inside the dry cabin, started the machine, and then returned back to the office. He quickly went into the kitchen, grabbed a coffee, and returned to his desk to wait for the truck driver to bring in the delivery documents.

"Hey man, you're ten minutes late! Get your ass in gear and prepare to unload that pole trailer!" Terry instructed Andrew, as the young man slipped into the office.

Terry was extremely jumpy and unusually nervous for a Monday morning. "All I can think about is Slider and that shipment out back!" he mumbled, watching the loader begin removing poles from the flat deck outside. "I can't go through the whole day this way—I'll be a wreck!" he picked up the phone and punched in Candice's extension number.

Candice saw the caller's name on the display of the ringing office phone. "Not already!" she grumbled, picking up the receiver. "Morning Terry, what's up? I'm very busy today!"

"Look, I'm feeling all cranked up with the shipment in the back and all. I need a way to release my stress caused by *your* problem with Giermo!" he told her in a high, tense voice. "You owe me, and today's as good as any to pay up, Candice!" Terry paused and quickly continued, not allowing the woman to comment. "One good turn deserves another and I want to collect today! I'm stressed and I'm so wired that I might do something stupid, and you don't want that!"

Candice thought for a moment before she answered. "Hmm ... yea ... ah, I don't feel much different than you do by the sounds of it. I guess we can help each other and I can finally meet my commitment I made to ya!" she replied, not surprised at the implied demand; Terry had tried before to collect on the commitment that she had made when Terry introduced Giermo to her. "Can you get away at lunch time?" Candice asked, thinking about the unexpected opportunity.

"Yep, the shop's busy and a lunch break would be the only opportunity anyway. Where?" Terry asked, smiling.

"The *Fraser Head Hotel*. Get a room and text me with the number," she replied and then hung up.

Candice hadn't slept much the past few nights, fussing about Giermo's shipment and having to get Terry Peters involved in her business again. She knew that Terry would always be a lingering risk, as he knew way too much about her activities and personal problems. She had thought about talking Brian into doing something to help her, but she had decided to deal with the man herself. She had been thinking about the agreement she had made with Terry, and had spent all weekend trying to think about ways to get out of it. The call from Terry sparked a new idea that she hadn't considered before, and she realized that she had been handed the opportunity to fix her problem. She knew that it would be unpleasant, but she hadn't devised any other plan to get Terry off her ass, so she leaned back in her office chair to consider her course of action.

♓

The windshield wipers of the *Bug Busters Computer Services* van were running out of control, trying to keep pace with the downpour. The driver looked like a drowned rat, as he rolled down the window to get approval to proceed through the security gate alongside the *ComTek* warehouse.

The driver was irritated. He'd gotten a flat coming in that morning and had been forced to change the right side front tire while parked on the soft shoulder of the expressway. To make things worse, the vehicle had only one of those "God-Damn" tiny tire spares that required the driver to proceed at a reduced speed until replacement. "I hate those damn things!" the driver grumbled, as water continued to run down the back of his rain-drenched coat.

The driver turned into the shipping dock of the IRD building, and poured himself out of the driver's seat, which was now soaked from the man's water-drenched clothes. He sloshed into the office looking for the receptionist. She wasn't there! "Jesus Christ, where is everyone?" the driver bellowed, now more pissed-off than before, looking around for someone to help him before he exploded.

Candice looked up from her computer monitor at the sound of the angry voice, and saw the wet man peering into each green cubicle seeking a breathing person to help him. She stepped out of her office. "Can I help you?" she inquired, avoiding irritating the man further.

"Yea, I need to make a pickup. It's *Bug Busters Computers*. What a God-damn day to be out! You got a towel or somethin'? I'm a mess and soaking wet!" the man growled.

"Sure, the bathroom's over there. Leave your pick-up documents with me."

He handed Candice the authorization document, now a little damp, and turned toward the bathroom. Candice found that it was hard not to smile just a little at the poor man, so she turned and reentered her office with his paperwork. "It looks like it's going to be one of those crazy days!" she thought, putting the waybill on her desk.

The driver reappeared in a few minutes, in a better frame of mind. He poked his head into Candice's office. "Sorry for earlier, it's been a bit of a bitch this morning. I'm ready to take the shipment now, thank you."

"Here's your documentation. Just give it to the store man in the back," Candice replied, handing the man his limp documents back.

The man tried a smile, and the squishing of water from his wet boot steps could be heard as he returned down the hallway toward the outside dock to load his cargo.

"Hey man, I'd go home and change if I were you!" Stewart remarked after completing the shipment transfer.

"Yea ... I can't work all day soaking wet. Damn, I'll be very late back to the shop with this load and I have to fix that tire, too! I'd better let Darryl know I'll be late," he replied as he jumped into the truck and headed back to where he'd started a few hours earlier. He picked up his cell to update his waiting employee as he stopped for the security guard to open the side gate.

※

Her anticipation was high as Kelly entered the detectives' office. It was Monday morning and things looked great. She wasn't sure if she felt energized because of her extraordinary date with Ricardo, or as a result of the expectations of the reports concerning her first detective's case.

"Great morning, eh Simon? Shitty weather, but a new day! Have we got the reports yet?" Kelly spoke quickly as though she'd already consumed a gallon of black coffee.

"Wow, we're upbeat on this miserable morning! What are ya on anyway?"

"I'm expecting some hot leads today on the bad guys. Hot leads, cold day!" Kelly replied with a big smile.

"You always like this on Mondays? If so, I want what you're taking!" Simon poked.

"Ha, ha ... we get our reports yet? Let's call downstairs," she replied, picking up the phone.

"Yes KO, one packet has just been received, addressed to you two detectives," the receptionist answered with a small cough.

"Great, I'll come down and get it ... ah, you okay? You sound a little under the weather."

"Damn rain and cold! I usually get something each year at this time. I hate flu shots, so I don't take those—anyone dressed in white with a needle is bad news so far as I'm concerned. A couple of days, and I'll be Ms. Sunshine again! Thanks for askin'."

Simon went downstairs, retrieved the delivery, and opened the brown, large, sealed envelope that had "RCMP Lab" stamped on the upper corner. The names "Detectives O'Brian and Chung" were printed on the bottom. "Let's see what we got," he muttered as he worked his way up the stairs, back to the second floor.

He pulled out the contents onto his desk. "The lab's got prints off the computer cases and a hit on the database on the Elvenden Row case. An Antonio Castillo has been identified. His prints are on file from his immigration application. He's from Medellin, Colombia, the same area as those two stiffs in the morgue. No rap sheet, so he's been very careful to stay under the radar. We do have an address, though. Let's pay Antonio a visit later," Simon said, reading the forensics first.

"That's about all they got at the Elvenden site," Simon continued as he flipped through another page. "There's a note about the owners—Maria and Ramondo Dominguez. They're retired, living in Cabo, Mexico."

"Maybe we need to check the Dominguez couple out, too. Strange to have such a beautiful house left alone long enough to have such a sophisticated grow-op installed and running," Kelly remarked.

"The rest of the package contains the photos taken at the scene. We can study those later. Let's pay Antonio a visit first. He's on Pandora Street, just east of Nanaimo," Simon suggested, noting the address in his small notebook, then he slipped the materials back inside the envelope.

Kelly's adrenalin began to pump and she was wired to go. "I knew we'd get a hit today!"

The pair reached the Taurus and settled in for the ride. Simon punched the address into the navigation screen, and turned the directing voice off. "I know how to get there and don't need any computer to tell me! I just like seeing the progress on the screen. It's a novelty, I guess."

The rain began to subside and turned into a drizzle, as the detectives joined the traffic headed toward the expressway. "The Second Narrows Bridge should be the quickest route from here, even with the heavy traffic and slow road conditions," Simon outlined his intended route. "I don't know what that navigation thing's going to say, but that's where we're going!"

Kelly just smiled, said nothing, and followed his instruction.

The drive was miserable, and the number of accidents witnessed on the trip only stood to prove the lack of attention local drivers had toward roadway weather conditions, and their disregard for defensive driving. The traffic cleared after passing Hastings Park, and they quickly found themselves across from their destination address. Homes in the area had been built in the fifties, and Antonio lived in a basement suite of one of the single level houses.

Both detectives approached the basement entrance doorway, and Simon loudly knocked. "Antonio Castillo, it's the RCMP. Open the door," he demanded.

There was no answer and Simon looked at his partner, waited about a minute, and repeated himself in a louder voice. "Antonio Castillo, it's the RCMP. Open the door!"

The upstairs door of the main house opened, and a little, elderly lady poked her head out. "Officers, I don't think he's home. I haven't heard him downstairs for a few days now. Is he in trouble?"

"Oh!" Kelly looked up. "We just want to talk with him, Madam," she answered, not wanting to alarm the woman. Simon climbed up the small set of stairs and handed the woman his card. "Please call us if you hear him return. My number's on the card. Thank you."

The woman took a moment to stare at the card and then returned inside without saying anything else.

"Well, we'll find him. Let's go to that computer place, Bug Busters something," Simon suggested, turning back toward the car.

Once inside the car, he pulled out his small black notebook and flipped the pages to the note that he had made earlier in the morning. "Here it is, *Bug Busters Computer Services*. It's on Dyke Road in Surrey." Sitting in the sedan, Simon punched the address he had in the notebook into the navigation.

"The place is quite a distance from here, KO. We need to go into Surrey, just under the Pattullo Bridge. The address is in an industrial area along the Fraser River. Let's hit the road!"

♓

Ricardo Sanchez got out of bed early. The rain was pelting on his front window, as the wind ran up the Fraser River and pressed the downpour directly at the front of his apartment. A spread of two-story concrete luxury condominiums skirted the Fraser River on the New Westminster side. The view of the mighty Fraser was breathtaking on a clear day, but this morning the rain cloud seemed to engulf the water and the opposite shoreline wasn't visible.

A Quayside Drive address was one of the best in the old city, and the restaurant at the entrance to the side road was frequently packed. Ricardo often walked along the public pathway to the large market that specialized in fresh produce and seafood.

Hunter, Ricardo's companion, enjoyed an early walk before Ricardo left him in the condo for the day. The dog was a two-year-old Australian shepherd that had gray and black hair. People often mistook the dog for some kind of wolf, as the animal had piercing wolf-like gray eyes that seemed to study every new face. Hunter was being trained as a police dog, even though the dog was small for the standards of the RCMP;

Ricardo enjoyed participating in the training and watching his smart dog move through the program with ease.

The dog watched his master remove his jogging outfit and get dressed for work. The dog tried to snuggle Ricardo's hands with his large cold nose as Ricardo finished getting dressed.

"I know Hunter; I'll put out your breakfast before I go," Ricardo talked to the dog as though the animal would answer. "Maybe I'll bring Kelly out here to meet you later this week. See ya later, Hunter!" Ricardo closed and locked the condo door and left for the underground parking lot.

"I should drop in and have another visit with Will Richards this morning and see how he's doing. That man seems to know everything that's going on at *ComTek*," Ricardo thought as he began to plan his day. He wanted to get more information on the activities of the logistics group, and recalled from their last talk that Will knew a lot about what was happening around that operation.

✵

Candice Parks had received Terry's text, and was pulling her white *ComTek* vehicle into the rear parking lot of the *Fraser Head Hotel*. She took out her personal hotel key and entered through the back door, as she had done many times before when she met with Brian Quest. It was just past noon, and the prior night's customers had already checked out. She proceeded up the back fire escape staircase to the third floor, and headed down the long hallway to room 311. She looked about, to ensure she hadn't been seen, and then knocked on the door.

Terry opened the door and Candice slipped into the room, quickly shutting the door behind her.

"You can never be too careful," she said with a grin.

Her blond hair was windblown and a little wet from the blustery morning. Candice wore a black, turtleneck sweater that almost covered her chin, a black, tailored, knee-length skirt, and she carried a small, black purse. She had been in no mood to be provocative when she got dressed that morning, and a sexual encounter had been the last thing on her mind.

"I've been anticipating this all morning, Candice!" Terry said nervously, his heart pounding as he approached her. He kicked off his loafers and took off his cap, pitching it onto a side chair.

Candice threw her purse down on the bed and allowed him to caress her waist and run his hands down to her buttocks, pulling his body toward her. He was a lot shorter than she, and she began to massage his boney shoulders. "Does this help with your stress, Terry?" she whispered in his ear.

He smelled her strong alluring perfume as she pressed her body close to his, and his face became pressed into the fabric of her sweater at the top of her chest. He slipped a hand up the front of the tightly knitted top, reached her full breast, and began to rub it through her sheer bra cup under the surface of the sweater. "Mmm ... this sure feels good!" he muttered as his other hand continued to feel her buttocks as it ran around the back of her tight skirt.

"Let's get more comfortable!" Candice suggested, carefully pushing him away, and starting to pull her sweater up and over her head.

Terry smiled, began to unzip his pants and pull his blue jeans to the floor. Candice moved toward him, and gave his groin a gentle rub as he stood up. "Ohh! Took your Viagra® I see! Stiffer than I thought for a guy your age, eh Terry?" she teased, feeling his hard erection through his shorts, and then backed away as he began to unbutton his denim work shirt and climb out of his pants, which had crumpled at his feet.

He just smirked, as Candice slowly unzipped the side of her black skirt, and seductively wiggled her behind until it dropped from her shapely hips to the floor. She stood motionless for a moment and deeply inhaled, so her breasts further strained inside of her thin lace black brassiere, as Terry stood staring at her arousing body.

She climbed out of her skirt, sat on the edge of the bed and methodically removed each heeled shoe, and then leaned over, allowing her partially exposed breasts to tantalize him, as she picked up her skirt from the floor and laid it on the bed.

Terry grinned, peering at her lace black panties, his heart pounding as he pulled down his briefs, and he smiled as he noticed that his erection was much larger and harder than usual. "Hmm, just like when I was younger!" Terry thought as he stood naked in front of her, ready to get started, as he craved to touch her naked skin and finally have the sex that he had so long dreamed about.

He grinned and moved toward her, preparing to unclip the front clasp of her low cut lace bra that matched the sheer arousing panties. Her nipples now stuck through the thin fabric, and the breast support strained to contain her bosom, as it pushed her breasts together, enhancing her cleavage and her erotic figure.

"No, not yet, I've a better idea!" she paused and pushed him away, eyeing his surprisingly hard erection. "Go into the bathroom and sit on the edge of the toilet! Put your cute ass on the front edge of the seat and stretch out so I can straddle my butt on you. I'll follow in a moment," she said softly grabbing her purse and pulling out a small package, "put this condom on!"

"Hmm ... that sounds like fun and something erotic!" Terry replied, as his heart pounded and he walked into the bathroom to put his naked body on the toilet's edge as instructed. The position was a little uncomfortable as he sat his small, bony behind on the edge of the open faced plastic toilet seat, placing the back of his neck on the front edge of the cold porcelain tank. He stretched his legs out, and he couldn't wait to have a lap dance that he knew he would never forget, and simply ignored the cold porcelain tank that now pressed against the top of his tense weak shoulders. He didn't notice the awkward position for long, as Candice joined him, still wearing her lace panties and bra that allowed him to see the soft skin of her sensual figure through the fabric, teasing him as she sauntered toward his wanting aroused body.

Candice slowly straddled her way up his stretched-out frame, "Ohhh!" he moaned, as she slowly moved her buttocks on him, and unclasped the front clip of her bra.

Terry grinned; his heart pounded as Candice moved her pantie crotch back, aligned his erection with her hand, and lowered her soft buttocks slowly back down onto him. "Ah!" she sharply exhaled as she felt him inside of her, fantasizing that it was Brian. She clenched her legs around him, and moved her hips in tight shallow motions, as she watched the satisfying expression rush across his face.

She felt his heart racing and his breathing had become labored, working hard to draw in the oxygen to feed the blood that rushed through his veins as she sustained her rhythm, moving to her own sensations that radiated within her. "Ah ... ah ... I've wanted you ... ah Candice ... AH!" Terry labored through each word, the strain and perspiration showing on his face. "Ah … ah!" he groaned, as he closed his eyes to focus on every sensation shooting pleasure into his brain.

She ran her hands slowly along his shoulders, worked her hands up his neck toward his ears. "Ah … ah!" she gasped as her hands clutched his throat and he labored to catch his breath. She began to squeeze her thumbs, cutting off his airway. Ah … ah …" she groaned, squeezing her fingers harder and harder on his windpipe.

Terry's eyes opened wide, and he tried to push her off him while fighting to catch his breath. She was in a dominant position and she had no trouble restraining his weak, panicking body. He grabbed her shoulders and tried to push her back, but she pressed harder and downward, pushing his back into the toilet tank while restraining his legs with her tight thighs that were wrapped around him. He couldn't make a sound, and his eyes bulged, staring through his glasses at her as she pushed his erection deep inside of her, her legs clutched to the side of the toilet. Terry took all the strength he had, and partially raised his head making a last effort to push her off balance. She responded by slamming his head back down onto the edge of the toilet tank, still continuing her grip on his throat, leveraging her legs around the base of the toilet to constrain him.

It didn't take long before his efforts subsided, and Candice continued to breathe heavily as she clutched Terry's throat. He lay motionless beneath her as she gasped for air; his pulse no longer throbbed though her clutched fingers. She took a deep breath, lifted her highly aroused body off his, and withdrew him from her as her adrenalin mixed with her sexual tension.

"Ah … ah … ah!" she continued to gasp from the strain and the sexual stimulation, pulling her soaking wet panties back into position. Candice took another calming breath as she clipped her bra back into place and climbed off the dead man's outstretched, limp limbs. She leaned over, slipped off the semen filled condom from Terry's still partially stiff erection, and pulled his body off the toilet seat. His dead corpse fell onto the floor with a thump.

She quickly put the used condom into the toilet bowl, took a strip of toilet paper and covered the handle before she flushed the prophylactic away. She returned to the bedroom, quickly pulled on her clothes, grabbed the torn open condom package off the bed, and stuffed it into her small clutch bag. She took a tissue from the bedside table, wiped the inside door knob and picked up the "Don't Disturb" door sign, ensuring she didn't leave any fingerprints.

She took a deep breath as she opened the door a crack to check the hallway. It was empty. She quickly moved into the hall, closed the door, and put the sign on the knob. She clutched the tissue in the palm of her hand and walked quickly toward the staircase where she had entered.

Candice rushed down one flight of stairs and with caution, opened the heavy door to see if any cleaning maids were in the hall. She fumbled around in her purse, found her FH 210 room key amongst the others on her key ring, and darted toward the room before anyone appeared. She inserted the key, entered the dark room and quickly shut the door, without making a sound.

She was again breathing in hard short breaths, and her heart felt like it was going to pound itself out of her chest. "Ah … ah … it had to be done, he would've exposed me, and ah … it just had to be done!" she kept telling herself, gasping as she began to strip off her clothes to get ready to shower and clean her body of the whole ordeal.

She sat naked on the bed as she pulled her BlackBerry® from her purse and selected a number on her cell. "Giermo," she huffed out, still trying to contain her heavy breathing. "Hey ... ah, it's Candice," she gulped. "It seems that Terry Peters is really tense and I think that he might do something stupid. He called me in a very agitated mood this morning, ah ... ah ... even for him. I ... ah ... suggest that you plan to get your stuff tonight from his office without telling him!" She swallowed, trying to contain her stress and regain her composure. "It's too risky if he goes AWAL on us, nerve-wise," she exhaled the words, now breathing rapidly as her hormones rushed around through her tense body.

"Shit, it's past noon already! I'll get things in motion. Thanks for the heads up!" Giermo replied, flustered, not noticing her labored speech, and then hung up.

Candice heard the call disconnect, and as she sat on the edge of the bed she realized that she was still highly aroused from her stimulating experience upstairs. "Ahh ...." she gasped and exhaled, not knowing if she felt excited from her sexual encounter with Terry or the rush from strangling him to death.

She took deep slow breaths in the dark room as she slowly regained her composure. "Ah!" she took another deep breath, pulled her perspiring naked body from the bed, and headed for the shower so she could get ready to go back to work.

⚹

Ricardo Sanchez entered the 66th Street turn and stopped at the *ComTek* security shack.

"Good afternoon, Mr. Sanchez. Good to see you," the guard said, standing in the doorway of his shack, acknowledging Ricardo's arrival.

The rain had subsided as Ricardo drove to the pole yard office looking for Terry Peters. The log loader was idle, as it was still lunch time and Ricardo realized how late it had become. "Hmm, I can catch Terry on my way out later," he muttered as he decided to head toward the recycling mill.

Will Richards was operating a small excavator, and moving a load of full-length poles onto the larger pile. He spotted Ricardo's truck, stopped what he was doing, and stepped out of the sun-bleached yellow machine so that he could meet the oncoming vehicle. "Hey Ricardo, great to see ya. I need to have a serious conversation with you. That okay?" Will asked, talking through Ricardo's driver side window.

"Ya, sure. I wanted to talk to you anyway!" Ricardo replied with a smile.

"I'll be just a few minutes finishing this job. Wait for me in my office," Will replied with a smile. "The guys are finishing their lunch, but they won't bug ya," he said and turned quickly, reentered the cab of the track machine and returned to finishing his task.

Ricardo Sanchez hadn't been in the trailer before; he climbed the wooden stairs and opened the door, noting the large steel deterrent housing over the keyed handle. He entered the trailer, and Ray Patterson noticed him looking around.

"The boss will be in shortly to take your order. He's finishing some clean-up work out there," Ray said as he pointed toward the excavator that was still grasping pole lengths.

"Thanks, he knows I'm here," Ricardo replied, eyeing the surroundings and the messy office desk. "Things back to normal, guys?"

"Well, as good as it ever gets around here. There's always something going on," Ray replied, and hearing that the sound of the excavator had stopped, he began to put on his gear. "Back to work, and I'm sure glad the rain has let up! It can be a shit-hole out here in the pouring rain," Ray commented, exiting the trailer and putting his ear-protective headset around his neck.

"Great to see you again, Ricardo. What brings ya to this place?" Will asked as he entered the trailer.

"Just checking that all's secure! How's the restart goin'?"

"Not so good! *ComTek* has my log loader which is critical for me to do my job, and the weather's marginal to keep the boys working." Will paused, "Can we take a late lunch and talk? I need some advice." Will asked, looking frazzled. "Ah ... I don't want to talk here. Can I meet you at the *Seventy-Sixth Pub* on King George? I haven't eaten yet, have you?"

"I'm ready to have something. Separate vehicles, or go in mine?" Ricardo replied as he looked out the front window at the crew working in the light drizzle.

"It's probably better if we go separately, so you don't have to come back here. You know the spot?" Will asked and turned to go out the door.

The pub was very busy and very noisy. Ricardo arrived first, and selected a booth away from most of the noise. He sat waiting for Will to join him, thinking about what information he might be able to gather about *ComTek* and the CLG. He realized that Will seemed to have a pipeline into *ComTek* and was well informed, and was a perfect source for gathering the information that he wanted.

Will followed about ten minutes behind, and looked for Ricardo as he entered the crowded pub.

"Sorry, I needed to ensure the guys had clear instructions as to this afternoon's tasks. I selected this place because very few *ComTek* people come in here. There're many closer establishments for them to have a quick lunch away from their offices," Will said as he sat on the other side of the large table.

The waitress recognized Will and came to the table just as he seated himself.

"A pint of Bud® and a menu please ... Ricardo?" Will asked, as he always started every lunch with a pint of Budweiser®, the beer he preferred. The waitress already knew his preference, and just smiled as she turned to face Ricardo.

"Same for me please," Ricardo told the waitress, and then focused his attention on Will. "So what did you want to talk to me about?"

"Oh ... I've been fussing for some time as to what to do and when to come and talk with you. Thomas Howe suggested that I not wait, and talk with you the next time I saw you, so it seems now is as good a time as any!" he answered nervously.

The two pints of beer appeared and two menus were left on the table top. The waitress knew that it wasn't time to take the order, and returned to the front to welcome another group of people.

"It's Terry Peters. He's been blackmailing me for some time now!" Will blurted out. "It's not right, and I can't afford it, either."

Ricardo peered at Will for a moment. "So what's Terry holding on you that makes you feel you must pay him?"

Will quickly updated the security manager of the story and he looked down-mouthed and ashamed as he spoke.

"I must report this you know, Will. *ComTek* has a code of conduct that every employee must abide by," Ricardo said, concerned what the fallout of such an exposure would bring.

"Yea, I know. That's why I've waited so long. It's going to be a mess!" Will replied as he continued to look down at the table, avoiding eye contact as he muttered the words.

"Does anyone else know about this?" Ricardo inquired.

"Only my wife, Helen, who's pissed to say the least, and Thomas Howe, of course."

"Who's Thomas Howe?" Ricardo asked, not having heard that name until Will first mentioned it in this conversation.

The waitress returned to take their orders and Will quickly scanned the menu and ordered. Ricardo selected a salad.

"A couple more pints, too, please," Will added, and then outlined who Thomas was in the scheme of things.

Lunch arrived and Ricardo changed the conversation topic. "So Will, what's the story with Brian Quest? I haven't been with *ComTek* very long and I've heard various mixed opinions about him."

Will looked up and stared at Ricardo. "I think he's a conniving prick and he's leading a plan to destroy me personally and my company! Terry told me that fact to my face while I was rebuilding the mill. I also think that there's someone else involved in the scheme, but I haven't been able to find out who that is yet. I just don't trust that son of a bitch."

Ricardo was amazed at the passion and direct assessment. "Well, Will, I'll think about the best course of action here, and I'll get back to you shortly. Okay?"

Both men started to eat their lunches and nothing else was said.

♓

Detectives Kelly O'Brian and Simon Chung finally worked their way to Dyke Road along the Fraser River, and found the *Bug Busters Computer Services* office building. They walked to the front door, but the office was closed and locked.

"It's unusual for a repair company to be closed on a Monday. Let's check the back," Simon said as he headed for the rear of the building.

The light industrial park had rows of small companies that occupied the string of single business fronts. They had rear storage or working shops separated from the front by thinly constructed walls, and *Bug Busters* occupied the end unit. The detectives found that the rear door was also locked and no vehicles were in the marked assigned spots either.

"Looks like we'll have to come back another time—no one's home today!" Simon said, shrugging his shoulders. "It'll be late in the afternoon before we get back to the office. There's nothing new for us here today, KO, so let's take a gander at the photos when we get back."

⁂

It was well past five in the evening before Ricardo Sanchez had reached his apartment. He had again stopped to see Terry Peters, but apparently Terry hadn't returned from lunch, so Ricardo headed home. It was time to let Hunter out, and the rain had stopped, leaving behind large water puddles everywhere.

Hunter was waiting by the front door and licked Ricardo's hand when he entered.

"Okay, I get it! Let's go for our walk along the promenade," Ricardo said as Hunter jumped up and down, eager to get out. The evening was getting colder, but neither Hunter nor Ricardo noticed as they strolled along the walkway. Hunter met the occasional dog that he recognized and he encouraged Ricardo to allow him to make his greeting. After a good walk they headed back.

Ricardo grabbed something from the freezer, tossed it into the oven, and got settled to make entries into his computer. He found his file, opened the document to complete his diary of the day, and while it was still fresh in his mind, recorded the information that he'd gathered from Will Richards.

Chapter Seventeen

The prior night's drizzle had passed, and the very early morning cold penetrated Antonio's jacket. He'd been dropped off next to some construction site. Giermo continued down the road toward the manager's entranceway in front of the *ComTek* warehouse office. The employee parking lot was secluded in the dark, and he parked the rental truck facing outward toward the entrance.

Giermo Hernandez sat in the darkness of his truck and reviewed the critical elements of his plan to get his drug shipment from the *ComTek* building across the street. He was very concerned with driving a rental truck at this very early time in the morning. He knew it would definitely attract the curiosity of any cop who might be patrolling the area, should he be seen.

Earlier the prior day, Giermo had paid cash for a room at the nearby *Fraser Head Hotel,* and had been given the key to room 309. He concluded that going to the hotel was his best-bet solution to minimize the risk of having his rental van look out of place after the heist. He had requested a quiet room that overlooked the rear parking lot, the place he planned to leave the truck overnight. He decided that he needed to be back at the hotel before the bars closed at two that morning.

Antonio carried a small, dirty, denim bag as he crept in the dark with his flashlight. He walked past the construction area that had a gravel access road leading to the back. He reached the end of the temporary road, and turned right toward the fence line that was somewhere ahead. Large, abandoned piles of earth hid him from view, but the heavy rains of the past few days left the area like a mud swamp, and

he hugged the side edge of the dirt piles trying t
sloppy muck from his boots.

He found the fence gate that had been left op
cut chain hung limply down the side of the metal post. Antonio slipped through the opening, and continued to head for the fence surrounding the back of the property. Giermo had seen the area when he had delivered the shipment the prior week, and had told Antonio the route to take. They were both worried about setting off any alarms, as their experience had taught them that there would be sensors looking for intruders.

Antonio came across a small wooden lean-to covering a large saw blade, and walked carefully behind the structure. He followed the side of the wooden wall and he almost tripped over a large, tin pipe sticking out that ran across the surface of the ground. "Shit!" he muttered under his breath as he continued ahead. He finally reached the metal fence that ran toward the front entrance of the *ComTek* building where their shipment was stored.

There was no early light from the morning sky as the heavy clouds still lingered, threatening to drop another load of rain. Antonio pointed his flashlight closely toward the ground, and allowed only enough light to illuminate his next step. He held onto the wire fence to keep from falling, and chose his steps carefully as he walked behind a large, blue tent structure and then behind a work trailer. Antonio came to another wire fence and he almost walked right into it, face first.

He knew that he was moving too slowly and that there was a tight timeline. He had to get to the front of the building before the security guard started his next round! Antonio fished around inside his bag looking for the wire cutters, and upon finding them, proceeded to cut the fence so that he could pass through.

"This is harder than it looks and a bitch on my hands," Antonio mumbled to himself. "I hate these shit jobs," he growled, thinking of Giermo sitting in the warm van, waiting for the hard work to be done by someone else.

Pulling his body through the opening, he realized that he was going to become exposed to the guard shack as he got closer to the metal-clad building at the end of the fence line. All kinds of steel pieces lay in small stacks along his route, but they didn't provide any cover of his approach.

All Antonio could do was to keep low and hope that his black outfit would hide his movements along the fence line. Giermo had figured that any motion detectors would be focused away from the perimeter fence and onto the open yard, and that it was unlikely there would be any detectors at the back of the building, as the guard was only a short distance away.

Antonio knew that he needed to be hiding in the darkness of the office building before the guard started his rounds. He was almost in position when he heard the guard's movement, and the unlocking sound made by keys, and locks releasing the chain they bound. Antonio checked that he had his weapon in his zipped pocket; the pocket was zipped because he didn't want the pistol falling out somewhere along the route, especially since it belonged to Giermo.

The guard was coming! Antonio's heart started to pound as he unzipped his coat pocket and withdrew the 9mm Glock, and stood motionless, waiting for his prey to unlock the office door. He pulled on a knit black ski mask and clutched his bag. He waited quietly, and in the dark the rattle of the guard's keys announced the guard's approach.

The large security guard had reached the front door and was selecting the key from his ring. The sound of the key inserting into its lock triggered Antonio to act, and he quickly jumped out and stuck the barrel of the gun into the ribs of the surprised guard. "Get in and close the door!" Antonio growled in a muffled voice through the mask. "Walk very slowly. Don't be stupid." Antonio reminded the guard by pushing the Glock harder into the man's side as they both entered the building. "We're going to have this dance together and be very close partners. Understand?"

Antonio watched the guard nod his head. "Great, so far!" he said in the muffled voice. "I want all the alarms turned off. You lead, there's not a lot of time." With a thrust of the muzzle, he encouraged the man to move forward.

They moved together like one body as the guard reached the security alarm panel and punched in the necessary code. The green light indicated the alarm had been disabled.

"Very good, stay extremely still!" Antonio commanded as he placed his bag on a desk next to him. "I'm going to step back about a foot, so don't get any dumb ideas. Place your hands behind you and stand very still." Antonio knew that the size of this man meant the guard could overpower him in a second if he got a chance, so getting the guard contained became his first priority.

The office was dimly lit only by a single light that was placed over the security shack. Antonio fumbled in his bag for the roll of gray duct tape and pulled it out. Holding his weapon, he pulled the leading edge strip from the roll and began wrapping the guard's hands and wrists with the tape. Once he felt the guard was secure, Antonio placed a large strip covering the guard's mouth. The guard had a large beard and the tape had to go completely around his head with a couple of passes to ensure that it was secure.

"Okay. Let's walk to the bathroom. Lead the way." Antonio pushed the man forward, moving as less of a couple now. The door was open and he shoved the bound man into the room. "Look dickhead, if you want to be breathing in the morning you'd better stay in here and keep quiet! Sit on the can and you'll survive my visit." Antonio pushed the man as he muttered, "Now straddle the seat and face the wall."

Once the guard complied, Antonio pressed the gun barrel into the man's neck.

"We're almost done here." Antonio pulled another strip of tape and placed the end on the tank of the toilet and pulled it around the man's back, maintaining the gun presence. The tape was pulled around to the other side and wrapped behind the tank. A second wrap was completed.

"Okay, now. Enjoy your visit." Antonio closed the bathroom door and grabbed the disposable burn phone that Giermo had placed in the bag. Antonio keyed the number and within two rings he heard Giermo on the line. "Ready! Let's get this done," Antonio said in a whisper and disconnected the call.

Giermo quickly drove the rental truck across the street and had to slide the yard gate open wide enough to slip the vehicle through. He had the truck in position at the pole yard office in less than two minutes and he backed the vehicle into the same spot as on his prior delivery. Antonio had opened the back office door and waited for his partner to lift and slide the rear door of the rental truck open.

"We're behind schedule! What took so long?" Giermo grunted as Antonio turned on the lights in the back storage room.

"Let's get this finished and we'll talk later!" Antonio replied tensely, his heart pounding in his throat.

It took fifteen minutes to load the truck and Giermo knew that the guard would be expected to report back to his office headquarters after each round. Giermo decided that they should take the computer, printer, and any other loose electronics to make the heist appear as an office robbery. They had to hurry.

Traffic was almost nonexistent as they pulled from the stop light onto 148th Street. Both men were pumped, and Giermo headed directly to the *Fraser Head Hotel*. He pulled the van into the rear parking lot and within ten minutes of their completed heist had found a parking space. They'd not heard any sirens yet, indicating that the guard hadn't yet been discovered.

The two men vacated their front seats, locked the truck, and slipped into the lobby of the *Fraser Head*. Giermo waved his room key at the desk clerk and they took the back stairs to the third floor. The pair of men found and entered room 309, quickly shutting the door.

"Christ! That was crazy!" Antonio exclaimed as he flopped exhausted onto one of the single beds.

"You got that right!" Giermo replied, noticing that the bedside clock displayed one thirty-five in bold green numbers.

⚜

It was one fifty-two in the morning when Ricardo's phone call pulled both Ricardo and Hunter from their nightly rest.

"Sorry to call you, Mr. Ricardo, at this early time in the morning, but one of our guards has failed to report in following his last scheduled round," the young caller advised. "We need your approval to call the RCMP."

"Ah ... hold on a minute!" Ricardo replied, a little groggy as he sat up on the side of his bed. "Ah ... sorry, which guard hasn't reported back to you?"

"Our security guard at the *ComTek* pole yard, sir. He's fifteen minutes overdue now, sir!"

"Hmm ... the pole yard, eh? You'd better advise the RCMP and I'll drive out there!" Ricardo replied, now fully awake.

Two RCMP cruisers were at the security guard gate by the time that Ricardo and Hunter arrived at the scene. An ambulance had been called to attend to the guard who had to be cut from his bonds. He wasn't seriously injured but was quite shaken up by the ordeal.

The guard was explaining to one of the responding officers, "I'm sure that I heard the intruders loading something from the back room for most of the time that I was tied up in the toilet."

"Do you have any idea what they were taking?"

"No, Officer. Once the two men finished loading what was in the back room, they came into the front office and took the computer and things," the Indian guard replied as he shook his head.

"Two men?"

"Ah, ya! I heard two men only. One of the men bound me and took me into the bathroom and I could hear another voice in the back while they were loading." The guard thought about the evening's event. "The man that held me by gunpoint and bound my hands had a Spanish accent. That's all I remember. Can I go now, please?"

Ricardo noticed that the guard had finished talking with the RCMP Officer, and walked over to the visibly shaken guard. A paramedic was placing some ointment on the guard's face and hands to ease the pain from the removal of the duct tape.

"Sorry, Mr. Sanchez, I was taken by surprise." The guard hung his head, feeling that he had failed in his duty.

"It's not your fault! I'm just glad you aren't hurt. Have you seen anything unusual around here at the office in the past few days?"

"Hmm ... the only thing I recall was a courier van that made a delivery for Mr. Peters. It stayed longer than most couriers, but it didn't seem out of place. There's a lot of traffic coming and going from here, Mr. Sanchez."

"Okay, for now. Don't worry about this, and go home," Ricardo replied, placing his hand on the man's shoulder. Ricardo took a breath and turned to look for the officer who had interviewed the guard. He noticed him standing inside of the pole yard office, and quickly walked in that direction.

"Officer, I'm Ricardo Sanchez, the security manager for *ComTek*," Ricardo said as he entered the office.

"Oh, yes, Mr. Sanchez. We've a strange situation here. The thieves were certainly after more than the computer hardware, because there're a lot easier targets than this one for that kind of stuff! We'll have to bring our lab boys down here in the morning to see what they can find, especially in the back where the guard heard the intruders loading something else."

"Perhaps I can talk to your team in the morning?" Ricardo asked, knowing the tasks the officers had to complete that night.

"Sure, I'm going to tape the area off and have a squad car sit here until the morning shift arrives," the officer replied as the RCMP crew started their containment of the scene.

Ricardo decided that there was nothing else for him to do until morning and climbed back into his truck. "Hmm ... I wonder what was going on here tonight, Hunter," he said, starting the truck's engine.

The six o'clock morning alarm seemed unusually early for Ricardo; for Hunter, too, who was spread out at the bottom of the bed. Ricardo knew that he was going to have a busy day, and quickly got ready for his morning walk with his dog. The morning was clear and the rain clouds had dissipated overnight, but had left a cold chill in the air.

The walk was uneventful, and Hunter was happy to cut the trip short and return to his cozy spot on the bed. Ricardo prepared for work, wondering what information the officer had gathered at the pole yard scene four hours earlier.

⋇

Giermo and Antonio didn't sleep well throughout the night as they were still pumped and tense from their heist. They planned to leave the hotel at the beginning of the daily morning rush, so the sight of the rental truck wouldn't look out of place. The first light of day was their signal, and since neither man had a change in clothing, they decided to have a *Tim Hortons*[R] takeout instead of going to a restaurant for a sit-down breakfast. The men left the room, pulled the door closed, and left the key inside. They jumped into their truck and started on their way toward Port Coquitlam, where Giermo had taken a sublease on an industrial building the day before.

⋇

Will Richards was up much of the night thinking about what he should do at the mill, should the loader not be returned by that morning. He'd almost completed the annual tally of pole deliveries, and it continued to look like there wouldn't be the annual subsidy payment. He worried about the resulting financial pressure the loss of the payment would place on things at home and on his business, now that the extra payment wasn't likely to happen.

Will walked by the mess on his desk as he started his morning routine getting ready for work. He peered out the back window and saw that the weather pattern had changed. "At least something's starting off in my favor this morning," he thought with a sigh, noting that it was finally going to be a dry day. "That loader had better be waiting for me when I get there!" he mumbled, knowing that the machine should've been repaired by the close of the prior day and there hadn't been an indication that he should think otherwise.

Will arrived at the pole yard gate and saw the sea of police vehicles and the common yellow warning tape cordoning off the pole yard office. He spotted Ricardo in the crowd, and pulled his truck over into one of the pole access laneways designed for the loader. "Hey, Ricardo," Will yelled as he vacated his truck. "What's going on?"

"You have to stay back away from the office, Will. There was a break-in here last night and the guard was taped and put into the bathroom at gunpoint. We don't know what the intruders were after, though," Ricardo replied, holding up his hand.

"What does Terry say?" Will asked, looking for the man.

"I don't know. He hasn't shown up for work yet. He hadn't returned from lunch when I looked for him yesterday afternoon, either. Strange, eh?" Ricardo asked, walking toward Will's green truck.

"Hmm ... not good! Terry must've been caught with his hand in the cookie jar and split. Well about time he got his balls caught. It couldn't have happened to a nicer guy!" Will thought as he considered the situation and grinned unsympathetically just as Ricardo reached the truck.

"I'll bet he's involved. Terry's always got a scam goin'. See ya later, Ricardo!" Will said and headed his truck toward his shop, curious why Terry would do something so obvious and stupid; it certainly wasn't his style.

"Damn, the loader isn't here yet! I'd better call *Ernie's* myself and find out what's going on. I need that damn thing today!" he exclaimed loudly, annoyed, as he entered his office to call the repair shop to find out the status of the missing loader.

♓

Kelly and Simon arrived at the West Vancouver precinct office by 0730 with a cup of coffee in their hands. Kelly was surprised that Ricardo hadn't called yet following their date. She knew that he was excited with their outing and she had expected a phone message, if nothing else.

"Hey, Simon, do you think we should revisit that computer repair place again this morning?" Kelly asked.

"You bet. Finish your coffee while I finish looking at these photos from the crime scene on Beach Avenue," he responded with his head faced downward looking at the pictures.

"I see you both are now here! Please come into my office, Detectives," Captain Hollingsworth called across the room and held the door open for the two detectives. He waited for them to grab a seat, and then closed the door. "How are you two doing as a team?"

"We're a good pair, Cap, and we seem to be jelling as partners," Simon replied with a smile. "She's a little aggressive but I can deal with that!"

The captain snickered. "Well, I'm glad to see that it's working out. Where's my progress report on the Elvenden case?" Hollingsworth asked seriously.

"We're just finishing up our notes on last week's activities, Sir," Kelly replied without expression. "We've a few new leads that we believe will shed more light on the case."

"Hmm ... okay then, keep on it," Hollingsworth replied as he eyed the woman. "Thank you!" He turned his attention to the next case folder on his desk.

The detectives understood the cue to leave. "'Report almost ready,' what's that? We haven't had time to put that report together!" Simon exclaimed as the pair returned to their desks; he looked surprised at Kelly's suggestion that they had.

"Ah, sorry. You've got to keep the Captain happy and we'll have time later this afternoon," Kelly replied, trying to reassure her partner who didn't look so pleased with the deceptive comment.

The trip to the Dyke Road industrial complex required patience with the traffic, and it was almost 0930 before the gray sedan pulled in front of the address. The detectives arrived at the computer repair operation and found the front door locked as before. An old Toyota hatchback was parked outside in a designated space, and the two detectives knew that someone must be at work inside.

The old hatchback had a bleached, red paint job and looked like someone was living in the messy back, indicated by a sleeping bag and a package of open potato chips shoved by the wheel well. They walked to the rear of the building as they had done the day before. The large bay door of the shop was closed, so they approached the man-door on the side.

"RCMP, please open up. We need to talk to you." Simon pounded on the steel door, and peered through the small safety window. He saw movement inside, but the person quickly disappeared from view.

"He's going to bolt! Go around the front and I'll stay here," Simon yelled at Kelly.

She turned and started to sprint for the front of the building. Her daily jogging was paying off and she was in the front of the building in a flash. She saw a man run through the open front door and try to unlock the Toyota in the parking lot. Kelly pulled her service weapon and yelled, "Stop! RCMP. Put your hands on the hood where I can see them. Now!" she screamed as she continued to move quickly toward the suspect, and heard Simon coming behind her.

"Hey, what's the big hurry, bud? We're not your type of customer?" she asked the man who had his hands placed where he had been instructed, and was a little winded from the dash. Kelly reached the captive, her firearm pointing at the shaking man beside the car.

"Put your hands behind your back!" Simon commanded, and pulled his handcuffs from the back of his belt and shackled the suspect. "You're not very friendly. We just wanted to talk to you. Hiding something in there, are ya?"

Kelly quickly grabbed her cell and called the dispatcher requesting backup and a ride for their collar.

Simon called out to Kelly, "Let's secure this guy onto his car's steering wheel and take a look around while we wait for backup." He yanked the prisoner around and took the car keys from the guy's clenched hand.

Having the man under control and shackled to his car, the detectives entered the building through the open front door. There was a small counter placed in the entranceway and the space looked like it had been used by another business that had obviously failed. The back wall had holes where some old logo signage had hung, indicated by the dark patch on the sun-bleached wall. The place obviously hadn't been repainted after the prior tenant had vacated.

"Doesn't look like a retail operation, anyway. Let's look around back," Kelly said, noticing that there wasn't any customer reception setup.

The two partners walked to the door that was open at the edge of the room and entered. The rear of the building was a large open space, concrete on both side walls and the open steel girder struts carried a few halogen lights. There was metal racking along both sides of the walls, each running about twenty meters from the wooden temporary front wall to the chained dock door.

The storage racks were loaded with sealed boxes and stacks of new unopened cardboard box packs. Kelly walked over to the sealed boxes, looked about, and found a razor blade-box cutter. She pulled a box from the shelf, placed it on the concrete floor and cut the tape with the razor. She noticed the *Bug Busters Computer Services* label affixed to the top. Simon joined her, and they already knew what they were going to find, as they had seen the packaging at the house on Elvenden Row.

"I bet I know what's in here!" Simon smiled as he helped Kelly pull the computer casing from the box. Cutting the rest of the box away from the computer shell, Simon spotted the two smaller boxes inserted between the motherboard and frame. "Yep, I was right! We'd better have the lab out here. Call it in," Simon instructed. Kelly stood up to pull her cell from her pocket and dialed.

An officer appeared and joined the detectives as Kelly finished with her call. "We've the suspect safe in the squad car, Sir."

"Good news. You and your partner stay here with him until the crime lab gang gets here. We'll contact the Surrey detachment about your guest later," Simon said as he stood up.

"You know, Simon, you did a great job figuring out that those computer cases and boxes went together! Hmm ... you know, this looks like it's likely more than a single-man operation. We'd better have the lab look for prints of any partners, too," Kelly remarked, looking about the warehouse.

"Okay. Maybe we can get a lead on the bigger picture here. Let's go," Simon replied as he led the way out.

※

It was almost noon and the cleaning staff was waiting to finish their morning rounds at the *Fraser Head Hotel*. The "Don't Disturb" sign was still on the door knob of room 311 and it was already past checkout time. The hotel manager rang the room a number of times without an answer. He decided that the guest must've already left, and since the room had been paid for in cash, the guest hadn't been obligated to formally check out. The manager instructed the cleaning staff to knock one more time before entering and then complete their room preparation for the next guest.

The chilling scream could be heard throughout the hotel complex.

The front parking lot of the *Fraser Head* was jammed with RCMP flashing police cars, the coroner's vehicle, and the ambulance from the *Surrey Memorial Hospital*. The two maids were sitting in the front lobby of the *Fraser Head Hotel* looking traumatized, giving statements to the attending Surrey officers on scene. The crime lab team had secured the room and was gathering evidence. From his employee identification card found in his pants pocket, they'd identified the body as Terry Peters.

"It looks like the time of death was around noon yesterday, according to his body temperature," the Medical Examiner said as he continued with his examination, dictating his findings into a digital recorder. "He was definitely strangled, and the victim's head was hit hard on the back of the toilet tank as well. I'll need to further study the body at the lab. Maybe I can find some more evidence about his murderer."

The forensics team was dusting for prints, and looking for any other clues that could help identify the killer, as Detectives Nick Haslow and Terrance Greenwall watched the proceedings.

"Hey Nick, go down to the manager's office and see if they've any surveillance footage from yesterday, and get us a copy," Detective Greenwall suggested to his partner. "Maybe we can get an eyeball on the killer."

The body bag was carted out the front door of the hotel and the news media had already gotten a tip on the latest murder in Surrey. The reporter pressed the coroner as the body was loaded into the ambulance. "Can you tell us anything about this latest murder?" the woman reporter asked as she shoved a microphone into the corner's face.

"You know I can't comment on this homicide until we've finished the preliminary evaluation. The RCMP is still gathering evidence. Sorry, I can't comment further," the coroner replied, and pushed aside the microphone so that he could carry on with his business.

"This is Surrey's nineteenth homicide this year and the mayor will need to improve that record if she's going to get control on the increasing violence in our neighborhoods," the reporter commented, facing her camera crew on the spot. "This is Vanessa Hill for *City Pulse TV News* at the *Fraser Head Hotel* in Surrey."

♓

Ricardo Sanchez received a call on his cell and answered it after its second ring.

"Mr. Sanchez, I'm Detective Haslow of the Surrey RCMP. I understand that you're the manager in charge of security at *ComTek*. Is that correct?"

"Yes, I am. What can I do for you, Detective Haslow?" Ricardo answered, assuming the call was about the break-in at the *ComTek* pole yard.

"Terry Peters, an employee of *ComTek*, has been found murdered this morning at the *Fraser Head Hotel*. We thought that you'd be the best person to contact in this matter," Haslow continued. "There's no answer at his home number."

"Murdered! Ah, why yes, I'm responsible for security at *ComTek*. Do you know anything about his death, Detective?" Ricardo inquired, wondering how Terry Peters' death linked with the break-in.

"No, not yet! Would you please inform *ComTek* management? I'll call you back if I need further information, Mr. Sanchez."

"Okay, Detective. Thanks for the call. I'll advise head office," Ricardo replied, hanging up the call.

"My God, there's a lot more going on here than I was looking for," Ricardo thought, trying to think of scenarios that could lead to Terry Peters' murder. "I need to see what the Surrey lab boys have found concerning the break-in last night. Maybe there's a connection." Ricardo pondered the likelihood, as he was still at the scene of the break-in, and then placed another call. "Larry Langstone, please, Carolynn. It's Ricardo Sanchez," Ricardo requested of the receptionist.

"This is going to be an unpleasant call," he told himself while waiting for his boss to answer.

"Langstone."

"Larry, this is Ricardo, and I've some bad news." Ricardo explained about the break-in first.

Taking a deep breath he continued, "And there's one more thing, Larry. I've just received a call from the RCMP that Terry Peters was murdered yesterday afternoon at a hotel in Surrey."

"Murdered ... Jesus Christ! Do the police know what happened or who did it?" Larry blurted out.

"No, nothing yet, Sir. How do you want to handle this?" Ricardo asked calmly.

"Uh ... leave it with me. I'll tell Brian Quest myself. Just keep on top of things and keep me updated," Larry replied and abruptly hung up.

♓

Kelly and Simon returned to their West Vancouver desks by 1330. They'd taken the opportunity to stop and grab a bite of lunch at a diner in New Westminster. Simon's cell phone rang as they were beginning to prepare the report that Kelly had promised earlier. "Hello, Detective Chung here."

"It's Detective Terrance Greenwall at the Surrey detachment. We've finished processing your Dyke Road collar and have filed charges of possession with the intent to traffic. You asked us to keep you in the loop."

"Thanks, Detective. Can you call when his case hearing's scheduled? He's a link to our active case in West Vancouver and we need to keep tabs on what he's up to," Simon requested.

"Sure thing!" Simon heard the answer and then hung up the phone.

"Hmm … better get these reports done before something else drags us away!" Simon glanced at Kelly who was pounding away at the keyboard. "Our *Bug Buster's* guy just got charged in Surrey for possession."

♓

Giermo Hernandez needed to replace his two guys, and racked his brain as to where to find new replacements. "Shit, the timing sure stinks," he mumbled his frustration at Antonio. "I'll have to deal with that later, once we finish getting this stuff unloaded."

The rental truck was parked in the back of a building in a light industrial park in Port Coquitlam. Giermo didn't want an operation out that far from his place in Vancouver, but it was a long way from the Elvenden Row place, and he thought that was a good thing.

The building was a nondescript, standard, fast construction, precast concrete structure that was similar to many going up around the city. It was nothing fancy, and the large complex of cookie cutter buildings was only partially occupied, which was one of the reasons the sublease rate was low.

The two men finished placing the last box of the shipment on the floor of the new facility.

"I think that's enough for today. Let's go back to my place and have a beer and rest. I can decide later what to do tomorrow," Giermo suggested as he huffed a little from the strenuous work.

Antonio was happy with the suggestion and worked rapidly to get the place closed up.

♓

The late afternoon sun was winding its way across the clear cold sky, and the bright sunlight was streaming into the West Vancouver detectives' floor. Simon's phone rang and he sat listening and taking notes. A large grin appeared on his face.

"Bingo! That was Detective Greenwall in Surrey. We've a winner!" Simon teased Kelly by waiting a second before continuing. "They found Antonio Castillo's prints at the break-in at *ComTek* last night. The Surrey guys were entering his information into the RCMP database and our open case popped up!"

"We should let Ricardo know there's a link to his security breach. He's heading security at *ComTek* and should know," Kelly suggested as she punched Ricardo's cell number into the desk phone.

"Hello, Ricardo Sanchez."

"Hey, it's KO. Just thought I'd keep you updated. We've received a call from the Surrey office that our friend Antonio Castillo left prints at your break-in last night, and ..." Kelly hesitated, "you haven't called me!"

"Uh ... things have been nuts and I planned to give you a call later tonight. Anyway, one turn deserves another. I just got word that Terry Peters, the foreman of the break-in site at

ComTek, was murdered yesterday. That's too much of a coincidence for me!"

"That sure is strange indeed. Thanks ... talk later!" Kelly hung up and stared at Simon. "Hmm ... the foreman of that operation where Castillo's prints were found was murdered yesterday afternoon. I wonder if Castillo had anything to do with that?" she paused, "I think that we should let the Captain know about Peters and get his thoughts about us getting more involved out there," she suggested, testing Simon for a reaction.

"Yes, that's a good idea, Kelly," he replied and got out of his chair. The pair walked across the room and knocked on the door frame of the back office.

When acknowledged, Kelly addressed the captain, "Hey Cap, all our leads are pointing to events taking place in Surrey. Do you think it would be a good idea for us to be assigned out at Surrey for the duration of this case? It seems that the action on our case is there, and it's our case and we should lead the investigation. I don't want to step on anyone's toes, but .... "

Sam Hollingsworth interrupted her. He knew where she was headed, looked at Simon closely who had a slight smile on his face, then replied. "I'll call Surrey and see what they think. I'll get back to you ... ah, got my update report yet?" he asked, smiled, and returned to the reports on his desk. He waited a minute, glanced up from his report and noticed that the two detectives had returned to their assignment, so he got up from his chair, closed his door, and made a few phone calls.

♓

The buzz was out! Will Richards had got wind of Peters' murder and felt awful at the way Terry had met his demise. "I'm glad that blackmailing bastard's out of my face, but this is certainly not the way I thought things would play out ...

murdered … he sure pissed off someone with balls!" Will mumbled as he received the news on the phone from one of his contacts inside *ComTek*.

Will was saddened by the event, and allowed his workers to go home early. He decided to remain and continue cleaning up the site, happy to be left alone. The loader had been returned later that morning following his call to *Ernie's Equipment Repairs*. He climbed into the cab.

He noticed the substantial increase in pine pole species that now had to be sorted into another pile, one that he was preparing for direct disposal. "You know, I don't get it! *ComTek* trucks these things all the way from the Interior, dumps them here and then I cut them up and dispose of them. What a waste of time and money." As his thoughts raced, he became increasingly annoyed with the idiocy of it. "They spend all this time and money just to increase the pole count so they don't have to pay me! What bullshit. It costs more to handle and ship them here to me than to pay the pole subsidy. It's stupid!"

Will continued with the sorting, and turned on *CKVR Radio* to listen to the talk show some more. "So I wonder what's the story on Terry?" he mused as the talking chatter carried on in the background over the noise of the loader.

Chapter Eighteen

Terry Peters' corpse lay stiffly on a cold slab in the basement of the *Surrey Memorial Hospital*, partially covered with a white sheet. The coroner was noting evidence, and taking samples from the body. He'd already bagged pubic hairs that were a blond in color, certainly not those of the corpse. The strangle marks on the body's windpipe were more evident now, and the bruising appeared darker on the pale skin. The body had large bruising on its buttocks in the shape of the edge of the toilet seat, which apparently had been made by the weight of the woman sitting on the top of the man's thighs.

There were indications that the man had used a condom during intercourse, and that it had been removed post-mortem. The condom hadn't been recovered at the scene, so it was likely that any evidence on the latex surface that it may have had was disposed down the toilet. These findings were photographed and logged.

"The bruising on the windpipe shows signs of long fingernails, as the skin has been punctured in a number of places during strangulation," the corner continued with his report. "The back of the skull has been cracked indicating that it hit the edge of the toilet water-tank lid with some force, but this wasn't the cause of death. Considering all the evidence, asphyxiation caused by strangulation is the primary cause of this victim's death."

The corner took a breath as he looked at the corpse. "Hmm … an interesting way to go!" the practitioner thought to himself, as it was clear that the man had been strangled during intercourse. "Hmm … I wonder if this was a crime of passion or premeditated. It's difficult to tell from the evidence."

Abused Trust

⚓

The news of Terry Peters' murder spread throughout *ComTek* like wildfire. The information age definitely has to work hard to beat the gossip network. Brian Quest had told his managers and staff about Terry Peters' tragic death at a quick impromptu meeting, immediately after receiving Larry Langstone's call.

Privately, Larry was a little concerned with the microscopic attention that the whole situation would likely bring to the operation as a whole. "Brian needs to be diligent about that," Larry thought, wondering what Terry was really up to, as he considered the pole yard break-in and subsequent murder. "Humph! Brian should've known about what was going on at his operation, too," Larry muttered as he continued to process all the facts now coming to light. "Brian's a sloppy manager at best, and could be dangerous if not kept on a tighter leash. Hmm …."

⚓

Candice Parks struggled with keeping her composure once the news about Terry had been released by Brian to the staff. She had been stressed all day, and continued to go over the events of the prior day, looking for something that she might've missed. She finally convinced herself that she was in the clear and that there was nothing to get concerned about.

"I saw you with Terry the other day from my window. What was that about?" Brian asked Candice following the meeting; the news had prompted him to recall the prior day and the image of Candice talking with Terry in her office.

"Oh … he just wanted to check about things that Will had taken to repair the mill and verify that I'd approved all the items. Nothing unusual for Terry—as you know, he had a passion for harassing Will Richards."

"Well, Terry was just trying to do his job!" Brian remarked coldly. "I'll have to be very careful who I select to replace Terry. Let me know if you have any ideas, Candice," Brian requested as he turned back to his office, thinking about the predicament that he had. "Tragic, and a pain in the ass! That setup was perfect for making Will Richards' life a hell on earth. Damn anyway!"

♓

Ricardo Sanchez headed home with the day's events spinning around in his head. He kept reminding himself to call Kelly, especially since she sounded disappointed and it was important to keep her interest.

Hunter greeted him at the door as usual, and was excited to have the walk that he'd wanted for most of the day. He was an energetic animal, and needed to run to burn off the energy that built up during the laziness of the day and hopefully, to get a chance to play with his best friend.

The evening was perfect for both of them to enjoy, and the walk worked wonders for Ricardo, who was able to put his thoughts aside for a little break. Hunter's many friends were out for an evening stroll as well, and any opportunity for "bum sniff" was always a good way to check out friends and meet new visitors on the walkway.

"Come on, Hunter, let's get something to eat," Ricardo called his companion, as it was time to organize dinner. The dog returned immediately to his master's side and trotted back, happy to have burned off some of his pent-up energy.

"Hunter, remind me to call Kelly after dinner later," Ricardo patted the dog as they reentered the apartment complex.

♓

"Ugh ... paperwork's so tedious sometimes ... but it can stimulate fresh ideas to pursue!" Kelly tried to convince herself to keep going, as the reports were now late for Captain Hollingsworth.

"Simon, do you think the Captain will let us go to Surrey to work from there on this case?" she asked, looking up from the keyboard at him.

"Well, you're right that our case is heating up in Surrey. I guess the detectives who have already been assigned by Surrey will have a say in that decision," he thought out loud as he spoke. "To be honest, it would make getting information easier and quicker for us if we were officially involved out there, though."

"Okay! I've sent the Captain an e-mail informing him that the report's completed and is in his case file folder. He can read it all in the morning," Kelly replied happily, as she logged off the computer. "Okay partner, ready to go home?"

Kelly O'Brian was glad to be home. It had been an eventful day and she needed a break from the Elvenden Row case. "It's funny how things take twists and turns and one thing leads to something else. I guess that's why I joined the RCMP in the first place! Humph, it's all about unraveling the mystery and getting to the truth!" she muttered as she entered her apartment. She noticed that the answering machine was flashing, so she pressed the play button.

"Hey KO, it's Ricardo. Sorry it's been a few days but I'd like to see you again. Please return my call when you can. Bye for now."

"Hmm ... I'll call later," Kelly thought as she made a note on the pad by the phone.

She was a typical single person living in the big city. The meal selection for the evening was often a challenging choice between going out alone and having a quick meal prepared by someone else, or struggling with some unplanned menu and messing up her own kitchen. She was tired and not in the mood to go out again, even for a quick bite, and chose to ramble around in her own kitchen and prepare something.

"So what to make. Hmm ...." she muttered as she opened the refrigerator to see what lurked inside, and then closed the door. "Nope, I'm cold and want to feel warmer." She chose to leave the meal decision for later and went into the bedroom to change.

Kelly reappeared from her bedroom about ten minutes later. She had put on her nightgown and a warm pink robe, looking like she was at some girls' sleepover party. She'd a spiral notebook in her hand, and placed it on the dining room table alongside her running Apple® computer, and headed for the kitchen.

The apartment often seemed too quiet, and Kelly enjoyed having music playing in the background to drown out the silence. She made a Christina Aguilera selection on her iPod®, which was connected to her stereo, and pressed play.

She did enjoy making her own meal and often had a great time in the preparation, but not tonight. A simpler menu was in order and she pulled eggs, red peppers, and cheese from the fridge and tossed them all together to make a simple omelet.

She placed her meal beside her, opened the laptop computer's lid, and reviewed the latest entries that she had made in her spiral notebook. The biggest mystery of all was her own, at least in her mind. Her mother's words "she's not my child" had haunted her for years, and her quest in determining who her parents really were had been a sporadic one.

Her mother and father had divorced when she was fifteen and her mother had moved to Toronto where her sister lived. Her mother was now in a nursing home, was in poor health, and refused any family contact. Her father had Alzheimer's, and no longer remembered her or any past events. She loved her father, and found this illness cruel and devastating.

Her search had started with fractured information that she'd gathered from her father's things following his admission into a care home. Kelly had already discovered that the cause of her parents' failed marriage was the bankruptcy of her father's business, *DigiCast Software*. His partner had embezzled large amounts of cash and had used the company assets as collateral for his personal use.

The business collapsed once creditors began demanding payment. Her father lost everything, including the house in Kerrisdale and his dignity. The embezzled cash had never been recovered. There was little detail on the business failure, but she knew how it had dramatically impacted her life. She had been withdrawn from *Croften House*, a private school in Kerrisdale and transferred into a public high school.

She recalled that there were other events that had taken place following the scandal, but as a teen with her own self-focused issues, the events went unnoticed. Kelly recalled the difficulty of the situation as a teenager, entering a new school, having no money, dealing with her parents' divorce, and wondering who her parents really were. She became driven; she was determined and self-reliant, and trusting people became difficult.

Her father did what he could to work through the devastation of his marriage and his business. He was a caring man, and had felt personally responsible for his employees who had lost their jobs and for those creditors who couldn't be repaid. Kelly grew very close to her father, and became very angry with her mother, who in leaving had forced both she and her dad to rebuild their lives alone.

It had taken many years before Kelly was able to face the horrid past and try to find an explanation that would ease her soul. She'd not been able to spend much time looking into her past, as the demands of her job with the RCMP plus detective school had consumed all of her energy.

Kelly thought that the clues to her mystery might be found through finding employees who had worked in her dad's firm. There had been little information in her father's papers that identified those employees, and she recalled that the search for them had been her last focus.

She sat staring at the laptop screen, fingers tapping out their instructions while she poked at her meal. "The Internet's a wonderful tool if one has the patience and discipline to sift through websites and links," Kelly thought, as she noted another possible website in the small spiral notebook.

"This process will likely take forever," she sighed, thinking that she must persevere. "Just one solid clue, that's all it takes, just one!" Kelly reminded herself as she tapped her nails on her dining room table, thinking where to look next.

"Maybe that prick who embezzled the money from *DigiCast* may know something—after all, he was Dad's partner." It came to her, pushing the keys, "Yea, I wonder what I can find out about him! Hmm ...."

ℋ

Giermo Hernandez was driving back toward Vancouver and soon ran into the heavy traffic of the rush hour trek from Port Coquitlam. He'd returned the rental truck and had retrieved his own courier van and was now stuck in traffic.

"Holy Shit! I never thought it'd be this bad going into Vancouver from here," Giermo uttered his frustration as he sat at the Cape Horn Interchange that led onto the expressway heading west.

"I don't think there's any place that doesn't have gridlock, no matter where you're goin'," Antonio replied, trying to turn down the stress level of his driver.

"Well, we'd better plan our comings and goings better in the future. Three to six in the afternoon is pure hell out here!" Giermo grunted, frustrated at the two-car-per-light progress at the intersection feeding the ramp. "You know, I think I'll drop ya off at your place and I'll carry on home."

"That's a good idea. I can get a change in duds and do my own thing tonight," Antonio agreed with the change in plan. "Besides, listening to you bitch about this traffic all the way to your place will drive me crazy!"

"Ya better settle in and put earplugs in, it's going to be a long trip and my bitching has just started!" Giermo growled, exasperated, moving the van two more spaces ahead.

♓

Kelly O'Brian's phone rang as Kelly continued to sift through Internet websites.

"It's Simon. I know that it's late, but I just got a call from the lady living above Antonio Castillo's. He just got home!"

"Great, I'll pick you up in thirty," Kelly replied. She closed her spiral notebook, shut the lid on the computer and got ready to go out again.

Simon was waiting by his stop outside of his apartment in Chinatown. Kelly stopped to pick him up where she had before and then quickly pulled out, headed for Hastings Park.

"Hey, Simon, what a break, eh?" she grinned. "Well, at least we had time to eat!"

"Yea, a detective's work never sleeps," Simon replied, and then both sat silently, lost in their own thoughts as Kelly worked her way through the evening traffic.

Kelly parked the vehicle a half block down from the Pandora Street house.

"Kelly you take the rear and I'll take the front!" Simon directed as the pair slipped out of their vehicle.

"RCMP ... Antonio Castillo, open the door!" Simon yelled as he used his fist to pound on the door of the basement suite.

Scuffling sounds could be heard in the small suite, and Kelly saw the back door fly open and a man stumble up the old concrete staircase. "RCMP ... stop right there!" she commanded at a man in his underwear trying to flee the basement of the house.

Antonio froze in his tracks.

"Lay down with your hands behind you. Now!" Kelly yelled, her weapon in her hand.

Simon joined his partner as Kelly promptly cuffed the suspect and yanked him to his feet.

"Good evening, Mr. Castillo, glad you could join us!" Simon smiled and pushed the handcuffed man toward their waiting car. "Looks like you're going to be our guest tonight!"

Kelly eased the partially clad man into the back seat of their car, and the pair of detectives prepared for their trek to the West Vancouver lockup.

Chapter Nineteen

The weather was warming up and the cloud cover reappeared, foretelling more rain. It was still dry when Kelly's alarm announced that it was time to get ready for her morning jog. She had retired the night before pumped with the anticipation of questioning the suspects incarcerated the prior day. She had lain awake most of the night with the Elvenden Row case facts racing through her mind, as well as thoughts of the next steps she would have to take in locating her father's business partner.

The West Vancouver detachment lock-up cells had a houseful of overnight guests; two cells were occupied by Kelly and Simon's collars. The suspect captured at the Dyke Road warehouse had decided to use a public defender, and refused to say anything until his lawyer appeared. Antonio Castillo had elected to delay his call to his lawyer until the morning.

"It looks like we're going to have fun today," Simon remarked as the pair reached their desks and started to settle in.

"Yup, I see that Darryl Finlay's lawyer's already here. We'd better start with him first," KO replied as she looked at her empty coffee cup and grinned at her sidekick.

"Good morning, you two!" the Captain said with a smile, as he interrupted the conversation. "I got your pass to the Surrey operation. I spoke to Captain Christopher Anderson about your desire to follow your case from his shop. He spoke to his assigned detectives, and they had no problem passing their file onto you two. You still need to process those two guys downstairs first, and keep me informed though, as it's still our case." Hollingsworth smiled, "By the way, good report, a little late but complete. Get going!"

"Thanks, Captain." Kelly couldn't think of anything else to say. She had gotten the temporary reassignment she wanted and was busting to get going.

She called the reception desk to have the log checked to see if Antonio had obtained a lawyer yet. She was told that the log indicated that Karl Kuntz had been contacted and that he was expected shortly.

"We'd better talk to our Dyke Road guy," Kelly said as she turned to face Simon. "Castillo's mouth piece is coming in shortly—it's the same guy that Rodriguez and Vergara had—you remember him, Kuntz is his name."

The two detectives got up from their desk chairs and headed for the cell block, carrying Darryl Fraser's rap sheet. They entered the familiar interrogation area and saw both Darryl and Antonio had been brought out and placed into their own private rooms. O'Brian and Chung entered Darryl Finlay's room first, and Kelly placed the man's folder on the desk as she and Simon sat down. A public defender was standing in the back of the room, leaning against the large front window.

There were no introductions and Kelly wanted to get started. "I see that you've been a busy boy, Darryl. You've a rap sheet as long as my arm," Kelly said stiffly as she peered over the tabletop to face the young man, while sliding the arrest file across the table toward Simon. "I wonder what we'll add to this list after our little chat." She peered directly at the young male, who acted uninterested in the conversation.

Darryl was a thin, lanky man about thirty and looked anemic. He sported two diamond earrings in the same left earlobe, a ring pierced through the right side of his nose, a large, fading tattoo of an eagle on his right forearm and dirty, jet-black hair that had been tied into a ponytail at the back and banded. He slouched in his chair, wearing frayed blue jeans and a dirty, short-sleeved t-shirt that had *The Grateful Dead* imprinted on the front; the lack of long sleeves exposed needle tracks and bruised skin on both arms.

"We currently have you on possession of a controlled substance with the intent to traffic," Simon started the conversation and showed Darryl the photos taken at the Dyke Road warehouse with the computer cases and boxes that had been opened.

The man grabbed the photos and raised his head to face his accuser, "That stuff's not mine! I was just sitting at the warehouse waiting for James—that's all, I swear," he blurted out, in a teary tone.

"Who's James?" Simon pressed.

"Don't know his last name, only James. This was supposed to be a clean gig and he said he would supply me if I helped him out," Darryl continued to whimper. "My supplier came to me and asked if I wanted a free hit—he said all I had to do was a few easy things for this guy. I said sure, why not! All I was to do was to help unload boxes and wait for James to tell me what he wanted next. I didn't know what was in the boxes."

"What did this James guy look like?" Kelly asked as she leaned over the table.

"Uh ... he's ah ... not tall, has closely cut blond hair, and uh ... a tongue ring and a pitted face from some type of childhood thing, a large scar, and a huge tattoo around his neck." Darryl sniffled as he looked over at his lawyer who was standing silently through the questioning.

"Sounds like a little bullshit to me!" Simon responded, turned, and left the room. Kelly followed and closed the door.

"I guess we'll have to do more digging for this guy James. We'll file our charges and leave this guy with his public attorney. Good luck, I'd say!" Simon glanced back and shook his head. "What a screwed up guy, eh?"

"Yea, I'd say. Let's go upstairs and wait for Kuntz. I can't wait to see what Castillo has to say!"

Karl Kuntz eventually appeared at the West Vancouver RCMP precinct about ten o'clock. He requested an immediate conference meeting with his client before the arresting detectives could join the meeting, a courtesy that was granted by Captain Samuel Hollingsworth.

Antonio Castillo was dressed in a bright orange cotton top and pants. He had been arrested wearing only his undershorts, so he had been provided with the colorful outfit after his booking the night before. Antonio's meeting with Karl Kuntz was short, and within fifteen minutes the arresting detectives were invited to his interrogation room for their questioning period.

Kelly thought that Karl seemed like he hadn't changed his clothing since his last visit, and his slicked-back hair still needed a cut. His loafer shoes were having their own challenge with the wet weather, and seemed to protest with every step.

"You seem to get around a lot, don't you, Antonio?" The scrawny man looked directly at Kelly but didn't reply to her question. "You're going away for a long time. We have ya at the scene of a marijuana grow operation in West Vancouver, and we've proof that you were at a heist at a *ComTek* facility in Surrey last week. Do ya have anything to tell us about either of those events, eh Antonio?"

Antonio looked at Karl, and the pre-discussed head movement told the prisoner to stay quiet.

"Eh, Kuntz, up to your old tricks, eh? We got your client cold and it would help him if he helped us in telling who his boss is. We have him for B&E and forced confinement, including an assault of a guard at the *ComTek* office on 148th."

"My client has nothing to say," Karl Kuntz replied flatly.

"Okay … it'll be harder later, and when we tie him to the smack trafficking, he'll wish that he'd had a better attitude today," Simon responded, and watched Antonio to see if this message caused a change in his thinking.

The conversation generated nothing new, and Antonio sat motionless, eyeing the top of the table with the occasional glance up at his lawyer.

"I think we're done here," the stocky lawyer stated in a drone voice.

The two detectives realized that there would be no value in pressing further, so they filed out of the meeting room, leaving Castillo and Kuntz by themselves.

"We'll have to see if that scumbag gets bailed out, then we can go from there," Simon sighed as he shook his head in disappointment.

"Hey Simon, let's wrap things up and find our new digs in Surrey. The Captain has approved that we can take our assigned set of wheels if we go together to Surrey each day!"

"Great deal, KO. That sure beats the bus!"

⚛

Brian Quest scheduled a management meeting for nine in the morning. He wanted to see what Allen Harwitz had come up with to get around the distribution software problem, and accommodate the direct delivery of transformers from the Chilliwack supplier. He also wanted to see how everyone was coping with the death of Terry Peters.

Brian entered the conference room that didn't have its normal pre-meeting chatter. The solemn atmosphere was gloomy, and it was evident that the tragedy was lying heavily on each person in the room.

"This isn't a meeting to push buttons today," Brian thought as he entered the room, "but I've an agenda that must be delivered regardless how everyone may feel about Terry Peters."

Brian took his seat at the head of the meeting-room table. "Good morning. I'm sure everyone's feeling as bad as I am about Terry, but we've things to do." Brian didn't have too much empathy in his nature, and getting things straightened out to handle his arrangement with *BC Transformer* was much more important to him than the tragic death of an employee. "Allen, what things have you been able to come up with to help us with our systems problem?"

Allen's expertise was in procurement, and not business software problem-solving. He worked well with others and was not an aggressive person, but working under unrealistic timeframes was new, and he found dealing with Brian stressful and frustrating.

"Uh ... I've worked out a work-around. It's messy and not very productive, but I think we can accommodate our contract agreement with *BC Transformer* until we can figure out a better solution," Allen replied, looking very tired and stressed from the pressure to find a business solution, and of course, from the murder of Terry Peters.

"Excellent work, Allen! I want the description of the process on my desk this afternoon, including the identification of each employee who'll be impacted and their specific practice changes." Brian's tone was business as usual and direct.

"Sandra, I want recommendations as to who you feel should replace Terry along with their employment history. That's a critical position across the street, and the person must be able to operate with little supervision. Have your suggestions to me by the end of the day." Brian looked stone-faced and eyed Sandra to ensure she got the message. "If any of you others can think of issues concerning the replacement of Terry, send me an e-mail outlining your thoughts. That's all."

♓

Kelly O'Brian loved driving the new Taurus SHO, and was ecstatic to be able to work in Surrey for a while. The drive from her apartment in Kitsilano to Chinatown wasn't too bad, and Kelly pondered about the best route to take to Surrey after picking up Simon.

Vancouver's Chinatown is the second largest Chinese community in North America, and its unique culture could be seen everywhere in the area. The brightly painted, red and green building fronts, the Chinese-character business signs, and the open markets that sold traditional foods and goods, made this area a major tourist attraction.

Even though Kelly had grown up in Vancouver, she didn't know the area very well. She drove the sleek gray sedan southward on Colombia Street, and as she approached the light at East Pender, she called her partner. "Hey Simon, I'm just about at your place. See ya in a moment or two." Kelly hung up and concentrated on the many pedestrians that haphazardly crossed the busy street. The car travelled eastward along East Pender through the streets that were alive with people going about their daily shopping for fresh produce, or poking into the many shops that sold specialty goods that were made in China.

Kelly stopped the gray sedan, and she put on the emergency flashers while she waited for Simon to appear across the street. She sat a car length back from the *Kam Gok*

Yuen Restaurant, which displayed a large red awning that was directly in front of the crosswalk where she waited.

"It looks like our daily trip from here to our Surrey office will be longer than going to our West Vancouver precinct," Kelly commented as Simon jumped into the car. "We'll be pushing lunch time by the time we arrive, so onward." She pressed the accelerator and pointed the car eastward.

The Surrey RCMP had a huge area to police, an expanse of territory that bordered the Fraser River at the north and Mud Bay to the South. Delta lay to the west and Langley the east. Surrey was the largest city in the province and was a melting pot of cultures with a wide diversity of lifestyles and affluence.

The two detectives were getting hungry as they neared the vicinity of the Surrey headquarters just before noon. The car's GPS provided a feature that showed gas stations and restaurants in the vicinity of the vehicle coordinates, and Simon activated the capability.

"Ah … there's a shopping area with a restaurant just minutes down this highway," he said as a large complex of shopping restaurants and community service buildings appeared at the approaching crossroads.

"Looks like the place—let's find some lunch and get to headquarters about one." Kelly turned the vehicle into a large parking lot and spotted the restaurant.

⸎

Will Richards had arrived at his mill site late. On the way to work he'd spotted a full load of used poles headed out of town toward the freeway, the opposite direction from what it should've been going. As the *White Western Star* truck and its load passed him, Will turned around and followed at a safe distance behind. The load worked its way onto the

TransCanada Highway and he followed the route eastbound. The driver took the 264th Street ramp and headed north toward the Fraser River. About half way between 72nd and 88th Avenues, the driver swung into a dirt side road, in the middle of nowhere.

Will couldn't see through the dense brush, and parked a hundred or so meters up the road, lifted the hood of his pickup truck to indicate engine trouble, grabbed his digital camera, and locked the door. He walked to the turnoff and carefully hugged the perimeter of the dense brush to avoid being detected.

"I knew these bastards were taking the best wood! I told *ComTek* that I get the crap and someone else gets the cream. I need proof that these good poles are being diverted!" he muttered as he crouched down, proceeding along the dirt roadway. Will eventually saw the parked log trailer and the truck driver was talking to a short, stout man, overweight and dressed in logging-type overalls. Will moved a little farther ahead, and he spotted a portable mill setup. The operation appeared to have been operating for an extended period of time, as there were large piles of saw dust and wood cuttings aligned along the perimeter of the bush.

Will had heard stories of loads that had been redirected to small mill sites that processed the prime wood without environmental controls and authority from *ComTek*. The stories told of scams that were orchestrated by line crews and job foremen, selling the poles for cash. The prime product from the job sites was sold privately and Will received the lesser quality and construction junk.

He took his photographs with his camera, and returned to his vehicle before he was seen, slamming down the hood of the truck. "I knew this activity must be going on! I wonder how many more operations there are, screwing me out of my profits."

Will jumped back into his vehicle, started the engine, and continued driving along the road past the illegitimate mill site. He glared angrily at the road as he turned at the next stop sign and headed back to his office. He was pissed off, and wondered what he should do with this new evidence, and wondered if *ComTek* even cared.

⚹

The Surrey RCMP's head facility was located in a new, concrete, two-story building situated in a large municipal complex that housed the School District's administration offices, the Provincial Law Courts, and the Surrey Municipal Government Operations Centre among others. RCMP employee parking was at the rear of the building, and was controlled by an electronic entry system. Kelly parked in the visitors' parking zone on the west side of the building, and the two detectives proceeded to enter the lobby of the precinct.

Simon approached the receptionist. "We're Detectives O'Brian and Chung and we've an appointment to see Captain Christopher Anderson. He's expecting us."

"Please take a seat and I'll tell him that you're here," the young woman directed.

The large open foyer was well appointed, and was busy with the comings and goings of all types of people. The two detectives waited in silence as they watched the parade of activity pass through the lobby.

"Detectives, Captain Anderson can see you now," the young woman called out.

The detectives returned to the counter for directions.

"Go down this hallway and take the elevator to the second floor. You'll find an officer in the lobby as you exit and you'll be directed from there." The young woman smiled and pointed toward the hall, then returned to her duties. The two detectives followed their instructions and found the officer as they had been told.

"We're here to see Captain Anderson," Simon said with a smile.

"He's expecting you two. Please follow this corridor to the front of the building, turn left, and proceed to the end office," the officer replied, returning the smile and pointing in the general direction.

The pair of detectives followed a concrete wall toward the front of the building. The hallway turned along the face of glassed-in offices and ended at the large office situated on the front corner of the floor. The door was open, and Kelly knocked on the lacquered pine surface.

"Come in, please," the voice from the room invited. "Ah … Detectives O'Brian and Chung, come and sit down."

The warm tone in his voice helped ease their tension. "I'm happy to accommodate Captain Hollingsworth with your investigation, Detectives. We don't often get a request from West Vancouver to work a Surrey case!"

The head man was in his early forties, had a slim build, sandy hair cut close to the scalp, and a well-trimmed mustache. He wore a light, sandy-colored suit, white dress shirt, and striped, beige tie.

"We appreciate being allowed to camp here while we try to crack our case, and the support of your detectives turning over their current filings, Sir," Simon replied as he returned the smile and looked about the tasteful surroundings.

"Well, we've a few offices that we reserve for just this type of situation, or to accommodate the Feds when they're here. You've been assigned the office two doors down from mine. See Officer Olson who greeted you when you arrived, and she'll provide you with things that you'll need during your stay. I believe your case files are waiting for you on one of the desks inside the office, and I expect to be kept current on your progress. Good luck, Detectives."

"Thank you, Sir!" Simon replied, and he and Kelly left the office.

They wandered back to the officer outside the elevator.

"Here's your package that contains all the information you'll need during your stay with us." The woman handed Kelly the envelope. "It includes your parking gate code and your personal passwords for computer network access. Let me know if you need anything else."

"Okay, great, Officer Olson," Kelly replied taking the envelope. "Thank you!"

The pair walked back to their assigned office. It had large, glass windows that opened onto the side street in the front of the building. There were two executive-type office desks, a book case, and each desk was outfitted with individual computers, which shared a printer sitting on a table placed between the desks. The stacks of reports were waiting for them as described. Each detective selected a desk and they hung their coats on a coat-tree that was behind the door.

"Wow, what a setup!" Kelly exclaimed, looking about the office.

"You'd better not get too comfortable—this is only a temporary gig, remember!"

"Yea, let's unpack and look at these reports to see what we've got," Kelly replied as she turned to face two small piles of reports on the corner of the desk that she had selected. "Here're yours." She grabbed one of the piles and placed it on Simon's desk.

They both took their seats and began to review the materials and documents in the files.

"Hey, look at this report from Detective Haslow. The investigation of the B&E at *ComTek* where they found Castillo's prints indicated that Castillo and a partner were after something unknown in the back office, according to the guard. The lab wasn't able to find any substance on the floor of the storage room and the loose end is still outstanding," Kelly said, reading the first report and continued to read out loud to Simon. "Another report possibly ties Castillo to a murder the day before the B&E. The victim is a Terry Peters, the foreman of the *ComTek* office that Castillo and his unknown partner burglarized." Kelly glanced over at Simon. "Ricardo Sanchez told me about Peters' murder when I told him about Antonio Castillo's prints that were found at that pole yard break-in."

"That explains why there're files here on the Peters murder and the evidence collected to date. Apparently there's surveillance video from the hotel where Peters was murdered, too, but it hasn't been viewed yet. Also there's a note that some evidence of blond pubic hair from the murder scene has been gathered and sent for analysis, but no reports on the findings are here," Simon said, still reading notes from Detective Greenwall. "It looks like it's a woman and some sexual encounter that went wrong. No murder suspects have been identified yet, though."

"Hmm ... all this sounds too coincidental for me!" Kelly muttered. "Look, it's getting late in the afternoon and we should see what the traffic will be like returning back to downtown. What do ya say we shelve this until the morning?"
"Okay, there's a lot of stuff here that we've got to sort out. We need to determine our priorities, and try to piece the entire

picture together before pushing out in some direction." Simon sighed, and placed the reports back onto the side of his desk.

Chapter Twenty

It was already Thursday morning and the week seemed to be rapidly disappearing as the two detectives arrived at the Surrey RCMP office. The two *Tim Hortons*® coffees had been finished long before the partners had arrived and parked in the secure RCMP lot. It was going to be a busy day, and the partners knew it.

They both sat in their comfortable surroundings and began to make notes of interest, pulling information from the myriad of reports and photographs supplied by the Surrey teams.

"I don't see much that's going to help us with Antonio Castillo, as there's nothing on the reported accomplice that the guard said he heard in the back room of the *ComTek* pole yard building," Kelly commented as she put down another file folder.

"I think we should work on the Terry Peters homicide then and see where that goes. Maybe Castillo's involved with the suspect woman or something. Let's get the *Fraser Head Hotel* video files and review those first. There must be some connection, as the *ComTek* B&E appears to be a common factor between Castillo and Peters," Simon suggested, looking for the folder that had the video CD disks.

"Ah … here we go!" Simon said, "KO, there's a cover note that says, 'This data disk contains video streams from the Fraser Head Hotel taken from multiple video feeds, which have been burned onto this one CD. The video clips cover the twenty-four-hour period beginning the morning of the estimated time of Terry Peters' murder, which was set at noon Monday. The only cameras recording activity are placed in the front lobby, viewing the reception counter and cash till, and one for the front parking lot and one for the rear.'"

"Hmm ... the hotel supplied only one copy, so we'll have to share a monitor to view the data files." Simon smiled as he pulled the CD from its white paper cover. He inserted it into his computer's CD reader as Kelly dragged her chair next to Simon.

"Ah ..." Simon remarked as he looked through the listed set of files, "let's pick the front lobby first." He clicked the file and started the video player.

"Okay ... there's Peters at eleven fifty-two according to the time stamp, taking a room key as he hands over cash." Kelly pointed to the screen as the video continued to play. "He heads toward the elevator and moves away from the camera."

The video continued to play as the pair of detectives studied the footage up to the twelve-thirty time mark, then Simon paused the play. "Humph! The only thing we've got in this time period is one brunette, female, teenager, about eighteen who's dressed a little provocatively."

"Hmm ... she's likely a hooker, considering the type of hotel that we're dealing with. We'd better check her out though, she may be wearing a wig or something, and really be a blond beneath that getup," Kelly suggested as she noted the data stream file number and time stamp, and then she pressed play to resume the video. The teen reappeared twenty-two minutes after she had arrived and headed out of the hotel. No additional females appeared before one fifteen that afternoon.

"The hotel manager's statement said that the rear entrance door of the hotel was locked, and only special customers that keep rooms on a monthly arrangement have access keys," Kelly continued, as she recalled one of the investigation reports.

"Hmm ... we'd best look at the rear door file then—it's the only other entrance into the hotel," Simon replied as he pointed to the file displayed on the monitor. He selected the video and the stream began. "Hmm ... this is really poor footage. The camera seems out of focus," he sighed, peering at the images.

"Yea ... hmm ... it's interesting that it's the surveillance feed at the back of the hotel where the special monthly customers have access," Kelly replied, as she frowned while checking the images that provided little detail. "Hey, look! I think we've got a blond female with a key at twelve-o-five. Isn't security a wonderful thing! Stop the feed, Simon!" Kelly remarked as she took a closer look at the figure on the screen. "It's impossible to tell much about her features, as the camera's out of focus and pointed toward the parking lot, but maybe she's our gal."

"Humph!" Simon muttered, taking his turn to peer at the blurry image. "She may be a hooker with a key or one of the regular patrons. Funny, she had a key and our victim rented a standard room. That doesn't fit if regular room-holders already have a designated specific room!"

"We need to get a list of all the key-holders and assigned rooms," Simon concluded, knowing that it was their only lead.

Kelly made a note of the task and noted the file and time stamp of the rear video feed as well. "While we're out at the *Fraser Head Hotel*, we should pay the medical examiner a visit and check on the progress on the hairs extracted from the victim. I believe that the hospital's just up the road from this hotel."

Simon's cell rang, breaking the pair's concentration. "Hello, Detective Chung here." He listened to the caller for a moment, hung up, and displayed a wide grin. "We've prints from the Dyke bust and our mystery James' last name is Gobbles. He's got a rap sheet and we've an address! He lives in Burnaby." Simon grinned. "We can go past his place later on our way home, so let's work on the local Surrey stops we've got first and then pay Mr. Gobbles a visit."

Kelly recalled that she was expected to return Ricardo's phone call from the prior night, and dialed his number. "Hey big boy, thought that I'd forgotten ya?"

"Well, I know how it gets. How're you doing, KO?" He paused, then asked, "Would tonight be a good date night? I'd love to see ya again."

"Love to, but I think I'll need to tail Antonio Castillo tonight when his lawyer gets the bail documents completed and posts the bond. Tomorrow's open, and besides I'm working out of the Surrey detachment for a while and I might be able to see ya later this afternoon for a quick coffee."

"Hmm ... don't know about that! I've a report due and I've got to get it finished. Let's connect tomorrow," Ricardo replied, sounding very busy.

"Yea, okay. We can see if that works tomorrow." Kelly sounded surprised and disappointed.

"What was that all about?" Simon asked when Kelly disconnected the call.

"Oh ... I remembered that Antonio Castillo's likely to be released tonight and we might have a chance to see where he goes when he's released. Want to come along?" she replied with a grin.

The detectives retrieved their vehicle and headed for the *Fraser Head Hotel*, about fifteen minutes away from the precinct. The desk clerk was not at the check-in counter when the detectives arrived. Simon rang the desk bell, hoping to arouse some attention, and a minute later a middle-aged man appeared. "Can I help ya? If you need a room I can give ya a better rate if ya need it for less than two hours," the man offered with a devilish grin, noticing that his guests didn't have any luggage.

Kelly pulled out her gold shield and placed it on the counter, a little surprised that he thought Simon and she were there for a room. "RCMP, we're investigating the homicide here on Monday. We're Detectives O'Brian and Chung," Kelly growled as though she had been insulted.

"Ah ... we do get a lot of short-term customers in here and we do have overhead to cover ya know. Besides, I've already talked to the cops. What are ya two looking for?" the clerk asked, peering at Kelly's badge and then glancing at her shapely figure.

"We understand that you've a special rate for long-term customers, is that correct?" Simon redirected the man's attention from his attractive partner as Kelly grabbed her badge from the counter.

"Yea that's right, and they're privileged with confidentiality and private access. They're provided their own room key that's coded and designed to look like any other house key," the man explained, trying to keep his voice low so others couldn't hear the conversation.

"Does that key provide entrance through the rear door of the hotel?"

"Yea, it's cut to provide the private access from the back, as many of our customers don't wish to enter through the front lobby. It also allows access to the specific room that's dedicated to that client," the man answered, returning his inquiring stare to again ogle Kelly.

"Hey man, I'm talking to you!" Simon said annoyed. "Do you have a list of these clients that we can look at?"

"No, that's privileged information. You'll need a court order to see that list. Besides, most of those clients pay in cash, and there's no registered name. So long as we receive their payment on the agreed date, they continue to have access. If we get a client who decides the room's no longer required, and we don't receive payment, the room's lock is changed."

"Hmm ... that unpaid client will still have access to the rear entrance, though," Simon picked up on the gap in security.

"Well, maybe only for a little while, but not the room. We'll change the keys and arrange an exchange with the other clients. They'll have thirty days to exchange their keys before we activate the new master rear door lock. Not perfect, but acceptable for around here and it's never been a problem. Any more questions, Detectives?" the man asked, glancing up at Simon.

"We'll be back with that warrant for your list," Simon replied, as he pulled his cell phone from his pocket and selected the number as he and Kelly left the hotel.

"Hello, Officer Olson, it's Detective Chung. I need a warrant for access to the *Fraser Head Hotel*'s customer lists and records of clients for the last ninety days. It's in regard to the Terry Peters murder and we need to see that information. Can you arrange that for us, please?" Simon paused to listen. "Ah yea, the *Fraser Head Hotel*, that's right. Thanks." Simon sighed and hung up. "She knows the ropes around here, so hopefully that won't take long. I noticed the Provincial Court is across the street from our office."

The *Surrey Memorial Hospital* was only a short drive up the street from the hotel, and the duo determined that a chat with the medical examiner was the next stop. They found the ME doing his job in a large theater in the basement, a room much larger than the one in *St. Paul's*. Simon knocked on the swinging door and they entered.

"Good morning, Doctor, we're Detectives O'Brian and Chung and we're here to discuss the Terry Peters case. Have you completed the tests on the blond hairs that were found on that victim?" Kelly asked as she looked around the sterile white room.

"Yes, I was about to send my findings to your office, but I have it here," he replied as he stopped peering at a cadaver stretched out on his table. He removed his surgical gloves while he walked to a small desk and snatched a folder. He opened the folder, and extracted a sheet and read the results of the test. "The blond hair was definitely a woman's and I extracted a DNA sample for you. I found tadalafil in the victim's system in an amount that indicated the victim took Cialis® shortly before he was murdered. That drug is prescribed for men with erectile disorder, not uncommon with men his age. The dosage in his system was higher than the common daily prescribed amount, so that indicates that Mr. Peters didn't expect to have sex regularly. I also doubt that the blond woman was petite, as the bruises on his buttocks caused by her sitting on him while he was on the toilet seat would indicate a woman with good-sized hips and a weight of about one hundred and thirty-five pounds."

"Thanks, Doc. Can we keep this copy of the report?" Kelly asked, moving toward the man to take the document.

"Sorry, this is my copy. Yours will be at your office by noon."

"Okay, great!" Kelly replied as the pair left the room and stood in the hall. "Hmm ... men don't usually carry around prescribed doses of Cialis® at work, eh Simon?"

Simon smiled. "You're asking me?"

"Ah ... no!" Kelly laughed. "I mean that the ME said that the dosage wasn't the daily amount so Peters must've been expecting the sexual encounter that day—you know, the higher dosage when the opportunity presents itself."

"Hmm ... so you think that the sex was preplanned, and believe that it wasn't with a hooker because the woman had a backdoor key," Simon thought for a moment. "Maybe he had the Cialis® in his wallet, like some guys carry condoms, and that would rule out your preplanned theory, KO."

"Yea, hmm ... hey partner, it's already past lunch hour. How about grabbing a bite and motoring out to Burnaby and visit our James Gobbles lead?" Kelly suggested. "I remember seeing a *Denny's*® next to the *Fraser Head*. How about that place—it's just back down the street?"

The clouds began to sprinkle rain drops on the sedan's windshield as the detectives followed the GPS directions to James Gobbles' Spruce Street address. It was midafternoon as Kelly drove past a neighborhood cemetery, and turned into Spruce Street. She turned off the navigation system. "That thing can be a little annoying with that female voice. It's a great device, but it can be too much of a good thing sometimes, eh."

Simon bit his tongue as there was an opportunity for a smart comment, but this wasn't the time to make it. "I'm just glad that this sprinkle isn't a downpour. Let's get this done."

A *Bug Busters Computer Services* delivery van was parked in the street, telling the pair that their suspect was likely home. The residence was a small square pre-war single-story house, and looked just like all the others in the street. The majority of the homes were well kept with small lawns, and the street was lined with large oak trees, all of which had lost all their leaves.

Each detached home had a fence between the lots, some wire and some wooden. Simon worked his way around the back through an unlocked wooden gate, and Kelly took the front door.

She waited for her partner to get into position. "James Gobbles, this is the RCMP, please open your door." Kelly knocked firmly on the metal screen door. "We know you're in there, so come to the door."

The front wooden door opened and a security chain stretched across the frame as the man peered through the opening. "I'm James Gobbles. What do you want?" A pitted face eyed the woman standing on his stoop, who had opened the screen door and stood to the side of the opening, holding her detective's shield where he could see it.

"Come out, you need to come down to the station with us for a talk," Kelly demanded gruffly.

"Why, I've done nothing wrong. Harass someone else," the man growled and started to close the chained door.

"Open the door and come out where I can see your hands, or I'll kick the door in, your choice," she insisted, almost yelling at him.

"Okay, okay. Don't get your panties in a knot. Let me unbolt the door, and I'll come out."

"Don't screw with me or it'll be a big mistake!" Kelly growled.

The door closed and Kelly heard the sliding bolt drag through the channel and the chain drop. The door opened and the blond-haired man stood in the doorway, wearing drawstring jogging pants and a white tank top.

"All clear, Simon!" Kelly yelled as she held the door open.

Simon joined the pair, and the group entered the house. "It's time for a visit. Sit down!" Simon pointed to an old sofa in the living room that overlooked the street. The incoming rain clouds made the room dark, and Simon found a light switch. "You've an interesting computer repair business and it seems you find more than bugs in the motherboards, isn't that right, James?" Simon paused for a moment. "It looks like you and Darryl are distributing, eh knucklehead?"

"Look, Darryl's just a part-time helper moving the boxes for me. I just pick the stuff up and take them to the warehouse in Surrey and wait to be told where to take them next, that's all I do."

"Okay, go on, we're listening," Simon replied, peering at the man.

"I just get text messages as to what I'm to do. I don't even know what's in the boxes, and I don't care. I get an envelope left at the warehouse with cash once every two weeks," Gobbles continued with the story, and pointed to the BlackBerry® cell phone on the front table. "I've got it on vibrate, so not to attract any attention, and I just respond to the messages."

"Who's at the other end?" Kelly asked, picking up the phone.

"I only know his first name as Giermo, nothing else. I've never talked with him face to face."

"Okay, here's the program. We're going to take ya to the precinct until we check out your story. When do ya expect another text?"

"I should get something in the next day or so, to get instructions as to where to take the shipment that's already in the warehouse."

"Where did ya pick up that shipment that's now in the warehouse?"

"I get most of those from *ComTek* in Surrey."

The two detectives glanced at each other when they heard *ComTek*. "How did that work?" Kelly asked confused.

"I get a text, telling me that a shipment's ready for pickup at *ComTek,* and I go to the Investment Recovery building on 66th. The shipment's usually ready on the dock. I sign a release, really a scribble that can't be read, load the van and drop off the shipment at the warehouse on Dyke Road." James took a breath and then continued, "Monday was such a shitty day and I got a flat. I came home to change and didn't go back to the warehouse until Tuesday. I called Darryl and told him to go home as I decided to stay home. I knew something must've been up, as Darryl's car was still in the parking space when I delivered the shipment the next day. Knowing that Darryl's somewhat unreliable, I didn't think too much about it."

"Okay, James, we're going to give ya a ride to lockup while we sort all this out," Simon said. "Get properly dressed for your appointment downtown. Don't get any stupid ideas either!"

Kelly waited for the man to leave the sitting room. "Simon, that story doesn't fit with the break-in. I think that something else must be going on over at *ComTek*! Ya know, some of the facts don't add up for me. Why break into the pole-yard building and take something stored in the back and use *ComTek*'s recycling building as a transfer station for drugs as well? It looked like Antonio Castillo was the key to the drug activity and the break-in, but the shell computers were being processed across the street. We need more pieces," Kelly said in a low voice, and then sighed.

"Ah ... it's getting dark and wet," Simon replied with a frown. "I know that we were going to tail Antonio tonight after he's released, but ya know that was a long shot!" he glanced over at the BlackBerry® on the front table. "I think that it's a far better bet to get this Giermo character using Gobbles' cell phone. What ya say that we scrap the tail and go home. I'll keep the cell phone and monitor it for any incoming texts. If a message comes in, Giermo won't know it's me and I can set some type of trap. What do ya think, eh?"

"Hmm ... yea, that's a better idea. I'll take ya home after we drop off our friend here at the precinct." She nodded her head and got up and grabbed the BlackBerry®. "Hey, James! Get your ass in gear! It's time we got goin'."

Chapter Twenty One

It was about six thirty in the evening by the time that Karl Kuntz had posted the bail for Antonio Castillo. West Vancouver was situated close to the mountains, and it became very cold and the rain was heavy. Karl had agreed with Giermo to take Antonio home to his Pandora Street apartment. The quickest route was to proceed over the Second Narrows Bridge and backtrack to East Vancouver on Hastings. No route would be very fast in the rain, and six thirty was at the tail end of the rush hour. Taking the trip through the core of Vancouver via the Lions Gate Bridge was not an option, so Karl elected the least of two evils.

Karl had had to park on the street behind the West Vancouver RCMP precinct on Bellevue, and as they left the building, he saw that there were now a few more empty parking spaces than when he'd arrived, some thirty-five minutes earlier. He didn't notice the black Hummer parked a half block down the street, and certainly didn't notice that the driver was watching him.

"Damn rain—it sure makes a messy and slow drive in this city!" Karl grumbled to Antonio, as they climbed into the red, sports Mercedes. "Don't smoke in my car!" he snapped at Antonio, as the scrawny man pulled a cigarette from a pack.

"The quickest route to the expressway's back to 15th Street," Karl muttered, talking to himself as he buckled up. The red, sleek vehicle pulled out of the parking space and waited for the light on Marine. The black Hummer followed, windshield wipers clearing the pelting rain to allow the driver's view of the Mercedes.

Traffic began to thin out, as the sports car rounded the highway on-ramp and entered the fast flowing stream of vehicles on the TransCanada Highway travelling eastward. Drivers usually didn't alter their speed, rain or shine, and the sports car accelerated to keep pace, leveling out its speed at just over one hundred and five kilometers an hour. The black Hummer tagged along some six vehicles behind.

The low-slung sedan had wide sports tires, and the vehicle was prone to hydroplaning in the heavy rain, so Karl kept his car in the slower, inside lane.

"Look at that idiot!" Karl growled as a vehicle flashed by, far exceeding the speed limit.

"Well, man, you're drivin' like an old lady in this thing!" Antonio frowned in reply.

The expressway required both skill and attention to drive in the wet conditions, as there were curvy areas and there would be a steep drop in elevation as the roadway met the Second Narrows Bridge. Karl had reached the Lynn Valley Interchange and knew that the steep roadway decline was approaching. He felt his vehicle pick up speed as the gravity sucked the traffic down the paved funnel. Most vehicles continued to pass him in the fast lane, leaving his sports car in a mist of wet wash and dirty spray.

The black Hummer pulled into the fast lane, and like a bullet, swerved and hit the sports car just as the roadway curved in its approach to the framed, steel bridge. "What are you doing, asshole?" Karl yelled as he yanked the steering wheel back to the left, trying to bring his sports car back into the lane.

The Hummer swerved and hit the car a second time, just moments before the bridge appeared. "Holy shit!" Karl screamed, eyes bulging in his head as his red Mercedes jumped the soft shoulder barrier, hit the bridge frame, and careened down the embankment to the river bed far below.

The Hummer took the immediate exit on the right, and disappeared from the expressway. It continued along the narrow, ramp roadway under the highway and slowed down to the posted speed limit. The driver checked to see if he'd been followed off the expressway, and noted that no obvious observer seemed to have followed. Brake lights at the scene near the bridge lit up the accident site as the Hummer driver proceeded up the service road, past a pub and moved into a deserted area bordered by dense bush on the right. A sign marking the entrance to the Inter-River Park pointed toward a side road to the left.

"That fixed that problem!" the driver muttered, stopping the Hummer in the empty parking lot of the park. The driver climbed out into the dark, wet night, and set a small paper fire under the front seat of the vehicle, and then set out quickly on foot.

Ten minutes later the Hummer was engulfed in flames and the driver had boosted a parked green Honda from a nearby condo complex. The Honda took the approach ramp, and proceeded onto the expressway and over the Second Narrows Bridge heading east.

The driver looked back at the snarled interchange through the Honda's rearview mirror. "I've promised to watch Giermo's back!" the driver muttered, as he accelerated the Honda down the highway and blended in with the stream of commuters rushing to get home.

♓

Kelly O'Brian approached the bright night lights of Chinatown, thinking about the events of the day as she drove Simon home.

"When's the last time you've had Chinese?" Simon asked the woman, who was navigating her way through the gridlock of the evening rush.

"It's been a while for the authentic stuff!" she replied as her eyes stayed glued to the traffic.

"Well, I'm not a cook, but I do know the places to go. How about parking this car, and the two of us can enjoy an evening together as friends?" Simon asked, testing to see if she would spend some time outside the office. "No talking about the case. It's a rule of the evening!"

"Man, you're going to be a tough date, eh?" Kelly grinned.

"Park behind my place, there's usually at least one spot. I'll put my ID in the window and the car will be okay there."

Kelly followed his direction and found a suitable parking stall.

"You know, the place across the street with the red awning has great food. I often do take-out, but the atmosphere's an experience," Simon suggested, thinking that it would be good to know Kelly on a more personal basis, and Chinese food was a wonderful way to share dishes and stories.

The restaurant owner knew Simon, and greeted him as though he was his own son. The couple was taken to the best table in the house.

"I don't order here, the owner just brings things. I love the surprise," Simon said with a smile as he settled into the small booth where they had been directed. "So KO, you seem to love the chase and the discovery. You have keen intuition and you're going to be a great detective one day."

"Yea, well I'm intrigued with solving mysteries, and I've grown to be patient in the process of gathering and considering any new finds or clues," she replied, sitting in the old, red leather seat as a waiter appeared.

Simon ordered some red house wine. "Chinese goes best with red," he said, "at least I think so."

"Yea, I like red." Kelly grinned. "It's my turn ... what's your story, Simon? You like to break in green detectives?"

Simon laughed. "Well ... my father passed away many years ago and I stayed in Chinatown to look after my mother. She's seventy-two now, and lives in the next block over from my apartment. I appreciate my heritage and the community way of life. It seems to calm me, and it gives me an escape from the tragedies we deal with every day," he continued after the waiter brought the wine to the table and poured two glasses. "As far as breaking in new detectives, well I enjoy the enthusiasm of new blood and I get challenged, too. That keeps me sharp!"

Kelly studied the man for a moment. "Hmm ... never married? You're a good-looking guy," Kelly prodded and took a sip of her wine.

"Ah, no more questions tonight," Simon replied as the food arrived, and it was time to enjoy the feast.

It was almost nine before Kelly reached home. She had enjoyed the day but found that she was tense. There wasn't any phone message from Ricardo, but she really hadn't expected one since they had connected earlier in the day. "Hmm ... it would've been nice to hear his voice anyway," she muttered, wishing that it had been Ricardo, rather than Simon, who she had shared dinner with.

She turned on her iPod®, selected Celine Dion from her play list, pressed play, and dimmed her sitting room lights. She wanted to relax, and the lower lighting and soft music created a soothing mood for her.

Kelly quickly stripped from her work clothes, washed her face in some soothing cream, and slipped on a sexy top. She pulled down her bed covers and went to the kitchen to find a pair of scented candles and a lighter, and lit the wicks so the flame could melt the aroma from the wax. Humming to the music, she let her mind wander and float to the rhythm and beat of the music.

The music faded from her consciousness as she relaxed, crawled under her bed covers and closed her eyes, just for a moment.

♓

Ricardo Sanchez arrived home late, which he had known would be the case. Hunter was waiting patiently as his master entered the apartment. "How're you doing, Hunter? Let's take our walk," he said as he placed the leash on the dog's collar, and grabbed a rain-resistant overcoat and baseball cap to protect him from the driving rain and wind that was now running up the river.

He had taken Hunter out for a walk earlier that afternoon, anticipating the late night that would be required to complete his business. Ricardo's *ComTek* office was located at *Central City Towers*, just fifteen minutes away from his New West home, which made it convenient to check on Hunter as situations dictated.

The walk was long enough to allow Hunter to take care of his needs and both were happy to return to the dry protection of the condo. Removing Hunter's leash and his own rain gear, Ricardo refilled the dog's food bowl and refreshed his water. "I'm going out for a short while. Be a good dog and I'll see you in a bit," Ricardo told the dog as he stroked his companion's back, and then went to the bathroom to freshen up.

Ricardo changed his clothes to a casual, open-necked shirt and dress pants. He pulled on a jacket, grabbed his keys, and left the apartment, locking the door behind him.

He left the *ComTek* truck in its stall and opened his Audi R8 silver-gray sports Coupe. The *Paddle Wheeler Bar and Casino* was moments down the road, moored at the key at the end of his road. The old paddlewheel boat had been retrofitted into a hot spot for singles, and was open until two in the morning. He often walked to the key, but with the driving rain and the possibility of returning with a companion, he chose to drive.

The bar and the casino were buzzing with patrons looking to have a lucky evening. Ricardo found an empty bar stool, ordered a Scotch and water, an appetizer of nachos and guacamole, and began looking about the bar, noting the single women of the evening.

In less than an hour Ricardo was leaving the bar with a tall blond on his arm, who was laughing at some story that he had told. He opened his car door, allowing the woman to get into her bucket seat. The trip back to the apartment was short, and the pair rushed inside, removing their coats, dumping them on the floor as the apartment door closed.

"Lay down!" Ricardo instructed the dog as Hunter came to the door to great his friend.

The seductive slim woman was inviting, and as they kissed and kicked off their shoes, they embraced each other's inner mouths with their tongues. "Ah!" Ricardo exhaled, as the woman unbuttoned his open shirt, pulling it aside and yanking it off his body. She invaded his mouth again, and grazed her teeth along his lower lip as he found the zipper of her long, sleek, red dress, guided it down her back to the top of her buttocks.

"Mmm!" she murmured as he artfully peeled off the dress from her shoulders, letting it drop onto the floor as she feverishly undid his belt and unzipped his pants.

Both displayed large grins as he pulled off his pants and stepped over them, pressing his body into hers, feeling her heart pound with desire. She ran her hands under his shorts, caressing his hairy buttocks as he reached behind her, unclipped the red, laced bra and slid the straps to the front of her shapely arms. "Ah … ah!" the woman exhaled as she pulled off the brassiere, and their bodies slammed against the foyer wall, Ricardo cupping her breast that loomed large and inviting in front of him.

"Ah … ah!" Ricardo pulled himself from her grasp, pulled his shorts to the floor and quickly led the lusting woman to his bedroom. She grinned, yanked off her lace panties, pushed him onto his back on the mattress and climbed onto his intoxicating frame. The dog jumped off the bed and curled up in the corner of the bedroom floor.

"You … ah … live around here?" he asked, but she didn't stop to answer.

Chapter Twenty Two

Kelly O'Brian woke to her alarm bellowing that a new day had begun. The candles had burned themselves out and the iPod® player had shut itself off. She felt refreshed and all the tense feelings seemed to have been eradicated from her body.

This Friday morning was bright; the storm of the night before had surrendered, and the rain clouds were dissipating, allowing strips of light blue to bleed through the sky. Kelly inhaled the cold brisk air as she ran her predetermined jogging route, and pushed her endurance to its limit. She couldn't wait to begin the day and work on unraveling the *ComTek* mystery. Her breathing was labored as she returned to her apartment and prepared for work, refreshed and reenergized.

⋇

Ricardo Sanchez was awakened by the rustling sound of the naked woman gathering her clothing in the front room. From the corner of his eye, he saw her sensual body get dressed, and he watched her slip out of the apartment without a word. He sat up in the bed, and Hunter joined him, glad to have his space returned to him. The night before flashed through Ricardo's consciousness and he smiled as he jumped from his bed, noting the extent of the disruption of the bedding and realized that he didn't recall the woman's name. He'd only a few short hours of sleep, but he was energized nevertheless, and pulled on a warm jogging outfit to take Hunter out for his morning stroll.

The morning blue stripes in the sky reflected off the surface of the water flowing down the Fraser, to meet its destination at the mouth that feeds the Strait of Georgia.

⋇

Kelly found Simon at his Chinatown crosswalk, and grinned as he joined her in the car. "I think that we should go directly to *ComTek* this morning and interview the manager responsible for that Investment Recovery operation, and see what we can dig up," she said as Simon closed the passenger door.

"Good morning to you, too!" Simon smiled as they headed for Surrey. "Sure, let's see what's going on over there."

※

Will Richards had decided to arrive late to his mill, and phoned Ray Patterson to have him organize the startup and ensure that all the workers had all their safety gear on before they left the crew trailer. Will needed to complete gathering company paperwork to take to Thomas Howe, who had agreed to prepare the annual financials required for *ComTek* and the tax department.

While Will was stuffing documents into labeled folders, his cell phone rang. "*Service Pole Recycling*," Will responded, and listened to the caller without interrupting. His eyes grew wide, and a large smile pushed away the strained look on his face.

"That's wonderful news! When and where can we meet to discuss this opportunity in more detail?" Will asked excitedly. "Uh ... okay. Can I bring my accountant to the meeting? He knows the financials better than I do!"

Happy with the response, Will scribbled down the meeting place. "I must check with my accountant, but would six thirty tonight work for you?"

Will hung up and quickly dialed Thomas's home number, and heard the phone ring a couple of times before it was answered. "Hello, Will, what brings you to call at this time of day, bud?"

"I just received a call, and there's a group of people interested in purchasing the mill! I said that I wanted you to attend and they agreed. Can you join us for a six thirty dinner meeting?"

"Uh ... sure, what do you want me to do?"

"Just come, that's all. I don't know any details, so we'll have to see what they have to say, and listen to their offer. The meeting's at the *Kingshead Pub* on 200th. I'll meet you there." Will paused for a moment, and then asked, "So how's the consulting going?"

"Well, ah ... I've finished with the bank. They take too much of the client fee and I've lots of overhead in working with those guys. I'm looking at some other interesting opportunities, though. Let's talk later."

"Yea, okay. See ya later!" Will responded, then hung up to think about the unexpected proposition.

♓

The gray, unmarked police car pulled into the *ComTek* side road alongside the large warehouse, and stopped at the guard station. Kelly showed him her ID and the guard gave her directions to the sales building.

Candice Parks was in her office working on a report for Brian Quest, when Simon knocked on her doorframe. The front office receptionist wasn't at her station, and the two detectives proceeded to the only enclosed office, assuming it belonged to the manager. Candice looked up from her work, aware that a couple of customers were coming, as she noticed them through her large office front window. "Can I get someone to help you?"

"We're looking for the manager. Is that you, Madam?" Simon asked as he studied the attractive woman.

"Yes, I'm the manager, Candice Parks. How may I help you?"

"I'm Detective Chung and this is my partner Detective O'Brian. May we come into your office and talk to you in private?" Simon pulled his gold shield out and showed the woman, as the two took a seat. Simon glanced over at Kelly. "We're investigating Terry Peters' murder, and we want to interview his co-workers and the managers who work here. We don't want to disrupt the business operations, so we're asking if you can join us at our office where we won't be disturbed. We don't expect to have your morning interrupted for very long."

Both detectives watched closely the woman's reaction and body language. They sat patiently waiting for their answer. Candice became very nervous, and appeared a little flushed. "I've some work that I must complete—can this be done later?"

"We'd appreciate you taking the time now, please, Ms. Parks. We promise to keep this as short as we can," Simon rose, indicating that the conversation was finished and that Candice should comply with his firm request.

Candice considered the situation for a moment, and knew that it wasn't a wise thing to appear uncooperative. "Ah ... okay, I'll leave a note on my secretary's desk explaining that I'll be out for a while," she replied, and jotted a note on a yellow sticky note.

Candice climbed into the rear seat of the unmarked sedan, and the two detectives took their places and proceeded to the Surrey detachment. Kelly parked in one of the designated visitor's spaces in the secured lot, and the two accompanied Candice to their office on the second floor. No one had said a word during the short drive, but Kelly had watched the woman closely in the rearview mirror during the short drive. She felt that Candice appeared to be trying to maintain her composure, as she sat stiffly, staring forward without looking about.

"Can I get you some coffee while we chat?" Simon asked as the group reached the office.

Candice took a large breath, "Yes please, with a little milk. Thank you. I've never been around this complex before. It sure is bigger that I would've imagined."

"Well, we hope not to take too much of your time, Ms. Parks, and we'll be speaking with many of the employees working at *ComTek* in Surrey." Kelly paused, and then got to the point. "Had you known Terry Peters very long, Ms. Parks?"

Candice could feel her heart pound rapidly in her chest and tried to fight back the anxiety, "Oh, I'd say over fifteen years. We both have been working at *ComTek* a long time."

Simon returned with a single coffee, and handed it to Candice and then joined the conversation.

"Would you've any idea who would want to hurt Mr. Peters, or did you know of any problems he might have had?" Kelly continued with the questioning.

"I know that …" Candice hesitated while she searched for an answer that would direct the detectives in a direction away from her. "Terry wasn't liked very much by Will Richards who's running that independent pole recycling mill at the back of the *ComTek* pole yard. Something was going on between them, I think. Other than that, I can't think of anything else."

"Hmm … thank you, we'll make a visit to see Mr. Richards as well then, and see if he can tell us what the issues were between him and Mr. Peters." Kelly paused before continuing, "But we also have another problem here, Ms. Parks." Kelly waited before she continued.

Candice's blood pressure rose and she reluctantly responded to the leading comment, "And that problem would be?"

Kelly answered and studied the woman closely, "We found samples of a woman's blond hair on Mr. Peters' body during the coroner's examination, and we need a sample of your DNA to compare with our finding. After all, you did know him and you're an attractive blond."

Candice fidgeted in her chair as she searched for an answer, but Kelly decided to press. "We can get a court order, or you can offer us a sample voluntarily. Either way, we'll get one, Ms. Parks."

Candice took a deep breath. "Do I get a phone call? I think I need legal advice before I say anything else, or allow anything more. Your implication is ridiculous, of course!"

"We're going to detain you for now then, Ms. Parks, so you'd better make that call." Kelly pushed over her desk phone, allowing Candice to reach the device.

Candice grabbed the phone and dialed Brian Quest's cell phone, as she knew that he always answered his cell. "Hey Brian, its Candice. The RCMP's holding me for questioning concerning Terry Peters' murder and I'm concerned that my rights might get violated. They're crazy, but I may need a lawyer. Can you arrange for one through *ComTek* or something?"

Candice heard Brian curse, then he agreed to handle the situation and hung up.

"He'll make the arrangements." Candice sighed, trying to appear calm. "Am I being charged with something?"

"Hmm ... not at the moment. We just need that DNA sample and then we can talk further, Ms. Parks," Kelly replied and leaned back in her chair.

Simon called Officer Olson, and requested an officer to come to the office and take Candice to a holding area, pending further investigation and possible booking.

♓

Ricardo Sanchez was listening to his car radio and the morning news report.

"The two occupants of a red sports Mercedes were killed last night in a horrific accident on the TransCanada Highway. It appears that the vehicle lost control on the wet and slippery expressway and crashed down the river ravine. A witness is reported to have seen a large black SUV, which appeared to have been involved in the accident, then leave the scene, but no additional information has been released by the West Vancouver highway patrol. We'll continue our report at noon as further information is released."

Ricardo arrived at his office and saw that his phone had un-retrieved messages, indicated by the flashing of the message light at the bottom of his phone console. He pressed play and listened to each message, the last of which was left by his boss, Larry Langstone. "Ricardo, call me ASAP please!"

Ricardo picked up the receiver and pushed his speed dial for Larry's office. "It's Ricardo, can I speak to Larry, please, Carolynn? Tell him I'm returning his call from earlier."

"Ricardo, thanks for the quick return," Larry said when he picked up his extension. "I've received a panicked call from Brian Quest. He told me that the RCMP has picked up Candice Parks in connection with Terry Peters' murder. I've given legal a jingle and they are preparing a document for her release. She should be out in an hour or so, and the cops haven't charged her with anything that I know about. Can you take a drive to the Surrey detachment and see what they have and what's going on? She's being held at the Surrey complex on 57th."

"Yes, of course, I'm on my way. I'll keep you in the loop. Larry, call me when the legals are ready." Ricardo hung up the phone, surprised at the turn of events as he was interested in other activities of Ms. Parks.

The white *ComTek* truck quickly drew into the visitor's RCMP parking lot, and Ricardo jumped out, locked the door, and sprinted directly to reception.

"I understand that a Detective Kelly O'Brian is temporarily assigned here. Could you call her office and advise her that I'm here concerning the Candice Parks case? I'm Ricardo Sanchez of *ComTek* security."

The receptionist smiled at the attractive man and dialed the number. "Detective O'Brian, there's a Ricardo Sanchez here to see you about the Candice Parks case."

Ricardo was directed to the second floor, where the officer directed him to the detective's office down the hall. "Hey KO, nice digs, better than mine!" Ricardo exclaimed with a smile as he entered the detective's office.

"It didn't take long for *ComTek* to react. Good to see you. Sit down, Ricardo," Kelly replied coldly.

"What's the scoop? Murder, what's that about?" Ricardo asked, taking a seat.

"We haven't charged Ms. Parks just yet, but she looks like a good candidate for the Peters murder."

"Based on what?" Ricardo snapped.

"We know that the murderer of Terry Peters was a blond woman, based on the DNA and physical evidence gathered at the scene. We also have some poor video of a woman entering the hotel close to the time of the event, and the woman had a build similar to Ms. Parks. We've asked her for a sample of her DNA so we can either rule her out, or have imperial evidence for the charge," Kelly advised Ricardo without looking directly at him.

"Well, *ComTek*'s preparing the legal documents for her immediate release, and you'll have to let her out of here until you get a warrant for the sample, you know, KO."

Ricardo's cell phone buzzed and he answered. "Okay, great." He pressed end on the cell. "The documents for her release will be here within the hour. I know you won't get your paperwork for the forced DNA sample until the end of the day, tops, so you'll need to get her ready for release. You'll have to deal with your suspicions later, Detective."

"We anticipated as much, and we've Ms. Parks in a holding room until the documents are received." Kelly took a breath and then asked, "Anything else, Mr. Sanchez?"

"Ah ..." he peered at Kelly O'Brian, "it'll be an interesting date tonight, don't you think?" he replied bluntly and left the office. Ricardo left the building and headed back to his office, feeling annoyed at Kelly but he wasn't sure why.

✳

Candice's visit with the RCMP resulted in a lot of people becoming very nervous. The news reached the attention of interested parties in quick fashion. Tom Lee wasn't happy at all when Brian Quest called and provided a summary of events.

"You mean to tell me that cops are buzzing around your place? What does she know about our arrangements, Brian?" Tom asked, sounding very angry.

"There's nothing they'll find concerning our arrangement, Tom. If the cops find anything, it'll concern other activities that Parks may've been involved with. Besides, this is a murder charge and there'd be nothing to make the cops look at our business. We have a legitimate contract, one similar to many others we have, so don't worry about our agreement," Brian replied, feeling stressed.

"My backers won't be pleasant people to meet, should this go sideways. Call me with any new developments, and don't get involved!" Tom warned and disconnected the call without further conversation.

Brian sat in his office with the door closed, wondering what the hell Candice had done. "I wonder what else she's up to. I'd better find out, and fast!"

He decided to pick Candice up at the RCMP building when her release was finalized, and have a little chat with her in their private room, where no one could overhear the conversation.

♓

Giermo Hernandez received a cell phone call from an insider at *ComTek* that alerted him to Candice's visit with the police. He freaked out, and hung up. "That stupid bitch, she had such a good setup going, damn!"

He had to contain the situation, and knew that it was time for Pablo again, to shut down any risk of his relationship with Candice Parks being discovered.

♓

Detective Simon Chung glanced over at a cell phone that vibrated on his desk. It was James Gobbles' BlackBerry® indicating that a new text was being received. The phone travelled around the desk surface for a few seconds in response to the internal vibration and then lay silent once again.

Simon grabbed the phone and selected the keys to access the text. "I need some help recruiting three new guys to work on my next shipment. Let me know if you can arrange some help and text me back," Simon read the message to Kelly.

"Let's sit a while before we respond, and make him think that arrangements are being made. We should set up some type of meet later so we can collar this guy," Kelly suggested.

"Okay. Remind me in an hour or so and we'll respond then and see where this plan leads us."

The receptionist in the lobby called Kelly's phone. "I've a lawyer here asking for you or Detective Chung concerning Candice Parks."

"We've been expecting his visit. Please direct him up," Kelly acknowledged and turned to Simon. "Our *ComTek* lawyer guest is here."

The slim young man dressed in a dark pinstriped suit appeared at their office. "I'm *ComTek*'s legal counsel for Ms. Parks, and have a release for her unless you charge her right now, Detectives!"

"Take a seat," Simon replied, eyeing the young lawyer. "You know that we're considering charging Ms. Parks with the murder of Terry Peters, but wish to have a DNA sample before we do so."

"I understand that you haven't charged her. What decision have you made?" the man asked stiffly.

"We're expecting our court order to force the sample, but must wait until the judge signs the paperwork. You may take Ms. Parks for now if you wish," KO replied, but wasn't happy with having to wait for what she knew would be the inevitable.

"Good then, we've an understanding. Here are Ms. Parks' release documents. Tell her that Brian Quest will pick her up in about ten minutes," the man said calmly, handed Kelly the documents, and then turned and left the office.

"Well, that was quick and to the point, eh Simon! I hate those self-absorbed stuffed shirts. They must all have a rod up their ass before they're hired by the *ComTek*s of the world," she vented as she pitched the document on her desk and went out for a coffee.

The release of Candice Parks was anticipated by many who were concerned about her visit with the RCMP. A black Escalade didn't look out of place, parked along the 57th Avenue road across from the RCMP building. Brian Quest didn't notice anything of concern as he pulled his 310zx black sports car into the visitor's parking lot outside the RCMP Surrey headquarters.

No one noticed the man, laying low on the flat roof of the house on the corner of 144th and 58th Streets, either. His view of the front and rear parking areas of the detachment building through his binoculars was unobstructed, and he concealed his short range radio that was placed beside his right arm. The wet roof wasn't a distraction to him, and he watched with intensity.

They all waited in silence for Candice Parks to appear.

Brian entered the lobby of the police headquarters and emerged with Candice, walking quickly to his car that was parked a short walk from the exit. The occupant of the Escalade witnessed her entry into the sports car, and prepared for their departure. The roof observer's eyes were unable to see the front of the building, but had a clear line of sight of the adjacent street intersection and still waited for Candice to appear.

Brian withdrew his car from the parking lot, stopped at the intersection, and turned north on 144th Street heading toward the *Fraser Head Hotel*. "Are you okay? Did they hurt you in any way?" Brian asked as he looked at Candice, concerned to see how she was handling the ordeal.

The Escalade pulled from its resting place, and stopped at the corner before turning north to shadow the black 310zx. The observant on the roof reached for his radio and spoke into the microphone, and remained otherwise motionless.

Brian continued along his chosen route that included passing through a residential area, not wanting to say anything about her predicament until he reached the hotel. "I think we need to talk at our place at the *Fraser Head,* and it'll be good for you to relax a while."

A white closed-in van quickly slipped out of a side street, briefly stopped, and turned in the direction of Brian's vehicle, cutting off the black Escalade, but Brian only noticed that Candice was highly stressed and shaken from her experience with the RCMP. "I can get us to the hotel quickly from here and I'm really concerned about you," he said as he focused on Candice and didn't see the parade of vehicles tailing his movements. Candice nodded her head without saying a word, and stared out the windshield as the vehicle headed to their place of sanctuary.

Candice didn't know what she was going to say to Brian, and certainly had no idea what she was going to do next, either. "Hmm ... spending some time with Brian might help me figure things out," Candice thought as the familiar hotel came into view.

The black 310zx followed its familiar route to the rear parking lot of the hotel as Candice rummaged around in her purse to find her key. Brian parked his car in the nearly vacant lot and the pair exited the vehicle.

"I thought that some sex might help relieve that stress and we can talk after," he said with a smile as the pair walked toward the rear entrance of the hotel.

A white van squealed around the corner into the parking lot and pulled alongside Brian, as Candice inserted her key into the hotel back door's lock. Two men slid the van side door open, jumped out and grabbed Brian and Candice by their arms.

"Shut up!" a tall Chinese-looking man demanded, holding a small revolver. The driver of the van bolted from the driver's seat, joined his partners and pushed a hand gun into Brian's waist. "Get in the van and keep your yap shut!" he growled, as a black Escalade entered the rear parking lot and suddenly stopped unnoticed.

Pablo Dominguez remained seated in the black Escalade and watched, wondering what action he should take. "Chinga, man!" he growled, confused as he watched Brian be pushed into the white van and the driver slide the white door closed.

The remaining pair of men surrounded Candice, and pushed her toward the hotel's back door. "Open the door!" the shorter man growled. She fumbled with the key that was still in the door lock as the two men pressed close to her until the back door opened, and the group slipped inside. The white van then moved to a nearby parking space and the engine was turned off.

Pablo peered through his windshield and glanced around the parking lot to see if anyone else had witnessed what he had just seen. There was no one else. "Who's the prick in the van and what are the two guys going to do with my female target?" he asked himself, and decided to wait and improvise a new plan.

"What do you want with me and Candice?" Brian screamed from the back seat of the white van at his abductor.

"Shut the hell up or I'll shut ya up. This won't take too long." The driver glared at Brian through a plexiglass barrier between the front seat and the rear compartment. The van went silent as each occupant waited, thinking about what was going on in the hotel.

Candice and the two men worked their way up the concrete back stairs of the hotel, and Candice stopped at the second floor entrance.

"What's the holdup here?" the short bony Chinese man poked Candice in the back. "Our party's in room 210! Move your ass!"

"Uh ... nothing, just habit," Candice replied, terrified, and opened the hall door.

The hallway was vacant, and the trio quickly marched to the room. Candice nervously inserted the room key and turned the doorknob. The men pushed the door aside, shoved Candice into the room, and quickly closed the door.

The two men took a quick look around the room, and the taller of the two peeked through the window coverings, noting that the white van had moved to provide a direct route from the hotel's rear exit to the sliding side door. "Our ride's in perfect position, Ping. Let's get this party started, as I agreed that we'd be done in less than fifteen minutes."

Candice stood frozen at the foot of the double-sized bed as the short, bony-looking man pulled the covers off the mattress and dumped them on the floor. Room 210 was her private refuge that she enjoyed sharing with Brian, and now it was about to become the room of her ugliest nightmare.

"You're my monthly bonus! Make nice, and you may just get out of here and join your guy down in the parking lot, otherwise he's dead! Ya get the deal?" the tall man growled.

"Ah ... yea I get it! Ya do me, then what? I've got money stashed. I could give it all to ya," Candice begged nervously, glancing between the two men as they placed their revolvers on the dresser.

"Just shut up and take your damn clothes off. This get-together's the payment I've been promised, and I've been horny since I was told this mornin'," the tall thin man demanded as he grabbed the keys and purse from her hand, placing them on the dresser beside the pair of handguns.

Candice began to disrobe, thinking about how she might get hold of one of the weapons on the dresser. The two men smiled, and the tall, thin man started to strip his clothing off.

"Look at them tits, eh Jiang!" the short, bony man grinned. "I'd sure like a piece of that, too!"

Candice eyed the revolvers lying on the furniture by the door, as she unzipped her skirt and kicked off her shoes. "So ya like my breasts, eh?" she asked, pushing them together as she slowly walked toward the dresser and the back of the bed.

"Don't take all day! You take them panties off too, or I'll do it for ya, eh!" the scar-faced short man sneered as his partner stripped off his briefs. "Look, Jiang's got a hard-on already!"

Candice sat on the end of bed and seductively removed her lace panties, her heart pounding, desperately trying to formulate a plan. She was now naked on the back edge of the mattress, and her seductive figure was examined by two pairs of wide-open eyes.

"Just do her—we've got a time window here, Jiang!" the scar-faced short man growled, as Candice took a deep breath, trying desperately to find a way to separate the two men in the room.

"Look, there's lubricating oil in the bathroom. It'll be more fun for both of us if you use it! Ya wanta get me off don't ya?" she asked trying to buy some time.

"I don't care if ya gets off or not, and I don't need no lubricant either!" the tall thin man's black piercing eyes stared at her as he replied. He started to advance toward Candice and then hesitated. "Hey Ping, see if you can find that oil quick before I come just standing here." He glanced up, "we got enough time and I don't want to rush anyway."

Pablo continued to wait and watch the white van from his black Escalade. "What the hell are they doing in there? If they were going to kill her, the two guys would be done and out by now!" he mused at the passing time, getting anxious while waiting; he never got stressed with a job, but this job was different. He wasn't in control this time, plus he was sitting exposed in a parking lot in broad daylight. "Damn, I hate this situation ... but I'd better hold tight just a little longer."

The driver of the white van had turned on the radio and was listening to some rap music, keeping the volume down as he didn't want to attract attention. Brian sat silently worrying about what the two thugs were doing to Candice in the hotel, and worried about what his fate would be.

"Ah ... what's the hurry anyway?" Candice asked, easing her body toward the dresser while rubbing her groin, drawing the thin man's attention downward. As he glanced down, she lunged for the pistol on the dresser, her fingers grazing a gun barrel as Jiang grabbed her hair and tossed her to the floor.

"Ya wanta play, eh!" Jiang growled as he knelt down on the floor and dragged her to her feet.

Pablo's eyes widened as he noticed a gold-colored Cadillac sedan pull into a parking space at the edge of the parking lot behind him. He held his breath as he watched through his rearview mirror at a heavy-framed man stepping from the driver's seat. The man with unkept curly brown hair stood for a moment, and then smiled as a young shapely blond woman came sauntering out of the *Kings Crossing Pub* toward him.

"Hey Slider, ya need a little company, eh?" the petite, well-proportioned woman asked.

"Yea, I needed to get away from the guys and have some female companionship for a while!" he replied with a grin. "I'm surprised that you're not already screwin' some dude, as it's early Friday afternoon."

"Ah … it's early yet, and I'm always happy to get your call," she replied, as Pablo ducked out of sight and the pair walked past Pablo's car toward the rear entrance of the *Fraser Head Hotel*.

The large man placed a muscular arm around the young woman's shoulder, "Demi's got a client, though!" she said as she looked up at the man. "She's a different ride, that's for sure!"

The pair reached the back door of the hotel, and Slider's cell phone rang as he reached for his key. "Yea, Slider!"

"Hey man, its Philippe. I tossed that Peters' guy's place last night as ya asked. I found no cash, but he's got quite a portfolio of stocks and investments!"

"Humph!" Slider grunted, "I figured as much! I hear that the word around the pole yard is that Peters' funeral's tomorrow afternoon. That'll be a great place to find out somethin' about his family!"

"What do ya want me to do, Boss?" Philippe asked.

"Hmm ... I'll have to get someone at that service and get a name that we can talk to about Peters' debt. I'll get back to ya later," he replied and hung up as the petite woman stood and fidgeted by the rear hotel door.

"Eh Slider, ya got a problem?" she asked as the large man pushed his key into the lock of the hotel's back door.

"Na, nothin' that can't be fixed. Hmm ... maybe I've got another gig for ya tomorrow, Kate. We can talk about it upstairs," he replied, as he opened the door and the pair disappeared inside the hotel.

Brian Quest sat in the back seat of the van, terrified as to what was happening to Candice. He hadn't recognized any of the three men who had attacked them, and now feared for Candice's life. He was helpless to do anything about their situation and was forced to sit for what seemed an endless amount of time.

"Hey man, at least tell me who's doing this to us!" Brian screamed, thinking that he might be able to figure out something.

"Just shut up, or I'll put a bullet in your head right here!" the driver growled without turning around.

Candice felt smothered as Jiang quickly worked to satisfy his need. "Ah ... ah!" he gasped, knowing that he was running out of time as he noticed Ping walk away from the bathroom doorway.

She tried to catch her breath and could only face Jiang as the heavily-breathing man's hand suddenly covered her mouth.

"Mmm!" her muffled voice seeped through his hand as Ping grabbed her arm, pulled it so the inner elbow was exposed, and inserted a needle.

"This will fix everything, bitch!" Ping sneered, pushing a plastic plunger down as Candice tried to move her head to get free from Jiang's grip over her mouth.

Candice's eyes bulged wide open, looking at the man on top of her in disbelief. She couldn't move. Jiang's heart pounded as he worked to reach his organism, while muffling Candice's screams of panic. She then went silent, and stopped fighting as Jiang stiffly inhaled at the rush.

Pablo Dominguez decided that he'd waited at the scene in the parking lot long enough. He put his black vehicle in gear, turned it around and backed the Escalade into the parking lot so it became parallel with the white paneled van. Pablo opened his side window and faced the driver of the van with a smile.

Bang, a single shot burst through the side glass of the van hitting the driver in the head. Pablo then jumped out of his Escalade, slid open the side door of the white van and grabbed Brian. "Get into the back seat!" Pablo screamed, waving his pistol.

Brian jumped into the back seat, and the black vehicle squealed out of the parking lot, quickly leaving the scene. "You can't leave!" Brian screamed as the vehicle sped away from the hotel.

"Shut up!" Pablo glared at Brian through the rear view mirror. "I'll deal with your woman later! This situation's become too complicated!" Pablo turned his attention to his escape down the boulevard. "I'll use this asshole to get the woman back later if those guys don't kill her first!" Pablo muttered, as he reduced his speed and merged into the afternoon traffic.

The sound of the gunshot and squealing tires was heard by the two men in room 210.

"Come on man, we gotta split!" Ping yelled, pitching the used syringe onto the floor as Jiang climbed off the woman's motionless body, her eyes fixed, staring out in shock. He scrambled to get dressed as Ping pulled aside the window covering and peered out the second floor bedroom window. "Oh shit! That was a hit on our van, man!" he exclaimed, as he saw that the driver's side of the van window was cracked with a hole and had blood spattered on the glass.

"What the hell's going on?" Jiang yelled as he grabbed his weapon and slammed the room door shut, as the pair ran from the room.

Both men placed their weapons in the back of their pants, pulled their shirt tops out and over the extruding grips of the guns and rushed down the fire escape staircase at the end of the hall. Ping reached the emergency door first, pushed on the handrail, and peered through the small opening. "It's clear," he muttered.

The two men slipped outside and slowly just walked out of the hotel toward the pub next door.

"Some bonus, eh Ping!" Jiang grinned as he fished out a cell phone from his jean pocket and selected a speed dial number.

♓

"Hey, partner it's time to send that text," Kelly reminded Simon of James Gobbles' phone text message.

"Oh, yea ... so let's set up a sting operation for say, six tonight, what do ya think?" Simon grabbed the cell phone and placed it in front of him. Kelly shrugged in agreement.

Simon found the initial message from Giermo, pressed reply, and keyed a message: *I've arranged for the three guys you requested. Before I send them to you, I want a meet to discuss my fee and see the place where I'm going to send these guys. Text me your agreement, address, and plan for our meet for six tonight.* Simon pressed send and placed the cell back on the side corner of his desk. "I hope this works and we hear back soon."

"We should have our court order for Candice Parks by now. Let's talk to Officer Olson and find out when we should pick up that paperwork," Kelly suggested, still not happy about letting the woman suspect out of the building.

"Yea, sure," Simon replied and the pair got out of their chairs and headed for the foyer.

Officer Olson placed a call to the courthouse across the street and waited on the line. "'Hold' seems to be the best key on the phone these days," she commented, looking at the two detectives fidgeting at her desk. "Yes, I'm looking for the court order on Candice Parks for Detectives O'Brian and Chung."

"Oh! Great ... hold a sec please," Joyce asked as she held her hand over the receiver. "It's ready. By the way, your court order for the *Fraser Head Hotel*'s guest list is also ready and you can pick it up at the same time. Do you want to wait for the delivery or go get the paperwork yourselves?"

Joyce waited for an answer and then returned her attention to her call.

"The detectives will come right over and collect the documents themselves." Joyce smiled and the detectives disappeared and she heard a faint "thank you" as they pressed the elevator button.

Simon stopped and remembered Gobbles' phone. "Wait, we may need the cell phone if we get a message while we're collecting Parks."

Simon quickly returned to the office and grabbed the cell, placed it in his pocket and returned to the elevator, which was now being held open by Kelly.

The gray RCMP sedan had just turned into the *ComTek* warehouse side road when the Gobbles' phone began to vibrate. Kelly pulled the car to a stop before she reached the guard station, and Simon extracted the phone and looked at the incoming text.

Okay. I think we should meet and work out an arrangement. 23449 Kebet Way, Port Coquitlam, just off the Mary Hill Bypass. Noon tomorrow. Simon read the short note. "Hmm ... the text idea paid off, but the meet isn't until tomorrow. It looks like another Saturday date, Partner!"

Kelly smiled, and could feel the arrest in her gut. She put the car in gear, restarting the car's movement toward the attentive security guard; reaching him, she rolled down the window and flashed her detective's badge. The gate opened, and Kelly made the familiar short trip to Candice Parks' office.

The detectives could see that the woman wasn't in her office, and approached the receptionist who sat at a desk facing the door. "Do you know where Ms. Parks is?" Simon asked.

"Sorry, I haven't seen her all day. Can I leave her a message?"

"Ah ... no, that won't be necessary. We'll return later, but if you could call us when she returns we'd appreciate that." Simon handed the woman his card and scribbled his cell number on the back.

"Is she in trouble?"

"Don't worry, we just need to talk to her. Please call should she come back into the office," Simon replied as he left the receptionist's desk.

"Shit, I knew we should've never let that woman out of our grasp," Kelly growled, annoyed that they had to find Candice Parks all over again.

"Due process, KO, due process. We'll find her," Simon told his agitated partner.

"You know, I recall that lawyer saying earlier that a Brian Quest was going to pick Parks up at the station. He's on my interview list for Monday. Maybe we should make that call and see him now. He works in the main office up there," Kelly suggested as she pointed to the administration building overlooking their position.

"Yea, good idea. Maybe he knows where Parks is!" Simon smiled at his partner as they climbed back into their car.

Kelly maneuvered the car and headed for the front of the complex. She smiled at the guard as she passed through the side gate, and found a visitor's parking space in the front parking lot.

"It looks like our man's not here. We should see if anyone knows where he is," Simon remarked, observing that the private parking space for Brian Quest was vacant. Both detectives walked into the front receptionist area. "Is Brian Quest available today?"

"No, he stepped out a short while ago. I don't know when he's going to return, if at all. It's Friday afternoon and he often doesn't return from afternoon meetings," the receptionist replied.

"Okay, thank you. By the way, does he have any appointments Monday morning? We would like to talk to him then," Kelly asked as she looked about the quiet office.

Georgina looked up Brian's schedule. "I don't see anything scheduled for him first thing Monday. How long would you need?" she looked up over the top of her computer monitor.

"Ah … please book about an hour around eight thirty, okay?"

"Well, he often doesn't get in until nine, will that work?" Georgina asked, knowing that Brian preferred at least a half hour before seeing anyone in the morning, so she pushed out the appointment.

"Perfect, we'll be here," Kelly replied and turned to leave the office. "Hmm … I wonder where those two have gone," she muttered as her cell phone rang. The pair continued to head for their car, and on the second ring she answered. "Detective O'Brian here!"

"Hi, it's Ricardo. I think we were a little tense as we parted in your office, so is our date still on?"

"Sure, it's on. Things get tense in our business all the time. No sweat!" she replied, taking a breath.

"Great, dress casually and I'll see you about seven. Okay?"

"Yea, good." The conversation finished and Kelly looked at Simon. "What! I think he's a nice guy," she grinned.

"Why don't we go to the *Fraser Head Hotel* and look at that special clients list before we head home," Simon suggested as the pair reached their unmarked police car.

"Super idea." Kelly almost had forgotten about the list. They started back to the hotel.

Flashing RCMP vehicles were scattered about the hotel as Kelly drove into the front parking area. "What's going on now!

This place sure is busy," Kelly remarked, looking for a place to leave the car.

The detectives showed their badges and an officer permitted them to enter the cordoned off area. "There's been a shooting in the back and we've a dead driver. The boys are back there now," the officer said, watching the managed chaos.

"This doesn't seem to be a very safe place to stay, does it Simon?" Kelly smirked. "Let's focus on our client list first, and check on this crime scene after."

The reception manager was standing at his station and definitely looked unhappy with all the police about. Simon presented his badge.

"Ah yea, you two. What can I do for ya this time?" he asked, irritated.

"We've your court order here. We need to see that list of special customers we talked about on out last visit," Simon replied coldly as he placed the legal order on the reception desk.

The man scanned the paperwork that seemed familiar, and proceeded to his office that was a small room behind the counter. "Here ya go. All you'll see is a listing of the rooms that have been assigned a key, no names. I told ya we received only cash for those suites." He slid the single page list across the desk. "You can keep that. I knew you'd be back sooner or later," he said with a sigh and eyed Kelly.

Kelly took the page and scanned the listing. "Each room listed here has a key number. What does the number identify?"

"Each room key that's assigned has a number engraved on it, which is our code to identify the key. We place an F and H stamp on the key to help the clients find the room key amongst their other keys, but we don't put the room number on it, for security measures," the manager explained his clever idea, while checking out Kelly's figure again.

"Hmm ... interesting. I see room 210 has a number of keys, why's that?" she asked, ignoring his attentive look.

"Oh! That specific client requested multiple keys. It's not common, but we don't charge any additional fee for that service," the manager replied, now occupied with watching the activity outside.

"Can we get into any of these rooms and look about?" she grinned, hoping to get what she requested.

"Sorry, customer privacy. You'll need some cause to get entry, and the legal paper. Same dance, guys," he replied, returning his attention to Kelly.

"So what's the story on the shooting out back?" Simon inquired.

"I don't know, some crack head or something, maybe a deal gone wrong. It happens more that you think around here. You guys will have to tell me that one," the manager replied as he walked around the counter to see what else was going on outside.

"Well, this one's not ours, so we should let the Surrey guys look after the action outside. Let's go home, Simon. We've a big day tomorrow afternoon anyway."

"Yea, and you might have a big night tonight, eh KO!" he grinned.

She poked him in the arm but didn't answer.

Chapter Twenty Three

The *Kingshead Pub* was crowded; after all, it was Friday night. Will Richards had arrived early to ensure that he was able to have a booth large enough for everyone to sit comfortably and enjoy the evening discussion and meal. The big Canucks® hockey game was the following night and Will was pleased that this meeting didn't interfere with him being able to watch the game. Will was pumped with the possibility that he could unload the mill and get out from under the *ComTek* bullshit.

He faced the entrance of the pub from his vantage point in the back corner, and he already had his cold pint of Budweiser® in a frosted glass sitting on a coaster. He loved eyeing the waitresses and he wanted to strike up a conversation, but noticed Howard Naden enter the front of the pub with the two Chinese businessmen who looked like they had just removed their neckties before coming inside.

Will rose from his seat and waved in the direction of the men who were looking for him in the crowded room. He was able to attract Howard's attention, so the incoming trio worked their way through the chairs and tables to the back booth. Thomas Howe appeared in the entrance of the pub as everyone got seated, and he spotted Will waving down the waitress to place another drink order.

Thomas reached the group before the woman could leave and an additional pint of Bud® was ordered.

"This is my accountant, Thomas Howe," Will said, starting the introductions as Thomas slipped into the booth.

Howard Naden introduced his guests, Chad Siu and Peter Yen, as the tray full of beers appeared.

"We'll order something to eat later," Will told the waitress, and took a sip of his cold beer as everyone got settled.

A baseball game was playing in the background, running on selected flat screen TVs hung from ceiling hangers. Other monitors were playing KENO®, and a Nascar® race was roaring on a screen at the far end of the pub. Other patrons were sitting at the bar counter checking their strip tickets, looking for a winner while having their pints of beer.

"Howard called me this morning and said that you fellows are interested in purchasing *Service Pole Recycling* and you wanted to discuss that possibility." Will smiled, anxious to get the meeting started.

"Yes, Mr. Richards, we're very interested in your recycling project," Chad, the smaller man, replied. He had an oblong face, narrowing eyes, and unusually short black hair. He had a dark, plain sports coat, and his black shirt was now open at the collar. "We wish to send the finished product back to China as construction materials for new housing."

"Wow, what a unique use for these old poles!" Will exclaimed, intent on every word.

"Are you able to get the permits to ship the product out of Canada?" Thomas asked as he studied the businessman sitting across from him.

"Why yes, Mr. Howe, we've already been told of the regulations required for this type of export. We plan to place the processed materials into large forty-foot shipping containers that we'll seal shut before they leave the mill site," Peter Yen continued to outline the plan. "We also have a program to ensure the shipment is free of insects, as China doesn't want to import some type of infestation," Peter said softly; the two men looked and dressed very similarly, making it difficult to tell them apart, other than that Peter's dress shirt was gray rather than white and his hair was lighter.

The men's beers were disappearing rapidly, and Will alerted the waitress for another round. The pub was getting busier and the hum was increasing in intensity, causing the men to speak more loudly to be heard over the background noise.

"We'll continue to ensure all your environmental responsibilities are met and that any agreements with the participating companies are adhered to. In addition, we are prepared to invest cash to improve the business process and reduce operating costs." Chad watched Will's expression as the opportunity was described.

"So what are the terms of the offer?" Will asked in a loud voice over the noise and held his breath for the answer.

The pub crowd burst out into a cheer as some team scored in the game on the TV. The table conversation paused, waiting for the room noise to return to the lower background drone. The refreshed beers arrived at the table and were distributed.

"Ah … give us another ten minutes and then we'll order." Will smiled at the waitress who looked exhausted.

"We'll give you 250 thousand dollars for the company, but you must pay all outstanding payables from those funds. You must also guarantee us a minimum three-year contract with *ComTek*."

Will and Thomas looked at each other, knowing that there was going to be a catch somewhere.

"My company only has one year left in the current contract. Why don't you guys take that, and work out an extension with *ComTek* yourself?"

"Will, you've the relationship with *ComTek*, and you've been doing this with them for so many years. It's up to you to procure the extension before we'll sign a purchase agreement with you," Chad replied, peering at Will.

"Ah, yea, of course. I'll try to get a meeting with *ComTek* for Monday. Are you two available to attend?" Will asked, as he thought that the attendance of the two Chinese would demonstrate to *ComTek* that the opportunity was real and that, therefore, *ComTek* would agree to the extension.

Will waved down the waitress and the meal orders were placed. While the others made a quick pit stop, Will and Thomas stayed behind for a private chat.

"What do you think, Thomas?" Will asked, looking concerned.

Thomas sighed, "It's very short notice for *ComTek*, and Monday will be a push, Will."

"Look, *ComTek* gets a new owner willing to inject cash for improvements, they get me out of their hair, and it's only three years. It takes them that long to decide what color underwear to put on. Besides, they currently have no plan on what to do with the retired old poles when my contract ends, and they'll need lots of time to develop a new plan. The three years will give them that time!" Will explained. "It's the common-sense solution and a great opportunity."

"If *ComTek's* got the hard-on you think they have, common sense goes out the window and it's all about power and control," Thomas replied, knowing the internal politics quite well and having been screwed himself for misreading the political signs and picking the wrong players. "By the way, who the hell's Howard Naden?"

"Oh! He's involved in the wood industry and he approached me some time ago saying that he may know of a buyer who'd be interested in the mill. He wants a finder's fee if he brings a signed deal to the table."

"Hmm ... how large is the finder's fee?" Thomas asked, scrunching his face.

"Five grand. Not really a large amount if the deal goes through."

"Well, it seems a bit higher than I would've agreed to, but then, if you get out with your ass and a few pesos left over, that'd be good, too. It's your business, not mine, Will."

The Chinese businessmen began reappearing from the washroom, and Will and Thomas took their turn. Another score and the pub erupted again in loud cheering.

♓

Kelly O'Brian stood in her lace black bra and G-String panties, considering the correct casual wear for her date with Ricardo. She had her brunette hair pulled back into a single ponytail and wanted to look sophisticated, but not overdressed.

Second dates were a rarity for Kelly, and she looked forward in anticipation to this one since the first one went so well. She disappeared into her closet. "No, no, definitely not," she mumbled as she searched for the right outfit.

Finally the right selection was made, and she and the clothes emerged from her bedroom closet. After placing the find on the bed, she sorted through her jewelry box looking for the right earrings and necklace that would complement the outfit. Happy with her choices, she continued with face and eye preparation in the bathroom.

The finished product in the mirror reflected a black, cashmere, long-sleeved top; a black, fitted skirt; and low, high-heeled pump shoes. Kelly had a silver chain with a large, fired glass pendant set in a thin-ringed, silver frame that hung just above her alluring cleavage, and large, circular, silver-ringed earrings that dangled just below the jaw of her face. She had turned her service belt to the black side, and positioned the weapon holder to sit at her back so that it would be hidden by her dress coat.

The doorbell buzzed sharply at seven, and Ricardo was smiling as Kelly opened the door and invited him inside.

"You sure look hot in that outfit, KO. It's perfect! We're going to *The Mansion* on Davie Street for dinner. It's an inviting place that serves pasta and has a great, elegant atmosphere," he said, smiling; he was wearing a white jacket and an open, black dress shirt.

The destination wasn't very far and neither said a word until Ricardo parked the white truck on the street across from the restaurant. "Did you know that this magnificent building was once the house of the owner of *Rogers Sugar* in the early nineteen hundreds?" Ricardo asked as he opened the passenger door of the truck.

"No. I've never been here before—it's beautiful!" Kelly remarked as she stepped out of the truck.

"This house has had many different lives in Vancouver. The prior owner ran an exclusive high-end restaurant, but I guess he wasn't able to make a go of it, maybe because it's a little off the beaten path," Ricardo replied as the pair entered the large foyer and he confirmed his reservation.

"Yes, Mr. Sanchez, glad to have you as our guest this evening. Follow me."

The pair was placed at a window seat in what had once been the living room of the home; the character of the original mansion had been restored, adding to the romantic ambiance. The restaurant, now a family pasta attraction, had paper sheets lying on top of the table with a package of crayons placed in a can. The living room seating was held for adults, and the families were often placed in the large ballroom that was located on the other side of the front foyer.

Their waiter introduced himself, grabbed a crayon and wrote his name on their paper table cover, and left them the menus after taking their wine order.

"The pasta here's first class and the selection's extensive," Ricardo said with a smile, his dark brown eyes seductively focused on his attractive date.

The bottle of red wine was delivered and sampled by Ricardo before Kelly was served.

"This is on the edge of casual, Ricardo," Kelly commented, looking about at the elegance of the room.

"Family pasta talks casual to me," Ricardo replied, taking a sip of his wine, his studying eyes not leaving Kelly's face.

"If the pasta's as sophisticated as the surroundings, it shouldn't matter what we order," she returned his smile and studied the separate sheet listing the specials of the day.

"So, how's your first case as a detective going?" Ricardo asked before he picked up his menu.

"The case seems to get more involved and complicated at each turn. We've the mysterious car accident that killed Antonio Castillo and his lawyer, Karl Kuntz. You know about the third man at the Elvenden Row house. Then we've the murder of Terry Peters, the *ComTek* foreman of the building where Antonio did the B&E. Now we suspect Candice Parks, a manager at *ComTek,* may be Terry Peters' murderer," Kelly replied as she put the menu on the table.

"Do you wish to order now?" The waiter stood ready, extracting his pencil and paper from his apron.

The couple placed their orders and momentarily stopped their discussion to enjoy the wine and the atmosphere.

Ricardo asked, leaning back in his chair. "How's your research going on your own mystery?"

"Not very well," she sighed. "I haven't had much time to work on it as of late. I thought of a new approach that might lead somewhere, but that's still on my to-do list," Kelly replied and then looked at Ricardo. "How're you enjoying *ComTek*? You must be settled in and getting to know who is who in the zoo by now!" Kelly asked, turning the focus of the conversation toward Ricardo.

"It's interesting. Politics are politics, whether in the RCMP or *ComTek*! The same games are evident. It seems to be the way life is these days."

The evening continued with small talk and seemed to melt away as the two exchanged suggestive glances, and as they finished a second bottle of wine it was evident that it was time to take Kelly home. She invited Ricardo back into her apartment for a night cap.

"Grab a seat in there," Kelly said as she pointed to the living room couch. She grabbed two brandy glasses, removed her service hardware, and placed it on the counter where the liquors were stored. She kicked off her shoes and returned with the two drinks, placing the pair of glasses on the table by the sofa. Ricardo pulled off his white dinner jacket and placed it on an old Victorian chair by the table.

"You can hear a pin drop in here!" Kelly exclaimed as she moved toward an iPod® player, and selected some soft romantic music. "I find music relaxing." Her eyes searched for something in his as she sat next to him, her heart pounding as she found herself in unfamiliar emotional territory.

Ricardo leaned over, embraced her and kissed her soft, pink-painted lips. She shuffled closer, encouraging his approach as their lips locked and tested each other's desire with their tongues. His hand started to slowly run up and down her side, frequently touching the bottom of her bra through her top, as she caressed his neck with her right hand, not discouraging his suggestive motions. "Ah!" she sharply inhaled in a whisper, as Ricardo's hand slipped under her cashmere top and shifted to rub the outer side of her breast through her lacy brassiere. "Oh! Ah." She jerked her face back and took a deep breath, as she felt his caressing hand slowly move over her covered breasts and hardening nipples, now stiffly piercing through the low cut, lace bra, under her top, as he teased them with the tips of his fingers.

Kelly's blood rushed through her as she undid his pants button, pulled the zipper down and slipped her hand downward to stimulate the bulge pushing at the material.

"Mmm," Ricardo muttered as he moved his pelvis to her touch, and removed her black top, exposing the fine figure waiting for him beneath.

She leaned back on the sofa, and he quickly pulled his dress pants down as far as his knees, and continued to stroke her breasts through the low-cut brassiere while kissing her neck.

"Ah ... ah!" she exhaled as he lifted his head and smiled. She unzipped the back of her skirt, pulled it from her hips, and let it drop to the floor at her feet. He undid her front bra clasp, and peeled back the cups from her firm breasts that seemed to be inviting him to continue with their stiffened nipples. She slipped her hand under his briefs, and gently explored his growing erection.

"Ah ... ah," he exhaled at her touch, as his right hand migrated from her soft smooth breast, reached her panties, and his fingers found the soft place that waited under the G-string patch.

"Ricardo ... ah ... ah ... I," Kelly tried to gasp her words from her breathless mouth just as the ring of her cell phone interrupted her labored un-imaged request.

Ricardo eyed Kelly to see if she was going to answer the cell phone ring, or allow their desire to engulf them in the heating passion of the moment.

"Ah ... ah!" she panted for a moment, and the third ring broke the mood and she removed his hand from her wet panties. "Ah ... ah!" she took a deep breath. "I'd better answer that! It must be important if a call comes in ... ah ... at this time of night!" She pushed him away, and tried to regain her composure before getting up to answer the phone.

Ricardo moved his heavily breathing body away from Kelly's highly aroused gaze, to allow her to get up and answer the call, now on its fourth ring.

Kelly climbed off the sofa, rushed to the cell on the kitchen counter. She took a deep breath, "Hello, O'Brian here," she huffed, standing clad only in her black thong, with breasts exposed and her hard nipples visibly erect in the dimmed room light.

"Sure took you a while—disturb you or something?" Simon asked. Kelly pictured him smiling, but of course she couldn't tell for sure.

"Ha, ha," she replied, trying to catch her breath. "Do you have a life? It's late!" she asked, still breathing heavily. "What's up, Simon?"

"Uh ... I just received a call from dispatch. Candice Parks was found murdered in a room at the *Fraser Head Hotel*."

"You're kidding me! Murdered?" Kelly asked, turning her back to Ricardo who was staring at her seductive figure in the dim light of the kitchen.

"Not sure about the facts yet, but they found her naked in room 210, one of the rooms on the special guests list." Simon paused, suspecting that he had interrupted something. "I think we need to zip out there now, unless you have company!" He paused, "Uh ... you know!"

"Company!" She cleared her throat. "No, it's okay. Give me about half an hour or so. I'll call you when I get to Chinatown," she replied quickly, hung up, and turned to Ricardo. "Gotta go. Candice Parks has just been found dead," Kelly blurted out as she ran back into the sitting room looking for her bra. "Ah ... ya gotta go, Ricardo!"

Kelly said nothing else, and Ricardo pulled on his pants, looking shocked and disappointed. Kelly located her bra and pulled the straps into place. "Just as well, I think," she said, smiling, as she clipped the front of her bra together. "It was a wonderful night, but duty calls," she continued speaking quickly, and then gave Ricardo a quick kiss. "We'll need to pick this up some other time, okay?"

Ricardo didn't really want to leave, but the situation was clear and he knew that there would be no debate. "I'll hold ya to that!" he replied softly and smiled.

Moments later Ricardo was out the door. Kelly took a breath, and knew she had to change everything that she had on. "Saved by the bell, so to speak," she sighed with a breath of relief, as she grabbed her top and prepared to change, her body still pumped with adrenalin and racing hormones, still wanting the man who had just left.

♓

Chinatown was still busy. It was Friday night and the city was always ready for a party and an excuse to celebrate the end of another work week. Kelly picked Simon up at their standard place and headed for the *Fraser Head Hotel*. "What other information do you have that you know from your call, Simon?" she asked as she headed the vehicle toward Surrey.

Simon glanced at Kelly, and was going to ask about her evening with Ricardo, but changed his mind. "Well, it turns out that the *Fraser Head Hotel* manager checks each of the rooms that are assigned to their special customers once a week when the maids haven't reported a room to have been cleaned. It seems that not all the guests remember to place a 'make the room' tag on the door once they've finished their visit, and the hotel has learned to check to see if cleaning's in order. The manager was late this week in checking the room servicing file, as it's Friday and a busy night for business."

"He never told us that he inspected each room weekly." Kelly recalled their strained discussion with the manager each time they talked to him. "Besides, cleaning rooms in the evening is very unusual, isn't it?" she asked, looking confused.

"Hmm ... we'll have to ask the manager that question. It does seem strange," Simon replied pensively.

"Ya know Simon, we need to confirm that Candice Parks had one of those engraved special keys. It's interesting that room 210 is the one with multiple keys, as well. I wondered about that!" Kelly replied, glancing over at her partner. "Simon, do you know how she was killed?"

"The ME was still at the scene when I received the call, so I'm sure the cause will be established by the time we get there."

"Hmm ... I wonder how Brian Quest fits into all this. He's still unaccounted for, and there's the murdered van driver in the parking lot, too," Kelly remarked, trying to place all the pieces. "Maybe today's video feed will provide some answers. We'll need that footage ASAP."

"If that feed is as bad as last time, I doubt it will help provide much detail though," Simon shook his head.

Nothing more was said, and Simon chose not to interrogate Kelly about her date with Ricardo. He had a pretty good idea what was going on when he called, and he knew a little bit about his partner and how she sounded on the phone. She would tell him if she chose, but he was curious if his call had caught her before or after sex.

The detectives arrived at the hotel to another display of flashing car-roof-top lights and officers working the crowd.

"Looky-loos are always attracted to cop lights like bugs to a summer flame!" Simon remarked as he jumped out of the car.

Room 210 was taped off, and an officer was stationed at the open door. All hotel customers on the second floor had been moved and relocated to alternate rooms, and the crime scene had been secured.

"We're Detectives O'Brian and Chung," Simon announced as the pair passed under the yellow tape that stretched across the doorway of room 210.

The woman's unclad body was still sprawled out over the bed as the ME continued his examination prior to covering the corpse.

"I'll be finished here shortly, Detectives," the ME said as he looked up at the two new visitors.

Simon took the bedroom and Kelly the bathroom, looking for evidence to bag and tag.

"I've a syringe here at the side of the bed and I've an open bottle of lubricant oil as well on top of the dresser. There's also a needle puncture mark inside of the victim's right arm," the examiner reported loudly as he returned to his examination of the body.

"There are bottles of hair and body cleansers, perfume, and a can of shaving cream strewn all about the floor and ah ..." Kelly paused, "a large travel bag with uh ... woman's toiletries and uh ... hmm ... sex toys, I think!" Kelly announced from the bathroom.

"Lubricating oil is unusual for a possible OD!" Simon mused, walking over toward the corpse.

"There's semen all over her pubic area and lower body," the medical examiner noted, "as well as on the sheets, Detective," he reported as he looked up at Simon.

"Likely some type of rape and forced OD after, I'd say," Simon replied.

"Rape victims usually don't get the privilege of a lub job first, Simon!" Kelly said, returning from the bathroom. "Maybe it was consensual rough sex and she overdosed after her lover left!"

"Hmm ... I doubt it, as there wouldn't likely be semen left everywhere. Her position on the bed indicates to me that she must've been unconscious when the man ejaculated," Simon replied.

"Or dead already!" Kelly said as she looked sadly at the sensual woman sprawled on the bed. "We'll have to take prints from the lubricating bottle and syringe, and maybe the DNA from the semen will tell us more about the guy. We might get lucky."

"You know, there must've been more than one man in here. This crime would be difficult for only one perp to pull off. A needle on the inside of the arm and forced intercourse! Hmm ... even with consensual sex that would've been difficult to do without some major fight unless she was drugged first," Simon remarked as he looked at the location of the needle bruise. "Hey doc, do a drug test and check for stuff under her nails, too. Maybe the sex wasn't playful, ya know what I mean?"

"I wonder if Brian Quest was one of the attackers," Kelly mused. "He picked her up from Surrey when she got released and maybe he killed her for some reason!"

The ME covered the corpse with a sheet. "Well, you'll have to wait until Monday afternoon to get my findings and the results from the lab boys. Good night, Detectives," he said as a gurney appeared at the door to take the body to the morgue.

"Let's see if the manager will give us the video feeds without a hassle this time," Simon suggested, but was skeptical that the information would be handed over without legal prompting.

The detectives found the manager at his post, waiting to have the police clear out and not scare off any more customers. Friday night was usually a big night for last minute business from the pub patrons next door.

"Will you release yesterday's video files to us without a hassle?" Kelly looked at the man sternly.

"Well, the Surrey cops asked for it this afternoon in connection with the shooting earlier, but I've not released it yet to them. With all this disruption, too, I'd like to get back to normal business as soon as possible and get you cops out of my face!" He paused, looking at Kelly, and added, "I'll do you a favor and give it to you without the paperwork this time, though, Detective. Come back in the morning and I'll have your CD, okay?"

The manager looked tired and the discovery of the dead woman appeared to have shaken him up some. "I hate having my valued clients screwing up my business!"

"Ah … and who would that client be?" Kelly looked up quickly, hoping to get a name.

"Sorry, but that information I can't supply!" the manager replied, realizing that he almost lost the client who was actually paying for the room.

"Oh ... one more thing—it's very unusual to have cleaning staff working the night shift. I've never seen that in a hotel before, so why do you work it that way?" Kelly asked, peering at the man behind the counter.

The man leaned over the counter to reply, "I rent the rooms by the hour, remember?" he replied with a grin. "I must have a cleaning staff here twenty-four-seven, Detective."

"Ah, yes, of course! Thank you, we appreciate your cooperation. We'll see you in the morning," Kelly replied coldly.

"Not too early, it's going to be a late night and I still need to cut the video files—so say, after ten," the manager called out as the pair of detectives turned to leave the lobby. "I still have to clean up all this God damn mess from you guys, too!"

"Okay, we've done our duty tonight, let's go home. Remember that tomorrow we've got to be in POCO before noon, so how about I call about nine," Simon suggested, remembering about the Saturday plan.

"Yea, okay, it's been an active night," Kelly said with a sigh.

"I bet!" Simon smiled, entering the Taurus's passenger seat. "Yea, I bet!"

♓

Pablo Dominguez had to stash Brian Quest somewhere until he could receive instructions from Giermo as to what to do with the man. Pablo wasn't happy that he was unable to fulfill his contract concerning the woman, and knew he had to rethink the strategy on that hit. The whole plan had gone off the rails, and he couldn't think who else would want the woman anyway.

He already had a place selected in the event he needed to hide and stay low, should the cops get too close on any given assignment. He sat in an abandoned warehouse, a little way down from the Vancouver port, and Brian Quest had been taped and shackled to a post in the back of the derelict room. The space was dimly lit by the dockyard port lights, and an emergency sleeping bag had been unrolled on the floor.

Pablo pulled his cell phone from his pocket and keyed a text. *Giermo call ASAP. Problem with the job!* He knew that Giermo wasn't always in a place that a cell phone ring would be convenient, so a text was often the mode of initial communication.

The cell phone vibrated, indicating an incoming text, and Pablo grabbed it. The cell phone face lit up once Pablo pressed the text key, and he was able to read the message.

Okay. Call to explain. Pablo smiled and dialed the number. "Well, we'll see what the plan will be for you, my man," Pablo said as he grinned at Brian Quest.

"Hey Giermo, I couldn't get the girl, someone else was after her and her boyfriend, too. I saw a couple of Chinese-looking guys take the woman inside a hotel, so I grabbed the boyfriend. We need to meet and decide this guy's fate, soon amigo," he said, still angry at himself, "and what to do about the woman."

The conversation on the phone chilled Brian, as all he could do was sit and listen.

"Okay, I'll meet you about twelve thirty tomorrow afternoon in POCO. Text me the address," Pablo said, turning away from Brian.

Moments later the text arrived and Pablo checked that the information was complete.

"Well, it's lights out until the morning. Get settled and grab some shut-eye," Pablo commanded as he put the cell into his pocket and unzipped the sleeping bag.

Brian Quest settled down for a cold, stressful night, worried about Candice and about what was going to happen to him.

Chapter Twenty Four

Kelly O'Brian had tossed and turned all night, unable to sleep at all, and now the morning light had become an unwelcome invasion into her bedroom. Her mind had become consumed thinking about Ricardo and the interrupted, heated passion, as well as about the Candice Parks murder. Her brain was busy trying to fit all the pieces together, and the planned sting operation for that afternoon took a back seat in her thoughts.

She dragged herself out of bed and dressed for her jogging tour around the park. She glanced at the weather, and it looked like another picture-perfect Vancouver day working its way across the skyline. It was going to be crisp, and the winter chill was definitely in the air.

She cut her jog short and was almost ready when Simon's call came at nine.

"Hey, partner. Pick me up and we can grab a quick bite, or coffee to work out the details of today's plan, okay?" Simon asked cheerfully on the phone.

"Yea ... see ya shortly," Kelly replied, a little tired from lack of sleep.

✻

Brian Quest felt that his butt was frozen from the cold, and would've paid a fortune for a hot coffee and a ticket out of his predicament. The confined position did nothing for his body, and his bones ached from the awkward sleeping position and constrained movement.

His taped mouth had been freed before Pablo went to sleep, on the condition that Brian would keep his yap shut, or receive a bullet as a consolation prize.

"Well, if you're lucky, you'll be in your warm bed tonight. Remember, one false move and this bad dream will end very quickly," Pablo told Brian as he rolled up and tied the sleeping bag.

Brian's tied hands were released. His wrists were raw from the bonds, and he rubbed them as Pablo looked about to ensure there were no witnesses to their departure. The pair walked a block or so through the deserted area, and found the black Escalade hidden from easy view. "Sit in the back on the passenger side so I can see ya!" Pablo instructed.

The pair climbed into the car and Pablo directed the vehicle toward an empty service road.

"If you promise to be a good boy, I can get you some drive-through coffee and a muffin. Can ya do that?" the driver peered through the rear view mirror and saw an acknowledgment of the offer.

♓

Giermo Hernandez knew that he was going to have a busy day, and also knew he had to make some decisions as to what to do with the male captive that Pablo was going to bring to the warehouse. Giermo also had to decide what to do with James Gobbles and the deal that he wanted.

He began to feel overwhelmed with the total situation, the loss of the Elvenden Row place, the loss of his Colombian workers, his contracted murder of his cousin, and the bungled Candice Parks situation.

"Chinga, what a mess. Maybe it's time to close up and go home," he thought, feeling exhausted from all the decisions. "I don't think that I'm cut out for this stuff!"

♓

Simon and Kelly were having a coffee, reviewing the facts and the situation so that they could devise the best course of action.

"Let's see, James Gobbles is expected in Port Coquitlam around noon. Giermo knows that James drives that *Bug Busters* pick-up van, so Giermo will be suspicious if we show in this Taurus!" Kelly mused. "Since all communication is via text, let's send a note saying the van needed some emergency repairs and he rented a Taurus for the day."

"I don't see what else we can do, since we don't want to take James to the site—no sense putting him in danger," Simon replied as he sipped on his coffee.

"All I can think of is that we get close to the operation, park, and see if Giermo comes out. If not we'll have to go in and get him. Not much of a detailed plan, is it, partner?"

Simon shrugged his shoulders and pulled James's cell from his pocket and sent the text. "We need to alert the Coquitlam office and advise them of the situation, so they know what's going down. I think we should request backup and unmarked cars at each end of Kebet Way, just in case we have to contain any unexpected situation," Simon said as he dialed the Coquitlam office.

"Let's mount up, we've a trip to POCO to make," Kelly replied as Simon hung up the phone, and the pair finished their coffees and left for the scheduled meeting.

It was high tide, and the Fraser River was higher than normal for this time of year. The heavy rains forced the river to rise higher on the banks, and the river rushed by in the late morning air.

Giermo had been at the warehouse early, unloading supplies that were needed to process the new shipment of product that had been stored inside. He had to be ready to begin work on Monday with the new workers that James had promised to provide.

Giermo had decided that Antonio's share was going to be offered to James, hearing that Antonio was now out of the picture.

Pablo decided that he should park on the back side of the quiet warehouse and secure his captive before meeting with Giermo. He was anxious to terminate the boyfriend and wanted to see how important the hit on the woman was, too. Pablo had been exposed, and the boyfriend had seen his face and knew about his private refuge; that situation was unacceptable and he was angry at how screwed-up the entire contract had become.

He found a suitable place out of sight, parked, and stepped out of the car. "Hold tight, it won't be much longer. Don't do anything stupid now," Pablo growled as he re-taped Brian's mouth and wrists.

It was noon, and the detectives' program was executed. The gray sedan approached the concrete building and Kelly checked the unit number. "This is it!" she announced, ensuring her service weapon was ready and loaded. Simon checked his weapon, expecting a difficult arrest.

They parked about fifteen meters from the building. They sat silently and waited until Kelly decided to honk the horn, alerting Giermo that they had arrived. No one appeared. They waited; the plan required that they stand their ground and wait for the suspect to appear. Time seemed to stand still while the detectives waited for Giermo to make his appearance.

The Colombian finally appeared, smoking a cigarette, accompanied by another man with his arm over Giermo's shoulder. The two men were laughing while they approached the unmarked RCMP vehicle.

"Simon, that's Ricardo!" Kelly blurted out in shock. "What the hell's goin' on?"

"Don't know. We must be sure they're together. Let them come closer before we take action. Be ready, anything here can happen now!" Simon replied in a whisper, eyes trained on the pair walking toward the car.

"We've run out of time!" she blurted out without thinking, as the two men approached; Kelly instinctively knew the time for action was at that moment.

Kelly jumped out from the driver's seat of the car and pointed her weapon at the two men. "Stop, it's the RCMP!"

Ricardo stepped behind Giermo and fired at Kelly. *Bang, bang*, the gun made its ear-piecing sound as the two shots missed her and hit the open car door, shattering one of the windows. Kelly dove to the ground and yelled, "Get on the ground Hernandez!"

Bang bang, another pair of shots whizzed past Simon, who was now outside the car on the passenger side. Both detectives focused on the surprise assailant to their right. *Bang!* Simon's pistol replied as he shot at a figure emerging from the other side of the warehouse. "Christ! There're two shooters, KO!"

Bang, bang, Kelly's pistol rang out as Giermo Hernandez dove to the ground and she yelled "Stop Ricardo!"

Ricardo disappeared in the river bank foliage as the detective focused on the second shooter; he decided to sneak along the wet rocky shoreline of the rushing river. *Bang*, the gunman on the side of the building reappeared and fired another shot at Simon who was partially exposed, and hit the detective in the shoulder. Kelly returned fire, *bang bang* and the man hit the ground and lay motionless after the sound of the shots echoed off the face of the building.

Kelly refocused her attention on the initial pair of men. Giermo had lain flat on the ground, arms spread out and there was no sign of Ricardo Sanchez. She listened, and heard Simon moaning on the ground, but tried to block out the sound of her injured partner and concentrated on the river shoreline. It was the only place to hide, and she knew that Ricardo must be somewhere in the riverside bush. She listened, but all she could hear were the sirens of the racing vehicles of the backup police responding to the shots. She didn't hear Ricardo's movement in the weeds, but saw some brush move far to her right along the river bank. *Bang bang*, she took two additional shots, but didn't believe that she had hit her target.

The area swarmed with police vehicles, lights flashing as the backup units rushed to the scene. Kelly carefully rose from her position, and knowing Ricardo was out there some place, cautioned the other officers to take cover. She instinctively worked her way toward the river's edge, pistol ready, looking for Ricardo, and saw his footprints moving westward downstream, but he was nowhere in sight. "I'll get that bastard later!" she muttered as she quickly returned to the parking lot to check on her partner. "I hit him, I could see the blood trail, but I think he's been able to slip past us. How're you doing, Simon?" Kelly asked, huffing out of breath.

"Ah, not too bad, I'll be just fine. The paramedics have been called and the officers have Hernandez in custody. Go check out the other shooter over by the building, KO."

Kelly worked her way towards the gunman who was facedown beside the warehouse. "Great to see you guys!" Kelly said as she approached a uniformed officer standing by her dead assailant.

"This one's dead, Detective. I've secured his weapon."

She noticed the black Escalade parked around the corner. "Cover me while I check out that vehicle," she instructed as she approached the vehicle, weapon poised.

"Come on out, it's the RCMP! You've nowhere to go, hands in the air," she commanded loudly.

Kelly could hear some kicking sounds coming from inside the Escalade. She opened the back door to view the back seat where a trembling man dressed in filthy business clothing sat bound and gagged.

"You're okay. We'll have the paramedics check you in a moment," Kelly said with a reassuring smile. "I need a paramedic! I've a man here that needs to be cut loose and checked out!" she yelled.

"You're safe now." Kelly yanked the tape from the man's mouth. "Who are you?"

"I'm Brian Quest. I've been held captive by some big Colombian man since yesterday!" He paused, trembling from the ordeal. "I was grabbed by some guys who kidnapped Candice Parks ... then this guy ... ah ...."

Kelly interrupted. "Okay, okay! Relax. You can give me your statement after you've been checked out." Kelly glanced up at the paramedic who was running toward the Escalade.

"The gunshot wound isn't serious but we still must take your partner to the hospital," the paramedic reported as he reached the black SUV.

"Ah ... okay, good news. You need to check this man, too," she instructed as she vacated the vehicle, noticing Simon being loaded into an ambulance.

"That son of a bitch! He was playing me for information all along ... I'll get that bastard!" Kelly mumbled, feeling used, betrayed, and manipulated, as she watched the paramedic take Brian Quest to the ambulance to join Simon.

"To think that I trusted him and that I was going to have sex with that SOB last night! Augh!" she growled angrily as the ambulance left the scene, sirens and lights blaring. She took a calming breath and headed for her car.

"I'm Detective O'Brian," Kelly said to the medical examiner and lab crew. "I need everything you got on that warehouse, and send me the information on that dead guy over there, when you have it. I'm assigned to the Surrey detachment at the moment and you can reach me there!" Kelly instructed a lab CSI. "I'll be in contact with you Monday, first thing. I've got another fugitive to find."

"Certainly detective," she heard the reply as the CSI crew left and started their work as the ME headed toward the dead Colombian.

Kelly took a deep breath, pulled her cell phone from her pocket and pressed a speed dial number. "Hey Captain Hollingsworth, sorry to bug you on Saturday, but I need your help!" Kelly exclaimed, still pumped from the event.

"Any time, Detective O'Brian. What do you need?"

"It appears as though Ricardo Sanchez, the security manager working for *ComTek*, is a player for the Colombian cartel. The bastard tried to kill me less than half an hour ago at a stakeout in POCO. He escaped, and is on the loose, so have the guys be mindful. He's a pro," she continued, still breathless. "I need some units at his place in New Westminster and I need access to his apartment, if he's not there. I must get at any evidence that he might have at his place before he can trash it, and ... oh, he's a dog that will need some care, too."

"A stakeout! Are you and Simon okay?"

"Yea ... ah ... well Simon got hit but he's going to be fine, and I'm just pissed I got used by Ricardo and missed taking him down. He used me and I want that bastard!" Kelly replied angrily. "I'll drive out to New West. Can you have some info for me in about an hour or so?"

"Okay, I'll work on it and I'll call back when I have something for you. Oh, Detective, you can't go after him without backup, so I'll send a team to the address when I find it."

Ricardo Sanchez was able to reach his silver Audi. The cops had moved down the road as soon as the gunfire had started, allowing him to slip past and reach his car that he had parked down the road. His arm hurt like hell, and he covered the bleeding with his coat.

He knew he'd likely not be able to return to his apartment as Kelly would figure that out in a second. He'd one of Giermo's apartment keys, and he decided to head for there, as he thought that the cops wouldn't think of going to that address for some time. Ricardo needed to call Colombia and update the Hernandez family, and advise them that Giermo needed a new local lawyer, as Karl Kuntz was now out of the picture. He also needed a doctor, and knew one that would make a house call, no questions.

The Hernandez family had treated him very well since he joined them following his dismissal from the police force. Their connections in Vancouver had heard about his termination and knew that he'd make a great asset. He had been hired by the family to ensure that Giermo was protected and his business activities remained out of the RCMP radar. They had arranged to have him work for *ComTek* and keep tabs on Giermo's business and internal contacts. Candice Parks was an unexpected event that screwed everything up.

"Stupid bitch! She had a good thing goin'. I don't get why she screwed it up," he thought, heading for East Vancouver in his sleek sports car.

He hoped to beat the crazy traffic. It was Saturday, and another Canucks® hockey night was going to suck fans downtown in droves! It was almost two fifteen in the afternoon and he hoped that he would be ahead of the frenzy of fans, which usually clogged the roadways after four.

Kelly O'Brian received a text from Captain Hollingsworth with the address of Ricardo's apartment on Quayside Drive. The text told her that the building superintendant had been notified and would be able to provide a pass key he used to deal with any condo emergencies, should the owner not be available. The super's apartment number was provided. "Way to go, boss!" Kelly thought as she received the text. "Best boss ever!"

She arrived at the foot of Quayside Drive and met her backup team that had been dispatched by Captain Hollingsworth. She knew that Captain Anderson of the Surrey office would've been updated, but she knew it was proper protocol to advise him herself. She dialed the Captain and reported the situation; as she had suspected, he was already apprised of the status of events.

"Go get him and be careful!" Captain Anderson remarked before he hung up the phone.

Kelly outlined the situation about Ricardo Sanchez with her team. She didn't want to storm the apartment and create a big scene, as she expected that he wasn't going to be found there anyway. Kelly stationed one of the officers in the street, and took the other one with her. She located the superintendant's unit and buzzed the apartment's intercom.

"RCMP—it's Detective O'Brian, you're expecting me," she spoke into the small speaker at the entrance gate.

Buzz. The security door lock opened and the two proceeded to the described unit. The superintendant's door was open when Kelly arrived, and a gray-haired man greeted them. "Good afternoon, I understand that you need access to Mr. Sanchez's apartment. I've been told that the appropriate warrant has been issued so here's his key. Unit one-o-five is on the corner. Please return the key when you're finished," the man said softly as he handed Kelly the key. "I hope he's not in a lot of trouble. People like him and Hunter, you know."

"Thank you, we shouldn't be too long. I'll have the key returned as you requested," Kelly replied as she smiled and proceeded toward Ricardo's unit.

"Be alert in case he's here. This man's a professional. There's a dog in the apartment and I don't know how the animal will react, so watch yourself," Kelly cautioned as she knocked on the door. "RCMP, Ricardo Sanchez let us in!" she demanded loudly.

Barking was the only response, so Kelly inserted the key into the lock and partially opened the door. The dog growled, and the gray-colored eyes of the shepherd could be seen peering through the opening in the door.

"It's okay, Hunter—sit boy!" Kelly commanded in an authoritarian tone, as she recalled Ricardo had told her that his dog was being trained with other potential RCMP dogs.

Kelly opened the door a little wider and saw the dog sitting in the foyer close to the doorway, but still growling and eyeing the stranger closely.

"Good boy, Hunter, good boy," she talked in a calm low tone and slowly approached the animal who was still carefully watching her with its wolf-like eyes.

Kelly looked about the space looking for the dog's leash. She thought the most likely place would be the kitchen and she slowly walked in that direction, finally spotting it hanging on one of the door knobs. Hunter remained sitting in the foyer, head turned, studying every move that Kelly made.

She attached the leash to the dog's collar and patted the dog. "Hi, Hunter, I'm Kelly. Everything's going to be okay. Good dog." She stroked the dog, trying to make friends with him. "Okay, Officer, it's all clear, you may enter," Kelly advised as she held the dog's leash tightly and led the dog into the kitchen. She tied the leash to the refrigerator door. "Sit!" she commanded.

"RCMP ... Ricardo, come out!" Kelly called out again and listened. "Okay, Officer, let's check." The pair slowly checked each room in the apartment and confirmed that Ricardo wasn't there. "It's clear," Kelly said, "so take a look around without making a mess and see if you can find any weapons or information about this guy. You begin in the bedroom and I'll start in the front."

The officer turned toward the back of the apartment as Kelly walked past the dog that was watching her every move. "What was that bastard really doing at *ComTek*," she wondered as she poked around the living room. "Hmm."

She knew that the most probable source of information was usually the personal phone directory and computer. She looked and found the computer in the small den. She turned it on but it required a password, so she shut it down again, took the power cord and machine, and placed them all on a small desk in the foyer.

The two continued to search the apartment and found nothing else.

"Likely all the contact information's on the computer," Kelly remarked, frustrated that there weren't any other clues.

"I can't find anything useful, Detective," the officer said as he returned to the kitchen doorway.

"Okay then, let's go. I think we've all we're going to get here," she replied and found a bag of dog food, Hunter's stainless steel water bowl, and untied his leash. "Heel, Hunter!" The dog rose and stood by her side, as instructed. "Good dog!" Kelly looked at the officer, now joining her in the kitchen. "Here, take some of this stuff and help me carry it to my car," she said, handing the bag of dog food and bowl to the officer. Kelly grabbed the computer and power cord and the pair vacated the apartment. She locked the door and told the officer, "Okay, we need to return this key."

The pair walked back to the superintendant's ground floor suite and Kelly knocked on the door. "Heel, Hunter!"

The gray-haired man reappeared as the door opened.

"Thank you, here's Mr. Sanchez's key. Call your local police if you see him, and have them contact me," Kelly said, handing over the key as she juggled the computer in her arms.

"Okay, Detective O'Brian," he replied as he took the key, then closed the door.

"That's it—I guess that we're done here," Kelly remarked as the trio headed back to her car.

She popped the trunk of the Taurus, and placed the computer gear into the cavity. The officer added the dog paraphernalia and Kelly closed the lid, then she opened the car's back door. "Get in, Hunter." She waved her hand in the direction of the back seat and the dog entered. "Lie down!" she commanded and the dog took a place in the back and lay on the backseat peering at her.

The pair was joined by the third officer.

"Thank you both for your assistance. There should be an APB out on Sanchez by now, so keep a watch out. This guy's very experienced," she said, and shook the hand of each officer. "Stay safe!"

Kelly watched the two officers head toward their squad car and then joined Hunter in her car. "Well boy, we're going to have to be buds for a while. Let's go and see how Simon's doing," Kelly said as she pulled her cell and called Simon. "How're ya doing, partner?"

She listened to his reply then responded, "Not too bad eh, that's good. I can't say the same about our car! Where are ya—I'll come and pick you up and take ya home."

Kelly punched the address into the GPS. "I'm in New West, leaving Sanchez's place and should be there in less than an hour. Oh, you like dogs?"

✵

Terry Peters' funeral was held at a small chapel in Surrey. It had been arranged by Sandra Willows at the request of Terry's ex-wife, who now lived out of town. There had been a small reception before the service and the majority of people who attended worked for *ComTek*, or for one of their customers that was serviced by the pole yard.

"I know most of the people here, but who was that petite attractive young woman who came up to speak with ya, Will?" Thomas Howe asked, as the pair waited to find a pew in the small room where the service was to be held.

"I don't know. She said that her name was Kate, but I've never met her before. She asked me if I knew who was here from Terry's family as she wanted to introduce herself," Will Richards replied. "She's hot, that's for sure!"

"Hmm ... I don't see her now. I don't see any family here either and it looks like Sandra's going to run this service. Too bad, eh?" Thomas asked, looking about the room.

Kate stood outside the chapel in the parking lot, wearing a tight skirt, high-heeled shoes, a long-sleeved top that wasn't too provocative and a light jacket. "Hey Slider, Terry Peters has no family here at the service. His office manager's running the show." She paused and looked quickly about. "He has an ex-wife, but she's in poor health and didn't come out here. All I could find out was that she lives in Prince George."

"Humph!" Slider sighed, "Okay then, I'll call Philippe to pick ya up and bring ya back to the *Fraser Head*."

"Great—it's a downer here, and I'll need a boost when I get back!" she replied, and hung up the phone to wait for her ride.

♓

It was late by the time that Brian Quest got to his home in Richmond from the hospital on Port Coquitlam. He had a police squad car take him from the hospital to his car that was parked at the *Fraser Head Hotel*. He was exhausted and took a deep breath as he exited his black sports car, knowing that his wife was likely going to be very angry that he hadn't called earlier. She had seen him pull into the driveway and opened the front door as he slowly walked up the front walkway.

"Where the hell have you been? Screwing one of your regulars and lost track of time?" she bellowed as he entered the front foyer of their large custom-built home.

"I was kidnapped and held hostage since Friday afternoon!" he snapped back. "I wasn't screwin' around on you ... see!" He showed his wife the bruise marks on his wrists.

"Humph! That'll be a first! Looks like S&M to me!" she growled. "We were supposed to be at that Peters' funeral earlier today. What will people think eh, that his boss wasn't there, huh Brian?"

"I don't want to talk about this with you right now! I need a scotch!" he replied coldly, and headed for his study.

"You've a good job at *ComTek*, Brian. You mess that up with all your whoring around, I'm gone!" she yelled and stormed off.

Chapter Twenty Five

Vancouver was experiencing a continued high-pressure winter weather pattern, and Monday morning was clear and cool. The sun had risen and the rays were streaming through Kelly's front window. Her wake-up buzzer alerted her that it was time to get moving, and Hunter, who was lying on her bedroom floor perked up his ears at the sound.

"Good morning, Hunter—it's time for our daily run," Kelly said as she sat up and looked at the dog, now standing at her bedroom doorway.

It didn't take Kelly long to discover that Hunter loved a morning walk and that she enjoyed his company. Joggers stopped to pat or talk to the dog, and it took longer to complete her round trip with her sociable friend tagging along. It didn't matter, as her temporary companion's friendliness helped Kelly feel more at ease with providing a home for the dog until his future could be settled.

"I don't think I'll be late today, Hunter, it looks like a paperwork day," she told the dog.

Kelly knew that there was a pile of reports to complete, and with Simon's arm in a sling, the pair wouldn't be doing any investigating that required a healthy backup. "Besides, if I get a chance to locate your master ... well, you might just have to stay with me permanently, that's all!"

※

Will Richards was up early. It was very cold in Aldergrove. He was still pumped about the Chinese offer to buy *Service Pole Recycling* and wanted to arrange the meeting with Brian Quest as soon as he could. Will knew that the Chinese would need clean books and started to gather all his paperwork together, so that he and Thomas could have the financials up-to-date and ready by the end of the week.

He knew that Brian often didn't get into the office until almost eight thirty, and called Georgina to see if he could get an appointment after lunch. "Good Morning Georgina, it's Will Richards. How're you this fine morning?"

"Good morning, Will. Okay I guess—what can I do for you today?"

"I need to have a business meeting with Brian early this afternoon. It's critical it's today. Does he have some time available?"

"Ah ... I've an opening at one o'clock. How long do you need?" she replied as she checked Brian's Outlook® calendar.

"I think I'll need about an hour or so, and I've some guests I wish to bring, including Thomas Howe."

"Hmm ... okay. I'll schedule the large conference room in the building out back. Call me in an hour to confirm, please." Georgina knew that Brian often avoided Will Richards, so she had to check that Brian would even take the meeting.

Brian Quest was still shaken up with his abduction and the news of the murder of Candice Parks. He had been told about Candice by Detective Chung while he was being attended to at the hospital and blamed himself for the outcome. Neither of these facts had been made public yet, and he struggled with how to handle the situation when he arrived at the office. He called Georgina on his cell as he drove to work. "Georgina, good morning, this is Brian. I want a meeting set up with all the staff this morning, please."

"Yes, good morning Brian ... Larry Langstone called early this morning and he wants to see you in his office first thing. I don't know when you'll be back for a staff meeting, and Will Richards also wants a meeting with you after lunch with a group of people, including Thomas Howe. I've tentatively booked one o'clock for them if that's okay with you."

"Hmm ..." Brian sighed, "I don't think I'm in the mood for all that today, but I'd better see what Larry wants first. I'll advise you from Larry's office on the Will Richards thing later. Thanks, Georgina." Brian sighed again, as he was in no mood for any more surprises, but changed his route and headed for *Central City Towers* instead of his office. "I wonder what Larry wants—maybe he's heard about my ordeal and Candice. I doubt it's going to be fun. Man, I need a day off and it's only Monday!"

It was eight forty-five and Will Richards couldn't wait the hour; he knew that Brian should've been in contact with Georgina by then, so he called early. "Georgina, it's Will. Do I have confirmation from Brian on my meeting? I've others to get back to," he asked anxiously.

"I spoke to him, Will, and he has an unexpected meeting this morning, but didn't cancel yours yet. He said that he'd decide later in the morning. That's the best I can do at this point. Sorry, Will."

"Thanks, Georgina. I'll proceed on the assumption that everything will go ahead. I'll call about noon to check." Will hung up the phone and thought about what Georgina had said. "Hmm ... a panic unscheduled meeting Monday morning—that sounds strange, even for Brian!"

Will made calls to all those who had agreed to attend the meeting at *ComTek,* indicating to them that it might be cancelled, but it was a go for now.

☿

The two West Vancouver detectives arrived at their Surrey office to find that there were new files already waiting for their review on Simon's desk.

"You know, Quest wasn't that cooperative on Saturday when we stopped into his room at the hospital, eh Simon! The whole story of Chinese abductors and then the Colombian! There's more going on than he's admitting," Kelly remarked as she sat in her chair behind her desk. "He took the news about Ms. Parks' murder very hard. I think that there was some affair goin' on between those two!"

"Humph! I wonder what story he told his wife about being at the *Fraser Head Hotel* on a Friday afternoon," Simon replied. "A hotel to console an employee ... a woman no less ... give me a break!"

"Yea, if he had the balls to tell her that story!" Kelly grunted as she grabbed a folder from Simon's desk and opened the jacket. "Our DB shooter at the POCO warehouse was Pablo Dominguez. We don't have much on this guy, but we were able to get his prints from immigration. I hope that we'll get more information on him when we interrogate Giermo Hernandez—and more on the story on Ricardo Sanchez, for that matter."

"Hernandez has got a lawyer showing up here around eleven this morning. I'm glad we had Hernandez transferred here instead of us having to go all the way out to POCO for the interview!"

"Hey, we did get a hit on the guy shot in the head in the white van at the back of the *Fraser Head Hotel*. Some bottom rung hood working in the Chinese underworld, but there's really nothing else." Kelly pondered for a moment. "That reminds me Simon, we need to visit the *Fraser Head* about ten, to get Friday's surveillance video DVD concerning the Parks murder. That's in about an hour," she said and then glanced at her partner. "By the way, our ride will have to go into the shop later this week. It caught four bullets at the warehouse. Looks like you saved our vehicle from getting another one!" Kelly looked up from the report and grinned.

"The Medical Examiner's report's here on Candice Parks." Kelly returned her attention to the files on her desk, as she picked up a new file and opened the folder. "It says here that Parks' DNA did match the pubic hairs found on Terry Peters, and it's conclusive that she was the assailant. It also states that she did die from an overdose of cocaine, but there wasn't any other drug in her system. Rape wasn't conclusive and we have nothing on the male semen profile taken from Parks' body. Hmm ... they must've had a fun time with Parks before they killed her and I'll bet that they were likely interrupted by the shooting in the parking lot."

Kelly flipped through other pages of the report. "The prints on the lubricant bottle and syringe are new and we don't have any matches in the system. We're on square one on that front. There were also bruise marks around her mouth. It looks like she got in over her head, I'd say, whatever she was doing." Kelly looked up at Simon and then continued, "The ME also notes that a *Fraser Head Hotel* engraved room key was found on her key ring, so she is definitely one of the key-holders." Kelly sat and stared at the report. "You know, I'd bet Brian Quest is another key-holder as they were going there together! Hmm ... with the hotel not listing names with keys, we can't confirm that on him, and I doubt he'd volunteer the information—but we should press him later anyway."

"You know, he must be involved in what Parks was up to, and he'll likely be going back to whatever he was doing. We should advise *ComTek* about Parks, and have them take a closer look at Quest, too," Simon remarked, thinking about all the information in the reports. "How're things going with you and Hunter?"

"Really great, Simon! I find that I'm enjoying having him about, and he's certainly smart. I don't know if I'll be keeping him or not. I guess the outcome with Sanchez will influence that decision when we catch up with him."

"Well, our two captains will be pressing for our reports, so we'd better get them started, or should I say you should get them started … my arm and all." Simon grinned.

♓

Brian Quest arrived at Larry Langstone's office and stopped to talk to his executive assistant, Carolynn Gingell, before meeting with Larry.

"Good morning, Brian," Carolynn smiled and nodded her head toward Larry's office. "Larry's waiting for you," she said curtly.

Brian frowned at her attitude, and then proceeded into Larry's office.

"Close the door, Brian, and take a seat," Larry instructed, sounding more formal than usual as he stayed seated in his executive chair. "Things have gotten out of hand, Brian. People are very concerned with the police all over your operation and with Terry Peters and all. It's not a good business scenario. You have placed the *LM Distributors* operation at risk and Tom Lee is very nervous, to say the least."

"The Peters murder was out of my control. I don't even know who was behind that mess. I'm very upset with that, too, Larry. Did you know that Candice Parks and I were abducted on Friday, and that she's been murdered?"

Larry inhaled quickly at the news and then frowned for a moment. "Oh, really," he commented sarcastically and without emotion. "That must've been quite an ordeal for you, eh Brian. What were you and Parks doing, besides screwing I mean? Humph! Having sex with an employee in a room provided by Mr. Lee and not being discreet ... an employee! I trusted you to keep your act together and be smart. Christ, I can't even think about how many policies you've disregarded and the pressure all that information will put on the entire management team when it gets out!" Larry growled. "Besides, this conversation's about you right now, not Ms. Parks."

"I've got Will Richards on the ropes, Larry. That's working out!" Brian replied nervously. "Just as I said I would."

"I can't afford being connected to any of that stuff, you know that." Larry looked directly at Brian. "I think that it's best that you take an early retirement, effective immediately. I've discussed your situation with Peter Fisher and Tom Lee. You'll be employed by Mr. Lee, starting today."

"That's a little drastic, don't you think, Larry? I'd never roll over on you or Tom Lee!" Brian replied as he looked into Langstone's piercing eyes.

Larry slid a package over the desk toward Brian. "Look inside and sign the documents!"

Brian took a deep breath, opened the envelope, and pulled out the contents. A retirement agreement was all prepared and ready for his signature. A small envelope was also attached and he poured out the contents onto the desk. An engraved *Fraser Head Hotel* room key slid across the desk top.

"Carolynn and I believe that she'll no longer need that key. I suggest that you get your key and then return both of them to Mr. Lee." Larry's face was now stern and his eyes intensely focused on Brian. "If you've got Candice Parks' key, return that, too."

Brian sat and stared at the key with the FH stamp on the head, now lying on the desk. "How long have you known about Carolynn?" Brian blurted out, shocked, his eyes fixed on the *Fraser Head Hotel* key that seemed to stare back at him.

"I've always known, Brian! I needed to be kept in the loop about what you were doing and thinking, and Carolynn was such a good sport about it all. Executive assistants are critical in helping their bosses keep in touch with what's going on around *ComTek*," Larry replied smugly, and then continued, "I'm giving you a good package and an opportunity to get out unscathed. Tom Lee will be watching you to ensure that you stay out of trouble. You be a good boy over there, and all will be well for you."

Brian stared at the documents and the key in disbelief for a moment, and then took a deep breath. "One more thing Larry—something's up with Will Richards and he's pressing for a meeting this afternoon with a group of people including Thomas Howe."

"Sign your retirement and I'll take care of Will Richards! I'll have Carolynn call Georgina and get an update. Carolynn will arrange for you to get your personal belongings—I don't want you back at the CLG operation. Go directly from here to Chilliwack, and leave me your office keys and your company cell phone. Tom Lee is expecting you later this morning. You'd better learn from this and not screw up over there Brian! Trust is a fragile thing and Tom isn't as forgiving as I am."

Brian looked up angrily at Larry for a moment, and then looked at the documents, took a pen from his coat pocket, and signed the multiple copies. "This is a big mistake, Larry," he growled, pitched the BlackBerry® with a set of office keys, and then got up and opened the office door.

"Don't forget your *Fraser Head Hotel* key! Good luck, Brian," Larry said stiffly, and sat back in his chair as Brian vacated the office and slammed the door.

Larry took a breath, collected the documents, and looked up at Carolynn as she reopened the office door. "Carolynn, Will Richards is pushing to have a meeting with Brian after lunch. Call Georgina and see what you can find out, and get Pat Williams on the phone, please," Larry instructed coldly, and slid the signed paperwork to Carolynn. "Get this to personnel and put Brian's cell in a safe place. I'll have Pat pick up Brian's keys."

"Yes, Sir!" she replied. She grabbed the items from the desk and left the office. Moments later Carolynn called out, "Line one."

"Hey Pat, it's Larry. All things are arranged as discussed earlier. I'll have Carolynn call the CLG and have Georgina set up a staff meeting in about an hour. I understand that Will Richards wants a meeting this afternoon. Take the meeting, but agree to nothing. Call me after you're finished. Oh, you can pick up your new office keys for the CLG from Carolynn." Larry hung up and called out to Carolynn. "Carolynn, have Georgina set up a staff meeting in an hour and Pat will address everyone there at that time. Confirm the Will Richards meeting and Pat will handle that. We need to know what Richards is up to! If Quest has screwed things up I need to fix that right away!"

♓

Kelly and Simon arrived at the *Fraser Head Hotel* just after ten. Kelly found the manager checking out guests and she waited in the lobby until the counter was clear. The manager eyed the attractive detective as she approached the counter, and pulled out the data disk from behind the countertop.

"Morning, Detective, here're the files I agreed to hand over. Enjoy." The manager eyed another customer approaching with his suitcase. "Is there anything else?"

"Nope, thanks. We'll be in touch later," Kelly replied with a serious face, took the disk and returned to Simon who was waiting in the car. "I'd bet this will be interesting." Kelly turned the Taurus around and headed back to the Surrey office. "I don't like that guy, ya know! Your arm feeling any better, Simon? You still look like shit and you should be at home."

"No fuss. We need to get an eyeball on those video clips and we have Hernandez' lawyer soon after we get back to the office."

Simon had just gotten seated back into his office chair when a phone call from the first floor receptionist interrupted his discussion with Kelly. Simon pressed the hands-free key on the phone and then answered, "Detective Chung."

"Detective Chung, a Mr. Doyle is down here asking to see Mr. Hernandez. Mr. Doyle says that you and Detective O'Brian are expecting him."

"Yes, that's right. Please direct him to our office," Simon said as he hung up the phone and glanced at Kelly. "Call downstairs and get Hernandez into an interview room. I'm going for a coffee, you want one?"

"It's okay … I'll get it—your arm ya know!" Kelly jibed and quickly left the office.

She returned a couple minutes later and saw Simon had company in their office. "Good morning, I'm Detective O'Brian."

"Good morning to you, too, Detective," Doyle replied, peering over his heavy, black-rimmed glasses as he looked up at the attractive woman coming into the office with two coffees. "I'm Carman Doyle."

Carman Doyle was a middle-aged lawyer who had established his practice in New Westminster just after passing the Bar. He looked scruffy, and his long black hair was combed back in a 1950s hair style, held in place with a hair product that made his hair shine in the bright overhead strip lights of the office. His closely shaved beard completed the look he had of a deadbeat lawyer; but it was all a scam as Carman Doyle was cunning, observant, and highly successful at what he did.

"Coffee, Mr. Doyle?" Kelly asked as she placed the two cups on Simon's desk.

"No, thanks. I've a busy day, so may we see my client, Giermo Hernandez, please? His family has retained my services—what are the charges, Detectives?"

"Well, trafficking in cocaine and marijuana to start," Simon replied as he studied the man. "We waited to interview Mr. Hernandez until he had proper counsel, and he hasn't provided us with a statement yet."

The trio left the office area and joined Giermo Hernandez in the interview room, and each took a seat.

"Mr. Hernandez, I'm your lawyer, Carman Doyle. I was contacted by a Mr. Sanchez on Saturday, and he said that you would need my assistance. Is that acceptable to you, Sir?"

"Ah ... Mr. Sanchez, yes of course. He represents my family in Colombia." Giermo glanced over at the two detectives and grinned.

"So, Mr. Hernandez, we have statements that the marijuana operation at 905 Elvenden Row in West Vancouver was yours. Is that correct?" Simon asked.

"Ahh." Giermo looked at his lawyer. "Yea, so? It's private property and I pay my rent."

"Hmm ... were you processing cocaine at that location?" Simon asked, now peering at the man.

"No!" Giermo replied and sat back in his chair.

"What about all the coke at your warehouse in Port Coquitlam where you were arrested? Was that yours?" Kelly had her turn to ask.

"I ... ah, was visiting my friend, Mr. Sanchez, there. I know nothing about no coke ... talk to Ricardo!" Giermo replied and crossed his arms.

"Did Pablo Dominguez work for you, Mr. Hernandez?" Kelly pressed.

"No, he's just a friend who came out to see me. We were goin' for lunch with ah ... Ricardo, before you guys stormed in!"

"Humph! Lunch with a kidnapped victim, Mr. Quest, who was tied up in the back of Pablo Dominguez's SUV? Interesting arrangement. You order a hit on a Ms. Parks, too, huh?" Simon asked and leaned over the desk.

"Parks ... who the hell is Ms. Parks?" Giermo growled as he looked over at Doyle. "This is getting stupid!"

"What about Ernesto Rodriguez and his friend Juan Vergara. Were you involved in their murders?" Simon asked, leaning back in his chair.

"I have nothing else to say!" Giermo sneered, "Bugger off!"

"Okay ... okay. My client has nothing further he wants to say, so this interview's over," Carman Doyle said as he briskly stood up.

"All right, Mr. Doyle. There will be charges filed later today and you can go from there. Mr. Hernandez will be waiting in his cell pending anything that you feel you need to file," Simon replied as the trio filed out of the interview room. "Good day, Mr. Doyle."

Kelly and Simon returned to their office and their coffees were now cold.

"Any association with those murders will be hard to stick on Hernandez, Simon. I think we're goin' to have to live with the drug charges," Kelly said and smiled. "We got our Elvenden Row case solved though!"

"His comments about Sanchez were interesting, KO. We gotta find Ricardo!" Simon replied as he sat down and grabbed the CD with the *Fraser Head Hotel's* video clips. "Let's spend time on these."

"Let's start with the rear door video. It was the key last time, and everything took place in the area by the back door," Kelly replied as she loaded the disk and the clip started automatically.

"I need to get to the time after Candice Parks was released from here," she muttered as she fast-forwarded the video. "Okay ... here, look Simon, the video is just as shitty as before, but we can see the hostage-taking of Parks and Quest by the three men. The assailants' face details are blurry. Humph! The video provides no new usable evidence on the two men's identities who forced Candice into the hotel," Kelly growled, pointing to the image on the monitor.

"A tall man and a short, skinny one. Carry on, KO," Simon remarked.

Kelly played more of the video and again put the video on hold. "Look here, we can see Pablo Dominguez abducting Brian Quest. That's Pablo's Escalade that we found Quest in at the POCO scene! We can clearly see Pablo shoot the driver in the white van before he snatched Quest!" Kelly turned to Simon. "The big question that remains is, who are the guys in the white van? We only know that the dead driver was Chinese, but that's a dead end. The van plates were stolen and are a dead end, too!"

"Yea well, we know Hernandez and Dominguez were running a drug operation, likely based in Colombia, and Sanchez looks like he's involved in that. The other guys must be involved in a different scam that somehow involved Candice Parks! Hmm ... I wonder what that is! They did use cocaine to murder Parks, though," Simon remarked, looking puzzled.

⋈

Ricardo Sanchez decided to remain at Giermo Hernandez's place in downtown Vancouver for a while longer. He decided that he would try to get back to his apartment later in the day, now concerned about Hunter and his computer files. A doctor had extracted the bullet and patched up his arm, but it hurt like hell.

He wasn't happy about the cops capturing Giermo, either. It was his job to protect him, and the family had been really pissed when he told them. They weren't very happy about Karl Kuntz being eliminated either, and Ricardo told them that Carman Doyle was a better lawyer anyway. He hoped that it was true, but he wasn't sure.

"I'd better be careful and plan for my visit to Bogotá!" Ricardo muttered as he turned on the TV and went to the kitchen to grab one of the beers stacked inside. "Man, it stinks of smoke in here!" he grumbled, pulling the tab off the beer can. "Hmm ... I hope Hunter can wait for me a little longer!"

⋈

Pat Williams appeared at the *Central Logistics Group* reception area. "Georgina, where's Brian Quest's office?" he asked without introductions.

"Just around the corner, Mr. Williams," she responded in a cold voice, resenting hearing from Carolynn about Brian's sudden retirement and the unexpected replacement. "I've your staff meeting set up in the building out in the back yard," she said as she pointed out the window facing the storage yard. "It's in ten minutes."

Pat found Brian Quest's private office, placed his overcoat and briefcase on a side chair, and peered out the large window. He stood momentarily thinking about what he was going to say to the staff. The phone rang and interrupted his thoughts.

"A call for you on line one, Mr. Williams," Georgina said and hung up once she noticed that the line had been answered.

"Good morning, Pat Williams."

"Mr. Williams, I'm Detective O'Brian. I was looking for Brian Quest but have been told that I should speak to you."

"Yes, that's right, Detective. I have replaced Mr. Quest. What can I do for you?" Pat asked sharply.

"Replaced Mr. Quest! What happened?"

"Oh, it's just an internal reorganization. Why are you calling, Detective O'Brian?"

"I wanted to advise Mr. Quest that we found more information on the Candice Parks murder that took place last Friday. We're very sorry, and know that *ComTek* would want to be advised of our findings. We also thought that he might have some additional information for us."

"Murdered!" Pat paused and took a deep breath. "What happened, Detective?"

"I can't say any more, Mr. Williams. It's an ongoing case and we need to speak directly with Mr. Quest."

"Thank you, Detective, but I can't help you. Good bye." Pat slowly placed the phone receiver back into the cradle.

"Jesus Christ! What the hell was Quest doing?" he muttered and headed for his meeting in the outer building. "I'll have to get Larry to fill me in later."

The entire operations staff had stuffed themselves into the conference room. Everyone knew something was up, as this type of full staff meeting only happened at Christmas or at major announcements. Everyone thought the meeting concerned Terry Peters.

Pat Williams stood in the front of the room waiting for everyone to settle down, and eventually the room became silent. "I'm Pat Williams, and will be replacing Brian Quest as of today. He has elected to take an early retirement to allow him to deal with some personal issues," Pat said in a monotone voice.

The room buzzed with muttering by many in the room. Pat waited for the room to become quiet again.

"I'm also saddened to inform you that Ms. Candice Parks will not be returning either." He paused to collect himself, and continued, "She apparently was murdered on Friday and the police are currently working on her case."

The room remained still and without a sound. Everyone was stunned and shocked by the gruesome news.

"*ComTek* will provide any counseling should any of you request some help with all this tragedy. Any questions?" Pat asked as the crowd just stared at him in shock and disbelief.

No one uttered a word.

"Thank you. Everyone can return to their work," Pat said coldly, and stood and watched everyone file out of the room. "What a way to start!" he thought as he watched the last person disappear from the room.

Georgina was in tears by the time Pat had returned upstairs to see her about his next meeting.

"I'm very sorry, Georgina. I know you knew Candice and Brian well and for a long time. That was a tough way to be told, I know." He paused, then added, "After Will Richards and his group arrive, you may go home."

"Will Richards and his group will arrive in less than half an hour," Georgina replied, sniffling, her eyes red from crying.

"I'll be in my office getting settled until then," Pat replied without emotion, and turned to prepare his thoughts for the Will Richards meeting.

♓

Thomas Howe met Will Richards at his trailer on the mill site fifteen minutes before the scheduled meeting with Brian Quest. Will was on the telephone.

"My God! You've got to be kidding, Georgina! Are you going to be okay?" Will asked, shocked. "Yea, Georgina, everyone's coming. Thanks." Will looked distraught as he turned to face Thomas. "Candice Parks was murdered on Friday and Brian Quest has been replaced by a Pat Williams. Our meeting's still on, though," he choked out.

"Candice murdered and Brian's replaced!" Thomas exclaimed with a shocked face. "Uh ... I don't know if this is the right time for your meeting, Will. Maybe you should postpone the discussion with *ComTek*."

"I have to go ahead as planned! Chad and Peter have made additional plans for the next couple of weeks, and they want an answer before they go. I need to know today, Thomas." Will looked deflated and couldn't believe the shocking news. "First Terry and now Candice! What the hell's going on? I've got to get out of this God damn place!"

Thomas took a deep breath. "I don't know anything about this Pat Williams, but it's sure he has some authority in the meeting this afternoon. We must go now," Thomas urged, patting his friend on the back. "Let's see where this leads and go from there."

"Yes, you're right. This will be one of my few shots to get away from all these assholes. Let's go in your car—I need to get my head straight," Will suggested in a depressed tone.

The two men arrived at the office across the street before the Chinese guests, and stopped to visit with Georgina for a moment.

"I don't know what to say, Georgina. We're both very saddened by all this," Thomas said sympathetically, knowing the woman quite well.

"I know you got along with Candice well, and you both are as upset as I am. This place certainly isn't the same anymore. The best time was when you and Fred Hawthorn were here and you both looked after all of us ... the meeting's in the IRD building," Georgina replied and then began to cry, turning away from Thomas.

"Look, we'll wait for the others, you go and freshen up," Thomas offered and the pair waited by the door as Georgina left for the washroom. "She's such a wonderful, caring woman—I feel really bad for her," Thomas commented as the two Chinese men arrived at the front door.

"There has been some bad news here. I'll show you to our meeting," Thomas said as the rest of the people entered the office. Thomas and Will turned and led the men down a set of stairs and into the conference room in the outside building.

Pat Williams had already arrived and sat at the head of the conference table. He was more overweight than most *ComTek* managers, which was unusual considering he was only about thirty. Introductions were made all around, and each person took a seat.

"So, Mr. Richards, what's the purpose of this meeting?" Pat's loud booming voice filled the room.

"As I'm sure you know, I've an agreement with *ComTek* to process retired poles and extract the usable lumber in an environmentally responsible way. I've been doing this across the street for more than fifteen years now," Will replied, annoyed that he had to update a new manager at such a critical time. "Thomas Howe, sitting next to me, managed that project directly for *ComTek* for over five years and indirectly for much longer. My service agreement has been renewed each time before it expired, and the arrangement has been a large success for both of us. It has generated a strong public following, too."

"So why are we here?" Pat asked, looking confused and disinterested.

"I've an opportunity to sell my operation to these gentlemen from China, who have committed to abide by the recycling agreement and to invest capital to make improvements and increase productivity. The current agreement expires in another year and these people need a minimum of a three-year term so that they can justify the investment."

Pat turned to the two Chinese business men. "So what's so special about Mr. Richard's recycling operation?"

"We need lumber products in China to support the growing demand for housing. Using a lower-cost, recycled product would help serve that need more economically than purchasing new materials," Chad replied with a smile.

"We can't export contaminated wood," Pat said sharply, reaching for an excuse to reject the request.

"The Chinese government has arranged to allow this import, and we know that we can get Canadian permits as the finished product has very little, if any, contaminant after processing."

"*ComTek* doesn't have any intention of extending the agreement with Mr. Richards or anyone else. We want to reclaim the property where his mill is located and use it for another purpose," Pat replied coldly.

"That's the first I've heard of this! I can't believe that *ComTek*'s going to continue responsible pole disposal in any better form than we are now doing," Will said loudly, exasperated with Pat's statement.

"Well, that seems to be the current plan, Mr. Richards, so I don't think we've anything further to discuss. We don't intend to extend your agreement—period!" Pat stood up, indicating the discussion was over. "I've another meeting, so excuse me," Pat said and walked out of the conference room, leaving the remaining parties to find their own way out.

"What the hell was that?" Thomas asked in disbelief. "These guys don't know what they're going to do. I don't get this bullshit for a moment!"

"Well, I guess we can't do business, Mr. Richards. Too bad, we thought we had a win-win here." Chad shook Will's hand. "I guess you're going to have your work cut out for you!"

Everyone found their way out of the building. Georgina had gone home, and the upstairs office was deserted.

"Will, it's not too late. Let's go to *Kennedy's* for a pint, and think about this over a cold one," Thomas suggested, as he needed to think and discuss the past meeting.

"Thomas, with all this and Candice and Brian, I need to go home. Let's have our meeting tomorrow at lunch. See you here at say eleven-thirty?" Will suggested, depressed and shocked by all the news of the day.

Thomas dropped Will back at the mill site and left for home himself, stunned by the past events. "Hmm ... it must be Langstone, that bastard!" he muttered as he drove past the guard at the pole yard gate. "I'd better find out if this bullshit is Larry's idea, or if it really is Peter Fisher who's being unreasonable and trying screw Will! Humph, I don't trust either of them anyway!"

♓

Brian Quest turned his black sports car into the *BC Transformer* parking lot. He wasn't a happy camper, and didn't like the prospect of working in Chilliwack or for Tom Lee. Brian knew that Tom was a nice guy on the outside, but his true ruthless nature was dangerous and Brian also was aware that Tom was well connected.

Brian arrived on the second floor and Ho Lin pointed, directing him to Mr. Lee's office without her usual cheery greeting.

"Ah, Mr. Quest. Come in and close the door, please." Brian heard Tom's voice come from within, the moment Brian knocked on the open office door.

Brian took a seat and without the usual formalities, Tom looked up from the computer monitor. "I see that our arrangement's going to change. Too bad about your girlfriend ... ah, Ms. Parks. Murder's a messy business, don't you think?" Tom's eyes peered at Brian and recorded his every expression. "You'll begin working for me tomorrow, and look after some of the operation downstairs. We'll discuss those details including your role and salary in the morning. What information do you have about the person who killed that man outside the *Fraser Head Hotel* on Friday?"

"Why?" Brian asked, confused by the question. "How do you know about that, Mr. Lee?"

"I've got sources and am well informed, Mr. Quest. Just answer the question! I want to be sure that you didn't tell him anything that may harm our operation. I know that he took you from the *Fraser Head Hotel* after the shooting."

"Well, the cops killed him at the scene in POCO, but I think you need to find Ricardo Sanchez. He seems to be involved with the Colombians who took me that afternoon. Mr. Sanchez posed as the security manager for *ComTek*, but what his true interest is in all this, I don't really know." Brian paused. "Oh ... here are your keys to room 210. I told Larry that I would return them to you," Brian growled, and dropped a pair of keys on the desk and got out of his seat.

"Thank you for your cooperation. Mind your business, do what I tell you, and I'm sure you'll be happy here," Tom replied coldly, ignoring Brian's attitude; he stood from his chair and continued, "I'll see you here at seven sharp. That's when we start the plant. Close the door behind you."

Tom Lee watched Brian leave and then picked up the phone as the door closed. "Larry, this is Tom Lee. I've finished with Brian, for now. Tell me everything you've got on this Ricardo Sanchez. It seems that he's a loose end that needs my immediate attention."

He hung up the phone after receiving the information that he wanted, and smiled as he sat back into his chair. He hadn't told Brian that he had had Candice killed, and that she also had been a loose end. He knew that Brian and Candice had been having an affair and that now wasn't the best time to tell Brian why she had been eliminated; perhaps later the information could be a useful tool, but not now.

Tom also wasn't sure if he could trust Brian to keep his mouth shut. Having Brian close at hand was the best short-term solution until everything returned back to normal. He and his *ComTek* friends had agreed on that, and that Brian's long-term future would be decided at a later date.

︎

Ricardo Sanchez was driving his R8 Audi coupe back to New Westminster, as he had decided to pick up Hunter and his computer. He needed to figure out what to do with the dog before returning to Bogotá and wondered if Carman Doyle would be able to make the necessary arrangements. His current ride was certainly better than the Hummer he had boosted nights before, and while navigating the streets he realized that there was nothing more he could do in Vancouver to help Giermo. That would now be Doyle's problem.

He knew that there would be an APB out on him, and the police units would be patrolling his living area with a close eye, but he had to get back to his apartment. He took all the side streets possible, and in the cover of the night, he hoped it would be difficult for anyone to spot him.

Ricardo parked the silver gray coupe along the rail tracks, a block away from his condo, and proceeded on foot. He knew the RCMP and their street vehicles well, and he could recognize one of them long before they would see him. None were showing up on his mental radar, so he continued toward his condo's complex gate. He had his key out and inserted it into the condo's gate lock.

"Don't move or you're dead where you stand!" a deep Chinese-sounding voice demanded, as a short, boney man pushed the nozzle of a gun barrel into Ricardo's rear rib. "I'm not alone, so watch your step," the man growled, searching Ricardo for a weapon.

"Who the hell are you, and what do you want?" Ricardo asked, trying to think of his options, wondering if there really was a second man.

"Shut up asshole! We're going for a ride!" the man growled, pushing Ricardo toward a parked car across the unlit, dark street. "Over there!"

Ricardo was led to a car, and a beep sound preceded the trunk opening, just as a tall thin man appeared from the darkness. "Climb in!"

Ricardo saw no option, climbed over the bumper, and watched the trunk lid slam shut.

Chapter Twenty Six

It was ten on Tuesday morning. The high pressure system was weakening and a warmer cloud cover was moving into the Vancouver area. Kelly and Simon were still working on their reports as their assignment was wrapping up. They had been instructed to return to West Vancouver for an early meeting with Captain Hollingsworth on Wednesday.

"The Captain wants to give us a new case tomorrow, and the Ricardo Sanchez investigation can be done on the side, as our leads are currently dead ends. This was sure a doozy of a first case!" Kelly exclaimed, as she smiled at Simon who was pecking his case notes on the keyboard with one hand.

The office phone rang. Simon answered, looking for a reason to stop typing, and pressed the intercom button. "Detective Chung here."

"I'm Detective Quintz. We have you listed as the contact regarding a Ricardo Sanchez. We fished him out of the Fraser River this morning. He had a bullet to the back of his head and his body's in the morgue at the *Royal Colombian Hospital* in New Westminster. Our ME's report should be available tomorrow."

"Okay, thanks for the update." Simon hung up the phone with a surprised look on his face. "So our man Ricardo's fish bait. Suitable ending, don't you think, KO?" Simon asked, not sure how his partner would react to the short phone conversation.

She took a deep breath. "I guess we can close that loose end as well. I wonder who took him out," Kelly replied, visibly upset; she stared back at Simon, trying not to become emotional about Ricardo Sanchez. She was inwardly saddened somehow, even though he was a bastard, but didn't want

Abused Trust

Simon to know how she really felt about the man. "Ricardo really fooled me and him being a cop, I thought that I could trust him. I guess things finally catch up with ya, eh Simon? Well, I guess Hunter will be staying with me longer, anyway."

※

Will Richards always appreciated having lunch and a beer or two with Thomas Howe. It was a great time to strategize and let some steam off. "Helen shit when I told her all the messy news yesterday. I still feel very upset about Candice, though. I still can't believe that she's dead! I wonder what really happened" Will exclaimed quietly, looking sad and tired.

"Those *ComTek* guys are sure being king-sized jerks. I'm sure it's Larry Langstone behind your problems! He's a master self-centered bugger, and he didn't do me any favors in the past, either, when I was with *ComTek*. I've been working on a plan for some time to deal with all those who screwed me around at *ComTek*," Thomas replied as two cold pints of Bud® appeared on the table. "You know, I trusted those that I worked for at *ComTek*, but in the end, if they can use you, and I guess I let them, they will abuse that trust and screw you for their own gain. They did it to me and they did it to you, my friend. The people like Georgina who just do their jobs, do just fine most of the time, but if you have more to offer, you're a target for abuse by those who need what you have or are afraid of you."

"What options do you think we have now, Thomas?" Will asked, taking a long drink from his beer mug. "I could only come up with one last night, but you won't like it." Will took a breath, before continuing, "You know that *ComTek* hates public eyes on their bullshit actions. Any news about large BC companies is sucked up by the press, and I'm seriously thinking about that option."

"Hmm ... are you sure? That really puts you out there. You're not the most careful person when you get going talking about *ComTek*. Maybe you could go though the hoops and send a written claim asking for compensation. That's a safer initial approach for you, I think, Will."

"I know," he sighed. "The agreement was originally drafted by *ComTek*, so it's slanted. It wasn't an issue in the beginning, as it was supposed to be redone once the project proved itself—but it never was," Will grumbled, looking down at the table. "I guess I just trusted that they would do the right thing. I'm just a little guy trying to make a living and I don't think or treat people that way."

"Yea, it's a brutal world out there. I think you should give the written claim for compensation a run first, and if that fails, consider the media as a last resort. Not the best, but likely the only course of safe options left, my friend," Thomas replied and then took a drink from his beer. "Those bastards—Brian Quest and Larry Langstone, humph! I can help you tomorrow with the first draft, if you wish," Thomas offered, hoping to avoid a public spectacle. "I'd address it directly to Peter Fisher, even though I don't trust him either. We can see if he's involved in your demise or if he's a part of it with Langstone. It shouldn't take too long to figure out which."

"Yea, okay." Will looked up and asked, "What do ya think about Brian Quest being replaced so fast, huh?"

"Well, Pat Williams is a piece of work! You couldn't work with that bastard—even Brian was better in the earlier days. He sure must have pissed off Langstone! We'll find out why he's gone so fast, that's for sure."

The waitress appeared and the two men ordered lunch and a couple more pints.

⚹

A black, sleek new Lexus sat outside Larry Langstone's home in a wealthy area of Delta. It started to drizzle and the automobile blended into the darkness of the street.

Larry invariably came home late, and tonight was no exception. He stepped from his Mercedes and headed for his front door.

Bang, bang! Two shots rang out from the direction of the Lexus, hitting Larry twice in the chest, killing him before he hit the ground. The Lexus sped off before anyone knew what had happened.

The black coupe arrived in a rental lot in South Surrey less than fifteen minutes later. Thomas Howe stepped out of the car, picked up the two shell casings from the floor, locked the doors and walked a few meters to his parked blue mustang sitting at the Ford dealership next door.

He arrived back at his White Rock house and calmly walked into his office upstairs. He slid open the mirrored closet door and reached for a wooden box sitting on the inside shelf, above a small beer fridge.

"Hi, Dear. Home earlier than you thought, eh?" Jennifer Howe called out from the bedroom.

"Ah … yes. Will called and cancelled!" Thomas replied as he placed the 9mm Glock back into its box and put it on the top shelf of the closet. Thomas extracted a cold beer from the small fridge hidden inside, closed the sliding mirror door and sat in his office chair.

"Sometimes there's only one solution to deal with self-centered untrustworthy bastards," he mumbled to himself as he sat in his leather side chair. He pulled the tab from the cold can and took a long drink. Thomas knew that business life was just like a chess game. One chess player tries to outsmart the other by manipulating, lying, and cheating by using the unique attributes of each piece to confuse, disable, or misdirect the opponent.

Thomas also knew that Larry pulled many strings at *ComTek,* and that he had been a key player in bringing about his own fall and unwanted early retirement, just as Larry had done with Brian Quest, and was doing to Will Richards. Candice Parks tried to run her own game, but really was just Brian Quests's pawn, an expendable piece in the end, at least so it seemed.

Thomas smiled. "Every chess player has a move until one king is dead." Thomas picked up a black queen that stood on his office desk. "Hmm ... now I need to be patient and let the game play out just a little longer so that I can eliminate Brian Quest and Peter Fisher if he proves to be behind it all! I won't stop until I've got my revenge on each one of them."

The End.

The Painting

The next book in the Detective Kelly O'Brian Series

This fictional detective mystery story's set in the Gulf Islands and Vancouver British Columbia. Kelly O'Brian gets caught up in an investigation of a murder off the Coast of Bowen Island that leads to a case that had been closed fifteen years before. Her case takes many twists and turns and becomes personal for Detective O'Brian during her pursuit to find the truth, about the case and about herself.

See www.rushingtidemedia.com for more information about this latest Kelly O'Brian detective mystery.

CPSIA information can be obtained at www.ICGtesting.com
Printed in the USA
LVOW08s0756260713

344466LV00001B/5/P